PRAISE FOR
JIM CHRIST'S FICTION

" . . . a fast ride through the desert and grass country of Southern Arizona."

–Arizona Daily Star

"Jim Christ is a good writer, particularly of the western/thriller genre . . . the setting is well crafted and it is clear that the author is very familiar with the landscape of the Southwest. He pays attention to detail and evokes descriptive and realistic settings."

— Courtney McDermott, Tufts University

"Christ knows the Arizona/Mexico borderlands as few others do. His portraits of the characters are vivid and true. Who can describe a teenage girl better than Christ?"

— Margaret Savage, author of *Every Family Has a Secret*

"Jim Christ is a first class writer who creates his characters with such realism that you get to know them, grow to care for them and root for their safety. His style is clear and refreshing."

— Shirley Gray, author of *Roaring Mountain*

"This book is definitely a page-turner . . . The plot, characters and settings are enticing and original."

— Bonnie Edwards, author of *Deadly Patterns* and *Deadly Pairs*

ALSO BY
JIM CHRIST

Fiction

The Day Hal Quit

Non-Fiction

European Cabinetry

The Complete Guide to Modern Cabinetmaking

JIM CHRIST

Author of *The Day Hal Quit*

J&A
JOSEPH AND ASSOCIATES, PUBLISHER

WAYS TO BE *W*ICKED
by
JIM CHRIST

Joseph and Associates, 2018

ISBN: 978-0-692-97013-3

Library of Congress Cataloging Data has been applied for.

FOR JOSEPH

"It is not flesh and blood but the heart
which makes us fathers and sons."

– Friedrich Schiller

ACKNOWLEDGEMENTS

Sincere thanks to the following for their expertise and feedback on this project: Ellen Davison, Mary Hopper, David Ross, Jim Norwood, Alma Valdez-Peña, Roberto Thompson and of course, the Savage Writers of Tucson.

"You know so many ways to be wicked,
but you don't know one little thing
about love."

                    -Tom Petty, 1950-2017

ONE

Greg Valenzuela, editor of the Polk High School yearbook, had a giant crush on Usaré García and meant the yearbook to be a tribute to her. Instead, it turned out to be her epitaph.

There are thirty-four photographs of Usaré in this year's issue of the *Lance*, Polk's yearbook. But the one that's going to stick with me forever shows her leading a discussion in her English class, her teacher Chris Jameson over to the side in his vest and tie.

She looks much prettier in about a dozen of the other shots, posed ones with her smiling like she's about to give you a giant simpatico hug. She's there on the pages set aside for homecoming and prom royalty, plus mat maid captain, president of both Future Attorneys Club and the Mexican-American Studies Club. Also debate team secretary and senior peer counselor.

The rest are supposedly candids: Usaré relaxing with friends in the senior patio, Usaré shopping for formals with a couple other popular girls, and a bunch with her sitting in class or walking across campus. In the candids, the photographer somehow always managed to catch her in a fetching and bemused smile or at a good angle to highlight her figure.

The only exception is that one in her English class that I already mentioned, where she's behind a lectern and looking at some classmate, intense, almost angry. Pointing at him too, with her thumb and forefinger together. Even though she's wearing that fierce expression, she still looks damned good with her high Apache cheekbones and lustrous hair. She was going for a professional bearing that day, wearing a modest black and neutral houndstooth sweater dress. The caption says, 'Usaré García stresses a point about women's rights in her book talk about *The Awakening*.'

There are two photos of me in the yearbook as well: the obligatory head-and-shoulders shot in my coat and tie on the administrators' page and a candid where I'm doing game supervision, wearing a blue polo with the school logo—a charging horseman—nylon sweat pants and a pair of

Nikes—Lightspeed cross trainers to be exact. The caption reads, 'Mr. Tavish kicks back watching a boys' basketball game.'

The first time I was alone with Usaré was on a summer afternoon in my office. It was memorable for a lot of reasons, but what I remember best, beyond her startling good looks, is that she was able to make people want *her* to like *them*. That's why Mrs. Nelson, Mimi, had brought her to me, I think.

When Usaré came to Polk as a freshman, the first thing she wanted the counselor to know, wanted us all to know, was that she was going to be an attorney, and she needed for us to include her on the debate team. Our students are assigned a counselor according to alphabet, and since Usaré was a García, her assigned counselor was Mrs. Nelson, who had already explained to her that freshmen were not eligible to participate in debate.

But since Mimi's explanations were making no difference in Usaré's determination to join the team, and since Mimi is a pleaser anyway and wanted besides for this fourteen-year-old to like her, they both showed up at my office door. Mimi explained the impossibility of giving Usaré what she wanted, since the debate team advisor never accepted freshmen. Then she disappeared. Usaré came up close to my desk, so close that the frayed bottoms of her jeans-shorts were brushing the oak surface. I remember being glad I'd remembered to use mouthwash.

I listened as the girl pled her case, cautioning myself not to stare too long at the physical features she'd chosen to accentuate, finding it hard to remember that she was just a girl inside a woman's body. I thought of the first step—that I was powerless over my addictive behavior. I listened, then gave her the answer I'd known I would all along.

"Let me talk to the debate advisor, Mr. Maddock, and see if he can flex the rules a bit. I'll call you back this evening. We have your folks' number."

Still, she insisted I have her cell phone number, waited until I wrote it down, flashed her charming smile, and headed for the door. All predictable. I'd call the advisor, sure, give him a heads up, then call her parents' home number and explain to whoever answered that unfortunately Usaré would have to wait a year to participate on the debate team. But pretending I'd advocate for her got her out the door and allowed me the chance to be impersonal later on over the phone. Still, I had her phone number now.

But she paused at the door on her way out of my office, turned and said, "You know, it's remarkable, but I'm infatuated with you." Her voice was soft and cool.

I flushed, frozen, my mouth half-open.

She repeated, "It's really remarkable."

Then she was gone.

I was still grieving Maria then, so I was able to overcome the temptation to respond to her.

Still, I did call her back that evening. I tried the home phone first, twenty rings and no answer, no way to leave a message either.

Then the number she'd given me. I told her Mr. Maddock, the advisor, was happy to make an exception for such a gifted young woman. Forgot to punch in *67 too. That's how she got my cell number. Stupid 101. Can't wait to explain that to the cops.

The second time I found myself alone with Usaré, my urges were stronger still, but that came later.

*****

"The crazy thing is that our kids aren't *still* hysterical. It's like they're already over it," I say. "Everybody knew her. Hell, everybody adored her."

I don't mention the hollowed-out feeling inside my own chest. I know there is more to me than the good guy I put on display for everyone, and there are things I don't want anyone to know about the real me, not even those who think they know me best.

Burgoyne doesn't respond at first. He is sitting in a chair maybe twelve feet away, just below a portrait of my first wife Maria with our two kids. There's a space of seven feet or more between him and my desk, even though we are the only ones in my office. It is habit, I think, the place he sits when I am interrogating some kid about a bag of dope I found on him or the reason he had to wail on some dude for talking smack about his homies.

When I question kids about major rules violations, I have them sit right up next to the desk, Burgoyne listening from behind them and taking a few notes, getting ready. He always tells me I'm a great interrogator, that I should have been a cop, but I figure he's just saying that to prod me. That and he wants to take advantage of the school rules. I don't have to give Miranda warnings, not even for the most serious infractions, and the kid will usually think it's okay to talk to me, that the school resource officer is just sitting there for decoration, like it's only school trouble, a call to the parents, maybe a suspension at worst. I stay seated so my size doesn't intimidate the kid and do what I can to help him relax. I extract information, more than enough to arrest him for say assault, and then Burgoyne cuffs him and takes him away.

Most SROs call in a patrol officer, but not Burgoyne. He likes to haul kids down to the juvenile detention center in his own car so there's no chance of a patrolman just doing a paper arrest and turning them over to their parents without at least a few hours inside a cell. Then we never see the kid again, and usually that's a good thing, maybe not for that kid but for the rest of the school. Burgoyne loves that kind of bust.

And most of the time so do I, though there are not too many people I'd admit it to. I'm just feeding the school-to-prison pipeline, my boss would say. So would the kid's parents if they decided to sue the district, especially if they're working with one of the lawyers from CLED, the Center for Latino Education and Defense.

Burgoyne finally answers me. "Don't tell me you don't get it. Your students react just like their parents do with the twenty-four hour news cycle," sounding bored and moving his head side to side, very slightly, like the last tiny swings of a pendulum just before it stops. "That is if they even care about the news, figuring it doesn't affect them. If they're not continuously reminded, they're on to the next thing. The kids hear about your dead girl and they cry and blubber to each other and pile up flowers all around the crime scene, and that's all they can talk about until their cousin pulls up in his new ride. Besides, they're probably still yakking about it non-stop on Facebook."

Like I'm stupid if I don't understand. That's the thing about Burgoyne that annoys a lot of people, annoys me too sometimes even though I like the guy. He's merciless and critical and sarcastic most of the time, and he likes to remind you that he's smarter than you, that he's already figured it all out, no matter what *it* is.

He wears his Glock at his hip of course, but he's never dressed in uniform since being assigned to Polk, always in loafers and slacks and a polo with an embroidered PD badge, and he doesn't really look like a hardened ex-Chicago cop, if it's possible to look or not look a certain way. He is slender and not very tall, maybe five-nine if he keeps his spine straight, and he has an altar boy face, wrinkleless and pale and innocent-looking, except his eyes are gray, truly gray, colorless as the winter desert. He never smiles, at least not when I'm around, and if you ask me, I'd say his expression never changes. When he looks at you, it's like he's judging and kind of smirking at you, no matter what you're saying at the time. That's how you can tell he's an asshole cop from Chicago.

He's pretty young, not forty anyway.

Burgoyne's apparent coldness toward the murdered girl stings me, but I merely respond to his remark. "I know attention spans are short, but come on—this was outrageous. Usaré was about the best we had, and she winds up dead in a bathroom. I just don't want to accept it."

He doesn't react.

"And I got Augustine nipping at me like a Chihuahua because the school board is dogging him, even though he's wearing his famous smile the whole time. Half the teachers came up to me after the emergency faculty meeting yesterday to ask if it's safe to come to work. We even talked about closing the school, but Mrs. Nelson had already called in the crisis team so kids could come in for grief counseling."

I think back to the scene in the library the day before, Monday, kids flowing there in a stream of tears, then sitting at a table gushing out their emotions with one of the district's counselors and soaking dozens of boxes of Kleenex, talking about Usaré, writing about her, drawing pictures of their feelings with crayons or magic markers.

"Today, the only ones showing up are just there to get out of French class." I shake my head.

"Don't take it personal," Burgoyne says. "The best you had, hey?"

I can't admit to him how Usaré affected me of course, how she made sure she got my attention the first time we met and virtually overwhelmed me not too long thereafter, the next time we were alone in fact. She was impossible not to notice with her light perfume and her red nails, her full, tight-fitting blouses and her athletic legs, her waves of long, raw sienna hair.

And I won't tell him I attend sex addiction meetings almost every Thursday, something I've been doing since before my first wife died and that only she knew about. It is a story in itself, I suppose, that I do not relate these things even to Eloise.

"You need to get your sense of humor back," he says. "Was you who said all the tears were gonna restore the aquifer."

"Hyper-emotions don't seem funny today. Everybody loved her. Like Ophelia said, most people know what they are but they don't know what they will become; Usaré was the exception. She was a bright young Latina, and she knew she was going to be a brilliant Latina leader." I pause, in part to assess Burgoyne's reaction, which still seems blasé, and partly because describing poor murdered Usaré sucks at my spirit like river muck pulling off a boot.

"Half the kids here want to be an aide in the counselors' office, and she had a lock on it the second she applied. She was one of the peer counselors too, working with other kids, helping them sort things out. Smart, beautiful girl. Helluva good talker."

He says, "I thought counselors were s'posed to be good listeners."

"I want you to picture it. She worked right here in the office, a few steps from mine. Every day fourth period." I remember the image of her so vividly, I almost believe she could walk past my door. No one exuded energy the way she did; no one I know seized opportunity as eagerly as she had. No one in so short a life proved more forcefully that the seeds of victimhood can be rooted out and cast away.

"I remember seeing her. She did grab your attention," he says.

"It wasn't just her looks. She had a gift for leading; the kids looked up to her. The counselors loved her; the secretaries doted on her. Then these Levantes assholes haul her into a rest room and kill her. It's sickening."

"Nobody did her there," he says.

"How you know that?" Dumb question; he's the cop, not me. But I go ahead anyway. "There's a broken mirror, blood on the mirror. Her blood. And the scar on her forehead. Was you who told me it matched the cracked mirror. And Los Levantes' crazy-looking L on the mirror, claiming the place, claiming the murder for Christ sake."

"Yeah, that's how it first looked to me and the homicide guys. But the ME says she died before her head ever smashed into the mirror. So maybe that part was staged, the mirror and the big scar on her head, trying to throw us off, you know? Or maybe whoever it was thought she was still alive after lugging her in there and wanted to finish her. Makes you wonder if anything else was staged."

The first time I met Jim Burgoyne was when he was still a uniform guy on patrol. We all knew he was going to be assigned to Polk as our school resource officer, but until that day he was just a name on a letter, signed by our principal, Augustine López, and the chief of police.

He came on a 911 call, which I didn't even know till later, about an irate parent. I was in my office interviewing a black kid about his lunchtime fight with a Mexican kid over a white girl who'd been flirting with them both—your standard Tuesday fight. The kid was answering questions and I was jotting a few notes on my legal pad. I didn't know it until later, but I was the only assistant principal on campus, the athletics director gone to a rules meeting and the curriculum director over at the district office. I don't know where the hell our principal, smiling Augustine, was.

I could only hear some background noise from the outer office because my door was closed, getting louder though, and we were just getting to the part where the black kid was explaining how the serrated butterfly knife with his initials engraved "musta fell outta some guy's pocket," when there was this sudden banging on my door, then shouting, not background noise any more.

I was on crutches at the time, and it took me a half-minute to clear the door.

I saw my secretary, Santana, and one of the attendance clerks backed up to the wall where we keep the big master calendar posted. The women leaned together, huddling for protection, Santana holding her desk phone up in front of her like a shield, this gigantic Mexican guy leaning in at her and yelling.

"I guess any puta can get a job here," he said. He must have come all the way around the long counter where she usually greets people and conducts most of her business.

"Can I help you?" I said, not as loud as him but loud, thinking maybe the pro forma question might surprise him or make him think I was in command—something to take his eyes off the two women, but feeling like I was faking it. The guy could break me in half, I knew, me on crutches after knee surgery. I remember wondering why nobody had used their radios to raise school security, reaching to my belt for mine and realizing it was back there on my desk.

"If they let you work here," the huge guy still yelling, still bending in at the women, like I wasn't even there. Of course, I thought, crutching a step or two closer.

"When did they start letting putas run the school? I want my son here right now." Okay, I realized, his son is the other kid in the fight, who would be in a holding room down the hall, waiting for his turn in my office. Must've got a text out on his cell. It looked like the guy was about to shoot spittle on Santana and the other woman, the receptionist, if he didn't hit one of them first.

"I need you to step into my office, sir," I said, louder, stopping then about five feet away from him and willing him to turn toward me.

Didn't work.

"Maybe you estúpido, uh? Not a puta at all, just 'stúpido."

He'd obviously heard me now, purposely ignoring me.

And then his kid was standing there, jaw out, proud of his dad and egging him on. "Thass right, Papá."

Then they were both staring at Santana, the big Mexican guy and his son. Hell, the whole office was staring at the bunch of us, a high school tableau.

Santana suddenly moved the phone back and forth in front of the Mexican guy, trying to break the spell, right in front of his face.

His neck was bulging with blood and rage. And he tapped the phone then, tapped the hand that held the phone actually, like you would swat at an annoying fly that was starting to piss you off, shoo it away.

That's when I remember Burgoyne being there. I never heard him or saw him come in or approach our little scene as it played out. He was just right there sliding past me, clutching his baton. He didn't tell big daddy to turn around or leave the ladies alone, and he damned sure didn't say, "Can I help you?" He didn't want the guy to know he was there.

He just swung his baton in an arc, making a swooshing sound, twice, first on the side of daddy's knee and then, as he collapsed, to the right side of his head. Later, he said he'd missed on the second stroke, that it was supposed to catch the guy on the shoulder. "He moved, I think."

"You can be sure he moved," I said. "How do you like them—tied to a chair?" Remembering the way the big guy had dropped straight down, like a stack of cans when you've knocked the bottom ones away.

But daddy didn't move much at all after the second whack. He lay there grimacing and cursing softly. Burgoyne leaned close and said, "How you like that lady now, huh?" and put cuffs on him. Then, somehow, he got the six-foot-four guy to his feet and out into his patrol car. Charged him with threatening an educational institution, assaulting a public school official—class two felonies, and a couple other things.

Anyway, that's how I, how a bunch of us, met Jim Burgoyne. Santana thinks he's God now.

It's really the chief's call as to which cop gets sent to which site as SRO, School Resource Officer, but when the letter came, it was signed by both him and Augustine, as if López had had some input into the assignment. Professional courtesy, I supposed.

Augustine is the total Mexicano, the epitome of a stereotype I'd been avoiding since I was fourteen. I don't mean he's from Mexico or anything, because he isn't. No, I mean you can tell he's Mexican the minute you see him, even from a distance. Short, maybe five-eight, round-faced, medium-dark skin, and he's always smiling like the leader of a mariachi, and his hair is combed over. When he was young, he had slick black hair. I looked him up in one of my old yearbooks when I found out he'd gone to Polk too, graduated three years after I did. But now he's balding like somebody ran over his head with a planer, and he won't accept it, so he combs the hair over from one side. Most of the time he wears a guayabera shirt, white or blood red or light blue, and jeans or linen trousers that cinch up with a drawstring, which he can get away with because of the way the guayabera covers his belt line. And then black boots, pointy ones—the kind the Anglo kids used to call roach-killers when I was in middle school. Unaware of the taunting I'd receive, my parents bought me a pair when I was in eighth grade, which I wore to school only once. Anyway, the pointy boots are part of Augustine's look the same way my Nikes are part of mine.

The chief's letter, and López's too I guess, talked about Burgoyne's exceptional qualifications, which it turns out really are exceptional, but the main reason he came over so abruptly was that his predecessor, a woman named Watson, forgot her loaded pistol in one of the girls' restrooms. No one got shot or anything because the freshman girl who found it took it to her teacher, who then brought it to me, but the police department was pretty embarrassed and relieved that no one outside the school had found out about it. I didn't even report it to the superintendent. The chief told me he owed me one for that.

Burgoyne had served a few years on the PD in Chicago, which was such an insane job, he said, that he decided to move west. One time he and his partner were on Damen Avenue arresting a guy for robbing this little Polish café near the el station, and there was a gang shooting about half a block away, two kids winding up bloody and dead on the street, one fifteen and one nineteen, Puerto Rican kids, right when he and his partner were making the bust, like cops being so close hadn't made any difference at all to the gangbangers.

I wait for him to go on.

He says, "Like the double L for Los Levantes we saw marked on the mirror. Looked like theirs, but why they claiming it at all? They *want* the cops to come after them?"

"They've done it before. It's a message for Crips and Norteños, not for you guys. 'sides, they probably didn't figure the cops'd come too hard if it's just another gang killing."

He glowers at me.

"Just saying. About forty percent of the killings in the state are never solved."

"Come on, Hank. Let the homicide guys do their magic here, and we'll get this perp in the next couple days, and save good old Gus's job."

I chuckle when he says 'Gus,' Anglicizing and coarsening my boss's name right after doing the same thing to mine. I am Enrique. When I was growing up in this neighborhood, the other kids called me Ricky. When I started high school, I asked my teachers to call me Henry because I wanted my name to sound grown up, not like a mere 'Ricky,' and the teachers were almost all Anglos and couldn't pronounce Enrique worth spit anyway.

Besides, in those days I wanted to be an Anglo myself, like my Scots/Irish father, not Mexican like my mom. And I had heard this one black guy on TV talking about white privilege, which seemed like something worth having. It was pretty easy for me to come off as all Anglo too, because I am light-skinned, and I was already six-four at fourteen, almost done growing but taller than most Mexicans ever get. And for the most part, I gave up speaking Spanish then too, even tried to think in English all the time.

But after college, when I started looking for teaching jobs, I used 'Enrique' on applications for places where there are a lot of Spanish surnames. Places like James K. Polk High School, where the demographics include eighty percent Latino kids, an irony that nobody seems to get, and my alma mater for Christ sake. Burgoyne knows most of this and calls me Hank sometimes, for reasons he hasn't explained and I don't want to hear. 'Gus,' rather than Augustine, is funny though, I have to admit.

But Burgoyne is dead serious about Augustine's job being in some danger now, because of the murder. Mine too probably, because Usaré García was killed on campus during a Saturday night school dance, or maybe a little afterward, one of my nights for supervision.

Like wolves hunting, feeding and then regurgitating the contents of their stomach for their brood, media vans are perpetually stalking the perimeter of the campus now, occasionally disgorging a crew to gather file footage and interview anyone leaving the school who feels like commenting on Usaré or placing blame, and of course never locating a Rhodes Scholar who feels like talking for the camera.

In his comments about the crime, the school board president, a guy named Benitez, sounded angry and vengeful and condemnatory. During one interview for television, he said, "Administration has been lax in their approach to the criminal element as it affects our schools. Our kids need to be safe at *all* school functions." He didn't explain how the board's discipline policy discouraging suspensions and keeping offenders in school fits in with Augustine's supposed laziness or my own, and the reporter didn't ask.

Benitez and the rest of the board refer to their approach as restoration, whereby you take some offender, a bully for example, and instead of suspending him, bring him into a meeting with the kids he's harmed and try to talk it all over in hopes that the bullying stops. Restoration can work, I have read, when it is used in schools where the entire school is committed to it, but so far it's failed at Polk, at all the district's schools, because it's seen as a stand-alone alternative to traditional discipline, which I call separation discipline. After everyone has pretended the problem has been resolved through a restoration session, the offender invariably feels as if he's gotten away with something. He death-glares his victims, and they are still afraid of him.

When we keep some delinquent in school for threatening honors kids with a knife, we do get to keep the state aid we'd have lost for forty-five days if we'd suspended him, but we often permanently lose the tax dollars we'd have kept if his victims had not transferred to another school. We feel like unsuspecting sailors on the *Lusitania* as the school-choice torpedo zeroes in on us. All the AP's, all eighteen of us, refer to restoration as 'hug-a-thug.'

"So they got a new theory about what happened? The homicide detectives, I mean."

"Bet your ass they do, but they ain't telling me very much until they got something for me to work on. But tomorrow, the next day, they'll want me to run down everything I can on this gal's associates. Other kids, teachers, secretaries, you . . . everybody. Count on it. You'll be busy."

"Like I'm not. You're thinking it's people she knew."

"Might be one guy. More than one guy, maybe. Might still be a couple of these Levantes. They coulda wanted to recruit Usaré for a prostitute, or one of their bigs mighta had a hard-on for her. Everybody our gender drools when they talk about her. I get it, tits like that, Jesus. And she mighta led their guys on some, then ultimately didn't wanna play along. Sexual motive, seems to me."

He pauses a moment, checking my reaction I suspect. I've never confessed my attraction for Usaré to Burgoyne, to anyone, but I imagine he senses it. I'm thinking about how he must have seen her dead and naked in the morgue as if she were a dancer in some macabre titty bar. Part of me wants to tell him to be more respectful, but part of me wishes I'd been there too, God help me.

"But I'm betting not," he says. "I'm guessing it's somebody she knew."

"Which could still be Los Levantes. She knew everybody. Over two-thousand kids, half of them with hormone-charged dicks."

"Well, that narrows it down. Not only did she know everybody, but according to you everybody loved her, which I suppose means she had no enemies. Two thousand kids, two hundred teachers and staff. She goes to six different classes every day, in five different buildings. And the custodian finds her body in a men's bathroom where there's a couple days' worth of dirt and piss and DNA. It's fabulous!" He pauses momentarily. "Hey, when's the funeral?"

The sudden shift throws me for a moment, and I wonder what made him ask. "Viewing is Friday evening at the mortuary. Family and close friends only. Memorial the next day. They're expecting a lot of people, so we offered them the auditorium. Holds nine hundred. Opening the cafeteria afterward too."

"They Catholic? Her folks?"

I nod, and Burgoyne says, "Well, that's less than twenty-two hundred anyway."

I am about to ask him what the hell he's talking about when the intercom makes its little clicking noise, and Santana's voice says, "Mr. Tavish, it's almost three o'clock. You were going to meet Mrs. Tavish."

"Thanks," I say, taking the ID card off my shirt as I get up. Burgoyne gets up too.

He says, "You still looking for the right house, hey?"

I nod and force a smile. Burgoyne knows I am tired of house-hunting. When my wife and I began looking for a new place, I thought I knew what we wanted—bigger bedrooms for the kids, mine from the first Mrs. Tavish, some space between us and the neighbors, pretty rare nowadays in this town, and maybe a pool since the summers are hot and last about half the year. Anyway, that's what we told the realtor, at least that's what I remember telling him. But today will be the twelfth and thirteenth places we have looked at, because apparently the agent didn't hear me explain what we wanted. Then again, I apparently didn't listen to Eloise very well either.

As I leave the office, I look to count the number of kids who have been referred to my office for any number of mundane infractions: calling teachers bitches or stealing cell phones or throwing gang signs. There are six since Burgoyne and I closed the door to chat. Since I didn't interview any of them, Santana knows to look over the referrals to make sure we aren't turning a felon loose, and then she will send the kids on their way and add the referrals to my pile, which grows a little each day.

I am in a constant state of trying, not to catch up, but to keep within a couple weeks of the dates on the original referrals. Burgoyne may be correct that I am a good investigator, and I take some pride in that, but I am certainly not a fast interrogator, and I have evening duty at least once a week and thirty teachers to evaluate and twenty-six clubs to supervise, and I cannot hear the kids' stories and designate a consequence, let alone schedule a restorative conference with them, as fast as the kids are sent to me.

The other AP's get almost as many referrals as I do, but they handle things differently. Sally, the curriculum gal, with her brash energy and feisty tongue, would rather argue with a parent than listen to some girl's drawn-out explanation of how what she was doing was not really a lap dance for three boys in the basement below the gym, so she lets all the kids say a few sentences and then sends them home for three days or so. I sometimes tease her that she might as well have a suspension kiosk. Will, the athletics director, generally looks for a way to decide kids didn't do anything wrong, especially now that the board and the superintendent don't want us to suspend anyone, even though the teachers get pissed off at him for being soft and seldom assigning a significant consequence. One time a school bus driver sent some boys to him for fighting on the bus, and he judged that since they were almost home, the school didn't have jurisdiction, so they were home free, so to speak.

In any case, neither Sally nor Will has a pile of unprocessed referrals to rival mine.

When Dak, the real estate salesman, shows us the day's first house, he doesn't bother pointing out the big rooms or the pool. Instead, he tells us the house is the oldest in the neighborhood, which has always been a blue-blood neighborhood to begin with, and he names some supposedly-renowned local architect who'd built the place in the forties, some guy whose name started with a J.

Dak says the house is getting close to eighty years old now, but newly remodeled with a premium-grade kitchen by E Jay Cee, the best custom cabinetmaker in town, and a pool house with a full kitchen, cable connection, and a built-in Klipsch stereo system, if we happen to appreciate high-fidelity music. And everything wrapped around the pool, making for "an exquisite entertainment venue." I'm honestly surprised he doesn't say "Dahling."

I say, "There's only a carport, no garage," thinking all I need is somewhere to mount the seventy-inch flatscreen and a set of shelves for my shoes.

But Dak and Eloise are standing at the French doors that open to the pool area now. He says, well no, it's just a carport, but you can see how easy it would be to enclose. Like he and his chums can do it on a spare weekend. I ask when they can come over and get started, and he pretends he hasn't heard.

"Oh my god," Eloise says. "Look at this." She has walked out the French doors and she is at the entry to the pool house. I come up next to her to see what she's looking at. The granite is from the Rosa Beta quarry, Dak says. Subzero appliances. Eloise's mouth is in an O. I know we are going to buy the place. Dak knows it too, so he will try to talk me up if I try to put in a lowball offer, and Eloise will be on his side.

The pool is old-fashioned, a plain oval and over ten feet deep at the drain. The carpet in the main house will have to come up because Eloise hates carpet to begin with, and it is some outrageous turquoise, or maybe teal, and cigarette-burnt in spots. Then there is that carport conversion . . .

Doesn't matter. Eloise can see herself hosting an office party here, bank bigs from Frisco and Taiwan, and of course the stiffs who lock up local Astrobank branches at night like she was doing not too long ago, all of them sipping eighteen-year-old single-malt.

On the way home, I say, "Babe, that's an old house. It's gonna take some maintenance work. Need to replace a bunch of the pool tile. Some termite repairs I bet." We'd already given Dak a check for the earnest money. He'd said that the owners weren't going to take our offer seriously, and, though I don't say so to Eloise, I hope he's right because I don't see how we're going to afford it. Then again, she is being promoted into a vice presidency, so maybe I'm just being a cheap bastard. Right now, we are living in a two-bedroom frame and stucco that's about twenty feet from similar stick houses on either side, and we share a patio wall with neighbors all around. I don't like it any better than she does, but maybe for different reasons, it now occurs to me.

"Yeah, it's old," she says, "but it's on the map. Besides, NJ and Francesca will love having friends over to fool around in the pool. I hope the owners aren't insulted by your offer."

Francesca, nine now, was born eight minutes prior to NJ, short for Nathan Jerome, which is my dad's name too, and she continually reminds him of his second place status, not merely by telling him, but also by beating him to and at most things. When their mother would make chocolate chip cookies, Francesca always claimed the first blob of batter and the first hot cookie out of the oven. Somehow she always managed to get the last one as well. But that particular thing ceased to be an issue when their mother died because Eloise doesn't bake. Still, Francesca beats NJ mercilessly at checkers, old maid, Sorry and fist fights, even if she has to cheat. She is very bright, and she doesn't care about NJ's learning disability, his self-esteem be damned. She's almost Machiavellian. If she were to choose a quotation to live by, it might be Mark Twain's: "Tell the truth or trump, but get the trick." My hunch is she has a bright future in the modern economy.

My other hunch is that NJ will also do fine. His first school experience, Francesca's too, was in our parish school, St. Thomas, where their mom, Maria, was sure they would receive good religious instruction along with academics, but where the staff thought NJ was mentally retarded because he couldn't spell to save his soul and his manuscript looked like Wingdings. It wasn't long before St. Thomas wanted to keep Francesca but have us enroll our son "somewhere more suitable." Before she died, Maria and I agreed they would *both* go somewhere more suitable, so after they completed kindergarten I enrolled them in the public elementary down the street, making damn sure I got them placed with who Maria thought were the right teachers. NJ is too trusting certainly, or his sister wouldn't be able to cheat him so easily, but he has many gifts. Despite his learning disability, he is quite bright, brighter than either his sister or myself, or his mom or Eloise for that matter, with an IQ above one-sixty and ridiculously high functioning in math. Sometimes I fantasize about him counting cards for me in Vegas.

"Just want to have something left to pay for the remodeling," I say. The rest of the drive home is silent, and I realize the kids will probably have to switch schools.

*****

Maria, my first wife, had been dead just a year when Sally surprised me with an invitation to the annual Astrobank holiday party. I knew she was dating some bank guy, in fact waiting for him to propose, and that seemed to be all she cared about other than class counts and the master schedule. I'd hinted before about going to happy hour with her and her friends, since I was lonely and she's damn cute, but she never bit. I thought maybe she was finally taking pity on the poor widower. I was still depressed about losing Maria, and everyone could see it. But no; I found out later it wasn't even her idea to invite me, but Randy's, her bank heartthrob.

There was someone she wanted me to meet, she said, Eloise Lagarde, a stunning blonde, and a branch manager who was expected to get a corporate job soon.

I hesitated, feeling guilty about attempting a new romance. Indulging my fascination for sexy women on Tumblr was perhaps a compulsion, but it did not affect the way I longed for my deceased wife. I had no idea whether actually dating a flesh-and-blood female would allow me to hang on to those feelings, but I told myself Maria would want me to try it, and I accepted the invitation, hoping to get laid that first time out too, I admit, after my heart-torn and celibate year. As I showered, I wondered if I'd look better in boxers or briefs.

Eloise was leasing a loft downtown, and I had to buzz her from the foyer on the first floor. Through the squawk box, she said, "You're early, Ricky," some scold in it, the voice half an octave lower than I'd expected but melodious and lovely. So I'm back to being Ricky, I thought. "Yes ma'am, but I can wait down here in the Starbucks around the corner if you want." There was a little buzzing sound, and one of the elevator doors opened, and she told me to come on up.

When she opened her door, I could see she was wearing a purple dressing gown, trimmed in red and black, short enough so that it stopped a few inches above her knees.

"Nice to meet you," she said, and when I was in, she held my neck and pecked me breezily on the cheek, like it was a thing she might do whenever she met someone socially and apparently not realizing it might have an effect on me. Chanel Number Five wafted faintly from her, reminding me of Maria. She turned, accidentally exposing one of her sizeable breasts as she did and checking to see if I'd noticed, I thought, and saying, "I left some whiskey out for you."

I watched the dressing gown from behind as she moved away, twin buttock mounds switching under the fabric and the purple hem dancing at her bare thighs, and I wondered what kind of underwear she had on and then wondered if it was normal to wonder that. She went into her bedroom but left the door open and sat down at a vanity and leaned into a mirror and tended to her face, which was fair-skinned and mature and sensuous. I told her I appreciated her inviting me up, but she didn't answer.

There were two glasses and a half-spent bottle of scotch with a name I wouldn't care to pronounce sitting on a little wet bar. There was a newspaper there too. "I want mine neat, but there's some ice in the mini-fridge if you want," she said. "And you can bring mine on in please," she added as I poured, me wondering what she would think if I poured too much or too little into the glasses. A lush if it was generous, a prig if it was stingy? I tried to measure an airline-sized pour by sight.

When I brought her the drink, I saw her gown pooched out above where the neckline plunged to her bodice, and I could see her breast again, and I glanced a little too long, and she sensed it and looked up and smiled. I went and sat on a stool near the bar and sipped the whiskey and picked up the newspaper where the story above the fold was about the state budget deal, and I pretended to read it and snatched glances of her prepping in the mirror.

Sally had been right, if anything had understated her beauty.

"I see where the governor is stiffing you guys," she said. I wondered who she meant by us guys, and she said, "The schools. More budget cuts."

I said, "Yeah, we gotta punch another notch in our belt," hoping it sounded neutral. You never know what people think about political things, and I didn't want to get off on the wrong foot with her. And I didn't really want to talk about budgets or politics, or schools either for that matter, so I tried to change the subject. "I love your apartment. How long have you been here?"

"But it's no surprise is it? That's what he said he was going to do during the campaign, reduce spending, run the state like it's a business." She'd started the talking, so I figured it was okay to stare at her. She was sitting upright now, turning her face slowly side-to-side, checking in the mirror. The hem of her gown slanted back along her thigh to where it turned into her buttock. "I was reading about it this morning, with my oatmeal. It says he's stiffing everybody else too, the child protective division, health services, so everybody gets screwed fair and square."

I said that most people thought he was just throwing out the usual lines about cutting waste and inefficiency during the campaign.

She said, "Except the prisons of course. He wants several million more for prisons. The private ones. And some tax breaks for the tech companies. You'll get to the part he says it again, 'We need to adhere to strict business principles,' and so he's keeping his promise. But don't you think he should say, 'We need to let the businesses run the state,' since that's what he really means?"

I hadn't expected a rising star in the bank world to talk like that. I nodded. "Yeah, you're right. Best way to fill up the prisons is to starve the schools." I didn't really want to talk politics though, contemplating her figure. I took a longer sip of the whiskey, which tasted very good without ice to thin it.

"I don't know what your friend told you, but I'm not interested in anything that takes centuries," she said, staring at me now.

I wanted to say something about the past year seeming like centuries, but I didn't know if she'd understand what I meant or appreciate it, so instead I said, "Sally said you were stunning. That's the exact word she used. Stunning."

Eloise said she'd only met my friend once and it was very nice of her to say something like that, and I wondered if she was just fishing, but I still told her Sally was right. Predictable stuff, but she smiled anyway.

TWO

Tuesday evening I'm on the telephone with Burgoyne. As he explains what is going to happen next, I start to see what he means about me being busy, and I'm thinking I'll need to put some other parts of my job on hold for a few days or a week, until they zero in on a suspect for Usaré's murder. I consider talking to Augustine about shifting some of my discipline referral burden over to Sally and Will for a few days, at least the low-level ones, which are the kind I hate most, while I'm holding hands with Burgoyne and the other cops, figuring Augustine might be sympathetic because he's feeling as much heat as I am about the crime and wanting to see an arrest made as soon as possible.

Of course there's the matter of what to do about keeping the crime scene secured while the cops continue poring over it, and I am listening to Burgoyne carefully because I know I will have to explain to the E building staff, mostly English teachers, why it is they are still locked out of their classrooms, why they can't access books or media or computers until at least the end of the week.

The whole building is a crime scene. The killer could have hung around anywhere in there after the murder, or even before, and left some evidence, and it was even possible that the crime itself happened in one of the classrooms or in the English office. There are chalk lines on the linoleum tile in the bathroom where they found Usaré, and the police techs have placed evidence markers at several spots. There are even some smudges on the hallway floor that they think could be blood. I have already explained it once of course, at a meeting I pulled together late Sunday afternoon, with Burgoyne there lending his authority. The teachers did some grumbling about having to use emergency lesson plans, but there was no real argument as long as I had the cop sitting beside me. There was a fair amount of horror to go around, even though most of the actual shock had worn off by then, I suppose. I'd had to tell them about Usaré's murder as I called each of them, of course, or you can bet most of them wouldn't have come to a meeting at school on a Sunday afternoon. But they'd all seen the yellow tape as they'd arrived, along with a half-dozen police vehicles and the uniform cops at both entrances. Most of them knew Usaré and said how awful it was. So yeah, they sense the horror, if only through their imagination, but most of them still want to get back into their own rooms. So tomorrow afternoon, Wednesday, we'll meet again, and this time I know the teachers will rebel.

I say, "My people ain't gonna like it." Trying to make the argument for them now. He doesn't say anything, so I say, "And it doesn't make any sense, Jimmy. That building may have all kinds of evidence that the bad guys left behind, but it's also got fingerprints and spit and sweat from a dozen staff and two-thousand kids. What's the point of finding the killer's prints in say room twelve if there's a jillion other prints in there besides? I'm all about being thorough, but I don't see how your guys can get any more than they got in the last three days."

Chris Jameson, the English department chair, had brought this up to me Monday morning. He said, "Our hallway is like an autistic kid's brain—it contains tons of sensory data, but the cops are like the poor kid—with no way to tell the difference between what's important and what's not." I've been thinking about his point since then, and I have to admit I can't see anything wrong with it.

Burgoyne sighs through the phone. In his mind, he's explained the relevant police procedures to me adequately and doesn't want to have to do it again. I have anticipated his sarcasm, figuring he'll say something like, Golly Hank, did you just get your junior CSI license in the mail? Instead he says, "Know what I think? I think you'd see it different if you hadn't already decided Los Levantes did her." It sounds a little patronizing, but he's giving me an out. It's not that my argument, Jameson's argument, is ridiculous; it's just there's an angle we didn't consider, something we overlooked. He goes on, "Cause you're right, Tavish, it *is* hard to tell what's what with everybody's DNA all over the place." He pauses, for effect I guess. "But see, we got evidence from the unfortunate girl, on and in her actual body, and some of that evidence either matches something we find elsewhere in that hallway or it don't. Like if the DNA we find on this wonderful gal of yours matches some DNA in room twelve, and it doesn't match anything we find in rooms one through eleven, that's helpful information, don't you agree?"

Wonderful gal of mine? I consider, a tremor coursing through me, wondering again how much he senses the affinity I had for her. I say, "Maybe. But I gotta tell you. This is a gigantic disruption. I have freshman classes meeting in the weight room all day long, fidgety little fourteen-year-olds hanging on chin-bars, and I have one teacher meeting classes in five different rooms."

He says, "It'll only be a couple more days. I thought good teachers were flexible." I decide I'd walked right into that one and give up, and he moves to the next point.

"I need you to do a couple things for us." Fabulous! I think it but don't say it. "I'm wondering what you can get me on the teachers."

I say, "Get you?"

"I know you can't share stuff from their official file at this point, but I was wondering if you had your own stuff. And any personal cell phone numbers you got."

"To compare to what's in Usaré's phone, I guess." I wonder how he knows about my files—notes actually, on learning styles, social skills, family status . . . The union gets livid about it. It's against district policy and, according to some, statute, but some of us administrators keep our own files on staff members. I keep a file on every effing one of the people I evaluate, partly because I was a psych minor and I am interested in everything about my staff, and partly because of my experience as a first year administrator when I'd tried to non-renew two teachers. One because he couldn't teach slithering to a snake, and one because not only couldn't she teach but she also insisted, to her students and to their parents, that she had experienced intergalactic travel. I followed the book with both of them, but legal staff missed notice deadlines with them and they skated, then applied for transfers to get away from Polk before I got another shot at them the following year.

"Yeah," I say, "I have a few things I can share. Or I can get it from the other AP's. What sort of information you looking for? I'm guessing you don't want to see their sample lesson plans." I can't help wondering why the police are so interested in the staff right away, why Burgoyne seems to be dismissive about the local gangbangers.

"Tomorrow afternoon okay? Let's start with the E building people plus the teachers on the girl's schedule. Shouldn't take that long."

"Not till two," I say. "Staff council meeting." Then I realize I'd rather meet Burgoyne than sit through the biweekly gripe session and I say, "Well no, we could get going right after lunch if you want. Twelve-thirty."

He agrees, then asks if I'm considered a close family friend of the Garcías. He wants me to go to the viewing, which is not open to everyone, figuring I can keep track of everybody from Polk who shows up. When I say no, he asks if the school shouldn't send me as a representative anyway, and I explain that's probably something Augustine would do as principal, especially since it gives him a pretext for leaving campus early again. He finally drops it.

I'm relieved because one thing I don't want to do on Friday evening is spend three hours with the victim's disconsolate family. I feel loss, for a certainty, and I grieve for Usaré's family, but they would think it strange if

I spent more than a half-hour or so with them at such an intimate proceeding. Burgoyne already knows I'll be at the memorial service Saturday, and he'll be there too.

"The last thing is I'm wondering if I can talk to this custodian, this Benjamin." He says *ben·ha·MEEN*, which is pretty close to sounding right. "Just want to double check something with him. Something he told the detectives."

"He's the day-shift guy, so there shouldn't be a problem, but if it's official you're gonna need a translator."

"Nah, it'll just be a question or two," he says.

I think about Benjamin for a moment. He'd already been working at Polk for ten years when I first roamed the hallways as a freshman, but I didn't pay much attention to him in those days. What did a Spanish-yapping janitor have to offer an Anglo-looking kid named Tavish? He's older, pretty close to retirement now, working as much overtime as he can the past couple years, to nudge his retirement pay up a few dollars a month, which explains why he was working on dance night. It's impossible not to like him because of the way he interacts with the kids. He teases them and lets them tease him back and picks up their messes and hugs them and gives them playful pokes in the ribs, boys and girls and jocks and thugs and geeks alike, and they love him, respect him too. If every staffer could learn to enjoy kids the way Benjamin does, school would be pretty easy on everybody. I wish to hell he had not been the one to find Usaré; it wounded him some way. I could see the pain in his eyes when he came to get me from the gym early Sunday morning, and today I knew it would still be there.

"You need to take it easy with him too."

Burgoyne can tell I mean it, and he says, "Look, I ain't gonna pull out his fingernails, all right?" After a moment, we are about to ring off when he says, "Oh!" like he's remembering one last thing. "You know a kid name o' Andre?"

"Andre Carver? Yeah. Black kid, graduated four, five years ago. Kind of a no-nonsense kid. Had a rep and nobody fucked with him. Still comes to the school sometimes to pick up a kid brother. Why?"

"His number's on the girl's phone. A lot. Nobody fucks with him, you say? He was some kind of high school bad ass?"

"Never made it a point to look like a bad ass. I mean didn't dress to announce himself. Still doesn't. Just a couple of tats. Well put-together, but not huge or super-buff or anything. It's just stories that go around. Lives with an older cousin now—quadriplegic name o' LaShawn. Pretty close to the school."

I think of one of the stories then, involving Usaré actually, and her kid brother Jaime.

It was last year when Jaime was a freshman trying out for football. The older football players were punking Jaime mercilessly. One guy in particular, a linebacker named Eddie, was harassing him—not just giving him titty-twisters in the hall, but pressuring his girlfriend into sex and stealing his clothes and pouring acid all over Mr. García's Ford pickup in the middle of the night—classic asslete pranks. When Usaré found out, she jumped on his back in the hallway one day and wouldn't get off, rode him like a jockey, and started pounding on his head with her fists, which Eddie thought was pretty funny, being a stud linebacker and all.

But then Andre heard about it.

Next thing you know there's a party at LaShawn's house, a rager, a quarter of the school there, and Andre made sure that Usaré came and that she brought along her little brother, even though he was just a freshman, and of course made sure this asshole Eddie got an invitation. Before he left, Eddie had to get on his knees and apologize to Jaime and to Usaré and promise to pay for a new paint job on the Ford, and Andre told him he should expect another little get-together if anybody bothered Jaime again. Bullying over.

Because Andre had a thing for Usaré.

Andre stopped the hazing faster than I or the coaches could have, and stopped it permanently. No, nobody fucks with Andre, not at least, if you believe the stories. Then I think a story like that, even though it's over a year old now, might suggest a motive to Burgoyne and his detective pals, and I make a mental note to tell him about it tomorrow.

"Yeah, I can tell you about Andre too."

When I hang up, Eloise appears, wearing a floral robe and holding two glasses of champagne, and she is just as bubbly. While I've been talking with Burgoyne, Dak has called on her cell phone to congratulate us. There was not even a counter offer. The house is ours.

*****

In the morning, I am at work earlier than usual, thinking I will talk to Santana before the parade starts, thinking I'll give her detailed instructions about which teachers' files to gather, and tracking down Benjamin, and gathering whatever I can pull together on Andre. The trouble is there's already a couple kids in my office, resting on their rear ends with a security guard standing there to make sure they don't do any talking.

Santana tells me they saw a gun on campus, her voice even and low, no drama in it.

I must look dismayed, thinking about the delays, because Santana takes over. She pumps me for a few seconds. I tell her about the conversation with Burgoyne, and she smiles and tells me to go find the gun.

In an hour, I've confiscated a pistol, which turns out to be a soft-pellet gun, and I've written a ten-day suspension recommendation for the two kids in my office and a longer one for the kid who'd brought it to school in the first place and had it stashed in his locker inside a Spiderman backpack. The school attorney wanted me to go for expulsion, but I couldn't see it. "Damn the kid for all time for showing off his new pellet gun to his pals?" I'd said. She spends the rest of the day faxing me articles about kids who'd been badly hurt with soft-pellets, one who died even, but I don't change my mind. It reminds me of the teacher in *A Christmas Story* saying, "You'll shoot your eye out." Then it occurs to me the board president may be right—I'm soft.

It takes a few minutes to track Benjamin down because he never has his radio on. He truly doesn't understand what is being said on the radios except for the names, and in his embarrassment, he always pretends he forgot to turn his on. Ninety-nine percent of the time, no one is trying to raise him, so this strategy works for him quite well.

"Enrique to Benjamin," I say over the radio. No response. I try it a couple more times, and one of the security guards responds to tell me he saw him in the S building, so I call for him to give me a cart-ride to the far end of campus and find Benjamin, holding his broom and looking like he's expecting me, his effort to smile obscured by that same pain, which I now think reached into him and touched his soul, and I don't want to interview him at all. I almost tell Burgoyne to forget it. I don't understand how he can have any more information that the cops could want, and I want to leave him to his private pain.

"Siento molestarte," I say, sorry to trouble you, and I keep going in my half-forgotten Spanish. "The policeman Burgoyne has some questions. Policía." Benjamin's eyes have a kind of distilled darkness, but he nods. He gets into the cart with me and the security guard, and we ride back to my office, Benjamin holding the broom up like a flag in a ridiculous way.

Alerted by Santana, Burgoyne is waiting in my office, and he wastes no time with his questions. "Does he remember if the bathroom was locked the other night? When he first went in? We heard the staff keeps the bathroom locked over there to cut down on the graffiti."

Benjamin explains that it was unlocked on that particular night, but that it is usually locked on a weekend. The night custodian comes through and locks all the rooms on Friday afternoon, then starts cleaning the buildings assigned to him. Burgoyne wants me to ask if he's sure, but I stare him off.

"And that's his hallway to clean? E's assigned to Benjamin? So does he usually do that on Saturday night?" I know the answer to this, but I discuss it with Benjamin anyway, to make Burgoyne happy.

Yeah, the hall is assigned to him. He usually cleans it on Saturday morning, but since he took the overtime to clean up after the dance, he put it off and combined the regular shift with his overtime shift so he could sleep in on Saturday morning. He's a little sheepish about this, because he knows there are rules about such things, and he thinks he may have broken one or more of them. He probably has.

"Did he maybe disturb anything? Doesn't matter how small. I mean, he comes in and sees her right away and runs off to get you, or . . . what? Did he touch her at all? Touch her stuff. Her clothes? Her purse?"

I try to ask this as gently as I can, but the old man starts to tear up, maybe from fear or maybe from shame. In half a minute, his face is red and there are tears literally streaming down his cheeks, and I am wishing I were somewhere else, but I tell him it's okay and not to worry and just tell us what happened, and I wait.

Finally, he says, "Lo siento. Lo siento. Lo que dije antes fue un error. Al primer policía." I explain to Burgoyne that he's sorry and he made a mistake with the cops before, guessing that Benjamin's referring to things he said to the detectives who'd questioned both him and me Sunday morning.

"What kinda mistake?"

I assume Benjamin understands he's being asked to explain and I don't say any more. His tears aren't slowing down any, and his glasses are getting foggy, and he finally removes them. Now, he lowers his head, and he's shaking it slowly side to side.

"Lo siento," he says several more times, and we wait. Finally, he tells us how it was. He thought she was sleeping there on the floor at first, not regular sleep of course, but maybe the kind that comes after drinking too much, like maybe she and her friends had smuggled some tequila into the dance and she'd sneaked away to be sick, and had fallen and bumped her head, so he knelt to wake her. He remembered smiling at her, like a wink for being drunk, having been drunk himself once or twice when he was young. He touched her neck and then held her chin and moved her head, to one side and then the other, and he knew she was dead, and he rose and stepped back, then really seeing her as dead, seeing the pitiful way she looked. He was about to call me on the radio to say, '¡Tavish, ven aqui!' but then thought I wouldn't hear him anyway in the gym with all the music and noise. "Entonces pensé en mi hija."

I tell Burgoyne he thought of his daughter. "No quería que la gente lo ve de esa manera." He didn't want people to see her that way, I say.

"What way?" Burgoyne says, and I think about asking him if he's got a daughter, which I know he doesn't, and I think of Francesca for a second. But then I don't say anything to him, and instead, I ask Benjamin about how she looked.

I can see he's ashamed to even tell us, but he says, "Su vestido se levantó por encima de su cintura y sus piernas se extendió, y su lugar de secretos fue descubierto." I tell Burgoyne that the hem of the girl's dress was pulled up above her waist and her legs were splayed, and her vulva was exposed. Benjamin had called it her place of secrets, but I thought that the delicacy of the euphemism might be wasted on Burgoyne.

When he goes on, Benjamin explains he looked around for her underpants, so that he could dress her, but didn't find any. Then he saw her purse lying on the floor and thought maybe she had panties in there, assuming that modern Americanas sometimes find it necessary to take their underpants off at one time or another when they go out dancing, and so he picked up the purse and looked through it, but no, just make-up.

"And?"

He went on again, and I explained. He pulled her legs together and lifted her at the waist so that he could pull the dress down to cover her, and when he thought she looked okay, he touched her cheek and her hair.

"What'd he do all that for?"

"You got a daughter?" I say.

Burgoyne pulls up the left corner of his mouth while he looks at me, but he is tight-lipped, a signal that he is done questioning our custodian for now, so I apologize to Benjamin for how hard this has been and ask him if he wants to go home. When he shakes his head, I call the security cart back to take him back to S building. Just before he leaves, he turns and tells me that if it's okay with me he won't be doing any overtime for a while, and then he walks out, carrying his broom on his shoulder.

I say, "So I'm guessing he left some of that out when he first talked to the detectives the other night." When he nods, I add, "Well you guys couldn't think he's a suspect."

"Tavish, us guys think everybody's a suspect until he ain't. Even you, except the kids woulda noticed if you left the gym long enough to go kill somebody. Nobody there to put a stop to all the bumping and grinding."

I remember the beginning of Saturday's dance, talking with the chaperones and the security guards just prior to opening the doors and letting the kids in, making sure we all understood what we were supposed to do for the next four hours, which chaperones got the first break at nine o'clock, and that we all had radios and flashlights. And for this dance we were all wearing buttons which Mr. Mayer, the sponsor had made for us. The buttons had one word—HUMPING—with a cancel sign superimposed. I anticipated some parent calling me all offended about it on Monday morning, but keeping the kids from getting too physically attached in the darkened gym was our primary job, and the buttons at least gave us all a good laugh.

To Burgoyne I say, "Humping. We call it humping."

"Anyway, the lab guys will want his prints and a DNA sample."

"What for?"

"Elimination data. Make sure it doesn't match anything the perpetrator left."

I nod.

"You said you can remember the victim arriving the other night? To the dance, I mean?"

"Following up with me now? Like you did with Benjamin?" We stare at one another for what seems like a long time.

"We just want to know if you or anybody noticed something. And maybe forgot it. Like your custodian did."

I don't want to let this irritate me, but it does. I want to tell him I don't want to tag along on his investigation, to kiss my ass. I'm no teary-eyed old guy with a broom, and he obviously doesn't think I'm a suspect.

And of course, I don't want him to probe me about my feelings for the dead girl.

I look away from him and stare momentarily at my kids' photos hanging on the wall, their eyes umber and smiling and naïve; I sip my iced tea and consider the galloping cavalryman painted on my wall to represent our school mascot—the Chargers; I lean back in my chair and rock a little; I fold my hands.

"Proceed then," I say.

"So, it'd be good to know who saw her last, and when that was. Starting with the adults of course. We get lucky, one of you saw her leave maybe. Whether she left alone."

"That *would* make you lucky." I sip my tea again.

"Us, Tavish. It would make *us* lucky. Look, the detectives are expecting me to give 'em a lot of help on this, 'cause they figure I know something about the school. And that means I'm expecting you to give *me* a lot of help." The way he says it takes an edge off my annoyance, making it sound like he needs my help, even though I suspect Burgoyne is patronizing me, because I know he wants to be a detective himself, and he thinks the García case represents an opportunity for him to impress his superiors.

Burgoyne's motivation to leave Chicago was not just to escape the intensity of its violence; he's also mentioned that there were too many angels to please in order to get a promotion there.

I know him better than anyone, I think, except for maybe a few other cops and some people back in Chicago. He has an older sister who lives in Arlington Heights with a husband and two sons. His Polish mother, who still lives in the three-flat where she grew up, gets by pretty decently now on social security, rent from the tenants above and below her, and the remains of an estate left by her parents. Burgoyne's father is dead, run over on a sidewalk one Sunday afternoon by a stockbroker who'd drunk a few beers at a Cubs game trying to sober up from the flask of bourbon he'd brought along. The stockbroker, who was a connected guy in a city where it meant quite a lot to be a connected guy, paid a fine and went home. Mrs. Burgoyne paid the funeral bill and went to work in a department store. Jim carried groceries so he could pay his mom something for room and board and got into the academy as soon as he was eligible after high school. He has told me more than once, "I was either gonna get that stockbroker or a hundred sons of bitches that reminded me of him." He married his high school sweetheart after the academy, but it didn't last. Sometimes he'll say, "I wasn't the guy she thought I was, and I found out she wasn't what I wanted," but I wonder how his ex would talk about it. His innocent looks can be deceptive, and they are always disarming. He has a forceful side, after all. But at some point in every situation, I begin to trust him. Santana assumes he's right about everything from the very beginning, no matter what's going on.

"Okay. I remember her coming in just after eight. She was dressed to the nines. Well, you saw the black dress. But she was made up great, overdid it a little on rouge but not as much as some of the kids. Beads or pearls and big, blingy hoop-and-pearl earrings. Patent heels, but ones she could dance in. Came in with friends, three girls and a guy. Course you see groups a lot more than you see couples or singles nowadays."

"Who were the kids?"

"The girls were Mona Bracamonte, Chevy Harris . . . Rachel Cruz. The guy was Marcus Lee, Chinese-American kid. He was probably their ride." He pulls out his note pad and writes, asks me if Chevy is the full name, and I say it's Chevelon.

"And all the adults were right there in the lobby watching them come in?"

"No. Me and Mr. Mayer, who was handling the money, and Amin the security guard, who was hovering around the money as well, and Mrs. Rocha, who was trying to control the crush at the front door. The others had gone on into the gym or up above to the second level."

"Second level?"

"Yeah. Kids will sneak up there if we don't police the area, and get a little too friendly for their own good. We don't want little junior Chargers nine months down the road. And it's also the best place for us to see into clusters of kids down on the dance floor."

"Clusters."

"Yeah, the kids get into circles to watch dirty dancing and to hide stuff."

"Hide stuff."

"If a fight is gonna start, or if there's a bottle going around. We shine a flashlight beam into the mix and it usually dissolves pretty fast.

"So did you see Usaré later on?"

"Couple times."

"She with the same kids?"

"Not Usaré. She worked the room. One time I remember seeing her talking to the DJ, who's one of the teachers too, Mr. Nuñez, probably making a song request, and once over at the punch bowl, which is also supervised— Mr. Trujillo there. And once she was getting a lot of attention dancing nasty with a kid named Keanu till I shone my flash beam down there into the mix. Keanu Jones."

He writes again, and while he does I picture Usaré on the dance floor, butt to crotch with Keanu like two fluid spoons in a drawer. The hip-hop music comes back to me too—"Drop it Like it's Hot." Not stopping their dry hump in the glare of my FlashTorch either, not until Amin comes through the cluster that surrounds them.

"What else?" he says.

"Didn't see her slip out, but we monitor all the doors so nobody can get in for free. Fire department won't let us chain the doors, of course. One of our people probably remembers seeing her leave."

"So how many of those chaperones are outta E building? Got a key for it I mean."

I see where he's going with this, but I also know that over the years, some of the teachers from that building, from most buildings actually, have lost their keys. My office is in charge of issuing keys, and Santana and I are more frustrated than anyone about it. It used to be standard procedure to rekey the building when that happened, but since we started using restricted keyway locks, it has become cost-prohibitive. And teachers wait days, even weeks, to report lost keys, hoping they'll turn up, apparently afraid I will have them executed.

Besides which, if a kid takes a fancy to something in one of the rooms, say a Samsung computer monitor, he will sometimes slip a wedge into the classroom's emergency exit door so that it's closed but not latched, figuring he'll come back after hours and snag the thing. Now we depend on the security cameras as a deterrent. I explain all this to him.

"Yeah, we looked at those security videos—nothing there from that night except the custodian, 'cause it only monitors one end of the building. The wrong end obviously. But we need to look at the straightest line first, so, tell me anyway."

I explain that most of the cameras were set up to monitor people entering and leaving campus. Only a few are set up to view on-campus activity. The camera installed in E building monitors the building's east entrance, which faces Park Avenue. He waits, a little impatient.

"But to answer your question about the chaperones, me and the security guard have master keys. One E-building teacher, Babs McNally, 'cause she needs access to the auditorium. And Mrs. Rocha too, I'm pretty sure, 'cause she's special ed and needs to get into three or four different buildings. She team teaches with Jameson, the department chair."

"Anybody lose their key since the last time you rekeyed?"

"I'd have to check, but like I say they don't necessarily report it right away."

"Would you mind checking then?" He sounds polite suddenly, like he's made some kind of shift inside his head. I nod, and he says, "Here's the other thing. Can you go through all this with the chaperones? See if anybody saw her leave and such? If they noticed her spending more time with someone in particular." I nod again, and he says, "Sorta pre-screen them for the detectives, without tipping what's going on of course."

"No tipping."

"Now what about this Andre? You think it's the same guy? Last name wasn't in the phone, but he called her a couple hours before she died."

"Yeah, probably the same guy." I tell him about Andre's anti-bullying campaign on behalf of Usaré and her little brother. "She call him or the other way? I don't see how she could have talked in the gym with all the noise. Well, maybe in the bathroom."

"Last call was an in-call; she didn't answer; no message either. There was a text from him, but it was later, like two AM. Asking her if she needs a mocha or anything."

"Later?" I say, the hollowed-out feeling in my chest seizing me again.

He nods, "After the custodian found her."

"You'd think there'd be a lot of texts. Specially if they still had a thing."

"Just like what we do, you know. Texts and emails when we want documentation, calls when we don't." He's right of course. Andre, anybody, could have texted Usaré knowing he wouldn't get a response.

And now, nothing will do but for us to go talk to Andre.

THREE

When we get there, Burgoyne observes that Andre has security cameras. "Better coverage than you got at the school too," he says. We're in my Camry because Burgoyne didn't want to pull up in his Crown Vic.

"Lashawn's probably got more money than we do," I say. I tell Burgoyne that in 1998, Lashawn was the king of Polk High School, every girl's fancy and expected to go to UCLA or Oregon the following year—led the conference in scoring, steals, assists, and shooting percentage. B-plus average besides. But over the summer, a guy in a Suburban T-boned his Honda and rewrote his future for him. Instead of a couple years' preparation for the NBA, Lashawn got a huge settlement. He's in a wheel chair, but he's got a red Caddy with hand controls in the garage, and he pays for everything in cash nowadays.

Burgoyne says, "So if he could still walk and feed himself, it would have been as good as winning the Powerball. Must be in his thirties now. So Andre lives with him? Takes care of things?"

I nod.

After we ring the buzzer, a male voice speaks to us through an intercom speaker in the wall and says hello and asks us, "Whass up?"

"This is Enrique Tavish from over at the high school. I'm here with our SRO, and we'd like to talk to Andre Carver if we could."

There is a pause, twenty seconds or so, and we hear voices, because somebody's apparently holding the talk switch open, and then a second voice says, "Hey Mr. Tavish, this is Andre. I'll come let you guys in." I know the calm voice right away, not eager, but accepting.

When the door opens, Andre says, "Y'all just getting around to this? I thought I'd see someone way before now." He's wearing blue and red workout clothes, and he's sweating like he's just finished a workout.

Burgoyne is showing his ID as we come in, saying he appreciates Andre seeing us, and they are sizing each other up. Andre's appearance always surprises me a little because it doesn't seem to fit the stories I've heard about him. He looks . . . well, pretty ordinary. He's solidly built for sure, not lean but not even starting on a gut; his muscle masses are rounded, not cut, and he's not quite six feet. His wiry hair is barbered, you can tell, and short.

The front room has a high ceiling and it's huge, and some walls have been removed to get it that way. There's a black leather sectional in one corner, and a huge flat-screen, and in another corner a bar and black leather stools, but much of the room is set up as a gym. There is a rack of dumbbells, a set of parallel bars and some kind of machine that looks like a stationary bike, with a Theracycle label. A basketball goal, glass backboard included, juts out from the wall.

"So you wanna sit down?" Andre says, motioning vaguely toward the bar stools. When we do, he sits on the seat of the Theracycle and swivels it around to face us.

"The García girl was quite a bit younger than you, wasn't she?" Burgoyne says.

"That's like me asking if I can get you a beer or something." Letting us know the answer is obvious. His skin is dark umber but otherwise his deadpan face matches Burgoyne's exactly.

"Actually, I was kind of hoping you could give me a water." Andre looks peeved, but he gets up and asks me if I need one as well, and I say no. When he hands over the bottle of water, Burgoyne says, "I'm wondering if the two of you were seeing a lot of each other lately."

"You wondering too, Mr. Tavish?" I remember questioning Andre in my office one time, my first year as AP, about which group of kids owned a particular stretch of hallway. He wasn't very forthcoming during that little chat either.

"It was on my mind, yeah."

"Being five years younger," Andre says, "doesn't mean she didn't know what she wanted. Usaré talked a lot about what she's gonna do, who she's gonna know some time soon. Seems like she didn't remember how hard it's gonna be getting outta a place like this."

"Place like this?" Burgoyne says.

"Y'all know what I mean. Sometimes she'd forget about her whack folks, this neighborhood, this here town, that lousy school of yours. Somethin' was always there to remind her, but she didn't pay it no mind."

Burgoyne says, "Yeah, some people don't wind up too far away from where they start out, but it sounds like she was going in the right direction."

Andre gives out a little laugh then, and a sudden knot in my gut wants me to tell him to stop, but he goes on before I can. "Usaré was gonna go somewhere, that's for sure. Y'all need to read between the lines a little. You probably know we had it going for a while, me and her, but I was never gonna be the one for her. She was saving it for the big ticket."

"So she *was* seeing you exclusively for a while? When was that?" Getting back to the original question.

"I guess you could say we's together around Christmas for a few weeks."

"And then she broke it off? Or you?"

"They's no breaking off the way you mean. Nodody announce nothing. She just quit coming around, and I know they's somebody else."

"And how'd that go over with you?"

"Wasn't crazy about it, but they's other girls." His tone is one of observation, not ego defense. I wonder momentarily if he's continually flirting with women, the way I do when I'm not at work, or if women are simply attracted to him.

"You seeing someone else now?"

"I thought you wanted to talk about Usaré. How 'bout if I ask you if you's seeing someone?" Not angry, I can see, just teasing Burgoyne, and I have to admit I'm enjoying it. You can tell Andre knows what's going on, why we are here, and he isn't worried about it. He hasn't even bothered to look at the Glock on Burgoyne's hip. I think he wants to smile but pictures Burgoyne as a dumb white boy, so he puts his tough face on. He's a guy you're definitely going to call Andre, not Andy or Ray.

"We couldn't help seeing you called her Saturday night, while she was over dancing. Called and texted her a lot the last few days actually." Burgoyne wearing his altar boy face.

"Then you saw she called me a lot too. And you saw she's the one started the string o' texts. 'bout last Wednesday, yeah?"

Before Burgoyne can follow up, there's a whirring sound, and we look left toward the hallway.

Seconds later a wheelchair rolls in, black guy driving it, ball-shaped hand controls between thumbs and forefingers, but coming sure and fast, like he's made this drive ten thousand times. I know, and I'm sure Burgoyne knows, it's Lashawn. He's an odd mix of features: cut pects and shoulders, solid neck and arms, but then long skinny fingers that look frozen. Sinewy legs attached to twisted ankles and feet. It's easy to see why he's got the all the gym equipment. He's wearing a Polk Chargers tank tee and gray shorts, like he's about to get out of the wheel chair and play hoops for the school. Then you remember he can't walk.

"What's goin' on, cousins?" Lashawn's voice is a tenor but meaty and sure. "We got the man heah in the neighborhood? You offer the man some refreshment, Dre?"

Andre keeps looking at us but says, "I kinda hinted at it." After a little pause he says, "You guys need somethin' more?"

I shake my head. Burgoyne stares.

Andre says, "Mr. Tavish and the officer come to talk about that girl, the one who died over to the school."

"Yeah, terrible thing, that." Lashawn is nodding his head gravely. "You on to who done her yet?"

"We're looking at some people," Burgoyne says. "Mr. Carver here was just now trying to help us on that."

Lashawn is nodding his head, saying hmmm. "Maybe my man heah need a lawyer."

"It's cool, L-man. Mr.Tavish ain't here to hang me. Let 'em finish." Andre thinking I've been brought along to lower his guard. And I'm sure Burgoyne hatched it that way.

Burgoyne says, "Your text you ask if she's gonna come by for a mocha. You expecting her after the dance then?"

"More like hoping."

"Maybe you were hoping enough you'da gone on over to the school and give her a lift, hey? In the Caddy to impress her and the other girls maybe?"

Lashawn says, "That ain't the kinda thing my man Andre do, know wha'm sayin? Go chasin' a kitty like that one. He take her sugar but only if she bring it to him, same as I would. And anyway, he don't take my Caddy out 'less I'm along." I think about this and decide it's probably true. Any time I see the Cadillac in the school parking lot, when Andre's come to pick up his little brother, Lashawn is in it, although it's usually Andre driving. "You wastin' you time. You dogs barking after the wrong tomcat."

"So who should we be chasing? In the interest of saving time and all." Burgoyne is letting this get under his skin a little, I can see, since he didn't think he'd be tag-teamed.

Lashawn sees the irritation too, and he smiles. "Well, you know as well as us them Levantes left they callin' card." He lets this sink in, since no one is supposed to know about the gang sign marked on the mirror. Then he says, "And if not, they's always her papa. He always got a thing for her. Everybody know that why she was the way she was."

"The way she was?" I hear myself asking this, and asking it the same way Burgoyne would for Christ sake, not liking the implication. All three of them are looking at me now, my face reddening I know.

"He means the way she always got herself to the front of the line," Andre says.

The knot twists tighter in my stomach, and I want to say, What the hell does that mean? Instead, I say, "Maybe it would help the police if you explained that."

"What's the point?" Andre says. Then Burgoyne asks why not.

Andre's voice is deep and calm. New Year's Day was supposed to be the day he and Usaré were going to leave. South to Tumacoccori, where they would swear vows to one another in the old mission, cuz that's how it had to be if she was gonna be with him for several days like that cuz her parents wouldn't like her running off with him, and the ring would help when she come back; he'd already bought the ring, only four hundred dollars. And then south to Nogales and then farther south to Santa Ana and Hermosillo and Guaymas, where the water is. The water was always important to her, the ocean, getting out of this stupid desert for a few days with someone she cares about, she says. Not really married yet, but sworn to each other. What the hell, never done that before and she's a fine girl.

But there was a hard freeze on the twenty-eighth, and again the next two mornings, and he'd gone over to her house on the thirtieth to help her father with a burst pipe. It was half-inch copper that ran across the roof, and Mr. García was afraid to go up on the ladder for fear of falling, and besides there were sheets of ice on the roof from the water that had collected, easy to slip on, and Usaré assumed he was good at fixing that kind of thing since he worked part-time for Joorgensen, the construction company, Usaré not really caring about the difference between grading roads and mending copper pipes. He would have just as soon seen the old son-of-a-bitch fall and break his neck, but if he didn't go, it would be a two-hundred dollar service call from a plumber because it was the holidays and all, and plumbers could charge whatever they wanted, and they didn't have that much to spare at the Garcías'. Besides, maybe it turns out Usaré's alone, like she is sometimes at that house, and that would be just fine with him. Andre took his toolbox.

The sky was bright and clear, but it was bitter cold. Since his old Mustang was having some kind of trouble, maybe the fuel pump, Lashawn let him take the Caddy. He didn't think it would be a problem, even though it was a claimed neighborhood, because he could pull into the driveway to park, get it off the street so them Levantes would leave it alone.

Besides that, he's Andre. He's used to people giving him some room— white, black or Mexican—anybody who knows him and anybody who's heard of him. And almost everyone this side of town has heard of him, at least if they haven't hit thirty yet. Los Levantes, this street gang, is no match for Andre and his friends.

Andre's speech sounds more and more like Lashawn's. "Besides," he says, "I know going over there I ain't gonna do a copper pipe replacement 'less I have to. That take too long. Mess with flux and solder and a torch and all like that. I's gonna look at it, go to the hardware store and get a couple Sharkbite fittings. Get outta there in twenty minutes. Car wouldn't be there more'n five while I check it out."

It didn't work out like Andre hoped.

Usaré wasn't there alone, he could see when he pulled up, her papa there to make sure Andre understood what needed to be done, he guessed, and his pickup parked in the driveway besides, so he had to leave the Caddy on the street. And across the street, five or six cholo-looking guys sitting on they porch, no jackets even though it was cold, wearing they crack-ass plaid flannels buttoned at the collar but open below, showing they crack-ass starchy tee shirts. Sitting around a smoky chimenea and drinking forties, you could see, and smoking bud, you could smell, with a couple puta-loca girls, all of them staring at the Caddy when he pulled up, checking out the chrome wheels and then sizing him up when he got out. And he thought he shouldn'ta brought the Caddy.

But what the hell. He gonna say hi to Usaré and her old man, climb up on that roof and see what up and come back down and leave for the hardware store. Five minutes tops, and he'd see the car all the time from the roof anyways. And that was pretty much how it went, 'cept Usaré wasn't there at all; some guy from the weekly paper had come and picked her up to interview her about what it meant to be a peer counselor at Polk High School, and it bothered him some that she wasn't there, since she asked him to come help and they was planning to go off together in a couple days, so there was just the old man, who was sorta faded from Coors already. Andre was probably only there four minutes, truth be told, so no trouble, except kinda pissed at Usaré.

I remember seeing the article now, which appeared in *Arizona Times* about the middle of January. Usaré's photo was on the cover and her name in the headline, all above the fold, even though it was the MLK Holiday edition, the King remembrance relegated to a banner on the cover that told readers to go to page two. And I remember the reporter coming to the school to do some research, shadowing Usaré most of the day and interviewing Mrs. Nelson, the peer counselors' advisor. He had an unusual Ionian name, because his family was from one of the islands there, he said, Laskeris or something like that. The article was very complimentary of Polk High School and Mrs. Nelson and of course Usaré. Mrs. Nelson was very proud of her peer counseling program and of her girl, so she had the article laminated and posted it on her bulletin board. Usaré brought a bunch of copies to school, too, since it's a free newspaper, and they circulated on campus for a couple weeks or so. And I know her Facebook page buzzed about it quite a bit, her friends' too.

Andre's trouble started when he came back with the parts from Lowe's.

His mistake was thinking the cholos would leave the Caddy alone as long as he could see it. He'd just finished the repair and tossed down the unused piece of tubing, and the leftover insulation and tape he'd used to wrap the pipe, and he had the cutter and the funny-looking little C-shaped tool in his pocket. Heading for the ladder to go down again, he heard sounds from the street, a couple whacking noises, and he looked over and saw two of the cholos swaggering away from the Caddy, one of them carrying a baseball bat.

He shoulda called his brothas, he said, since he had his cell phone the whole time. But it surprised him, they being so dissy and brassy like that, hammering the car with the bat and not even bothering to hide it, and him still pissed at Usaré, and he didn't think to call anybody, maybe Lashawn, who'da had ten brothers there in two minutes. Stupid, he knew pretty soon after, and still knew.

He could see where they banged the car, once on the hood and once on the roof, and all he could think about was how the girl wasn't there when she shoulda been, 'steada off with some reporter, and how pissed Lashawn gonna be.

"Sho was, man," Lashawn chimes in.

And they's sitting over on that porch with they putas locas and they crack-ass plaid shirts and they fucking Louisville Sluggers and they tough-looking grins. But he's used to fixing this kinda disrespect his own self, and he stopped to lift the trunk lid where his tools were and took out the sleever bar he used sometimes on the job, pissed off but still thinking clear enough to leave the trunk open, and crossed the street. They was six of them, not counting the putas locas, and they all stood up when he came. And he started thinking then that it was a bad idea, him, Andre, going over to give six guys a beat-down by himself, even if he did have a sleever bar. But he kept walking, thinking at least a couple of them had to be chicken-shits, and they probly too stoned to do any harm anyway. Then they came down off the porch, fanning out around they boss man, the one they call Memo, the only one not wearing plaid, most of them with hands hanging down at they sides, and two of them holding bats. He was close enough now to see some tats, that fucking fancy double-L for Los Levantes, 'the lifts' in English for fuck sake, what they lifting, they limp dicks?

And then he was standing on they yard, which was just crummy weeds and dirt that nobody ever did nothing with, and they was still pot-smell hanging in the air, and mesquite smoke from the chimenea, and he said he just needed that motha-fucker right there, pointing, who just hit the car and the rest of them could go chew on tacos and putas and keep smoking weed while he killed the stupid one. But now he knew that none of them would run scared because they had their crew together and none of them had to face him alone, and if one was a coward, he could fake his way through and pretend later that he was a tough guy. It woulda been nice to have his own crew, he realized, but he hadn't called anybody, so he didn't have them there, and it was now and he couldn't go back a few seconds and make a call, so he would just have to do what he could, damn that motha-fucker with the bat, who was just showing off for his dick-wad cholo friends anyway, and Usaré, who needed to see her photo in that fucking weekly rag, and her half-drunk papa, all three.

Besides, in the toolbox was his strap, a Beretta nine-millimeter, loaded, one in the tube, if he needed. And if he could get to it before these guys smashed his skull in.

"They boss-man come first, big bastard, Memo, but it was just a juke, and the bat guys come next, two of them at once, and I waited a half-second till they started they swings and then I stepped toward the one on the left an' poked him hard with the sharp end of the sleever so's I know he needs a doctor, and glad cuz he's the asshole done Lashawn's car, while the other guy swung short, and then I came back and got that one in the side with the edge of the bar, while he's still trying to recover from the swing he took, knowing right away I'd broke a couple his ribs, the dumb ass. They wasn't feeling so much like holding they bats then, and I seen everybody else jus' standing, like they'd all expected those two to handle it, 'th them just there for show, and I knew it was time to go."

"You was crazy goin' over there like that," Lashawn says.

"So then I's walking away, quick but not hurryin' cuz I know that start 'em sooner, but listening, cuz I expect 'em to come. I switch the bar to my left hand so I could reach in for the piece easier. I's about half-way back to the car, thinking maybe they wasn't comin', and thinking I maybe shoulda done the rest of them with the bar. But then one of the putas locas holler 'Get him, you bitches!' which is funny now, ain't it, cuz they's too stoned to come after me 'thout their putas yelling at 'em, even they boss. So they come, and I run and reached in the trunk and got the Beretta and turned and put it on Memo's head jus' when he come up, and it stop him, stop them all, jus like it shoulda, right where they standing. I's still holding the bar in my left hand, so now I swung it and got their boss man on the leg, trying for the knee but maybe missing cuz o' wanting to keep my eyes on they eyes. But he went down anyway, and the rest of 'em all too stoned and too smart to do anything. Then I thought it be funny if I talk to 'em like they putas done, and I said, 'Get *him*, you bitches!' and I drop the bar into the trunk then to let the rest of them know they bones is safe, and they got him outta there."

The knot in me is untying itself, but it's still there. Burgoyne is nodding and waiting for Andre to go on.

"I got a text from her in the afternoon asking me what happened over to the Martinez house, meaning the cholo neighbor I figured, but I didn't want that going out in a text so I didn't answer. She called me later, the evening actually, and I's thinking she's gonna thank me for fixing the pipe, cuz her family got water again. And I's gonna ask her about New Year's and the trip, cuz we talked about leaving New Year's Eve, since that would be a time she'd normally go out and her folks wouldn't miss her till the morning."

"And?" Burgoyne says.

"She's angry wit me . . . wit how it went down. She couldn't go no more. She don't know how I could slam those boys like I done, sendin' three boys to the clinic, making it hard for her family now, cuz the Martinezes is neighbors you see, cousins besides, and her dad don't want trouble wit them Martinezes. And I's thinkin', well it's out the window then, I don't want no more of this shit."

"You done come to yo' senses, nigga," says Lashawn. "Never unnerstood why you's thinkin' bout running off 'th that gal . . ."

"Didn't you tell her about the Caddy?" I say, and Burgoyne snaps his head around at me.

Andre says, "I ain't 'splaining nothing to her. I know what she's saying is bullshit. I know she lookin' for an excuse to stay here, get her name and her face in the weekly, besides knowing her daddy already ain't likin' her going around with a black dude. It's okay. I'm already thinking I got two weeks to return the ring. I thought maybe I's lookin for a way out too, 'fore things got too regular. Really didn't wanna make them vows."

"Seems like you had every right to break it off," Burgoyne says. "So you reckon she took up with the reporter?"

"What choo think?"

"So when did you hear from her again?"

"Never did."

"Till last week."

"Yeah. Last week."

"Mm-hmmm."

"So why'd you respond?"

Now Lashawn breaks in again. "You'd a got back to her too. Tavish too. We all would." I think of his disability—arms and legs, nothing else, and he's rebuilt those mostly. Yeah, he would've got back to her.

"She say everything gonna be all right. And I like her. Her mom and her little brother too," Andre says.

"When was the last time you saw her?"

"She come by last Thursday after school. She text me on her lunch time asking if she could come over."

"And you let her come . . . after all that." Burgoyne trying to rile Andre now, and I'm thinking it's a waste of his time, that he won't respond, Andre too calm and proud for that.

But he says, "It's crazy, right. Waiting on her then, wondering if she ever arrives. She always good at making dreams though." The way he phrases it surprises Burgoyne and me both.

"So why you think she got hold of you again? After all that time?"

"She need someone on her side again." Lashawn talking.

Andre looks at him but answers Burgoyne. "I think she having trouble with them Martinezes."

"Levantes?"

Andre nods. "You don't find the guy pretty soon, I will."

Back in the car, Burgoyne produces a plastic bag from his pocket and slips the half-drunk bottle of water into it and seals it.

*****

"So what did you make of all that?" I ask.

Burgoyne is sitting across from me in a booth at Mija's, which has the reputation of making the best chorizo in town, which in turn explains why so many south-side politicians meet people here for early breakfast—businessmen who need influence on the city council or at the legislature or union guys who need the same thing, or somebody who wants the ear of a school board member. If it were breakfast, I wouldn't be here because there's a good chance somebody would spot me and report me to the board president as MIA, which I am. I am also hungry, however, with nothing to eat before work, and the lunches at Mija's are not famous for anything, so there are only a few diners in the place. It smells of roasted onions, Ancho chiles and lard. We are sipping coffee that tastes like it's been sitting too long and waiting for our taco plates. "Sounded like Andre agrees with me about the Levantes."

He's ready for my remark, and he answers on the next beat. "Yeah, well Pontius Pilate blamed Herod if I remember the story right." A guy who's never heard of Occam's razor. "What else did it sound like to you?"

"Like he's a guy who wanted to do stuff for her. Still does," I say and look at him as hard as I can. "He *will* go after them you know."

"Not if he left prints or DNA at the crime scene."

"Well, she's the moveable part of the crime scene. How long can her body hold onto semen?"

"Can be a couple days in the vagina. They can even tell how long based on the condition of the sperm."

"And he said she came by Thursday, so the better evidence is fingerprints, yeah? Or DNA on her clothes? I mean, if he's the one."

He nods. "But the thing that helps rule him out is no match at all."

"Honestly, I don't think they'll find any sign of Andre on her." Maybe inside her though, from Thursday. I frown.

"You've made it plain what you think. So who do you like so far *besides* the Levantes?"

"Well, not her dad since it happened at the school. That's just Lashawn being disgusted about some old rumors. And not Lashawn 'cause he'da needed help. And not Nick Laskeris, 'cause he didn't have a motive."

"Probably not, but worth talking to. Tells us more about the vic. How she thinks. Who mighta wanted to do her," Burgoyne says, and I remember what he said about everybody being a suspect until they're not. "What you think about Lashawn's assessment of the girl? Makin' her sound kind of, well, fickle."

"Didn't strike me that way," I say, but admitting it now in my head. Burgoyne means something else though. He's calling her a whore and using a euphemism for it. Because he knows I liked her, the way she charmed people, the way I was proud of her, of what she brought to the school. I wonder if he's trying to protect my feelings or if he's looking for my reaction again, so I don't say anything more.

A beautiful dark-skinned, jet-haired Latina brings our taco plates, wearing a shoulderless black top. Her bosom is not large, not even as large as the average Latina, and I wonder what keeps the top from falling, and I make a mental note to ask Eloise about it. I study her and contrast her with Usaré, who was light-skinned, almost as light-skinned as I am, and who took pains to avoid the sun because she wanted to keep her skin light, and whose hair was ochre and so full-bodied and wavy that you wanted to crush it in your hand just to see if it would spring back. And whose bosom would have had no trouble holding up a shoulderless top. I remember Burgoyne's unsentimental remark about her breasts.

We eat in silence, and I reflect on Burgoyne's questions, on Lashawn's remarks. Fickle would not have been the first word I would have used to describe Usaré. Vain? Perhaps. Conspicuous certainly, because she wanted to be noticed. More than wanted—she was determined not only to be noticed but regarded. And not alone for her looks or for her flirtatiousness. Nearly all the girls at Polk are flirtatious and most have attractive features, and they have learned to make the most of them from Univision or from some Internet search. No, Usaré presented herself in some intangible way as qualitatively different from her peers.

When we finish eating, we head back to school, where Burgoyne decides to accompany me to the staff council meeting before he heads off in search of the reporter. He's suddenly more interested in talking to Laskeris than he is in scratching his way through the teachers' files. The meeting is scheduled to last an hour and a half, and I am an hour late.

Apparently, Sally is in the middle of fending off criticism from the English Department about the closure of their hallway. She looks relieved when I come in, so I know I'm up next. She is trying to hand the ball off, you can tell, to Augustine, who wants no part of it. He says, "Enrique, did you pick up enough of that to respond?" He rrrrolls the RRRR in my name more than he needs to.

"Sure. We were going to have a meeting about it after school, but we can address it here. The hall has to remain closed a couple more days so the police mobile team can get what they need. Still gathering forensics. I'm afraid it's the best they can do. Your people should be in there Monday, Chris. Sunday maybe." I look at Burgoyne, hoping this is true, but he's not looking my way.

Jameson responds. "Look, no disrespect to the police, but my teachers gotta get in there."

I let my impatience get the better of me. "Well, try some respect for Usaré and her family then." This shuts him down and the topic is over for now. One less goddamned meeting, I think. I know I am being unprofessional; Jameson's teachers really are going through a hellish week, and it's virtually a week of lost instruction for their students. I should go ahead with the meeting and listen to their wails and concerns, and tell them I understand and hug a few of them and mourn along with them, but my decision is made. Again, I look over at Burgoyne.

. . . who is staring at a new face in the room—blond, petite, hazel-eyed, not beautiful, not even pretty, but eye-catching somehow, late forties and trying to seem younger. When the meeting ends, Burgoyne is on her like a mosquito on a vein. I step over to introduce myself. She is Mandy Tung, the new chair for the department of English as a Second Language, ESL, also a union representative for the teachers. Burgoyne is talking about union business with her, pretending it's something they have in common. He's noticed she's not wearing a ring, I decide, and I wonder if I would be posturing and flirting with her if he'd not noticed her before I did. Something to talk about at my Thursday SAA meeting.

I still have about half an hour before school ends to work on my pile of referrals, so I head back to my office. I think of Usaré and Usaré's family, and I feel an unspeakable sorrow.

FOUR

The rest of the afternoon is routine. I talk to a handful of kids and suspend enough of them to risk the wrath of the superintendent under ordinary circumstances. JV Muñoz is an astute man, and he knows that reporters and parents alike believe a high suspension rate indicates a bad school, an unsafe school. And one sure way to keep the suspension rate down is to just not suspend any kids. At administrative meetings he has told us APs not to suspend anyone for fighting until their third fight. We need to provide interventions instead, he says, and restorative conferences between the combatants. Gotta hug those thugs.

But with the recent carnage in our bathroom, we do not have ordinary circumstances. Reporters and parents alike are looking past the suspension numbers now and asking what we are doing to remove dangerous elements from the district's campuses. Right now, no one is going to come down on me for being draconian.

With two kids, non-threatening offenders, I make an abeyance contract, signed by their parents and me, keeping them in school and then lifting the threat of suspension in a semester if they behave themselves.

I am about to log off my computer, but then I remember what Andre said about the Martinezes, the six he'd fought with, maybe not all of them Martinezes but at least a couple of them, young guys, maybe high school age or a little older, and I go to the student records program. Even if they're dropouts, they'll be in the current year's index. If they were registered here in the last five years, I can access their records without even getting authorization from central office.

And there they are. Three Martinez kids on the same street as Usaré. But with an even number, so on the east side of the street, opposite the Garcías. Two boys—inactive since October—Jhonny and Julio but no William or Guillermo, and a girl in ninth grade who's still coming to school most days. Then I do a search going back five years, and I find Guillermo too, last matriculated four years ago when he was eighteen. I study his photo for a minute, finally remembering him.

How'd I forget that kid? Then I log off.

As I'm leaving about six o'clock, it's still warm, but pleasant now, less heat rising from the sidewalks. The sky is a washed-out blue.

I run into Jameson. He's a lean guy in his early fifties who tries to look hip: rapper sunglasses, always with a dark slimming vest and black slacks and a trendy tie, a faux leather jacket when the weather's cool enough, full head of dark hair that I know he colors, combed straight back, all Anglo but tan enough that he's darker than most Latinos. In fact he occasionally needs skin surgery to remove carcinomas.

"I just talked to Augustine." He takes off the sunglasses, to show his grit I suppose, but it doesn't work all that well because of his eyes. They always look a little droopy, like he's been smoking bud, which I know he does on occasion, and which helps him look hip but not intrepid.

"Kinda late for him to be here," I say.

"You know what we talked about?"

"I got a pretty good idea," I say, now realizing that chopping him down at the meeting was not only unprofessional but also counterproductive.

"He said I should talk to you informally. On behalf of the department. See if you can resolve the department's grievance before we put it in writing." He has blue eyes, and it seems to me his dark skin accentuates the blue, makes it seem glossier somehow.

"How come you need to get in there so bad? You leave the last issue of *Rolling Stone* behind?"

"It's a pretty good rag. You should try it some time instead of *People*."

"Look, I know I was outta line before, back at faculty council. It's just I know there's no way to—"

"You need to make *something* happen, man. This is two pounds short of a ton of bullshit, Tavish. You said it'd only be a couple days."

"Well, tomorrow, it'll be four. Which I can't do anything about right now. Or even Friday, for that matter, which'll make it five, if you want to see it the way it really is."

"See it any way you want," Jameson says, "You know you can get us in."

I widen my eyes, trying to show innocence.

"I know you have the key to those padlocks they put on."

I am surprised he knows this, but I say, "Ain't gonna happen, but I'll talk to the cops again for you."

"Lotta good that'll do. Cops with their siege mentality." Jameson is a hardcore liberal, so this comment is not just about his frustration with the hallway. I see elements of what he's talking about in Burgoyne, though, reflected in his violent entrance at Polk High School. Burgoyne's shield means a lot to him. He wears it, and it is him, his identity. He is the force of law, and in his mind that force is the barrier against barbarism and chaos. He sometimes mentions something about another cop that he doesn't like, some not-quite-ethical thing he knows about going on inside the PD, but never getting too specific, and you can tell he still feels a brotherhood with other cops, ethical or not. So, yeah, Burgoyne probably does think of himself as a segment in the thin blue line between us and the beasts. Hell, maybe he is.

"I can only do what I can do." And with that I turn and go. The day is starting to fade.

*****

As I drive north to the crosstown parkway, I realize I'm passing Usare's neighborhood, what used to be her neighborhood, and I decide to drive through it, wondering what the family has done to express their mourning. I drive slowly and a neighbor's Doberman yaps about me.

It's a painted stucco bungalow, like most of the houses in that barrio, where the yards are often enclosed with chain link or corrugated steel, to keep people out and dogs in. Some have only the dogs, chained to stakes or trees in the front yard. The García house needs some stucco repair and a new coat of turquoise paint, and the front yard is open, with no dog at all.

Memorials overwhelm the front porch: rose and carnation arrangements as well as flowers in bunches, candles inside red glass, rosary beads hung from the porch beam, sacred heart paintings, dolls and skulls and baskets and blankets. Usare's framed photo on the door. I glance across the street and find the Martinez house.

At the end of the block, I make a U-turn and crawl the curb until I am within a hundred feet of the García place and park to watch the Martinez porch, wondering if the detectives have gotten around to talking to any Levantes. I know they have more information than I do, but I go over it in my head anyway.

So Usaré was in the mix with at least a few of these Levantes, and a cousin to these Martinez guys. And one of the things we know about Levantes is they run a few whores, according to Burgoyne anyway. What did he say? 'Coulda wanted Usaré for a prostitute.' And that's something like what Andre talked about, unless the putas locas are just slutty-looking girlfriends. But if you're a pimp, you probably don't worry too much about keeping your slutty-looking girlfriend chaste and pure and cleaving to you only.

And isn't that how they recruit their working girls anyway? Treat them sweet and bring them roses and make them girlfriends first. Get them away from their family. Drugs and a little force as time goes on. Get 'em to sleep with a friend or a brother, and then more drugs. That's what people say anyway. Or maybe the movies have ruined me.

Why isn't Burgoyne buying that angle about Usaré then?

'Cause Usaré was maybe too smart and too independent to be fooled. But the cops couldn't have decided that already, could they? They don't know her like I did.

'Cause there was no sign of drug use? Maybe, but that doesn't mean the Levantes weren't *trying* to recruit her, right? Memo or one of the younger ones trying to make her a girlfriend, and not succeeding, running out of patience. Doesn't that make sense to Burgoyne and his plainclothes pals?

Besides, there's the calling card, the funny looking L. Ain't that something to get the cops at least sniffing?

Something pops into my head. I remember what I used to teach my players when I was still coaching basketball: you can't just sit back on defense—you have to get up in your opponents' face. Make them uncomfortable. Force the action.

"Activate the basketball," I used to say.

Nobody's going to notice my Camry like they would a Cadillac, so I get out and head for the Martinezes' porch.

A brunette girl wearing a 4/20 T-shirt and hipster panties opens the door, in heels, attractive, but needing a shower and a hairbrush. There's music playing, hip-hop, but so new I don't recognize it.

"Hey. Wondering if Memo's here." Trying to look nondescript. Should be easy for a school principal.

She rotates her head a little and calls, "Ay, Jhonny." Her head comes back to look at me, with that cat-like look girls can get when you don't know if they're smiling or getting ready to eat your liver. She holds onto the door a foot above her head and tilts her body at the waist so that you have to look. I wonder what the geometric angle would measure if you had a protractor. She reminds me of a junior-high girl, but she's standing there in panties and heels, and her face is too hard for a thirteen-year-old. She says, "Nice tie," sincere enough that I wonder if she really likes it, a yellow Save-The-Children tie.

"Who's there?" the voice coming from behind her. Jhonny's dark-skinned, and his hair ripples back in tight waves. He's wearing a sleeveless tee shirt and baggy cotton slacks with chiseled creases and bunches at the ankles, barefoot, adjusting the bunched-up pants around his belt as he walks in.

The girl keeps looking at me but talks over her shoulder. "Straight guy looking for Memo."

So I'm straight, wondering if that's good or bad.

"What's he need Memo for?"

To me the guy looks like a Harris's sparrow that's spent too much time preening and not enough feeding, with a slick black crown, brown skin and a slight frame.

The girl says, "He's standing right here, dude. Ask him your own self. I ain't no servant." I make her for the sister then, too smart-alecky to be one of Memo's girls, and she moves away, her butt twitching with the rap beats, or it seems like it in my imagination. The doorway is vacant now and I pretend it's an invitation and step inside. There are pizza boxes and Colt 45 bottles next to the sofa and on the coffee table, a burnt-weed smell. "I wanted to know if Memo talked to Usaré last week. Is he here?"

Jhonny picks up a pair of cross trainers, orange Nikes with black trim, and sits down to put them on, making a show of it. "Why you wanna know who Memo talk to?

"Why don't you just tell me if he's here?"

"It's their drongo no snitching thing," the girl says. "I seen you over at the school, right?"

"Yeah, I'm one of the principals," not bothering with the assistant distinction.

"BFD," Jhonny says, his shoes on now, ignoring me and heading out the front door to the porch, then lighting a cigarette and leaning against one of the stone pillars and looking out at the yard like it's his fiefdom. Striking a pose. It pisses me off, and I wonder if this is one of the guys who squared off with Andre.

"My brother acts tough, but he's just pretending," the girl says. I wish I'd thought to pay attention to her name. "I don't know why he's so unsociable wit you. He's usually friendly to guys who drop by wit money to spend." She's smiling, but only a little—Mona Lisa sans innocence.

Jhonny draws on his cigarette and blows out a long smoke plume, agitated now. I walk out and stand behind him, waiting for him to turn, thinking it would be easy to pitch him off the porch, which is about four feet off the ground. I look again at the shrine across the street, the faded color of the García house, and then the neighbors' houses, some of them bright and freshly-painted—turquoise, banana yellow, even a magenta. I can see the Doberman behind chain link, sniffing and staring but silent right now. It's an old neighborhood, built in the forties. There are WPA sidewalks, buckled here and there by mulberry roots. A couple of the yards have sprinklers throwing water on desperate Bermuda grass.

I hear the girl behind me again, and I say, "It's not like school, is it."

"No. I'm learning lots more here."

"Not from this one, I'm guessing." I watch Jhonny take another draw, fidgeting now.

The girl says, "He don't know nothing worth learning."

I face her again and say, "So where's Memo? Maybe he knows something."

Jhonny turns now and says, "Rosa, you don't tell heem nothing, see?"

She says, "You don't tell *me* nothing, see?"

I can see her school record in my head now, the name. "Rosa, I just want to ask him about the last time he saw Usaré. When that was. Stuff like that."

Jhonny says, "You ain't no cop. We ain't gotta tell you nothing."

"I ain't talking to you any more, friend. Maybe you just need to finish your ciggy." I face Rosa again, and say, "Maybe I could have his cell number? Talk to him on the phone instead of in person?"

She stares, thinking about it.

"It's just a couple quick questions." I wait. "About Usaré. You knew Usaré, didn't you?"

Jhonny snorts and says, "That García chica was nothin' but a tease." I'm burning when I look at him, and he turns away again and huffs his cigarette.

Rosa recites the phone number and asks me if I need for her to write it down.

I repeat it and tell her no thanks. I think about telling her she has somewhere else she can go. "You okay here?"

"I'm fine."

I thank her and turn to leave.

I can't help myself though—I grab Jhonny's belt with my right hand and throw him as far out into the evening air as I can. He lands in the dirt harder than I thought he would and for a second, I worry that he will be the one to call in some cops, but then he rolls up and looks at me, surprised and hurting, but not really injured.

"You need to show better manners about people who have passed."

He calls me carajo as I walk to my car, and I realize I have let one of my old demons overcome me again. The sign of a life that's become unmanageable . . .

But I know I have activated the basketball.

*****

In my car, I call the number that Rosa gave me. No answer, so I leave a message. "Hey, Memo, this is Enrique Tavish from over the high school. Can you call me back please—got a couple questions for you." I figure he has caller ID, but I leave my number anyway.

When I pick up Francesca and NJ from Abuelita's condominium, they are arguing about who won some überpatriotic online video game where the players try to protect the homeland by blasting armed border crossers carrying drugs and Uzis, and I'm thinking it might be time to arrange for professional child care. Maria's grandmother is a sweet, wise woman, but no match for Francesca's wiles.

At home Eloise is packing for a flight to San Francisco for a meeting with some Western-state Astrobank executives, which I'd forgotten about. I'm going to miss her, for her loveliness especially, because I do not expect a lot of help from her with the kids.

I know I should not compare, but I can't help thinking about Maria and the way things used to be, oddly grieving Maria's absence right now when Eloise is the one leaving, selfishly, because I miss the parent partnership I had with Maria. Partnership—wrong word. Maria did the majority of the parenting, and when she died, it all fell on me. I hoped it would get easier when I remarried, but it hasn't, given Eloise's career path. I focus on her wavy blond hair and her curvy shape, and I plot bedtime fun.

She says she'll be back Sunday afternoon, so we can celebrate our second anniversary together on Monday. Eloise is a good stepmom when she is not at work, though she is a little too strict I think, much more direct and less patient than Maria was, and much less permissive than I. But she is not available to them all that often—Sundays and mornings, and I get the kids to school most mornings anyway, because they are used to me rousing them and because their school is right on my way to work. Then I get them from Abuelita's in the late afternoon because Eloise is usually still working till six-thirty or so. Even when I have evening duty at school, once or twice a week, I get the kids home and get them fed before I head back to campus. And I admit, my kids have not yet warmed to Eloise in the way I'd hoped.

NJ wears his emotions on his sleeve, and my months grieving for Maria were marked by hours soothing him. He still has quiet, teary moments when he's alone, or thinks he's alone. On the other hand, Francesca cried only one time over losing her mother, when I first told her the terrible news. Afterward she refused to speak about her loss unless someone forced the topic on her, but I sense it tore her inside even more deeply than it did NJ, certainly more than she will admit.

You can see the different grief reactions in how they behave around our dog Ursa too, probably because they sense, as I do, that Ursa was mainly Maria's dog.

Maria bought Ursa from a breeder, supposedly to be the kids' dog, but fed her every meal, walked her almost every walk, picked up all her dung, and trained her as well as a stubborn Rottweiler bitch could be trained. She named her Ursa, Latin for she-bear, for her prodigious head. She loved that dog, and though I used to tell Maria that dogs can't really love, that love is an exclusively human emotion, I have to admit now that what Ursa offered to Maria was something very like love.

While I pretended to be unshaken as my Maria's life ebbed away, in some kind of foolish effort to protect Francesca and NJ, Ursa unashamedly did everything she could to comfort my wife after she became ill, sleeping next to her, padding along next to her around the house, begging to ride along in the SUV whenever Maria picked up her keys, and finally lying listless on the floor in Maria's last days and for a month after the funeral. It was NJ more than anyone who rallied to comfort poor Ursa for the loss of her mistress, and he is the one who tends to her now for the most part, and I sense Ursa is appreciative.

I have this feeling, though, that Ursa desperately wants Francesca to love her, but Francesca more or less ignores the poor bitch, as if to show anger that the damned dumb dog could not save her mother any more than the doctors or Father John or the rest of us could.

While Ursa's visible grieving lasted for weeks, I paid my official respects to Maria Chacon de Alastair Tavish for over a year, too long and too much she'd probably say. But I know, and she knows too, in her imperishable place, that it was less than she deserved. There is still a void inside me that Eloise can't fill, and now I know it will always be there.

We are in the kitchen after Eloise has her bag packed, almost seven o'clock. I am having a ginger ale, and she is sipping whiskey, both of us trying to figure out what to get for dinner, Mexican or Chinese. But then she asks me if I've ever thought of living somewhere else. "Another state I mean."

"Somebody say something at work?" But I'm thinking, No.

"Burke hinted about it today when he called." When I raise my eyebrows, she says, "Senior vice-president."

"What did you say?"

"Caught me off-guard, you know. I said it depends."

I sip my ginger ale and she tastes her whiskey, she with her thoughts and I with mine, not in a hurry to get into it more.

After a while she says, "Can you imagine leaving here?"

"Well, St. Augustine said those who don't travel read only a single page in the book of life. Or something like that."

"But can you imagine it?"

"It depends." I watch her react, then go on. "Can I imagine shuffling off to Lordsburg, for chrissake? Or El Cajon?"

"So it depends on the place?"

"That's one thing, sure. And the timing. There's my job. New schools for the kids. House hunting again." She's watching me.

"What are you thinking about?" she says.

"All the changes."

"Least you didn't have to change your name."

"I know," I say, nodding. "You like Tavish for your name?"

"I'd never change my last name again, but yeah, I like it fine. Sometimes I wish I could change my first name."

"How come? I like Eloise. Means warrior, right?"

"It's okay. My dad wanted to name me Victoria, after the queen. Daddy thought kids should be named for who he hoped they'd become. My brother was named after Douglas Macarthur, and he's career army now. My mother wanted something feminine, like Adrianna. Eloise was the compromise."

"I'm glad it wasn't Cinnamon—that would've limited your career choices."

"Me too."

"I like names that are pleasing to the ear. Francesca, say."

"You like your name, Ricky?" She smiles.

I smile back. "Better than Carajo, anyway. Who's getting dinner?"

"You call it in. I'll go get it. I want Mexican."

"I've noticed that," I say.

When she stands up, she says, "Burke's remark was real oblique, so maybe nothing comes of it. Just thought I should have something to say if it's a topic. You know?"

"I do know." In a moment, she's headed for Molina's. I call in the burritos and enchiladas and head toward the fake laughter of some sitcom rerun to urge homework and threaten doom.

*****

On Thursday, Burgoyne texts me at 5:15, and I roll over and look at my phone: 'Murder dicks arriving 1200. Your office. You & me preview at 7.' Eloise is already on her way to the airport.

I don't arrive till 6:45 because I have to wait for the kids' school day care to open, and Burgoyne is already there, talking conspiratorially with Santana as they look at an open file.

At times like this, I suspect that Burgoyne is sleeping with Santana and it makes me envious. She possesses perfect Andalusian features, with fine brown skin and hair like sable and ink-black eyes. She has an attractive figure too, which, to please her possessive husband, she attempts to disguise with loose, long pants and oversized sweaters. Nothing can disguise her low, provocative voice, however, which would probably be alluring enough on its own to seduce most men. It amazes me that I haven't succumbed.

It looks like Santana has already pulled together my unofficial files. When they see me, Santana closes the folder, puts it on a stack she has assembled and carries the bunch into my office.

Burgoyne settles into his usual spot as Santana exits, Burgoyne watching her ass, and I pick up the first folder, but Burgoyne says, "Some stuff you need to know." When I look up at him, he says, "Stuff you'll probably have to know to help us with this . . . only I don't want anyone to know you know . . . get it?"

Not really, I think. I understand that he doesn't want me to leak information, but I get the sense that he is not quite following procedure, and I don't know why. I nod my head anyway, because I want to know whatever he is going to tell me.

"Your girl wasn't killed in that bathroom, like I kind of hinted to you before. Homicide is pretty sure it happened in the teacher lounge across the hall, 'cause they found hair and fibers in there to match hers. On that sofa in there, more than you'd find from a casual sit-down too."

"Something violent."

"Or intimate. Or both, hey? There was a semen stain there. Diluted, like somebody tried to wash it off, but it was there. And they found samples in her vagina too, from two different men. Spermicide too, which might indicate a third guy in her last couple days."

"A third guy?" I shake my head, and I feel the skin on my face getting warm.

"It was spermicide like condoms have most of the time. The lab can even tell which brand. Might be one guy does her once with, and then a second time without, or something like that, but most guys wouldn't do that, right? It's one way or the other. If you think a gal's a skank, you put one on every time."

"She wasn't a skank, goddamn it. Condoms are as much for avoiding pregnancy as for STD's. And anyway, this couldn't have all happened there. Three guys?"

Burgoyne smiles, as if I'm slow to catch on, and says, "No, she coulda brought along one or two samples inside her. But she obviously was partly undressed while she was bouncing on that sofa." He considers me carefully for a moment, then goes on.

"And the techs think she died there. The perp carried her into the bathroom and smacked her head into the mirror and maybe wrote the big L to distract us. The perp hoping we'd never find the crime scene across the hall. There wasn't much blood from that gash on her head 'cause her heart had stopped. As far as the tag, maybe one of the Levantes had left his mark before the carcass was even dumped, and it's got nothing to do with the crime at all."

"Or the Levantes killed her in the lounge and carried her in there," I say, pausing to consider the look on his face now, which tells me nothing. "You know that sofa probably *is* the best location for sex in the E building."

"You know from experience?"

"You're killin' me."

He pauses again. "There's at least a couple holes in your theory."

"Like? . . ."

"The girl was smothered. They found her snot and saliva on one of the pillows. Which is not a gangbanger's weapon of choice, a knife or a Glock being lots quicker—takes at least three minutes to smother someone like that, maybe longer. And you gotta think that the pillow was just the handiest thing to use, that the perp made a spur of the moment decision to finish her after their moment of romance passed." He smirks more than usual when he says this.

"Well, I don't know near as much as you do about murder, but I know plenty about gangsters, so I wouldn't count them out."

"You want it to be them for some reason, 'cause you don't want it to be Andre maybe. But this guy was emotional, angry with her. Not just pissed off 'cause she wouldn't turn tricks, but outta-control, mad-dog livid about something, or scared. He doesn't even face her and push the pillow down on her face; he pushes her down into it and holds her there from behind. Which is smart too, because it's easier to do it that way. Way harder for her to fight back."

"Well then, it coulda been a smaller guy too, right?" I don't say it but I'm thinking of Jhonny Martinez.

"I s'pose. Position of power from behind like that. Your gal was pretty tall. Not skinny either, hey?"

"Yeah. Like five-eight."

We stare at each other for several seconds, then I say, "So what are we looking for here?" Nodding toward the files.

"Motive, I think. We got some confidence that the perp was a guy . . . that he had a key to the hallway . . . and the room too . . . 'cause it's the same key. Even though, like you said, a kid coulda wedged one of the doors. So we look for motives and motivations that might point to an outta-bounds relationship."

The first file belongs to Babs McNally, not a guy, the drama teacher, and I set it aside. Next is Chris Jameson, and I tell Burgoyne about him, what's in the file and what I remember: How he thinks he's Mr. Cool and tries to act that way.

"He's married with two kids, seems happy enough in his marriage—to a woman who works over in the social studies department, no complaints from staff about him except he has a temper and a sharp way of voicing his disagreements. One time a female student came into the office to report that he'd brushed her bare leg when their class was working in the library—made her feel funny—and she wasn't sure it was on purpose, but according to the girl Jameson followed it up by looking at her kinda funny, and she felt it was like checking for her reaction—not aware of any witnesses."

"What did you do about that?"

"Not a whole lot *to* do, since she wasn't even sure it was intentional. Called Karla, the attorney for the school district. Who had me interview five or six kids in the class with real oblique questions: See anything recently that made you uncomfortable in any of your classes? Any teachers do anything you thought was outta line? Stuff like that. Pain in the ass because some kids tell you about teachers raising their voice or using inappropriate language or whatever, and then you gotta look into that as well."

"Nothin relevant turned up?"

"Not about Jameson. One female said something about a science teacher trying to look down all the girls' tops—physics and physical science teacher name o' Smith. Those rumors fly around about him every year, and I've decided it's bullshit."

"Assuming Smith don't have a key to that hallway, we'll come back to him later maybe. So did you ever talk to Jameson? Or follow up with the girl."

"Yup. Had to stick to oblique questions with Jameson too, to protect the girl's identity. And of course he didn't know what the hell I was talking about, or pretended pretty well. Only thing I thought was funny was that he wasn't real inquisitive about it. Just answered my questions and left.

"Most guys would ask where the complaint came from. And the girl, I just got back to her and urged her to let me know if anything else happened. She said she'd almost forgotten the whole thing anyway."

"No other flags?"

I shake my head and I pick up the next file. "Anthony Navarette. Only Mexican on the English staff. Maybe a misogynist in that he glorifies Hemingway." I smile. "Teaches juniors. He's a snob and a lazy-ass. You heard o' the coach who just rolls the balls out and tells the kids to scrimmage? That's him, but with books. Doesn't even bother to keep track of which kid gets what book. Drives Jameson crazy 'cause it eats his budget like a great white shark. Drives *me* crazy, 'cause he does just enough that I can't nail him. Sorta *wish* he was the perp." Burgoyne doesn't smile.

"Jared Wilson. Out there, religiously. Born again or on the edge. Wife and special ed kid. Absorbed in his family. Doesn't have time for an affair and wouldn't have one if he did. Church, Boy Scouts, all that."

Burgoyne says, "I think of English teachers, I think of gray-haired women with bifocals."

"Yeah, we're unusual with all the men." I wait a moment, then say, "Robert Paxson. Everybody gets along with him. No complaints from kids or parents or colleagues. Main problem he's gonna be seventy when his kids graduate college. He'll die before the debts are paid off. Crazy fucker stopped using birth control when he was forty-five."

WAYS TO BE WICKED

Burgoyne smiles a little.

"Mac Gabello. Small-man's complex. Cruises singles bars on the weekends and gets lucky a lot to hear him tell it. Rough around the edges, but most of the kids respond pretty well to him. Rides a Harley. Also teaches over in auto technology part of the day."

"He have your gal in class?"

"No. Mac teaches all freshmen, but he probably had Usaré when she was in ninth grade." I want to tell Burgoyne to quit calling Usaré 'my gal,' but I don't quite have the nerve. I set aside folders for Nikki Sullivan, Helen Dunham and Nancy Horwitz.

"John Klein. Little guy, but full of confidence. Probably the best teacher in the department. Up for teacher of the year a couple years ago. He and his wife can't have kids so they both work their asses off in their jobs. Sublimation, I guess. She's a teacher too, in another district, or maybe admin now, I don't know. And that's all the men in the department."

"Nothing exactly tantalizing there. Who had current ties to the girl?"

"Well, Jameson was her English teacher . . . And she'd been seeing Klein lately because she wanted his help writing her senior essay." Burgoyne allows me time to search my brain. Nothing else.

"Why Klein for the essay and not Jameson? Is that a little odd?"

"Not really. Klein gets all kinds of seniors coming to him for help with their senior essays. The way he teaches more or less makes them dependent on his method. The smart kids worship him, and so do the kids that wish they were smart. It gets to be time for their senior submissions and they come back to him. He stays late most afternoons for tutoring."

Burgoyne looks at me quizically. "You got any idea how many after-hours visits the girl made to this Klein fella?"

"No, but I know he makes kids sign in when they come to tutoring. Very careful too. Props the door open when students come after school. Worried about rumors. Paranoid, really."

"So assuming you're just a cop, no other interest in these teachers, who do you look at?"

I think about it for a minute, then say, "Los Levantes." I wonder if my visit to the Martinez house is going to generate anything to attract the attention of police.

He shakes his head and says, apparently finding me amusing now, "Tell me about the E building women then. Anything we should look at with them?"

"Not quite as obvious if we're honing in on motive."

"Somethin' may jump out at us. Worst you can do is bore me a little."

I pick up the women's folders. The first belongs to Cynthia Flores. "Department clerk—like a department secretary, but they don't pay her as much. All I got on her is paperwork from when Jameson and I nominated her for an award—Office Professional of the Year, which she got, and more paperwork we did trying to get her reclassified as a secretary, which she didn't. Kept copies so we'd have a head start when we try again. Hard-working and friendly. Frustrated with her job situation though. No real relationship to Usaré . . . Then there's Nancy Horwitz. No interest in men. May be a lezzy or may just be too busy with other stuff. Helps her parents out a lot and pretty serious about horseback riding."

"But maybe a lesbian? Would she have contact with the vic?"

"Probably not for a couple years. When Usaré was a sophomore. And she maintains pretty consistent detachment with all the kids. Her friendship with 'em begins and ends at the classroom door. Can't see how she's involved . . . Helen Dunham, married and divorced, but that was ages ago, when she first started here. She's only a couple years from retirement now. She got a degree in psychology a while back but decided to stay in the classroom. Enjoys teaching the way an elementary teacher does."

Burgoyne raises his eyebrows, asking a question.

"It's a theory of mine. Most high school teachers became teachers 'cause they like the subject matter, science or English lit or whatever. Most elementary teachers started 'cause they like kids. That's Helen, enjoys seeing kids learn and grow up . . . Nikki Sullivan—"

I guess the look on my face tells him something. "What about Nikki?"

"It might be a stretch. I don't see how it would fit."

"You're holding up a good man here."

"She may be a little on the wild side, sexually. She did her semester of student teaching here, working with Klein. Did great, like they all do student teaching with Klein. We had an opening midyear, so we hired her. But it's not long before she's taking Mondays off or coming in late. Turns out she's left her husband, living with some doper. Started partying every Friday afternoon and then couldn't shut it off in time to recover for work. Helen talked to her, Klein too. Got her in rehab and most of it straightened out by the end of the year."

"Most of it."

"Left the boyfriend, or I guess he left her when she was doing her twenty-eight days. Kicked the cocaine."

"But . . ."

"Well, hubby didn't want her back. And not sure it's true, but some people tell me she's on one of these hookup sites. Grownupfun dot com or something. Exploring fantasies."

Burgoyne nods. "You ever try to verify it?"

"Didn't think something like that would fly for a school administrator. Picture me explaining it to the governing board: Yes, sir, I joined that site in the interest of pure research. Just wanted to see if any of my staff have overactive glandular impulses."

"Be fun to check it out, I bet." Deadpan look. "Maybe *I'll* look." He doesn't say anything, trying to figure out a connection.

I go on. "Babs McNally. Teaches drama and junior English. Screwy but harmless. Came in one weekend and painted all the ceiling tiles black 'cause she doesn't have a performance room. Adopted a kid whose parents had kicked him out. Kid screwed her over later. Kinda teacher who'da lent her keys to a kid though. To have him run an errand you know, figuring he's gonna bring it right back. But just as likely to forget. Not a genius."

"So which one now? Man or woman. And if you say Levantes, I'll drop-kick you."

"Maybe you don't have the whole story."

"Okay," he says. "People who got keys and motives, since you insist."

"There's the administrators. Who I guess you're ruling out right now, including me." I wait.

He waits too, then says we're low on the list.

"The security guards. They got keys to all the buildings. Four of them. Amin's the lead."

"You got info on them too?"

"Not so much. Will supervises the security personnel. But Amin does a lot of overtime. You know him. The black guy. Religious but very sincere about it. Embarrasses me sometimes quoting scripture when I go into an expulsion hearing. Gird up thy loins against the serpent and all that."

"Interesting, but they'll be down the list. Who else?"

"The coaches. They were never supposed to have master keys, but they weaseled them out of one of my predecessors way back when. I've tried, but I can't get 'em back without pulling rank, and Augustine won't let me. Afraid Quiroz will quit."

"Quiroz is football?"

"Yeah. But no connection to Usaré there either. But—"

Burgoyne waits.

"Wrestling is big here."

He nods.

"Rusic is the head wrestling coach. Usaré didn't play any sports, but she was a mat maid."

"Mat maid."

"Like a cheerleader but for the wrestlers. They sit on the floor and pound on the mats and holler guttural encouragement. Get towels and water. Usaré was their lead."

"So what about Rusic?"

"Wins a state championship almost every year."

"That doesn't make him a suspect."

"Rep is he's had some girls here. Will's guy to supervise, so I don't know a lot about it, but I wouldn't be surprised."

"You gotta be kidding. Nobody gets away with shit like that anymore."

"State titles still matter. There have been some investigations, but nothing ever stuck."

"Who did the investigating?"

"Will and Augustine. Fox and the henhouse."

"What do *you* think?"

"I think he should be in Florence prison with three-hundred-pound Crips and skinheads taking turns raping him," I say. "You want to hear about the other teachers on her schedule? Math and whatever?"

"Not right now. Most likely didn't have keys, right?" he says. When I nod, he goes on. "How you feel about talking to some of these E people? See if they stumble . . . or say anything relevant. Without making it seem like that's what you're doing."

"Aren't you and the detectives going to start talking to them today anyhow?" I feel odd about trying to catch my own people in a lie.

"Yeah, but they trust you, hey?"

"Not so sure about that."

"More than they do the police."

"If they ever got a speeding ticket, I guess."

I must be wearing a quizzical expression because Burgoyne adds an explanation. "It points us to the right line of questioning, even if they're all clean."

"I'll start with Rusic then, since he was at the dance."

That's when the fire alarm goes off.

I know it's not a scheduled drill, so we either have a fire or a prankster. I am never prepared for the piercing sound. As I open my office door, it pounds shrilly on my eardrums, and I almost decide to return to my desk for the little foam ear protectors that I keep there. Burgoyne takes off for Augustine's office where, according to our emergency plan, he will help the principal set up a command center until emergency personnel arrive. I head for the north parking lot to count heads, but as soon as I come out the main door of the administration building, I see smoke pouring from the door to one of the boys' bathrooms. Its door is propped open with a wedge, and just inside is a plastic trashcan now belching flames that lick at the walls and the ceiling tiles. I report this to Augustine and everyone else who has a radio.

FIVE

I notice several boys standing close to the inferno, watching the smoke and flames, their backs to me, though I think I recognize the Cano twins. As hundreds of our students stream from the hallways toward the parking lot to gather around their teachers, a couple dozen drift toward the scene and join the gawkers, ignoring the procedure they've supposedly practiced every month since they were five years old.

Even with a crowd gathering though, I see Benjamin walking directly toward the fiery doorway, not in a great hurry but not hesitating either. He has a red handkerchief tied around his nose and he is carrying a canister-type fire extinguisher. I'm thinking he's acting on a really bad idea fighting the fire like this, but I also realize he's done this before. Standing in front of the doorway, he sweeps the carbon dioxide plume at the ceiling flames first, then advances and aims the spray at the base of the fire, the piled-up paper towels in the garbage can. Like it's nothing. Like he's wearing an airpack, a flash hood and a face shield.

The fire doesn't yield. The flames fight back because the base of the fire is now deep in the can, which is stuffed with a couple days' paper towel waste, probably melting and igniting the plastic too, and he can't really spray it directly. It reignites simultaneously on the ceiling and in the can, but Benjamin moves in again, spraying above first so that the flames don't leap out at his face, I'm guessing, then blasting directly at the can. I'm thinking that he underestimates the explosiveness of the plastic, and I'm sure that the kids who are standing close have no idea they're in any danger. Finally, Benjamin is right on top of the fire. He sprays the carbon dioxide plume straight down into the mouth of the can, then above him at the ceiling. The can flares again, and he sprays down into it, then at its sides, and into its belching mouth again.

Finally, the fire seems to subside and he pulls the handkerchief from his face and wraps his right hand with it and grabs the misshapen plastic container and drags it outside. He is as calm as I've ever seen anyone, though

I know there is still danger from the molten plastic and aerated paper in the trash bin.

The teachers are trying to get their classes in a semblance of a line so they can take roll, but there are still too many kids gathered near the smoldering fire, as many as twenty now, who ignore their teachers' exhortations to report as required. A couple teachers venture close and order students into line, without much effect. Frank, one of the security guards arrives in a cart to assist. The sound of a fire truck wails closer.

The damned alarm screams on.

Benjamin has pulled a garden hose from a nearby closet, connected it to a hose bib and is now spraying water into and on the trash can. Over the radio, I tell Augustine, "We're not all clear yet, but cut the alarm. The fire's out."

When I get close enough, I assist the security guard in directing kids away from the immediate area around the bathroom door, but I am also trying to identify a suspect, searching my memory for details about those first boys watching at the scene, mainly remembering shirts—a couple of red tees, a white one with a skateboard name, and a plaid. 'Fucking stupid plaid,' Andre would say. And it is stupid, since there won't be more than a half-dozen plaids on campus. I scan the groups of kids clustered around their teachers, but don't see any checkered flannel.

Then Benjamin is right there next to me, waiting for me. He says, "Robert Wood, Neto Arregon, Keanu Jones, Billy y Freddy Cano—los wrestlers." Even with his accented pronunciation, the names are clear. No need to scour the campus looking now. And Neto will be the one wearing Levantes plaid.

*****

Robert Wood is the portrait of terrified when Amin brings him into my office. His schedule tells me he was four hallways away from class when the fire broke out, something like six restrooms he could have used before he got to that one. No discipline record for him shows up in the computer though.

He's obviously never been called to the office for questioning before, white as plain paper when Amin brings him in, but I sense his fear goes deeper. He knows I'm after information he has, and he doesn't want to give it to me, partly because of the kids' code of silence of course, but more practically, because he is frightened of Neto, or the Cano twins or some other guy—whoever tried to incinerate our bathroom a few minutes ago. He's setting his jaw against me, thinking he'll be able to tell a partial truth but leave off before implicating someone, understanding that good lies are grounded in truth, but his eyes are wide and his skin pale. He stands stiffly, waiting for me to ask something so he can say he doesn't know what I'm talking about. I tell him to sit down.

"Robert, you were seen over by that fire, by the boys' bathroom, right?" I wait.

"Yes," he says, trying to smile.

"Standing there with some other boys."

"Yes. But we were there before the alarm went off." Like this explains everything.

"So do you know any of those other boys?" I say.

"No, I don't know them." He knows this is the easiest answer if I accept it.

"Really? Couple of them said they know you." Half a second later, I say, "What about the Cano boys, right? The twins? I thought everybody knew those guys. Can't tell 'em apart. On the wrestling team." He doesn't know what to say. I'm guessing he's starting to wonder at what point he has to quit pretending he knows nothing and make up a few lies, trying to think of stories that sound plausible and that are hard to disprove. I go on. "They were standing right there. You were talking to them at the fire scene, right? They sure know your name by the way. Why do you think we sent for you?"

He stutters.

"You might not know the other two, but you know them, right? The Canos?"

"I seen the twins around. I didn't know their name."

"But you know 'em. So you couldn'ta missed them standing a few feet away from you over by the fire. Did they tell you who lit it? They were thinking it was maybe you, but I don't think so."

"I didn't light no fire."

"Maybe not, but I gotta go with what the witnesses tell me, you know? If they all say it's you, all five of them say it, then what have I got? I mean, then you did it right? No matter what you say."

His face is reddening now, the way it does with a scared dough-faced kid, his freckles getting pink. "How 'bout it? You feel a little frisky this morning and toss a match in there? Step back and watch it?"

"No." He's nervous, bringing his knees together, and I wonder if I'll need a custodian to clean his chair after we're done.

"But then why would they tell me that? I'm trying to see it, you know? It's like they're coming out of the restroom and they see you tossing in matches. I mean, two student athletes, state champs, and you're gonna say something else? Who's the hearing officer gonna believe? Who you think the cops are gonna believe?"

He thinks he might be going to jail now, and he is too if he started that fire, so he raises his voice. "I didn't start no fire."

I lower mine, speaking slowly, like everything is going to be just fine. "You know, people who start fires aren't bad people. It's just they get an urge and make a mistake." I use my hands like a shrug, and I wait. "But, it wasn't spontaneous combustion, right? So if you didn't start it, you must've at least seen who did, right?" I lean back in my chair now, consciously relaxing my shoulders. "I wanna help you here, believe me, son. I don't wanna see Burgoyne haul you off."

He's fighting to keep his hard face on, like he's seen tough guys doing a hundred times in the movies, trying to be Russell Crowe or some other filmland bad-ass, but there are tears leaking from the corners of his eyes betraying the picture in his head, and he's mad about it because he can't hold them back, so his lips tremble a little.

"Am I in trouble if I tell you who it was?"

I let him wait for my answer, but I tilt my head a little and try to look sympathetic, and he rubs back and forth at his tears, fast, as if he's using an eraser. "Son, you didn't start that fire, you won't be in any trouble." Which is fairly honest. "But don't lie any more, okay? You lie and I can't help you."

"Will *he* know?"

"He?" I say.

"You know. The guy with the matches."

This is harder to answer truthfully. Burgoyne won't have any qualms about including the snitch's name in his police report, so eventually my firebug could find out who rolled over on him, no matter what I do. "Well, you can bet I'm not gonna tell him. He'll probably think the custodian saw him. Or the twins."

"Those guys always find out who narced," he says.

"*Those* guys?"

His eyes go wide now because he knows he's said too much. "I meant, you know, people. The other kids."

"Mmmm, yeah. But more than one then? Wasn't just one guy? You saying the twins did it?"

"No."

"Well, that leaves us with Keanu and Neto. Or you and some guys. Or a phantom guy and his ghost buddies. So did you mean black people when you said *those guys*? Or Neto's friends?"

"Are they gonna find out?" He's terrified.

"No way, son. What you say stays right in this office."

"It was the kid in the plaid shirt."

"Thought so. Tell me about it." I know he's still going to lie, but this version is going to have a few truth nuggets if I can pan them out. I start taking notes on a legal pad.

He heard sumpthin' was gonna happen for sure, early as the bus ride in. That's what that Mexican kid was talking about anyway, all flashed about how you, meaning me, was a punk-ass, and no shit like what you done was gonna stand.

"Okay."

Knew it was gonna be early, cuz the Mexican was all pissed off, you know. And he, Robert, thought it would be cool to be there for once, to actually see the shit breaking out from the start, whatever the shit was, and besides Miss McNally, she lets you go any time you need to go, you know?

"I *do* know."

Kept going through the halls, you know, up one and down the next, popping into bathrooms and peeping into classrooms looking for that Mexican kid.

"'Cause you figured he wasn't just talking . . ."

"Coach, that dude was high. I could smell vodka or whatever, and I figured sumpthin' else." The last vestige of an honor that few people understand, being called coach. I wonder why he calls me that, but I do not ask or react. "Knew he'd do sumpthin'."

"But you didn't know what?"

"Was getting late in the period so just about to go back to class but then seen him goin' into the D bathroom, the one opens right to the parking lot."

"The public restroom."

"Yeah, and so I went there to piss, no harm in pissing, like to see if the guy was still high or whatever."

"Or see what he does . . ."

He's pouring sumpthin' in the can by the time I'm coming in, dumpin' it really, outta this bottle. And I kinda scooch back. Then the twins come up behind me too. And they just stop to watch, cuz now he's throwing in a match. The first one doesn't do anything, like a dud or sumpthin', then the next one roars. Explodes like, you know? And the dumb ass Mexican jumps back, but like back inta the bathroom, so now the fire's blocking his way out. A few seconds later, this black kid comes out, crawling like a caterpillar, right down onna floor.

"You know his name, the black kid?"

"Seen him around but no don't know the name. And then the alarm is ringing, and I start to think the Mexican is gonna die in there. But then he busts out, not crawling but with his arms over his face, you know?"

"I think I get it, yeah," I say, letting my condescension show. No wonder half the kids hate me. I have him sign the sheet of notes and tell him I'll protect his identity from the Mexican kid, but that he needs to keep his mouth shut too. Then I send him back to class knowing that Burgoyne will call him in later and make no such promises.

Usually, when I know some little bastard has committed an expellable offense, I take statements from all the potential witnesses before I confront him, but not this time. "Security, I need Neto Arregon from D-twelve," I say over the radio. A husky voice crackles back that he's on his way. It's Frank, a heavy-set, dark-skinned Mexicano himself, and it surprises me because he is seldom the first to answer one of my calls. I think about reminding him not to let the boy use the bathroom or toss anything, but then chide myself for not giving Frank enough credit and keep my mouth shut.

*****

Neto Arregon, a medium-sized, good-looking kid with sleepy eyes and a Mohawk haircut that's got too much gel in the vee, comes in smelling of smoke and saying he didn't do nothing, man.

He's posing with his chin thrust out, standing with his hands straight down at his sides, but showing me the L tats on the back of them and holding them several inches away from his hips, like some five-eight action figure. He is still a couple steps away from my desk, and Frank remains in the doorway behind him, leaning heavily against the jamb. "Seems real interested in his right front pocket, Mr. Tavish."

"You standing like that so's to keep the starch in your shirt from crinkling?" I say.

His spine stiffens more. "Man every time sump'n happens, you call one of us in here."

"One of who?" I say.

"You know who I mean. Mexicans, man." I think about telling him my mom was from Mexico.

"This time it's just a coincidence. I'm talking to everybody who smells like smoke. There's only three—you and a black kid and Benjamin."

We are under the fluorescent lights now, cool and off-color, an institutional deity planted in the acoustical-ceiling-tile heaven.

"Thass who set it then, man. Benjamin." He's nodding.

"That's what I thought too, Neto, but turns out he's got a solid alibi." A few seconds later I say, "You got an alibi?"

He brushes back his shirt then and puts his hands in his pockets. "Djou got an alibi for going by Memo's house lass night?" He takes a step forward, and now Frank quits leaning on the door jamb.

"What you got in your pocket, Neto? Something you shouldn't have at school maybe?"

"Nothin'. It's what you call a gift, maybe." His Dickeys are a couple sizes too big, but I can see him fidgeting inside his right pocket.

"That's very thoughtful, but I can't really accept gifts from kids. And if it's an apple, I don't want it. I'm more of a burger and fries man."

"An apple? What I wanna give you a apple for? Besides, maybe it's for your kids." He glances at the photos of Francesca and NJ on the wall to his right.

I really don't think he has any realistic possibility of hurting my kids, but now I think he's ready to show me the gift, whatever it is, and I decide to move before he does. I launch around my desk and come right up to him, a foot from his face, and I say, "Tell you what, Neto. If it's for my kids, you can give it me and I'll pass it on to them."

Now he's hesitating. This wasn't what he expected, with a security guard circling like a raptor and thinking I'd stay put in my chair while he threatened me and my family, and then he'd make the next move, pulling out a knife or a pistol, or just pulling out a stick of gum and making a joke, scaring the bejeezuz out of me. He's pulled weapons on people before, I'd wager, for a drive-by or a beat-down, but not like this, not standing close and personal with his opponent eight inches taller and fifty pounds heavier. It never looked like this to him in the movies either. He was supposed to be scaring me, and I was supposed to be quivering over there behind my desk like some pendejo.

I'm scared too, I have to admit. I say, "Whatcha got in there?"

"Nothin'. It ain't nothin'. Jus a kinda surprise."

"Well, how 'bout you just empty out your pockets then. You can put your stuff right there on the desk." I lean into him a few inches. "I got an idea. You bring that gift out nice and slow. I don't want a surprise, and my kids don't either." I lean into him another inch.

"I . . . I got nothing in there." He's changed his mind now, not ready.

"Empty your pockets, Neto."

He pulls out his hands and shows empty. "I got nothin', man."

"Show me." I can see Frank behind, ready.

"I ain't gotta show you. You ain't got probility cause."

"Well, I don't need probable cause, just a suspicion, but if I did I'd just say I was looking for matches or a lighter. Chances are pretty good, you got those. Am I right?"

Now he wishes his hands were still in his pockets, holding whatever it is he's got, wishing he'd pulled, wishing he'd kept the power. I can see it, and I smile. I can't help myself.

He plunges his right hand back into his pocket, but Frank and I grab him at the same time. Frank has an arm around Neto's neck and a hand on his right arm, trying to lift the hand back out of the pocket; I'm holding the kid's left arm with my right hand while I force my left down into that right pocket. He has his hand around something, but I can't tell what it is. Neto is writhing and twisting, and in a few seconds the three of us go crashing onto the carpet. Frank takes the brunt of the fall, the weight of me and the kid on top of him. I'm thinking this all must look pretty ridiculous, the three of us on the floor like this, wrestling for control of Neto's right pocket, and I'm thinking it would be a great time for Burgoyne to drop by.

At this point, Neto is trying to keep his hand and its contents buried in his pocket, so I start pulling it upward, working with Frank to extract it. The kid is strong and sinewy, but there are two of us working against him now, and the hand finally comes out, and with it a gun, pewter-barreled, about five inches long. Neto's finger is around the trigger, and I wonder why it hasn't fired, but glad that it hasn't and hoping it doesn't.

"It's a gun, Frank." Since he can't see.

I bring my knee up and use it to pin the kid's left arm so I can free up my other hand. Then I reach over and keep his gun hand down with my own right, and I start prying his fingers off the frame of the weapon with my left—it's stubby, and the grip is only big enough for two of his fingers.

I get them off, but he still won't let go, his index finger wrapped tight around that trigger, so I put my head down and bite it, hard, so hard he finally starts screaming and releases his grip, and I've got the gun. I toss it onto my desk and then call for Santana. There is no direct line of vision from my office to her work area, but when I look up, she's already standing in the doorway, talking into her radio. She's obviously heard Neto's scream and probably most of the commotion that came before. I'm panting.

She says into her radio, "Activities office to Jim or Amin."

A pause, and then her radio squawks, "This is Burgoyne."

A second later, "This is Amin."

Santana says, "Mr. Tavish can use some help in the office, forthwith." I rest my knee on the kid's arm and wait, and soon they are both there. The two of them lift Neto off poor Frank, whose face is now red, tired of the kid's weight, and Burgoyne puts the cuffs on him. As strong as he seemed, as hard as he fought me and Frank, he is docile now in the cop's custody, and Burgoyne puts him in the chair at my desk. The kid stares at the pistol, and so do I.

"What the hell's that?" I say.

Burgoyne looks at it and says, "Ruger pocket gun. Little bastard, hey?" He looks at me. "Only a three-eighty so it just kills you . . . 'stead of tearing you all apart." He looks at Neto. "You the one started that fire?"

Neto stares up at him as if he is preparing to spit.

"Thought so."

I know that Burgoyne will take a statement from the kid, and I wonder if Neto will tell him about my visit to the Martinez house last night. For a moment, I am about to relate the story myself, but then I remember the shrine around Usaré's portrait, and the sorrowful look of the Garcías' porch, and I decide to let Neto initiate the explanation.

Activating the basketball is usually the best thing to do. This time, I'm not so sure.

*****

I don't know why it's so, but you can tell a guy is a wrestler just from the way he walks, something in his balanced gait or in the way he holds his shoulders, and you can tell Russell Rusic is a wrestling guy from two hundred yards away.

Since he's a head coach, Rusic gets last period off to plan lessons, which for him are basically weight training routines that do not vary from week to week or year to year, and since he's the PE department chair, he also gets a period each day to do department duties, like teacher observations within his department, which he signs for but does not perform. Instead, he tells his teachers to write up these phantom classroom visits, so that he can work with his number one wrestlers in the mat room. He lives for his sport, and no one is amazed that his wrestling teams have won fifteen state titles during his seventeen year stint at Polk, nor was anyone surprised when his wife divorced him in order to look for a companion with a wider range of interests. He has one child, a son whose mother raised him until he was promoted from eighth grade, and who then moved in with his dad to get ready for high school by adding twenty pounds of muscle, doing sprint drills and of course learning wrestling moves.

The son, Greg, is a sophomore, straight-A student, starting fullback on the football team, and already a state champion wrestler in his weight class.

The first time I met Coach Rusic, I was a high school freshman and he was trying to get me to give up the hardwood court for the wrestling mat. He told me he could make me a state champion, and I did think about it, but I told him my dad always wanted me to play basketball, though my dad couldn't have cared less about any sport. But at the time, I sensed Rusic wouldn't have accepted most other reasons I might have offered.

The real reason I said no to wrestling was that Rusic scared the hell out of me, the sport too—grappling with guys who were just as strong as I was but who'd been practicing wrestling moves since they were in grade school. The idea of being repeatedly slammed into a two inch mat didn't appeal to me, not to mention all the sweaty, hairy armpits on those guys.

When I came back to Polk as a teacher, Rusic was one of the first teachers to say something to me. He shook my hand when he welcomed me, clamping it tight like a set of handscrews so I'd know he wasn't going to let go until he said his little piece to me.

He said, "You gonna coach something, Tavish?" When I said yeah, he said, "Good. A lot of these goddamn teachers only think about their classes and their little lessons." I didn't tell him naturally, but I was already thinking about my own little lessons for advanced placement American history by the time he unclamped my hand.

I have no idea how I am going to start this conversation about last Saturday night, but I walk over to the wrestling room anyway, trusting to Providence as Huck Finn might say. Rusic is just as I expect him, kneeling on the mat in the cave-like room and talking to two boys, who are also kneeling, something about a guy named Granby and lifting your butt up to roll the guy, which might as well be Greek.

"Hey, Coach, can I have a few minutes?" I look at the boys, who understand it's time to leave.

When the steel door slams closed behind them, I say, "The cops are trying to track Usaré's last movements."

Rusic laughs, and I realize I've made a Freudian slip, fodder for him— Usaré's last movements, for Christ sake—and I wish I'd planned this interview better. Trouble is, I know I'm apt to look like a fool now, at least to Rusic. I hope my face has not turned red. He shifts and sits on the mat now, leaning back a few inches and putting his weight on his arms and hands. Then it occurs to me this actually may be better, feeding his sense of superiority. Whether he becomes a suspect or not, I do want to know if he ever slept with Usaré.

"So you get it then," like we are brothers, but it makes me feel like I've betrayed this poor dead girl whose only remaining trace is her reputation. That's when I lower myself to the mat, situating myself a few feet away from Rusic, adopting his lean.

He smiles, sensing where I am headed.

I say, "What do you know about her and this guy, Memo?"

"Memo?"

"Yeah. You remember him?—Guillermo Martinez . . . gangbanger. He was here at Polk a few years ago. You hear anything recent about him?"

Rusic stares at me but says nothing.

"I guess he's something of a Romeo. One of these damn Los Levantes. Pushes dope but runs whores now too. Usaré sent him some texts. Thought you mighta overheard something one of the wrestlers said . . . since she was a matmaid . . . or in one of your PE classes. Was he doing her?"

"How would I know that, Tavish?"

I look down and shake my head, sensing I've overplayed my hand. "Just hoping you'da heard something since she hung out down here some." I shake my head again, earnestly. "Longshot." When I look up, his eyes are still on me, and I realize he still frightens me.

"There were plenty of texts, you know? Burgoyne's hoping they'll lead us to the perp somehow. Wanted me to ask around."

He stares at me, wondering about the texts, I hope. I make myself stare back.

I say, "Because he thinks she was all about trying to move up, ya know? Like everything she did was about that."

"Pphhhh . . ." It's as if he's told a joke that I'm too naïve to understand.

I raise my eyebrows. "You think so too?"

"That girl, it was just a question of when she screwed over the wrong guy."

His remark twists my insides, but I press on. "You think Memo coulda been the guy? . . . all things considered?"

"Sure. Coulda been lotsa guys. Any texts from *my* guys in her phone?"

"I'd bet on it. Especially if they were seeing her socially. Phone's got hundreds of contacts. Some teachers even." It's hard to hold the eye contact, but I make myself do it.

"Yeah? Like whose?" he says.

"Yours," I say, "and mine." I pause. "And some of the women."

"They gonna find texts between you two in there, Tavish?"

I want him to think so, and I say, "Phone call records too, I suppose."

"She told me she deleted everything."

"Yeah, she told me that too, but Verizon or whoever can still pull 'em up."

He finally looks away from me, shaking his head, skyward if there were a sky in this miserable room, low-ceilinged and smelly. I start wondering how many years' sweat are in the mats, if they ever get sun, if there are still air molecules trapped in here from twenty years ago when they built the wrestling addition—it's due for renovation in the fall, and I wonder if they are getting new mats. He's not liking what I have to say about cell phones and text messages, and I try guessing how tech-savvy he is. At least as much as I am, probably.

He says, "I imagine the cops will get around to questioning me at some point then." I can see he's thinking back to Saturday night now, in earnest. It's hard to know if he's got some actual fear of discovery or if he's just annoyed that the texts are somehow discoverable. I'm guessing his point is that although he may be a seducer of underage girls, Usaré in particular, it does not make him a bad person. He doesn't see himself as someone who uses his authority to secure sexual favors; he figures the girls are willing, since virtually none of them are virgins, and he is just the handiest adult male available to them in their time of exploration and desire, far superior to the boys their own age, superior to me too, since I've led him to believe I am his tunnel brother. He believes he fulfills their need as no one else can, and of course he enjoys their freshly-pubescent features.

I say, "They will definitely want to have a chat with you. Burgoyne says everybody is a suspect, but I still think they're going to come back to Memo and the Levantes." I pause again. "But the sooner they go after those guys, the sooner they quit digging up irrelevant texts and phone calls. The main thing right now is to be covered for Saturday night."

"I'm good. Might be a bigger problem for you, huh?" So he has bitten.

He's referring to my being married I assume . . . or my administrative status. He understands discovery of such a thing as we are talking about is a marriage ender, which he wouldn't care about, or a career ender, which he at least understands is a problem. But I wonder if he's been stuck in this cave so long that he doesn't realize he'll go to prison if the county attorney can prove he had sexual relations with Usaré or *any* underage girl. Will and Augustine may have winked, but the police won't. Not nowadays.

"I should be all right," I say, then add, "never took much of a break—just a matter of people not remembering me being AWOL. So, about her last movements . . ." This time I smile as I say it. "Did you happen to see her leave the dance?"

He hesitates. He is a practiced liar, so I assume it's because he doesn't know the safer answer. "No, I didn't."

"You must've seen her though, right?"

"She made sure I saw her." The bastard can't help strutting. "Came up and talked."

"Alone?"

"One of her friends was with her. Chevy."

"What'd she talk about?"

"Asked me if I'd be cool and let them go out to Marcus's car. Said they'd be right back. Forgot their tampons."

"You let 'em go?"

"I told them they knew it wasn't allowed. I don't fall for their bullshit anyway. I figured they were probly gonna sneak in some vodka shooters."

"You remember when that was?"

He thinks for a few moments, then says, "Ten or so."

"Who relieved you for your break?"

"Amin." He answers right away, but his eyes narrow, knowing I can check his story.

"Just wondering if they coulda sneaked out during the switch or something. Which would give us a time. The cops think she left early. Any ideas which way she went out?"

He says, "Probably over the other side. How the hell I know?"

"When was your break anyway? Eleven?" hoping it sounds casual.

Rusic knows I created the schedule, but he also knows teachers tend to ignore it, work out their own arrangements. "Elevenish."

"Kinda late. You come back or just head home?"

He does not answer.

I say, "It's getting late, no one wants to be there, nobody's sneaking in after eleven anyway—I get it. We can cover each other when Burgoyne asks about it, 'cause I know it's gotta be those Levantes that killed her. But you gotta be straight with me." I'm not used to playing the good old boy, and I can only hope I sound convincing. My heart is throbbing.

He says, "I went out for a dip of snuff, ten minutes tops, and came back." Pauses. "But split after Amin seen me. About eleven-thirty. When did she get it?"

I say, "About then. Make it simpler if I say you stayed till the end? Midnight."

"I'd appreciate that, Coach." He uses the honorific, but I sense he doesn't have much conviction behind it.

"No problem." I don't know quite how to fish out the next one, but I blunder ahead. "They found semen samples in her, you know."

"Not mine," he says. "Bet your ass on that."

"Yeah," I say, assuming he uses condoms. "There's no covering for DNA."

He says, "You're not worried about that, are you?"

I shake my head. "I haven't seen her in a while. Except from a distance. Just letting you know though—they found samples *on* her body too."

"*On* her body?"

"Sweat and spit has DNA too. Stays on for more than a day." I have no idea if this is true, but I think he'll believe me. "If anything you tell me doesn't add up, I'll have to cut bait."

He hesitates. I sense that now he doesn't feel quite so superior to me as he did a few minutes ago. He says, "Been a month. That'll be no problem."

"So Saturday you were there till midnight?" I say.

"Yes I was, Coach."

"And you could see me the whole time?"

"I remember waving at you when the lights came on at the end of the dance." He winks.

"So about this Memo. His name ever come up among your guys?"

"What you want the answer to be?"

I realize the trouble with getting cozy with Rusic is that now he does think we're brothers. He believes I want him to fabricate more narrative with him now, whereas I only meant the reference to Memo as a lead-in. At this point, I think I've gotten as much truth from him as I'm going to get, but I don't know how to bring this chat to an end without ruining the little bit of credibility I've gained with him. I go ahead. "I only want what's verifiable."

"My boys were talking about the Levantes. Was maybe a couple months ago. At a pre-match durbar."

"Durbar?" I say. An obscure word, which I only vaguely remember. Middle Eastern or something, referring to a court.

"We do it the day before every match. It's like a council. Any wrestler can say what's on his mind. Anyone can talk. Everyone listens. Usually it's focused on the mat, you understand? Who they expect to wrestle the next day. Usually how confident they are—their pride, making weight, their dads, their girlfriends. Sometimes it's about other stuff going on."

I stay silent. He's tried to make everything unique for these wrestlers, to make them winners, to give them a world where *they* control success, not their parents, not the school or the cops, not the closest burger joint, and it comes through in the word—durbar. He's obviously chosen the word carefully, foreign and mysterious, and it's become this sacramental moment for his grapplers—their word, their private council, exclusionary and awe-filled—the perfect stage to rebuild shaken confidence, to boast, to encourage teammates. Durbar—a word nobody uses except for the Polk Chargers . . . the Polk crotch-grabbers. I fight my condescension to stay respectful. His methods work, after all.

"It's a blessed time." He keeps a straight face.

'Blessed.' My face almost breaks. I say, "But this one wasn't about wrestling. What was the drift?"

"I guess you could say Bobby Oropeza was looking for a few guys to step up and be men with him. He wanted a few wrestler buddies to go with him to teach somebody a lesson—one of them Levantes, it turns out, which is why he needs some back-up of course."

"Because thugs hang together," I say, wondering if Rusic ever thinks of himself as a thug, if these wrestlers stepping up to be men do.

"Right. Don't know if it was Memo, but it was a Martinez for sure. And it don't matter. The message has gotta be for all them assholes."

"A lesson regarding? . . ."

"Staying away from Bobby's sister. The Martinez boy was paying her way too much attention . . . even crashed her quinceañera the Saturday before with a couple other guys . . . all decked out in brown plaid."

"Recruiting her," I say.

"Yeah. And apparently she'd already tried some drugs supplied by Martinez. Not just grass, but something stronger. Meth maybe. Or heroin. Wanted more."

"So just warning her off was no longer enough."

"Bobby said his mom was worried, and he was worked up, rocking side to side, like he wanted to take care of it right then."

"Were there some volunteers?" I ask.

"All of 'em." He nods his head, barely. "You know how they are. Your teams woulda done the same when you were coaching—go beat down some little punk who's screwing with a sister."

His remark about my teams is gratuitous, but I believe him about *his* guys. It makes me feel inferior in some way because my teams never would have stepped up for each other like that. Or at least I'm not sure they would've. Face a street gang? Yeah, maybe two or three guys, but the whole team? I'm doubting it. Maybe that's why my teams never made it past the first round in the playoffs.

"So was the lesson delivered?"

"Not when he intended. We had Sunnydale the next day. Runners up last year and tougher this year."

I say, "So you intervened."

"Damn straight. I told them it had to wait a couple days. That Bobby needed their help, sure, but we had to focus on Sunnydale. Took Bobby home with me. Wrestled one of the twins at his weight. Kicked ass." For Rusic, no judgment mattered more.

I say, "But the Martinezes got the message later?"

"Don't really know. Bobby quit on us a few days later. Never heard any more about it."

"You must have talked to him though."

"Of course. Tried like hell to get him back. He was the best kid I had at that weight, but he said he had to take care of family business."

When I return to my office, I look up Oropeza on my desktop. Bobby dropped out of school a week before the state wrestling finals. Matilde, his fifteen-year old sister, a couple weeks prior.

The intercom buzzes and Santana says, "Mr. Tavish, a Mr. Martinez to see you." She pauses. Pretty common name in these parts, Martinez.

"*Guillermo* Martinez."

SIX

Mimi Nelson's specialty assignment at Polk is 'personal and social' counseling. And not only is she well-suited to it, but the other counselors are only too happy to let her keep that specialty, preferring 'career paths' or 'scholarships' or 'tech-support' specialties to dealing with a bunch of hormone-charged, oversensitive, teared-up teens who are usually upset over things that are meaningless in the adult world—best friends dissing you or insipid remarks on social media, which Mimi hears about daily and accepts as meaningful to *them*. She hears kids' stories of deep turmoil and fear and loss as well: the death of a classmate, the torment over a father who drinks too much and beats too hard, the worry that a landlord will hang up an eviction notice on their door. She looks carefully for signs of true depression, and sometimes has to have a child hospitalized to prevent a suicide attempt. There are several indicators that can let her know when one of our kids is in real emotional trouble; she says she starts to worry when she asks a kid about the future and whether he can see something improving in a few days or a month or a year, and the kid says no.

She gets really worried, though, when she asks about the past, whether he can remember better times, and he still says no. That's when it's time to ask him if he's thought about suicide.

After I lost Maria to that Goddamned cancer, the mornings came anyway, and when each one came, I told myself the new day would be less painful than the last. But when each evening came, I looked into Francesca's eyes and NJ's eyes, and Ursa's too, and finally into my own, looking back from the mirror as I flossed, and I admitted the pain was worse. Then I would try to look into the future and see that the three of us would feel better, four of us if you counted Ursa, and I honestly could not. And when I looked back in time, it was easy enough to remember both special and ordinary moments that were full of joy, but looking back at them only intensified my sorrow. I didn't think about suicide, but I worried that I'd start. So I worked, I helped

Abuelita comfort my kids, and I felt sorry for myself. Then, Usaré came along.

Mimi needed an administrator to accompany her on her annual retreat to train peer counselors, and once again she invited me, since I'm her supervisor.

She had already lined up a male chaperone to go, Mac Gabello, but Mac only agreed to go if he didn't have to participate in the training sessions. He didn't mind keeping an eye on the boys so they didn't try sneaking over to the girls' cabin at night, but he wasn't interested in learning any counseling skills. But the district requires someone with administrative certification to supervise any trip like that, someone to be accountable for a glitch or to be a scapegoat for a scandal. The retreat was at a woodsy resort about twenty miles south of the city, in this canyon renowned for its hummingbirds, though the term resort is something of an affectation for the four cabins and meeting hall. It was scheduled for the September after Maria died, and I was still in a lightless place, and I didn't want to go. I tried hard to get out of it, and I even had Sally talked into going instead of me.

Then I realized Usaré would be there, and I changed my mind.

I don't know the exact reason she affected me so completely, maybe the way she'd said she was infatuated with me—we men are so easily drawn in after all and me more than most, maybe the plush of her red-brown hair, or maybe the way she seemed to command the attention of any room she was in—what all the adults referred to obliquely as her leadership qualities. And of course, I possess compulsive feelings about any attractive female— that influenced me too.

I go to Thursday SAA meetings and hear stories from the other addicts, and sometimes they're so outrageous that I think, Well, I'd never do anything like that so maybe I don't need these meetings. Last Thursday, one married woman confessed to needing to meet a new man every week, making it clear that her interest in each one was carnal, which not only sounded outrageous but also caught the attention of a crowd of men who approached her after the meeting with offers to be her sponsor. I wasn't one of them, but I can't say the idea didn't go through my mind.

So no, I can't stop going to meetings and working the steps.

When I learned that Usaré would be attending the peer counseling retreat, I told myself Mimi needed me; I had accompanied her on all her previous trips after all, and she depended on me to play the heavy if a few kids got a little unruly. I told myself the topics Mimi picked were always enlightening, and the subject that year was leading by listening—appropriate for me. I told myself it was time to move past my loss and start connecting with people again, and that included young people at my school.

In Mimi's peer counseling program there are two boys and two girls at each level, freshman through senior. She tries to recruit kids as freshmen and then retain them as peer counselors for the entire four years they attend Polk, but of course that doesn't always happen. Consequently, she always starts the school year with a half-and-half mix of veterans and rookies in her program, so a lot of the activities during her retreats have to do with learning to work together. Still, the only name I recognized on the list of new recruits was Usaré's.

Three days, two nights in an aviary canyon with Mimi Nelson and Mac Gabello and sixteen young people, including Usaré.

As I watched the kids work at becoming a team, I couldn't help noticing that Usaré worked to stand out, somehow usually finding a way to bring up La Raza, the race, which was her political cause, during the discussion, so that Mimi or one of the upperclassmen had to remind everyone they were there to develop techniques for effective personal interaction.

With Usaré's hoop earrings and pearl pendant, her cotton blouses, her red lipstick and outrageous nails, her proud, large bosom and round buttocks, her hair—always the hair, I became entranced, ensnared really, so that I looked for characteristics in other girls and women that reminded me of her. God help me, I even started comparing her, feature by feature, to my dead wife. Bigger breasts, longer legs, a tighter butt showing through the fabric of her jeans, a wider and less comely back and torso but more fluid hair, not hazel eyes but brown ones . . .

Mimi always brought me into the mix as they worked, changing the group members again and again, so that every kid worked with every other kid. She and I were supposed to move around and monitor during the sessions, making sure her recruits felt like they had to stay on task, but I always lingered with Usaré's group, even to a point that I wondered if Mimi would say something, or worse yet, notice me doing it and say nothing to me.

During breaks and in the evenings we had plenty of time to be alone if we wanted, and on previous retreats I had sought solitude, heading to my room to call Maria or to read and get some time away from the adolescent chatter while Mimi and the other chaperone kept track of the kids.

That year was different of course, because there was no Maria any more. Dead-hearted as I still was, I'd linger behind after Mimi released the kids. To see what happened, I admitted to myself, to see if Usaré would show some sign of being infatuated with me, as she had said only a couple months before, and wondering what she meant by that.

The curiosity, the hope for a scrap of her attention, penetrated my consciousness from top to bottom in those moments, as if I were impaled on a spit, and there was very little space for another emotion, including my grief. I think it was then I truly began to heal from my desperation, but I thought I should feel ashamed about it too, that the possible attentions of a fourteen-year-old girl, along with my attraction to her, was the thing that was mending me. Anything to lift the gloom.

I'd never act on impulses about a teenage girl, I told myself.

My grief over losing Maria was like a nasty dope-low, like I'd had three tokes too many of some extremely potent grass and I was struggling to come back from the stoned feeling but couldn't do it. It's crazy to think of it that way, but that's how I felt, afraid I'd be stuck in a murky confusion forever, merely pretending to function as the world shook its head disapprovingly at me. I was performing all my duties rote and out-of-touch, but not sure my work was any use, like a carpenter's attempts to install new plumbing.

Usaré brought me back from the edge of an abyss, and I will always owe her for that. I don't like to think of myself as a Humbert who chases Lolitas, and I despise guys like Rusic, but I attended that retreat because Usaré was going to be there, a fact which I never shared—never will share—at an SAA meeting.

Usaré would dally in the meeting room after sessions, the same as I, and I fancied it was to spend a few moments with me, which turned out to be true. There would be an initial crush of bodies leaving the room, boisterous and laughing, and then there would be only a few of us, me staring out the window for a minute, Usaré schmoozing Mrs. Nelson, until there were just the two of us, me and Usaré in the big room that smelled of pine smoke and bleach and bacon—the room served as our cafeteria too—and a rhythm started, maybe just in my lifeless heart, but I sensed inside her as well.

The first day we talked about the team-building sessions, about her mother and father, about school and her future, about what she said was her passion—La Raza studies, and how Mexican-American kids should be exposed to it. But she'd always get around to saying how she admired me, the way I could think on my feet, which I wished I could believe, and my respect for Latino families like hers. She seemed such a singular mixture of things—traits. Characteristics you'd never expect to find in a fourteen-year-old.

She seemed older, of course, or I think she would not have had the same effect on me, but maybe that's just me reconstructing the past to minimize my sense of guilt. She did know she seemed older, artful in mien and more confident than most thirty-somethings. Rhythmic and composed, disciplined and charming. I can't remember her laughing—maybe her rules of self-control didn't allow for laughing—but her smile made you think she was laughing, even-toothed and perfected, with those Apache cheekbones.

She made me think I was the only man in the room, which I actually was most of the time now that I think about it, with Mac watching a DVD on his computer or jogging on one of the canyon trails. I think, though, she could have been in a room with ten men, and somehow each of them would have felt like he was her favorite, the only man in the room who mattered to her.

And bright. Intuitive enough to ask me if I'd ever seen myself as principal instead of 'just' an assistant, which of course I'd thought about a thousand times. Her voice, along with the things she said, always seemed smooth and confident and natural, as if all her remarks just popped into her head.

She could be tough too, hard even, but I didn't know it when we talked on that muggy September afternoon, the second day of the retreat.

"Let's see what we can find in the fridge," she said.

I followed through a set of swinging doors into the kitchen. I took out two cans of Pepsi, while Usaré rummaged around, used two fingers to taste the cold navy beans left over from lunch, seeming to like it, found a half moon of sharp cheddar and broke off a corner. "Let's sit and talk on one of the couches till the others come back; I'm sick of those stacking chairs." She carried the cheddar with her, along with a bag of celery she'd found.

Back to the meeting room, to one of the tan faux-leather couches that lined the north wall, below a painting of a grizzly bear fishing for salmon. She said, "Don't you think it's odd they have that kind of painting here? There's hardly ever water in the rivers here." She tore off a celery stalk and broke it in half and removed the strings that had come loose and munched at it.

"No salmon around here either," I said.

"You ever think you shoulda done something else? Besides being a principal, I mean." So here she was, this girl who was probably pretty self-absorbed, if she was like most high schoolers anyway, asking me about me. I found myself grinning at her.

"No, I never really did."

"How come?"

"I wanted to teach and coach, like this one teacher I had in high school." I thought of him for a minute—Coach Jimmy. "He wound up as an administrator too."

She said, "You would have made a good judge, I think."

"You really are going to be an attorney, aren't you?"

"No question."

"Why are you so sure?"

"Lotta reasons." She tore off another chunk of the cheese and nibbled at it. "Because my father never got anywhere. Because of La Raza and

CLED"—the movement to elevate the voice and the power of Mexican-Americans in the Southwest, which some people characterize as radical, and the Center for Latino Education and Defense. Her eyes were dolled up with shadow and eyeliner and mascara, but she was deliberate in her remarks, with an even, analytical tone. I didn't really want to talk about La Raza though. She put her left arm on the back of the sofa and faced me, and I swiveled my hips so that I could look back at her. Our hands were practically touching on the back of the couch. She smiled with her lips parted.

"You know what it means to have a thousand lawyers drown at one time?" I said.

"A good start." She smiled, but not with good humor.

"You know why lawyers don't worry about sharks?"

"Professional courtesy," she said. "I know a lot of lawyer jokes. You know the difference between a lawyer and a liar?" When I shook my head, she said, "The pronunciation." Trying to show me she knew everything she needed to know. Overdoing it, but it impressed me anyway. I liked the wittiness, adolescent as it was. Maria could pull off a joke, but it was always a guileless, harmless one, like a knock-knock.

I was sitting there with this audacious, bright and beautiful girl, and a guilty giddiness overcame me. I wanted to touch her hand, her arm, but I was afraid to. I could see myself looking up her schedule later, going to whatever classroom she was in, asking to speak to her out in the hall, tempting myself all over again.

Making me just like Rusic, I think now.

I was about to make some kind of excuse and leave, but then I noticed she was looking at me.

With the look. Her eyes were clear and bright.

I remembered what she'd said: infatuated. And I remembered what a friend had told me once: "If a girl gives you the look and lets you kiss her, you can bet she'll let you fuck her." I remembered too that he'd been talking about some forty-year-old he'd just met. Forty, not fourteen.

But there she was, giving me the look.

I didn't turn my head, but I sensed around, and I could tell there was no one there to see us. I thought about doing it, about covering her hand with mine, about watching her react and then, if I sensed she'd let me, kissing her. I may have sent some neural signal to my hand, releasing the chemical to make the hand move. Hell, I may have even started to move my hand.

But I didn't touch her. I froze. I wish I could say that my good heart took over, that my ethics and moral fortitude reappeared, that I became aware that reaching over those last couple inches to touch the lovely, bright-nailed hand constituted an emotional betrayal. But I don't think any of that passed through my mind.

I was just scared. Terrified, really, and of what—of an unintended consequence or of being swept away like a dove in a hurricane or of Usaré herself—I was not exactly sure. I heard a bird, some kind of wren I think, and the moment passed, but I didn't feel safe until I heard a couple boys laughing as they approached the meeting room. Part of me felt safe, another part disappointed. Her smile turned wistful.

The remainder of the retreat presented no more moments to be alone together. During sessions, though, I would turn sometimes and find her smiling at me, emitting the same wistfulness, holding my gaze without wavering, and I couldn't help myself from smiling back or nodding, though the whole interaction seemed on display, and her smile would deepen enough to show a dimple. Once I glanced up and caught her eyes boring into me with such intensity that I thought I could feel their warmth, and everything else, every external thought, drained from me.

In a way, that was the best part. Instead of the continuous awareness that I had lost Maria, I let Usaré's presence wash over me. I began to fantasize again. Not just about trysts but about conversations with her, about shared accomplishments, about aiding her to further the cause of La Raza. And always in the fantasy, she expressed this adoration of me. And showed it.

It kept me awake at night. I'd think back to the moment of the near seduction, whose and by whom I didn't care, and I'd see it playing out with a different ending each time, each less disappointing than the reality, my heart speeding up, my viscera reacting predictably, with a prevailing sense of incredulity. I searched myself for connections to the old Tavish, but not too hard. My image of the old Tavish was depressing—a guy who moped and spent his energy not breaking down in tears. I was actually afraid I'd wake up the next morning and that that old Tavish would be back.

But he didn't come back. The last day of the retreat, and for weeks afterward, I woke up with a sense of anticipation, thinking I'd make sure to conduct teacher observations in rooms where Usaré was in class, imagining I'd stop at her desk to ask her if she understood the lesson so I could smell the aromas from her morning shower, planning my cross-campus walk-arounds to maximize the chances I'd run into her as she switched classes . . . and always on the lookout for a signal from her.

And for months, I actually did those things, wondering if anyone noticed and never saying a word about it at my Thursday meeting. The gloom lifted.

I felt guilty, but it was a relief to leave Maria behind. Some part of me knew the insanity of my grief had merely been replaced by an obsessive madness for a young girl, but I was glad for it. I'd become weary of my woe.

Maria's presence didn't let go of me easily though. I still thought of her every few minutes, and her absence pained me, and it got so I would consciously remind myself of Usaré to drive out the hurt, changing the subject of my internal discourse. A memory of Maria's patience for my Nikes and my basketball obsession would pop into my head while I was supervising a girls' basketball game, and I'd conjure up an image of Usaré pounding on a rubber mat and leading a chant for our grapplers somewhere across town at a meet. I'd get an image in my head of Maria making a subtle sexual advance, and I'd drive it out by recalling Usaré munching celery and cheese on the sofa that day and somehow making it seem alluring.

I had met Maria in high school when we were both seniors. Her parents were going through a divorce at the time, brought on by her father's over-attentiveness to his secretary, a fair amount of gold-digging by the secretary, her mom's jealousy, and too much drinking by all three of them. Of course, the family's electrical contracting business was failing as well.

Maria was a straight-A student, but she didn't particularly like going home after school in those days. She'd go to these Alateen meetings down in the basement of the gym after school, to brace herself for the drama awaiting her at home. I'd be at basketball practice and I'd see her emerge from the basement stairwell, then watch her cross the hardwood floor and exit through the heavy metal doors. She wasn't eye-catching in the way that usually grabs the attention of high school boys, no big bosom or long legs, but she carried an armful of books and walked with a graceful gait, head up, full of purpose.

One day she came out of the basement and didn't cross the floor to the exit. Instead, she sat down on a folding chair and watched us practice. I had this hope that she was watching me, just me and not all of us, and I kept glancing at her, flexing and trying to keep my abs hard because we were going shirts-and-skins and I was wearing just my shorts and Jordans. We were doing what Coach Jimmy called time-and-score, which is situational scrimmaging: protecting a three-point lead with two minutes left, trying to get the lead when we trail by two with thirty seconds to go—it's mental practice as much as it is getting the execution right. After about ten minutes, we ran a play where I was going to get the first option to score—as if we were near the end of a game and down by a point. As we set up for the situation, I looked over my bare shoulder at Maria. She was holding her books on her lap, still watching. When coach started the clock, I was supposed to set a screen, forcing a switch so I'd wind up with a short guy guarding me with about ten seconds on the clock, then catch the ball and go to the basket to score and win the game. With her eyes on us, I made up my mind I was going to dunk, even though Coach didn't like us dunking in that situation, and even though I'd miss the shot about half the time when I tried.

Coach said go and we went live. The clock ticked down, and I set the screen, held it just long enough and rolled to the hoop with this five-ten guy trying to guard me. Anthony, our shrimpy point guard now matched up with our six-eight back-up center, fed me the ball perfectly with a bounce pass. I caught the ball, I went up with all the power I could muster and I threw that sucker down, even hung on the rim for a second like a chimp, showing off. When I came down and turned to look, Maria was smiling at me. Coach Jimmy came up and asked, "What the hell you doing, son?" but I kept looking at the cute brunette sitting in the folding chair and smiling back at her. She told me later that that was when she fell in love with me.

When she came to our next home game against Wasson Peak, she hung around in the gym till after almost everyone had gone home. I came out of the locker room and asked her out. She told me her eyes were hazel, which I guess means they could change colors depending on the surroundings, but to me they were mostly green, which is a color I don't even like very well, but I liked her eyes, so I said they were emerald.

After that, Maria appeared during basketball practice every day about four-thirty. I'd start watching for her a few minutes before, trying to catch the exact moment her brown hair appeared from the mouth of the stairs so I could see her emerge, hair first, then her bright face—almost golden in the bright light of the stairwell floodlights, then her shoulders and so on, rising in segments as she lifted herself on each tread. She often wore greenish tones, or tan, and I would pretend she was a flower, like a brown daylily, pushing her way from the earth and into the light of day. I'd nod at her with a faint grin if coach wasn't looking my way, and she'd smile back and go over and sit in one of the folding chairs and open a book and pretend to start her homework.

After I asked her to prom, we spent most evenings together, sometimes going for coffee at Jimbob's Family Restaurant, but more often than not just sitting in my family's backyard and talking and kissing. She asked me what it was like to play basketball in front of a crowd, and wasn't I ever scared? I told her that first of all there seldom was a crowd until we got into the state tournament, and then there was no difference between playing in front of fifty people and five hundred 'cause either way you made the killing or you fell down, and most of that was determined by trust. If you were going to fall down, I told her, you can't let it be from a lack of trust, parroting what Coach Jimmy always said.

"Trust?" she asked, raising her eyebrows.

"Trusting the other guys, yourself too," I said. She looked away, thinking about that.

I'd take her to the park to practice free throws, which I never got very good at, and she'd shoot some too, worse than me. I told her there was a lot of punking on our basketball team, hazing, and that the other guys teased me about her having my juevos in a vise, but I didn't care. I told her she was the best-looking girl I'd ever seen, but she didn't believe me. I could hardly wait to marry her. We dated all through college, though both of us went out with someone else after a spat or when we'd been talking about being 'too serious.' And sometimes I'd go out with a hot girl I'd met just because Maria was two-hundred miles away, attending a different school. I'd accepted an out of state basketball scholarship at a small liberal arts school. Maria went to the state university a few miles from where she grew up.

Her mom held me in some disdain, or maybe she was just so hurt by the ugly divorce that she didn't trust men anymore. She told Maria once that she could do better than me, and of course her mom was right. Maria told me she'd said, "These sports jocks think they're God's gift to women."

Maria answered, "Daddy was an athlete."

Her mom said, "Yeah, look how that worked out. The sooner I'm rid of him, the better. He hasn't come home sober in ten years. Ex-jocks drink. Jocks drink. Fool around too. I bet your boy is already drinking, even if he's not fooling around on you."

Maria said, "He never drinks," which was true at the time.

"They'll throw him out of the jocks' club then," her mom said.

Maria was the youngest in her family, and none of her siblings lived at home, so I seldom saw them. Drunk or sober, her dad liked me, so of course I liked him as well. I didn't know it at the time, but her dad liked everyone, trusted everyone too, which may have had more to do with the failure of his business than anything else. I thought maybe that was why she reacted the way she did when I mentioned trust.

Maria gave up her virginity to me on the floor of her parents' living room, actually her mom's living room by that time, just before Christmas during our sophomore year in college. I'd driven home for the holiday break, and we practically lived together while she house-sat for her mother, who was visiting a sister just then. Maria was not quite nineteen, an unusually late start on life's sexual adventure for a modern girl, I suppose, but that's how it worked out . . . or played out. In my experience, either phrase is right, depending on circumstances and attitudes.

We married in June at St. Thomas Church, about two weeks after earning our degrees, lived in a one bedroom apartment for a year, then moved into a brick veneer cottage in a subdivision called Montrose Heights, though the property was so low that rain water often came right up to our doorstep. Francesca and NJ were born in April just before our fourth anniversary. Maria blessed me for another five years. I hated God when she died. HATED Him!

Still do.

SEVEN

Memo is six-feet-five inches tall if he's an inch, athletic-looking, and my first thought is I should have recruited him to play basketball when I was coaching and when he was some gawky tough kid trying to figure out what the hell was going on. Too late for that now, but he's standing in my office.

His hair, combed straight back, is black, and his skin brown, but they take on an olive drabness under the fluorescent lights, and an almost-jaundiced yellowness suffuses his eyes, as if he's already drunk too many forty-ounce bottles of malt liquor for his age—early twenties. His nose is hooked down with a pointed tip, and he has black eyes, reminding me of a fierce kea bird,

"Can I come in?" he says, the smart ass, knowing I'm looking for him. He is very calm.

"You're in. Wanna sit down?" I'm indicating the hot seat where I interview kids, close to the desk, but he doesn't bite.

He closes the door, then sits in the chair that Burgoyne usually occupies. Might as well be on the telephone. He leans back in the chair and extends his legs to show he's relaxed or maybe to show off his hand-tooled boots, which I'm guessing are crocodile skin. He's got the damn L tat on the back of one hand, looking just like the ones we see on campus, and doesn't mind showing it.

"How can I help you?" I say, too late realizing it sounds stupid.

"I thought that'd be *my* question." He pauses. "You lookin' for *me*, right?" pauses again. "Came by and talked to my little brother."

"Your brother wasn't cooperative so I talked to your sister." I watch his reaction, which is not amiable.

"What you wanna know about the dead girl."

"Should I take notes?"

"We didn't have nothin' to do with it."

"We?" I say.

"Me and my family."

"Which family? Martinezes or Levantes?"

"Neither one. I'm here about the tag, actually." He leans forward, his elbows on his knees, conveying this relaxed attitude, which annoys me. "It ain't ours. Good rip-off maybe, but it ain't ours."

I figure he's lying, but I'm also surprised he knows anything at all about the tag. I decide to blunder ahead anyway.

"Sure looks like yours. Identical to your tat." I glance at his bicep where the calligraphic L is prominent, inked professionally enough that you might have thought it was put there by a medieval monk. "Cops thought so too." Thinking, let him talk some more.

"Yeah, you wanna say so."

"So tell me how you know it ain't yours," I say.

"It's chicken-ass. We doan claim no punk shit like that. We doan even *do* shit like that. Somebody puttin' it on us. And if one o' us did sign that, there'd be some kind of tag from the one who claimin' it." I want to tell him he sounds like a Mexican guy trying to talk black and not doing it very well, but I don't. I just want him to keep talking.

I wait.

"And there ain't one, is there!" He knows it, doesn't just suspect it. There were no initials or secondary tags with the funky looking L.

I take a moment to write down the remark on my legal pad. "You knowing that just puts one of your guys at the crime scene," I say.

"No, it just means I mighta seen a picture on some guy's phone."

I'm thinking about how likely it is that photos from that bathroom got out after Benjamin found the body. How likely that even a description got out. Not from any cops, for sure. The gang tag is what the cops call withheld evidence—something that only they, the thin blue line, and the killer or killers would know about. Presumably anyway. "Whose phone?"

"Another guy who didn't have nothin' to do with it. Just wanted me to see the tag."

"This other guy with such an interest in amateur photography—he mention how he was able to get access to a crime scene?"

Memo grins.

I have other questions too. Were there other photos? Was there a time stamp like there sometimes is? What else could you see in those photos: the splintery crack in the mirror? the smudges of blood? Usare's lifeless body? But I suspect Memo is not going to satisfy my curiosity with any truthful information. No, it's better to leave the forensics to Burgoyne's colleagues.

"So how many guys are in familia Los Levantes, give or take?"

He ignores even that question. "Wouldn't be smart for my family to do her, dude. You got the wrong idea 'bout us. We business people. One o' my guys do that, he wind up in a ditch somewhere."

"Running whores ain't a business. It's a crime. Look it up."

"We provide escorts, man. That ain' no crime. *You* look it up." He hands me a card then, glossy, embossed letters, black letters and a nippley silhouette on an orange background: Lift Your Spirits . . . Arouse Your Power. A web address and a phone number. "Maybe you like to try us out some time."

"So you all are just misunderstood entrepreneurs, raising up one man at a time."

"You could say that, yeah."

"You employ any underage escorts? That could be a problem for entrepreneurship."

He says nothing.

"Still, you were dating Usaré, yeah? She wasn't eighteen yet."

"I was seeing her occasionally. Lovely girl, but just friends. Neighbors, you know."

"Was she teasing you? Your brother Jhonny said she was a tease."

"Nobody teases me," he says. Cocky, but not aggressive.

So there it is. "Wow, you're gonna have to tell me your secret."

He pulls his head back at the neck, brings down his eyelids a notch, not liking my sarcasm. I think for a moment that it's time to back off, but then, after all, he's right here . . .

"Guy's gotta have an edge, right? Or else, anybody can get lucky." I don't blink. "What's yours?"

He still says nothing.

"Friend of mine, back in the day, used to get the gal to smoke a doobie with him. Made it easy he said. He'd say it was no fun if you had to hold her down, you know? A little wine . . . a little funny smoke, and there was no more teasing. That what you do?"

Memo smiles at me. "Nothing you say is gonna set me off, man. I didn't need no dope to get Usaré."

A safe and neutral answer. "Okay, but maybe Jhonny don't have your gifts with the ladies. Maybe, *he* needed an edge. Or some other Levante. Some guy who didn't get the memo . . . so to speak." I stare for a few seconds. "The cops'll come by with questions pretty soon."

"Already did, man." He likes saying this, grins more broadly, letting me know he's smarter than the police. And me.

I begin to wonder why he has come in to talk to me at all then, since he's not afraid of me sending the cops his way. "So then you won't mind telling me . . . Where were you Saturday night? . . . Sunday morning?"

"Don't mind at all. I's home . . . running my business. All right there on my tablet, you know? Saturday always a good night for us." Again he smiles. "My sister'll tell ya if you ask."

"And your families? Jhonny? He understand a dead escort ain't good for business? Not a Ph. D. your brother."

His face cracks. Just a little.

He looks around and finds my photos of Francesca and NJ, and then his eyes come back to me. "You got family? Mister?"

I suppose my face cracks too now, and he sees it, but I don't say anything.

He says, "You already met some of *my* family, right?" A few seconds later, he says, "You come sniffin' around last night like a DEA dog."

"Don't misunderstand me, Mr. Martinez. I don't care about any drugs you pass around. I don't even care about the whores until it affects my school."

"You sucker-punch my little brother like you done, same as disrespecting me."

"Jhonny needs to learn some respect himself, seems to me." After a beat, I say, "I'm wondering if you're related to the Arregons."

"Got some cousins name o' Arregon. Distant. Why you ask?" He's grinning again, needling me like that kea bird pecking into the back of a sheep.

"Just sent one off to Florence, I think. Least I'm thinking he'll get there. Guy named Neto. Wears his hair in a Mohawk and flashes L tats. He's one of yours, right?" I'm staring intently at his expression, wondering what he's heard about the fire and the tussle in my office. I see an almost imperceptible flinch, so I'm thinking there must be at least some part he doesn't know yet.

"I mighta seen him around sometimes," Memo says, "but we don't exchange valentines or nothin'."

"Wants everybody to know how bad he is, but hasn't quite perfected it yet. Few months from now, he'll be afraid to pick up soap off the shower floor. You assign him a job to do this morning?"

"Now you getting down to it, ain't ya."

"I'm not a cop, but I don't take to your ways. Or your businesses."

"You grew up aroun' here. You oughta understan' the neighborhood better'n you do."

"I put my nose in some books. You shoulda tried it," I say.

"You ain't no smarter'n us, gallina."

"Luckier maybe. Your boy came to school and tried to light us up. Talked about it on the bus first, so half the school was waiting for him to make his play. Then he comes in here with a little peashooter, doesn't even know how it works. Made a fool of himself. Spilling his guts to the cops right now."

"Neto way smarter than that."

"Maybe he's the one with no alibi on Saturday night."

He thinks about it.

I say, "You really a businessman, it'd make sense to give him up."

"If it was him, I'd do it, dude. Quick as a cockroach when the lights come on." I wonder where the simile came from but I don't say anything. "Except he couldn'ta done it. He was over in LA for the weekend."

"Cops'll be on your ass. Stop your business in its tracks. Them or maybe Andre."

He pretends he doesn't hear 'Andre.' "You tellin' me straight you think one of my brothers kill this girl?"

"Looks like, don't it."

This time, Memo pulls a pack of Marlboros out of his Dickeys, extracts one and lights it. I'm supposed to tell him it's a no-smoking campus, but of course it's irrelevant. "I know it wasn't my guys. What make you think that?"

"Wasn't just the tag. Was the meanness of it. The way the coward takes her, defenseless like that."

"My boys train girls. They don't kill 'em," he says.

"Some girls don't take to bein' trained." I'm close to pushing him over some kind of line. He's a strapping, handsome kid, once-upon-a-time high school dreamboat, a pimp who could have been somebody. "Mr. Martinez, I appreciate how you feel, but I'm gonna need to talk to some of your guys in the next few days. Anybody who knew Usaré. Save us all some time if they come by."

"You know," he says, "I always thought a guy from the neighborhood would understan' the way it is. The way it always gonna be."

"Usaré was from the neighborhood." I stare at him. "You and I both had choices. So did Usaré till Saturday night."

*****

"Your guys are full of it. You tell 'em that?" I say. "No way it was Andre."

"DNA don't lie, hey?" Burgoyne says. "Why'd you think I took the water bottle. Besides, it's not like they arrested him. Just picked him up for an interview. They're calling him a person of interest, not a suspect."

"You got identifiable DNA from a fingerprint on a water bottle? And it matches what they found on her?"

"Your man Andre sweats a lot. There's a lot of pressure to make an arrest 'cause the case is so filthy. You know that better'n I do. So the chief got 'em to use what's called an integrated microfluidic system for rapid DNA analysis—a chip test. Matched a sample they found inside her," he says.

"So it was probably from Thursday. Like Andre said."

"Relax, will ya. I agree with you. Andre's little swimmers showed significant deterioration."

I'm confused, and my face shows it.

"Sperm will remain inside a woman for a couple days, but almost all of them are dead after that long," he says. "The trouble with homicide detectives is they turn off the inductive side once they get a theory of the crime."

"Andre's in some trouble then?" I stare at him, waiting.

"For now, looks like. Once those guys think they got a suspect, that's it, hey. 'stead of looking at new theories, they try to make all the evidence fit the one they got: Andre put his semen in her, but she's sweating up the sheets with a couple other guys—there's your motive; besides that she's involved with gangsters who got a history with Andre; he texted her and called her, so the way they see it, he's obsessed; all he's got for an alibi is his cousin, who also had a thing for the girl. Any new facts will fit that scenario or they'll get tossed."

"What about Memo? The Levantes?"

"You listening to me? Andre's their guy until he ain't their guy. They may not even come over here this afternoon 'cause they'll be running down Andre's story. If they do come, it'll be to find out if your folks saw Andre hangin' around."

"What do *you* think?"

"I think their tunnel vision is as bad as yours." He sighs and regards me. "You know him better'n I do, but even I can tell Andre's too smart—no, too calm, to have killed her. Trouble is they could still build a case unless he comes up with a better alibi. Meantime, you can't see past Memo and his boys."

"What about Rusic? He's got a key. And motive too, especially if he thought she might tell somebody about their thing. Left the dance before midnight. I gave you what I got. He looks good for it. And even if he doesn't, he admitted to having sex with her. That'll send him up."

"Well, it wouldn't hurt if you got a sample of his DNA somehow, but he said he hadn't touched her in a month."

"Doesn't matter. I'm supposed to report immediately. In fact I should have reported already." After a second, I say, "This is my report, okay?" State law is stringent on this. A teacher or administrator has to report any 'reasonable suspicion' of abuse immediately.

He smiles. "Relax. I'll make a record of it . . . send some patrolmen by in a day or two."

I feel foolish, but only momentarily. A colleague of Augustine's was fired for ignoring gossip about a woman teacher who was 'too close to her students.' I come out of my fog and hand him the card that Memo gave me. "What about that?"

He inspects it for several seconds, and I think he's about to ask me where I got it. "Memo gave you this?"

"Not what I expected," I say.

"Gangsters with business cards," he says.

"And a web site."

"Speaking of which, I looked up your Ms. Sullivan on that hookup site."

"She's really there, uh?"

"Not too discreet either. She's got face photos on her profile. One of them is the same as on her Facebook page, and another one looks like her yearbook photo."

"So, you sifted through hundreds of profile photos till you found her? No wonder there's never a cop around when you need one."

He pays no attention. "No. You can narrow the search pretty easy. Zip code . . . age . . . physical features. All of which I had 'cause I knew who I was lookin' for. Plus you can filter out men, which is over ninety percent of the members. You really oughta have a look. Check out Memo's site too. We can use my computer." He rises abruptly and exits my office, expecting me to follow.

When I come into his office, Burgoyne is already sitting in one of the visitors' chairs at his desk; the other one, I gather, is for me and I sit down as he repositions his laptop so we can both see. In a few clicks, Nikki Sullivan's adult dating page fills up the screen. She's made no attempt to mask or conceal her face on her profile photo, and it's obviously her, though she calls herself 'playfulbrunette24_7'. After her profile name appear her age—twenty-six, her gender—female, and the classification—'Seeking: Men only'. There are about a dozen smaller photos on the page as well, under the heading 'Friends,' most of which display male features other than the face, guys with profile names like 'Rockinyerworld' and 'WouldLove2HaveYou'. It says she has a total of ninety-four friends, most of them here in the valley.

I read the way she introduces herself:

"Most important—NO STRINGS ATTACHED. I'm not interested in any long-term arrangements. I'm divorced, but I still need to be discreet because of my profession. Looking for handsome men for the occasional playdate, preferably at your place. I'm an educator, so if you're young, I might have had you in one of my classes or something. Let me know if you went to high school here in town or if you think you recognize me. I prefer men a little older than myself, 30-49 or so, but if you're especially handsome, well-hung or generous, or you think you have some special skill, please feel free to contact me. I play evenings and weekends only, unless it's summer or a school holiday.

"Doggie is my favorite position, but they're all good, lol. Think of me as that girl that loves to do the things your wife or girlfriend won't do. I can be coaxed into almost anything after a few glasses of wine. And by the way, I prefer married or attached men, since they can't really get possessive."

I say, "Jesus H. Christ. No wonder there's gossip."

"It gets better," he says, clicking to her photo albums, where there is an array of nude and semi-nude photos. With these, however, Nikki has made an attempt to disguise herself—head cropped off or with part of the face masked. Other members have attached comments to some of the photos, and Burgoyne scrolls through a few, which are blunt and crudely complimentary: "What a sweet young thing" or "Wish you were my teacher."

Burgoyne clicks back to the main profile page and says, "She's got Platinum status."

"Which means . . ."

"For one thing, it means she's very popular. She gets all these likes and cyber gifts from other members."

"Cyber gifts?"

"Yeah. Guys pay extra to send her things like cyber flowers or cyber jewelry so she'll pay attention and maybe set up a date with them."

"She must get a jillion guys sending her messages, way she presents herself."

"Ya think?" He looks sideways at me. "Young, attractive and slutty? Hell, I might email her myself."

I have to admit the same thing crosses my mind.

"These websites love having gals like her 'cause it keeps the men paying their monthly fee, so she gets a free membership, and they do all they can to promote her. The guys have to pay a hundred dollars a year just to belong, and they're willing to pay extra to get noticed, because there's not enough females to go around. Quite a scam."

"Wish I'd thought of it, but I'm not smart enough."

Burgoyne says, "You'd be a billionaire. I think one of the soft porno publishers owns the site now anyway. He clicks to a page of testimonials where seven or eight guys are swearing Nikki is the best hookup in the state and vividly describing her qualifications.

"Jesus."

"You said that already," Burgoyne says.

"Bears repeating. This is a CE unless she suddenly acquires some prudence.

"CE?"

"Career ender. Just a matter of time till the governing board hears about her somewhat unusual social network and fires her for moral turpitude."

"See any connection to your dead girl?"

So she's still *my* girl, at least for Burgoyne. "Maybe if Nikki wasn't so hetero, she mighta tried to get something going on with Usaré. Give her a motive like Rusic's."

"She's got a motive, just not a sexual one," Burgoyne says. When I look at him, he says, "Look at it this way: she mighta found out about Nikki's extracurricular activities . . . suggested she'd expose her for some reason. You fill in the blanks."

"What'd Usaré have to gain from outing a teacher?" I say.

"To demonstrate power? Moral outrage? Personal satisfaction? I don't know. But there could be something there. It's worth finding out, right?"

"Pretty cynical." I'm thinking about Nikki, remembering her crazy time with the boyfriend and the cocaine. I know she goes to NA meetings several evenings a week, and she has seemed straight. But I wonder about her mentioning glasses of wine and I wonder whether her hook-ups on this site are just a new compulsion to replace the cocaine, like an alcoholic's penchant for caffeine or cigarettes or religion, or a sex addict's need to watch porn.

"That's what looking for motive is—cynical." He looks back at the screen. "What we used to call a nymphomaniac, hey?"

"Maybe. Or maybe just a woman who behaves like a man." I know I am going to talk to her, if for no other reason than to tell her to be more cautious. "Let's see the Levantes' website. Since the PD apparently doesn't mind where you go on your cop computer."

"Difference between the PD and your governing board is they actually listen to explanations." He glances at the orange and black business card and types in the site, which turns out to be pretty basic. There's a spreadsheet with six columns, dressed up with suggestive photos. He scrolls down and up—seventeen women's names, mostly first names only—there's a Buffy and a Sandy, but some with first and last like Charity Lavender and Ariel Fire. Other columns are enrollment date, location, availability, rating and reviews. The names are links, and Burgoyne hovers on one, a certain Scarlett Blaze, white, nineteen, who does incall only at a southside motel. She has sixty-six reviews.

He clicks on her name and we get more information. She apparently enjoys pleasing generous gentlemen for one-hundred-fifty dollars per hour, doesn't accept dates with black men, and offers escort services only during the daytime, nine-to-four, while her husband is working she explains. She accepts invitations by text only, but takes Visa and Mastercard, no American Express, ten percent cash discount. Burgoyne clicks on her tiny thumbnail photo, and her tiny, bare-breasted frame jumps onto the screen. There's a five-two-zero phone number and an email address.

Burgoyne clicks back and then to another listing: Yvette, Hispanic, eighteen, who accepts dates with generous men of all races for two-hundred dollars per hour, day or night. "Bigger tits," he says.

"Same phone number and email though," I say.

He clicks through a few more. Most of the girls are Hispanic; all of them are under twenty-five, four-twenty-friendly, and according to Burgoyne, dirt-cheap, two-hundred dollars and under for an hour's labor of love. He says, "Memo's going for the low-budget guy here. Porn-star types get a lot more. Wonder if Memo has them paying into social security."

"Social security?"

"Yeah. Escorting is legal, but if Memo or his girls aren't paying taxes, we can bust 'em."

"It looks like Memo's only going after them eighteen and up."

"Don't be so sure," he says.

When I look at him quizzically, he nods at the screen and says, "This site they claim they are, but remember the Robinson girl?"

He's referring to Cecily Robinson, an eight-year-old African-American girl who disappeared about two years ago. She was apparently abducted silently from her own bedroom while her parents and siblings slept. Not even the family Doberman made a sound all night. Investigators responded and found an empty bed with mussed bed clothes, an open casement window with its screen tossed aside and nothing else—no useful fingerprints, no impressions in the soil outside her room, no fiber evidence.

At least that's what we found out in the newspapers and local TV. Maybe things were withheld.

The search for Cecily involved dozens of police officers, family friends, volunteers, finally the FBI. The neighborhood was canvassed multiple times, a reward was offered, Cecily Robinson's face appeared on posters and billboards and television news. The parents and other family came under suspicion. Cranks called the police department with ridiculous tips. Cecily is still missing.

"One theory is she got sold to some cartel down in Sonora or Sinaloa."

"I heard that rumor."

"Might be just a rumor. Did you hear the one she got sold to pay a drug debt the old man owed?"

I shake my head.

He says, "Some of my people believe those particular rumors. Robinson is kind of a shady guy."

"You think Memo's guys coulda done that? Got away with it? A guy like Neto? He'd probably fall and knock himself out trying to go through the window," I say.

"Sergeant of detectives I know floated the theory that Robinson was in on it—made things easy for the kidnappers. Left the door unlocked, drugged the dogs, gave a signal maybe."

"What do you think?"

"I think there's some crummy people in the world. And I know a couple hundred kids get snatched every year by strangers who do them harm."

The bell rings signaling the end of third period.

"I'm going to go talk to our playful brunette."

*****

Nikki is in the teacher cafeteria during her planning period, of course, because she is not allowed into her hallway, and she's one of the teachers who's been assigned several different classrooms while the police work goes on in the E building, roving from hallway to hallway and pushing a cart full of *Romeo and Juliet* books and an old cassette player. As I walk there, I become aware of a shift in my attitude about Nikki because of the provocative profile and photo array I have just seen, but I tell myself I won't be tempted.

When she first came to work at Polk five or six years ago, I automatically classified her as a needy rookie teacher. And since she came in midyear, I figured she'd need more help than most. But she didn't. It was partly because she was largely Klein's creation, of course. The teachers who came through a semester of student-teaching with Klein were always solid, and he was always right down the hallway as a resource for her anyway. But it wasn't just that; she was more independent than other rookies, almost rebellious about accepting help.

She conveyed the attitude she didn't need anyone, reminding me of some teenage boy.

She also seemed flirtatious from the very beginning of her time with us, which I found a little humorous because I never found her attractive. She was buxom and well-proportioned, and she wore tight-fitting clothes, but she was on the fleshy side, and she had the kind of eyes that seemed to be looking two different directions at the same time. All of which I told Maria, who told me I was being a terrible sexist and stereotyping the poor girl like a perfect American boor. That's why I always called her right-again Maria. Anyway, Nikki's flirts were easy for me to resist.

Then again, Nikki had not looked at all fleshy in the photos I'd just seen.

When I enter the cafeteria, she's sitting alone at a corner table, looking bored, hunched over a pile of papers, which she's marking occasionally and indignantly with a red pen. When I stand next to her table, she doesn't bother to look up.

"Can I join you, Ms. Sullivan?" I say.

"Why don't you just call me Nikki?" She smiles up for a second. "Wanna grade some papers?"

"Depends what they're about." I sit down, and I can't help noticing that she still wears tight-fitting clothes. She's in a black skirt, an orange leotard top and two inch pumps.

"I wish I knew, but they're so bad it's hard to say." She's looking down again. "Most of them purport to be about abortion, but they suck. If I read one more lead about poor little Johnny getting cut apart and pulled out in pieces, I think I'm gonna cut my *own* throat with a scalpel."

"Well, I'll pass then."

"Figures. You know, last year I meant to take abortion off the list of potential topics for the persuasive essay, but I forgot somehow. Jesus!"

"Yeah. When I taught American Government, I got tired of reading about the invisible hand."

She looks up and says, "I don't know what that is."

"Don't worry. It's bullshit. I'm really here to talk about your website."

It gives her pause, but not for long. "It's not a site; it's a page. And I'm not sure it's your business." She looks at me without flinching, daring me to disagree.

"I know it's not my business, but there are people who might see things differently."

She stares, looking more like forty than she does thirty. "I'm gonna have some more coffee. Can I get you a cup?"

"No, but I'll take an iced tea."

She rotates her legs and rises and shimmies showily to the stainless steel counter to pay Doreen the cashier, then sidles over to pour the drinks. She looks over her round shoulder at me, like she's in a photo shoot, and asks, "You like it virgin or corrupted?"

"Just a little sugar."

As she sets the glass down in front of me she says, "You know in Shakespeare's time, some people thought that coffee reduced a man's sex drive. Sort of an anti-aphrodisiac."

"Just the men?"

"Yeah, coffee shops were for men only in those days." She sits down.

"Really."

"Of course, coffee shops were usually attached to brothels, so it may have been just the wives noticing their hubbies had no desire after stopping off for a cup of coffee on the way home." She smiles now.

"Ms. Sullivan, maybe—"

"Won't you call me Nikki, just this once?"

"Nikki, yes, maybe you could be more discreet. If I found you, so will your students. Parents maybe."

"Dads?" She smiles more broadly, with amusement.

"More likely than moms," I admit. "Look, you're a good teacher. I want you to be here for a few more years."

"Who says I won't? Don't act so serious. It's just a dating site."

"Okay," I say, but her attitude surprises me. I came in here thinking she'd accept me as the wise uncle, but it obviously isn't working out that way. "But think it over. At least get some advice from some of your friends, will ya?"

"I will." Impatiently. "Anything else?"

"Well, yes actually. I'm wondering if you'd talked to Usaré García recently."

"That poor dead girl." She smirks. "Next, you'll wanna know where I was the other night." She grins like she's sending an LOL.

"Yes. I was getting to that. Where were you last Saturday night about eleven-thirty?" I know a cop would be more exact, but I'm thinking it'll have to do.

"That's when Usaré was killed, isn't it?"

"Yes."

"And you're asking me where I was then."

"If that's okay. We're asking everyone with a key to the hallway." Making an excuse, but realizing as I say it, that it's more than I should say. "You had Usaré in class as a freshman, didn't you?"

"Yeah, I did. They should all be like Usaré. That girl could write, and she didn't waste her time yammering about abortion."

"You had her as a freshman. You talk to her recently, like the last month or so?"

"Why would I?" She sips her coffee.

I shrug. "She goes past your classroom every day for senior English. You're out there in the hallway during passing period saying hi to kids just like Klein taught you to do. Along comes a young woman who seeks the advice of a more experienced young woman . . ." I taste the tea, which is sweet but weak and ordinary.

Sullivan hesitates for a moment but then tells me. "We'd gotten to be friends. It's shitty what happened."

"Totally shitty. You and she were friends?"

"Sometimes she'd stop by right after school, and we'd talk some. On her way to Klein's for tutoring. Not smart of me, I know, and I was pulling back from her. She told me she liked me for my independence. I admired her for her toughness."

"Are you saying you two had a lot in common?"

"Yes and no. I don't think she was able to enjoy her own life 'cause she was so obsessed with getting to the top. I'm just looking for fun right now, but she was always looking for an advantage, an edge."

"With men?"

"With everyone she knew, I think. You already know what her edge was with me."

"That she knew you were . . . having fun?"

Nikki nods, not smiling this time.

"Toughness. That her word or yours?"

"You must know what I mean. She was like a pit bull with lipstick."

"Pit bull?" I'm thinking of Ursa, our Rottweiler, one hundred pounds of stubbornness but whose mean streak only seems to appear once a week when the garbage trucks come to steal from us.

Nikki hesitates again, then says, "Usaré had an audacious side."

"She was bold for sure."

"Reckless."

I wait.

"Remember the MAS teacher? Not the guy we have now, the one before?"

"Mexican-American Studies? Mr. Canseco? Left to do graduate studies. Like a year ago."

"Usaré was in that class, you know. Fact is, she felt like the class wouldn't even be there without her. Like she was the one who forced the school district to create it. Taking all the credit." She pauses. "Didn't you think it was odd the way Canseco left all of a sudden?"

He *did* leave suddenly, but until now, I had bought what I thought was the insider story. Canseco was the rising star—young, handsome and aspiring to go into school administration, he had carried the water for the Mexican-American Studies movement, had presented its case to the governing board, had written its curriculum. JV Muñoz, the superintendent made deals to get Canseco into a national doctoral program because it made the district look good, made *him* look good.

Sullivan goes on, smiling faintly. "She had an advantage with everyone."

"I'm naïve. You're gonna need to be a little more direct. About her advantage over Canseco."

She touches my thigh under the table then, like it's a thing that's done.

"She'd told him it was time to come clean. It's a phrase she liked, 'come clean,' because of the lawyeresque thing she had going on in her head all the time."

I'm wondering what her hand on my thigh is meant to communicate. Sincerity? Availability? My body reacts in a pleasurable way. My sponsor would be telling me to move away from her, but I don't.

"How is any of that relevant? Canseco's been gone for months. He didn't kill her."

"His wife's still here."

"She's not with him back east?"

"Do you even know he's back east?"

"So where *were* you last Saturday night about eleven-thirty?"

"I wasn't over here in the E hallway killing a teenage girl, I'm pretty sure." Not taking me seriously.

"Okay, that eliminates one place," I say. Her hand remains on my thigh, but I tell myself it's okay because I'm leaving soon.

She smiles, but in irritation. "Had a date. Black guy name of Johnson." Her smile breaks wide then. "Subbed here in PE last week. Pretty easy to track down, you wanna take the time."

The cops will, I'm thinking, if they're not already sold on Andre. "Thanks for your help," I say. "But please, think about what I told you. About the web profile I mean." I slurp a little more tea before I leave. When I clear the door, I get on the radio and ask Santana to check on a recent substitute teacher named Johnson.

EIGHT

On my way back to the office, I pass the choir room door, which is propped open, and I see Jameson sitting in a tall chair at the director's music stand, which is substantial and wooden, like a lectern. He's been meeting two of his daily classes here this week, but there are no students with him right now, so I decide to talk to him.

It's a rehearsal room, and there are no desks, just a piano and a carpeted riser and the lectern. Jameson is leaning back in the chair, reading a paperback, but he doesn't look relaxed.

"I thought you had a class this period."

He sets down the book, *Troilus and Cressida,* on the lectern and looks at me with his droopy eyes, coming erect and smoothing the front of his vest. "I decided they might as well go get a Coke down at the Circle K, since this room sucks for teaching lit."

"Ouch!"

The reference to the Circle K is one of the bits of sarcasm Jameson uses with his kids.

He does try hard to keep students on-task in his classroom—engaged visibly if not always mentally. He plans activities with observable, on-task behaviors in mind, like guided note-taking, and it frustrates him when he sees his kids not participating, so he usually tries to pull them back in by using proximity—standing close to the non-compliant kid. If that doesn't work, he uses implied directives like "I need you to answer the questions on page two of the study guide." But he gets irritated when he can't get a kid back to work, so he sometimes says, "This is school. You're supposed to learn something. If you don't want to do that, you should just be sucking down sodas at the Circle K."

You have to admit he's got a point.

But his wicked tongue will sometimes backfire. Once, the security guards brought in some girls who'd been ditching his class at the Circle K, and they told me that they were just taking Mr. Jameson's advice.

Jameson says, "Rocha took my kids down to the little theater. They're watching *Troilus and Cressida* with Navarette's kids. I get to write the exam."

"*Troilus and Cressida?*" Betraying some confusion, since I've never heard of it being taught at Polk before, as well as some ignorance of the play.

He leans forward to look at some papers on the lectern. "Yeah, I got a copy of the video when PBS did all the Shakespeare plays. It's sexy as hell but the kids don't get it.

"So, what question do you like better: A. Identify a character whose name has come to mean 'unfaithful woman' or B. Who is slaughtered unarmed by Achilles?"

"I don't know the play, but I know Achilles killed Hector, so that one's easier."

"Okay, so we'll go with unfaithful woman then," he says.

"What's the answer?"

"Just about any female you can name, right? But in the play it's Cressida."

I wonder if there's trouble at home for Jameson, but I say nothing in response. "Hey, what do you remember about a kid used to come here name o' Guillermo Martinez?"

He answers almost instantly. "Course I remember him, the SOB. The archetypal gangstah-thug."

"Not that fond of him," I say.

"You ever have a kid you were afraid to turn your back on? That was Memo. I always kept two or three rows of desks between me and that asshole."

It reminds me that the world looks different based on a man's height. Memo is about six-feet-five. I am six-four, so stature alone gives him only the barest advantage over me. Besides, Memo knows I'm from the neighborhood—I have survived the pecking-order battles. When he was a student at Polk, he never would have tried to intimidate me with his physical bearing. But Jameson is not quite six feet. He is tall, relatively speaking, but he has to look up at me when we are standing close, and Memo towers over him by a good five inches. He's also an outsider to the neighborhood and doesn't know a damn thing about growing up Mexican.

"I see."

"Seriously, were you ever afraid of a kid when you were still an educator?"

This question in itself irritates me, but I say nothing.

He, says, "I don't mean 'ready for class to end.' I mean scared that a kid would crack open your head with a machete if you turned away."

I think about my morning, rolling around on the floor with Neto, about extracting the pocket gun. "Not exactly like that, no."

"Well, Memo was an intimidator. I'd scan the hall for him when I greeted kids at the door. Celebrate inside my head on those rare and wonderful occasions when he didn't show up for class but then hold my breath for the next ten minutes, hoping he didn't show up tardy. I even brought in an inch-thick birch dowel to use for protection. Used it as a pointer when I was lecturing at the whiteboard so kids would think that was why I brought it in. Carried it around like a cane the whole period when Memo was there too."

It triggers another memory. Our art teacher Mrs. Syndegard, who never had trouble with classroom management, used the emergency call button one day. The speaker crackled in my office: "Teacher in need of assistance." I recognized her voice, controlled but tense. "Student is belligerent and non-compliant. I need him removed." I jogged to the art room myself, figuring it would be just as fast as calling a security guard.

The non-compliant kid was Memo. He was acting stone-cold casual, talking to some girl and ignoring everything else, like they were the only people in the room, like they were at the mall. Mrs. Syndegard was pale as whitewashed chalk. It had only taken me about half a minute to get there, but I could tell she must have been struggling to hold on to her composure the whole time.

I said, "Okay Guillermo, let's go." Thinking back, I realize his actions after I arrived that day were a bit surprising. He simply turned and exited the room for me, no questions asked. He wouldn't have obeyed me today, back in my office, but that day in the art room, he complied immediately. A kid of sixteen or seventeen will sometimes do that—be defiant with a teacher but then obey an administrator—but it's not a predictable thing. It may be my size, I guess, but I've known Sally to get the same result. She's a tough woman. Barely five feet, but you don't want to cross her. I know I wouldn't.

I recommended a long-term suspension for Memo, charging him with intimidation of a teacher, but the hearing officer would only put him out for ten days, said the school board wouldn't support long-term. All I could do was impose the ten days and then make sure Syndegard didn't have to put up with Memo in class anymore, switched him to a different elective.

To Jameson I say, "He's gotten a little more sophisticated since his school days."

"Why we talking about Memo Martinez? You should be looking under rocks for him," he says, picking up his book again, opening it to read, indicating he's ready to dismiss me.

"Burgoyne's got me gathering background on him. I guess the cops are interested in him regarding Usaré."

His eyes pop back to me now, wider, suddenly not droopy. He puts his book down again and leans toward me.

"They think he might be the guy?" he says. He's excited, rooting for the cops. For the first time since they busted a couple bullies for stealing his bubble gum in fifth grade, I'm thinking.

"I wouldn't say he's their suspect yet, but they're looking into some connections."

"Yeah, I can see it." He's nodding. His eyes narrow, like he's thinking back. "And Memo's in that gang, right?"

"Which gang?"

His eyes flick away for a second as if someone else has come into the room, and I look over my shoulder. Nobody there.

"You know, the one that's always tagging us," he says. "Memo was with them, right? When he was a student . . ."

"I can't remember. Mighta been."

He doesn't respond.

"You notice something in the last couple weeks that would connect them?"

"I know she got texts from a guy named Memo 'cause I could see her screen when I'd circulate. Figured it might be him. Kinda pissed me off." He lifts his hands and rubs his temples, like he's trying to massage away a headache.

"Pissed you off? Bitter are we?"

His eyes narrow.

"You know what I mean," he says. "She's got everything in the world going for her and she hooks up with that . . . virus."

"She just had the phone out on her desk?"

"They all do . . . Hell, I quit trying to stop their texting in January." He's a little embarrassed about this. "It was driving me insane. Every other statement out of my mouth was 'Please put the phone away,' and I was losing the battle anyway. Told them the new rule was silence—no phone calls and low vibrate for texts. Seemed to get compliance with it and it saves my sanity."

"Mmm." Some of my teachers are effective at controlling the kids' cell phone use. Klein is one, Sullivan too, and I've always thought Jameson was pretty good at it as well. I wonder if his lost battle was because they wore him down like he says or if he thinks it's part of being the laid-back teacher who dresses hip and acts cool.

"You see anything in these Memo texts?" I say.

"Words, words, words."

I assume it's a line from Shakespeare. I wrinkle my lips and wait.

"Not much. Saw one with a couple hearts on it, something about getting together again."

"Again? You sure it said 'again'?"

He closes his eyes, like he's trying to see it inside his head. "Yeah, pretty sure."

"And it was from Memo to her, not the other way around?"

"Yeah, somebody name o' Memo. Name was right there at the top of the screen. Course, the cops can see the whole conversation, right?"

He curls his lips as if he's mocking me . . . or maybe someone he's thinking about.

I remember the way Rusic reacted when I suggested the cops would find messages back and forth between him and Usaré.

I wonder how many of Usaré's text conversations the police have pored over, thinking those probably contain some of the best leads, whether they've begun the process to surface her deleted texts, how many of them Burgoyne has seen. It's a relief to know Usaré and I never texted.

"Could you tell how long the text string was?"

"She didn't scroll through it for me, Henry." Like it's a stupid question. Then he adds, "But there were about four or five little text boxes on the screen when I saw it."

"You see Memo on campus lately?"

He shakes his head, and I decide it's time to go fishing.

"Well, you said you could *see* it, right? That Memo could be the guy. And I agree he's got criminal mentality. So let's do some supposing. Suppose he planned to meet her, and he had some way of getting into the E Building. But why'd he want to kill her in the first place? And why would he do it there? It's not like she was about to give him an F in English."

"Or kick him outta school." He pauses, then says, "I'm not Freud, but since we're supposing, why are we supposing he even needed a reason to kill her? Memo's pathological . . . like Iago . . . a motiveless malignity as Coleridge would say. And if he did have a reason, why we supposing he had it *before* they hooked up?"

"I see—the motive coulda developed at their meeting," I say.

His eyes have gone back to droopy, but I can tell he's interested in exploring the theory with me. He says, "He's not there to kill her, but because they have an arrangement to meet somewhere. Then they go into the building 'cause one of them has the key . . . Usaré probably. She was driven to succeed, we all know, but she could be coquettish too, when it served her purpose."

I don't like the way he's portrayed her, but I merely say, "I don't understand. I get it the other way around, but how would he serve *her* purpose?"

"Usaré always had a purpose. If she was seeing Memo, she saw an advantage in it. You can bet on that. But you can't condemn someone unless you give her a chance to explain, right? Or change her mind. Maybe Memo was giving her one last chance to redeem herself for something she did."

"Or wouldn't do." I think of the memorial for Usaré on the Garcías' porch. "So now Memo was somehow the victim? Sounds strange coming from you."

"That's not what I mean. It's terrible what happened to her. But she thought of herself as the new face of her people. Mexican-American Studies. Latinas. Latinos too. Their savior, for Christ sake. And she didn't think too favorably of machismo. Let everyone know it too. And Memo is about as macho as they come, impulsive besides. Psycho. C'mon, Tavish."

'Terrible what happened to her'—it's lip service to Usaré and irritates me. "One thing Memo does *not* strike me as is impulsive."

"You could say the same thing about Othello until Iago turned him."

"From what I remember about Desdemona, she was submissive, accepted her death sentence. That wasn't Usaré."

"No, she fought like hell, I bet," he says. "Her independence woulda just made it easier for Memo to commit the crime. Gave him a motive too. Assertive people make him feel threatened. He didn't like the way she was changing the rules."

"So your theory is Memo's involved with her, doesn't like her independent streak, and lets her have one last chance to behave like a good Mexicana, then offs her when she stays defiant. That doesn't explain why they'd meet at the school. Or how they'd get into your building."

He curls his lip again. "If they're intimate, he knows she's at the dance and then one of his little wannabes gives her a message to come outside. And you know there's probably a lot of ways they coulda got into the building, even without a key."

"Hell, you got a better theory of the crime than Burgoyne."

Jameson stares for a moment, then says, "Yeah. I told you I wasn't Freud. Or Sherlock Holmes either. But like you said, we were just supposing." He picks up his paperback again and starts scanning for a new test question. "But if you playing detective helps us get back into our rooms, I'm all for it." He smiles, annoying me further, so I decide to get his reaction to Usare's cell phone data.

"By the way, the cops found some teachers' phone numbers in Usaré's phone contacts. Phone calls and text strings both."

He doesn't bother to look up. Coolly, he says, "We both know some of our teachers have shit for brains. She was probably their Facebook friend too." Not concerned.

*****

The homicide detectives are Simpson and Bejarano, black and brown, male and female, and they want to interview the teachers who were at the dance before they all go home for the day. Burgoyne recounts what we've discovered about Memo's website and looks at me for confirmation. I nod. He doesn't mention Nikki Sullivan's adult dating page.

I give the detectives one of the rooms we use for holding kids prior-interview, and they set up their laptop and recording equipment. It's a sparse room, with an oblong table and six chairs, nothing else except a defaced Ronald Reagan poster on the wall. On the radio I tell Santana to get the teacher schedules and give them a heads-up that we're going to need to see them this afternoon, figuring Santana will know how to explain who 'we' is; I also explain planning periods to Simpson and Bejarano and how teachers will have to be paid for the preparation time they are losing, which they don't understand or care about. They ask if they can't just call teachers in and have me cover their classes during the interviews and I say no, silently adding 'and you go to hell.' Burgoyne smiles as I'm answering, and it lifts my tension some because I know he can read my mind and finds it amusing. I wonder if Burgoyne will be just as arrogant as these two when he makes detective.

I say, "Why not start with the folks that have afternoon planning periods. Maybe I can get some coverage for the others from substitutes in the building." I think for a moment about who was chaperoning the dance. "That would be Nuñez first, right after lunch. Maybe me and Amin, the security guy, since we don't have planning periods. Rocha during fifth period, then Rusic and Mayer during sixth." I wonder whether Burgoyne will tell the detectives about Rusic's history with the victim.

They are deadpanning me, so I ask how long they think each interview will last. Simpson answers. "Shouldn't be long. Twenty minutes tops." I call Santana down to the interview room.

"Santana, can you see if you can sweet talk one or two subs into doing some extra coverage? They get an extra twenty bucks or something, right?" She nods and I say, "Can you work it out so the nice detectives here can chat with Trujillo, McNally and Morales this afternoon? Oh, and tell Mr. Nuñez I need him to drop by for a bit right after lunch." She nods again, then sizes up the two detectives before going back to her desk.

Simpson and Bejarano grumble a little at each other in low voices and look up at the clock. Simpson says, "Can we get started with someone right away, Mr. Tavish? Maybe you or this Amin guy. Since your Nuñez can't come for another forty-five minutes."

"Wanna start with me then? I need Amin in the cafeteria till second lunch is over. He's better at preventing food fights than I am. You can see him after Nuñez."

They motion me to one of the chairs. Burgoyne puts his hand on the doorknob, preparing to exit, but Simpson says, "We figured you'd stay for these. Give us your on-site perspective." Figuring the SRO can tell if and when I'm lying, I suppose. Burgoyne looks at me, then closes the door and sits in a chair at the end of the table. Simpson, the talker, takes his jacket off and sits across the table. Bejarano, who's in a tight-fitting mauve turtleneck, is next to me and closer than I'd like.

Simpson is an even six feet, lean, with shoulders that you can see rippling with muscle inside his shirt. He is bald, and I'm guessing he waxes his head instead of shaving. His hazel eyes bore right in on me, looking green in the room's bare fluorescence. I glance at the poster mounted on the wall behind him. It's one with Ronnie's face, on which some kid has written 'A-Hole', and the rippling flag and a quote: "There are no easy answers, but there are simple answers," by which I guess he meant *he* had the answers. My predecessor hung it there, a big Reagan fan, thinking it might push kids toward the truth. I've left it there as a reminder that kids can usually see through an adult's phony bullshit, like answers that are simple but not easy.

Simpson turns on his recorder while Bejarano opens a document on her laptop and begins staring at me. Simpson speaks at the recorder with the date and time and our names, then says, "Thanks for meeting with us, Mr. Tavish. Few things we'd like to ask you about."

I nod. I know they want me to say something, but for some reason, I don't feel like it.

Predictably, Simpson says, "Can you make a verbal response?"

"You mean an audible response? Yeah I can do that."

Simpson is not amused. "Yeah, an audible response."

"You got it." I glance at Burgoyne, who's wrinkling the corner of his mouth.

"You were the one in charge at the dance Saturday night?" Simpson says.

"You could say that. I'm the one who assigns the chaperones . . . the one who approves all the paperwork for our dances."

"What's your job once the dancing starts?"

"Mainly I'm just another chaperone, keeping an eye on the kids. Keep the vodka out, and the drugs. Look for kids whose behavior is a little off kilter and such. Remind the teachers to stay on their toes."

"So you're really monitoring the chaperones too."

I hesitate. "Never thought of it that way."

"But you'd see any irregularities, yeah? Like if some teacher wasn't where he was supposed to be."

Tough question. If I'm honest and say no, it's the same as saying I'm not able to do my job. If I say yes, I have to pinpoint a problem, which I can't do. "Depends what you mean. I'd see most of them when I looked around for them."

"We mean breaches in the perimeter. Non-students at the dance. Strange students at the dance. People that shouldn't have been there. Anything unusual."

"I double check with the chaperones from time to time, but I'm not anal about it. They know it's a serious job. Non-students aren't allowed in without a guest pass. And nobody at all can come in through the side doors."

"How do they get a guest pass?" Simpson asks.

"A Polk kid has to vouch for them and give us a photocopy of their ID. And they gotta be age-appropriate; no junior high kids or twenty-five-year-olds." I smile a little, remembering when one of our seventeen-year-olds brought her thirty-year-old husband to prom. "We only issued two this time, somebody's cousins visiting from Silver City."

"How 'bout leaving? The kids allowed to leave through the side doors?"

"We discourage it, but it's not a rule. The main thing is they can't leave and return, no matter which way they go out."

"Well, somebody must've seen Miss Garcia leave then, right? Would they remember that?"

"Most likely, unless she stayed till the very end when the remaining kids leave en masse. But that's probably not Usaré. She'd leave a little early, just to be cool."

"Did you happen to see her leave?"

"No, I didn't." He stares, so I add, "One of the door people might have."

"Who was that?" he says.

"Rusic and Morales on the side doors. Mayer and Rocha at the front. And Amin would've relieved them for their scheduled breaks."

"So does everybody get a break?"

"They all have a break scheduled except the DJ . . . Mr. Nuñez. And Trujillo at the punch bowl. Most of them get out for a little air at some point, ten minutes or so. Santana can give you the schedule from our folder."

Simpson's eyes move deliberately to Bejarano, who rises briskly from her chair and leaves the room. Simpson goes on. "Anybody gone for more than ten minutes?"

I shake my head, then say, "Not significantly."

"So what's significantly longer . . . in your mind?"

"Ten minutes more. So maybe up to twenty minutes total. In my mind."

"And this Amin, he'd probably remember when such and such a chaperone went on a break?"

"I'd say so. Probably have a good idea how long they were out too, but you'll have to ask him."

"We'll try and remember to do that."

An audible response pops into my head, but I don't say anything.

"How 'bout you? Did you get out for some air?" he says.

I think about lying, or rather, I have thought about it since the moment it occurred to me that I would be asked this question. I'm pretty sure no one knows I slipped out. It's pitch dark on the upper level of that gym when Steve Mayer's senior class puts on a dance, because his kids want it that way. They cover all the windows with black paper, so there's no ambient light, and Steve has figured out a way to disable the emergency overhead lights without any alarms going off. The only light comes from the light strands strung around as decorations for the kids' Springtime-in-Paris theme, and the floor lamps that Nuñez sets up so he can see what he's doing at the DJ table, and of course the chaperones' flashlights. From my perch twenty feet above the dance floor, I can see a fair amount of what's going on, but no one can see where I am unless I snap on my flashlight. Of course, there's a chance Babs McNally saw the upper level exit door open from her vantage point on the opposite side, once when I left and once when I returned, and Amin might have noticed his golf cart missing for about twenty minutes, since I was too lazy to walk across campus that night, but I doubt it. The main reason I have decided to tell the truth, though, is that I'm not very good at lying; I can embellish or underestimate or skew things well enough, but if I try to float a complete lie, everyone in the room will know it, especially Burgoyne.

"Sure did." I sense Burgoyne tilting his head to look at me, since I never mentioned this to him. "Went over to my office and checked my email."

"What time was that? And for how long?"

"The dance had been going for about two hours, so I'd say ten-thirty, give or take. Like everybody else, you know, ten or fifteen minutes."

"Anybody see you come and go?"

"No idea. Maybe someone across the other side."

"And who'd you assign to the other side?"

"Babs McNally straight across on the upper level, Rusic down below. Maybe Amin, the rover."

"But no one relieves you. How come?"

"The kids would notice if one of my people abandoned a door on the ground floor or the punch bowl. Not much chance they'd notice me MIA for a few minutes."

He nods, considering me, and his partner returns and hands him the chaperone schedule.

"How about those emails? You answer any of them?"

I hesitate. This question shouldn't surprise me, but it does. I never thought once about the time stamps on emails, and now I wish I'd lied about taking the break. "I'll have to check."

"Do that and let us know, please." He takes a deep breath and says, "Okay. On to something else then. How well did you know the girl? This Use-uh-ree?"

"Usaré," I correct him. "I knew her fairly well. She was very outgoing. Made it a point to get to know her teachers."

"Likeable girl?"

"Very."

"*You* liked her then?" Like I don't see where he's going.

"Sure. Everybody did."

"Not everybody was in her contact list though."

I thought I was prepared for this, but I feel my face flush. I look up at Ronnie, who reminds me to keep it simple, even if it's not easy. "I'm sure you're right."

"What kind of relationship did you have with Usaré?" He still butchers the name, but it's closer.

"She was our student, very good student."

"Nothing beyond that? You ever see her outside of school hours?"

"Wrestling meets when I was covering. Club events. School stuff."

"Nothing else? A social event? You ever give her a ride home or something?"

"Nope." My mind wanders for a few seconds. I've driven kids in my own car before, especially when I was coaching, or when a parent refused to come pick up a kid I'd suspended. Coaches and club sponsors haul kids around frequently. I wonder if Rusic will stumble on this question when they talk to him later.

"So how is it she's got your name in her contacts?"

"You're gonna find very few actual calls or anything."

"I see. But the question is how she got your name and number."

I tell them about that first call to her cell phone, over three years gone since then. Part of me wants to add something like, 'It was a mistake, I know,' but I don't.

"You got a key that lets you into that hallway though, yeah?"

I nod. "Master key, yes."

"And all the rooms in that hallway?"

"Wouldn't be a master key if it didn't."

"How many people got access to that building, all the rooms?"

"Twenty staff, maybe."

"Anybody besides staff?" he asks.

I think about all the lost keys, the keys that teachers entrust to kids, but I don't want to explain all this, especially since I went over all of that with Burgoyne, so I say, "Not likely."

He stares at me for a long moment like he's giving me a chance to revise my answer, but I don't. "Waddya know about a guy named Andre? Used to come to this school. Lives nearby."

"Andre Carver? I know him. Has he been arrested?" Simpson stares, and after a moment, I start telling them details about Andre's time at the school that I know they probably don't care about, trying to decide what else I will say: his regular attendance, general cooperativeness with staff, grades all over the place from A's to D's. I go on to more recent history: his frequent appearances at the school in his Mustang or in Lashawn's Cadillac to pick up his brother, who's a sophomore, his caretaker situation with Lashawn. "Most days, I monitor the student pick-up area after the last bell."

Burgoyne is leaning forward suddenly. I'm sure he's already passed on a lot of what I told him about Andre, since he's turned over the water bottle for DNA analysis, but I figure they can ask more questions if they want more specific answers.

"He had a lot of respect among the kids too, he and his friends. Nobody stepped on his toes."

"You ever see him talking to Usaré? Maybe when he's waiting on his brother?"

"Not lately. I used to, but the last time would've been a couple-three months ago."

"Can you be more specific?"

"Not really. February. Maybe January."

"And before that? Would you say it was frequent?"

"No, I wouldn't. More like occasional."

"And these occasional meetings—any of them seem less than cordial?" I shake my head. "No."

Simpson considers me, then looks at Bejarano, who hasn't touched her laptop since she turned it on. "Partner, you got anything you need to ask Mr. Tavish?" Bejarano shakes her head. Inaudibly, I want to point out. Simpson says, "You, Sergeant Burgoyne?"

He looks surprised to be asked. "No, I don't."

Simpson fishes a business card from his shirt pocket and slides it toward me. "All right, Mr. Tavish. Thanks for your time. If you think of anything else that might be helpful, you can call me or just pass it on to your school resource officer."

NINE

In my office, I look at the digital clock. It was a twelve minute interview. I use the radio: "Enrique to Amin."

In a few seconds, he comes back: "Amin here."

I don't want to convey too much urgency. "Can you come to my office right after lunch, Amin? Was wondering about something you told me for the Valdez file." We'd found over a pound of marijuana in Eric Valdez's backpack, which he and his parents claimed must have been planted. In reality, we suspected his parents gave him the grass to peddle."

It's almost simultaneous: Frank says, "That was my bust," and Amin says, "I think that was Frank's bust."

Damned radios, I think. "Yeah, I know it was Frank's bust, but I need to see Amin." They pause, but then both of them roger me.

When he enters my office, Amin follows his ritual. He removes his yellow ball cap, which says 'He is Love' in red embroidery, and waits for me to tell him to have a chair. When he does sit, he always cites a bit of scripture, which used to annoy me but doesn't anymore because I've learned it is some text he has been mulling for a sermon and you can tell he is sincere. He ministers to a small group in his home every Sunday, twenty or so souls. Today he says, "Open for me the gates of righteousness, and I will enter them."

To which, of course, there is no good response, so I ask where it's from.

"It was Martin Luther's favorite Psalm, the hundred-eighteenth." Amin, whose first name is actually Heyward, is a self-educated minister and he loves sharing trivia that he encounters in his research. He's in his eleventh year as a Polk security guard, and unlike most of his peers, he has no plans of advancing to a better-paid line of work. Security at Polk High School is his career, a calling second only to his preaching. He is especially vigilant about, some would say tough on, our African-American boys because he believes anytime they misbehave, it is a reflection on him and on the black race at large. In return, many of them call him Tom. The first time he brought a black youth to my office for discipline, it was for shooting craps, which I didn't take very seriously. But with the sternest face, Amin said, "Mr. Tavish, don't forget they crucified him and parted his garments, casting lots. Proverbs says 'Wealth gotten by vanity shall be diminished.'" Then he referred me to our administrative discipline guide, which specified up to a five-day suspension for gambling. I confiscated the boy's dice and offered him OSIS—on-site isolation school, but he declined and went on vacation for three days.

"The cops are going to talk to you this afternoon about the dance last Saturday. What you remember and so on. Talking to all the adults first, looks like. They just interviewed me."

"About Usaré? Thass okay. I didn't really see anything important."

"Yeah, me neither. They're just trying to pin down when she left the dance. Maybe who she left with."

His voice is gentle and low. "Thass easy. Was just before eleven. Usaré and Keanu went out the south door."

"South. Was the chaperone there at the door?"

But now he's not listening. His brow has wrinkled, and I know his mind is somewhere else. "Mr. Tavish you don't think Keanu . . ."

"No I don't, Amin."

"I saw 'em dancing sinful, those two. When that girl dances, it's like the dance of Salome, somethin' bad sure to come shoatly. You shined your flashlight on them once and busted up the crowd aroun' em, and they separated, but they got to it again a few minutes later, and I guess you couldn't see them that time."

There's a sort of terror coming into his eyes. "I let that girl down, didn't I, Mr. Tavish. I should have followed her but I couldn't on account of having to stay at the door."

"No Amin. It's not on you. And Keanu sure as hell didn't kill anyone." I always hesitate a millisecond when I say something like 'sure as hell' to him, but I don't want him to start carrying Usaré's cross. "So, which door were you stuck at?"

"The north door. Mr. Rusic's door," he says.

"You sure?"

Amin says he's positive. Which, when somebody says, always reminds me of Ambrose Bierce's definition of positive—"mistaken at the top of your lungs." But this is Amin, who is always truthful and exact, perhaps the only person alive I'd trust with my soul if I hadn't already entrusted whatever's left of it to Maria.

Rusic had waved him over to the north exit at ten-forty, then at ten-forty-one and again at ten-forty-two. Amin had the relief schedule memorized because he had to relieve everyone, and he knew it would be too dark to read inside the gym. Rusic was early. At first, he pretended he didn't see Rusic's gesture because he'd just relieved Morales on the south door, and he thought he'd circulate for ten or fifteen more minutes before relieving him, but Rusic kept motioning him over. There's a class division between teachers and classified employees in most schools. Many teachers consider themselves professionals rather than workers, and teacher prestige has certainly increased in most places since the nineteenth century. This attitude can foster snobbishness in a teacher about clerks and custodians and groundsmen, but it can also create a sense of authority in a guy like Rusic. In Rusic's world, a teacher can give orders to a security guard. I've told Amin a dozen times that this is not so, but some part of him feels compelled to fulfill a teacher's requests as if they were commands. At ten-forty-three, he reported to Rusic and relieved him, assuming he'd be monitoring the north door for the rest of the dance.

Amin is frowning again, and I'm guessing he's back to feeling guilty.

"Tell you what," I say, "why don't you go get Keanu out of class. I'll check the video from that night. Try to see when Keanu left campus. Who he left with." To which he nods and leaves. Our security cameras don't cover the interior of the campus, but the system is fairly easy to use and it doesn't take me very long to spot Keanu as he goes out to the parking lot at eleven-twenty-seven.

When they return, Amin closes the door and sits in the chair usually occupied by Burgoyne.

Keanu is lanky but not tall, maybe five-seven. His skin is a glossy black, and the overhead light bounces off it, glowing like part of his perpetual smile. His hair gets regular attention from a barber's razor, with perfect right angles at his temples and sideburns that come to a point. He's wearing a white shirt, its long sleeves rolled above the elbows, red jeans and two-tone saddle shoes without socks. He's probably the handsomest boy in the school, and he knows it. He takes the interviewee seat in front of my desk and says, "Good afternoon, Mr. Tavish," and continues to smile.

"Thanks, Keanu. Mind if I ask you a couple questions about last Saturday night?"

The glowing smile fades, but traces of it remain in his eyes and at the corners of his mouth. "No sir."

"From what the chaperones tell me, you left the dance kind of early. Went out the south door. Is that right?"

"Yes sir. A little early. It was boring cuz Mr. Nuñez wouldn't play the beats we wanted."

"Yeah, he won't play stuff with X-rated lyrics. You notice the time?"

"Not really, sir. After eleven some time?"

"It's pretty important, Keanu. Could it have been before eleven?"

He shrugs. "It mighta been. I didn't check my phone."

"Who was the chaperone at that door when you left?"

"It was Mr. Morales, my government teacher. He reminded me we couldn't return."

"Mr. Cook, can you enlighten us about the time?" Keanu swivels to listen over his shoulder.

Amin says, "You left before eleven. I was checking my watch pretty regular all night."

I say, "Because you have to relieve different chaperones, right?" Amin nods.

"You leave with anyone, Keanu?"

He faces me again. "Not really, sir."

Amin stiffens and his voice takes on a certain rage. He says, "Keanu, guard the truth that has been entrusted to you by the Spirit who dwells within."

There is no smile on Keanu's face now, not a trace of a smile. I say, "You know Keanu, lots of young men lie to me when they're sitting in that chair. It doesn't upset me the way it does Mr. Cook here. I figure lots of kids got a good reason to lie when they're sitting where you are."

He hangs his head when he answers and the result is a mumble.

"I didn't hear you. Would you mind repeating that?"

He looks up. "Usaré left the same time."

"Thank you, Keanu. You want us to find out who killed her, don't you?"

"Yes sir, I do."

"Well, you have to tell us what happened then. Amin has you leaving the gym with Usaré at ten minutes before eleven. Mr. Morales will probably agree. The security cam shows you going out to the parking lot about eleven-thirty. That's forty minutes, son. You need to tell us what you know."

What he knows is Usaré wanted someone to walk across campus with her, where she was supposed to meet someone at the Park Avenue gate two hundred yards northeast of the gymnasium, some older guy, like Andre, Keanu supposed. But no, he wasn't sure if it was actually Andre. There are a lot of dark spots, scary places, she'd explained. Which is true. The campus is being renovated, and a couple buildings are completely without power. And she wanted to leave when nobody was looking because there were a few guys who would probably be jealous, so it had to be pretty early. She'd arrived with Chevy and Marcus, but she'd already told them she wasn't leaving with them, and "if you ask them, they'll probably tell you the same thing about her having a date with an older guy." By ten-thirty she'd danced with everyone she wanted to dance with, and the music sucked anyway, with Nuñez playing oldies half the time, stuff from when he was in high school like "Electric Slide," which he'd already played like three-thousand times, and she came and got him and said it was time to go. Keanu knew the rule about not reentering the gym, but he figured Mr. Meyer would let him back in since he was senior class treasurer. No luck with that as it turned out.

"Okay . . ." I say, "So you walked her to the Park Avenue exit?"

He says he did, except they stopped just short, in the shadows but in sight of Park Avenue then, and she said it was okay and he could go back to the dance, and he started back to the gym, except he was curious, so he came back, lurked in the shadows of the D building. He started watching to see who picked her up, still figuring it was Andre, and even if it wasn't maybe he'd see what kinda car the guy drove, since he himself has a pretty hot, souped-up Honda with a bad stereo and bass, thanks to his dad being a car salesman and all.

"So did you see the guy . . . the car?"

The girl, Usaré, was watching to see when he went out of sight, he says, and when she was sure he was gone, she came back, all the way to the west end of the E building, and she looked around again, making sure no one would see, and then she opened the door, like with a key, you know?

"I do know."

He says it made him wonder, since she stone lied about getting picked up on Park. He went back, waited a few minutes in case she was watching through the small window slot in the door, then ran from the shadow where he was hiding into the shadow of E building. At first, it was in his head to peek through the window in the entry door, but then he thought she might see some kinda shadow when he stuck his face up close to the glass. So instead, he went to the south side of the building, to see if any of the window lights were on.

"Smart move," I say. "What'd you see?"

"Well, Mr. Tavish, you know them rooms, right? The windows are all high up, like up by the roof, am I right? So I know I couldn't see nothing that was going on inside."

But what surprised him a little is that all the lights were on, lights on in every room, except one in the middle maybe, if he remembered right. Almost every room. He wondered about that, about why the lights would be on, and he started thinking that a custodian could be in there, since they gotta clean the rooms some time, though some of his classrooms seem dingy compared to others lately.

"Yeah, we've cut the custodial staff in half 'cause of budget cuts," I say. "So what'd you do?"

He says he was just gonna get up and go back to the dance and see if Meyer would let him back in, but then there were some little changes in the light that caught his eye. Like some movement in one of the rooms. So he decided to watch from a spot in the shadow of F building, which is closed down for construction and totally dark and surrounded by that temporary fencing, you know?

I nod.

"So I was figuring she was in one of them rooms, right? And the changes in the light had to be her moving around in the room. And maybe somebody else in there too. Since she went in there for some reason, am I right? She ain't no thief, Usaré, so why's she in there, right? Like why she going into the E building. She must be meeting someone in there, right?"

"I don't disagree."

So he watched the shifts in the light, shadows, quivers. Sometimes they were rapid, and sometimes they were slow, and sometimes there would be no quivers at all.

"How long did you watch?"

He's ashamed of this. It was twenty minutes or so, him wondering what was going on, wondering when Usaré would emerge from the hallway again, wondering who else was in there.

"Which room did you see the quivers?" I say.

"That was weird. It was two different rooms where I seen the lights shaking, like there was two different things going on, or whatever was happening was happening two different places. But first in one room and then another. Different times, right?"

"Could you tell which rooms?"

He says it was first in some middle room, E-4 or E-6 or E-8 or maybe E10, which would make it Helen Dunham's room, or Jameson's or Sullivan's or Wilson's. But then there was flickering in the first room, in E-2, which is the English office, which is every English teacher's room and where, Burgoyne says, someone killed Usaré.

"Then what happened?"

Before he can answer, Santana's earthy voice breaks through on the intercom. "Mr. Tavish, Francesca's school is on the phone."

For a moment, I wonder if I should step out to her desk and take the call so Keanu can't hear, but I decide against it. What's the danger, after all? "Can you find out what it's about?"

She answers right away. "She's got a fever of a hundred-and-two. They think it's flu."

"Okay, tell them Abuelita will come and get her in a little while." Then I remember Abuelita's Thursday garden club. "Or me. I'm almost done here."

There's a pause; then Santana says, "They say sooner is better, Mr. Tavish. She's very uncomfortable."

"Will do." With the intercom switched off, I say, "So what else, Keanu?"

"Thass about all, Mr. Tavish. It didn't look like nobody was coming out of E building, so I decided to scoot and see if I could get back into the gym."

"You didn't see anyone else go in or out? Or see anyone nearby? Or hear anything? Any sign of Andre's car?"

Keanu emphatically shaking his head.

"You sure?" Amin asks, his voice a warning this time. "You didn't start out here so troofful."

Keanu looks at me. He is not one of the boys who would call Amin a Tom, but I can tell Amin's follow-up has aroused his defiance.

"Please answer, Keanu."

"Positive."

*****

Francesca is lying on her side on one of the cots in the nurse's office when I arrive. She's holding her neck with both hands, like you'd hold a pet with an injured paw, not to heal but to comfort. She looks at me through her teary eyes but otherwise does not move. I wonder momentarily if she'd have acted differently for Abuelita or for Maria, if she'd have sat up and held out her arms perhaps, which is what I imagine she'd have done.

It's Mrs. Humphrey the attendance clerk sitting in a chair next to the cot and stroking Francesca's hair, since the school is staffed with a nurse only one day per week, not Thursdays obviously. Mrs. Humphrey smiles at me and reports, "We gave her Tylenol about half-an-hour ago, and her temperature stopped going up. Still a hundred and two."

"Thank you. Do I need to sign something?"

"The release. It's on the nurse's desk."

After signing, I lift Francesca and she wraps her arms around my neck, tighter than I expected, and presses her head against my cheek and starts sobbing as I carry her out. "You'll be okay, sweetie," I say, which is all I can think of, and her sobs deepen. I think of another scripture then, probably something Amin said sometime: "I have calmed my soul like a child quieted at its mother's breast," and I know my soul is not calm and that I'm unable to quiet my own child. It's a pitiful feeling. At the car, I ask her if she wants to lie down in the back seat or sit in front.

"I want Mama," she wails, clutching me tighter now.

I lean against the car and rock back and forth at the waist and say, "I know, sweetie," and I almost let out a sob too, thinking, Me too. After a minute or two, she sighs and slips down from my arms and opens the passenger door and slides into the seat.

"We'll wait at home for Abuelita." I know it's not good driving, but I call and leave a message for her while I'm navigating through traffic. I leave a message for our pediatrician too. "Do you want some sherbet?"

Francesca doesn't say anything but I pull in at the grocery store anyway and leave her in the car with the air conditioning on and trot in for the sherbet and cough drops and Sprite. It takes longer then I expected, of course, and when I return to the car, I can't see her in the front seat, and I get a spasm of panic for a few seconds until I check the back seat where she is lying down holding her neck again. At home, I carry her to her bedroom where Ursa appears after a few seconds.

Ursa is a dog who would happily spend all her time outdoors, but the sounds of our arrival have apparently alerted her and she has pushed in through the dog door to investigate. She barely turns her head as I leave the room and lies down with her throat on the floor between her forelegs and stares at Francesca, like some sad sphinx.

While I wait for return calls, I remember what Burgoyne said about me and the detectives both having tunnel vision, and I tell myself that I'm going to run through the facts I have, cold, like a soulless computer would, to decide if there's some way the cops can hang Usaré's killing on someone other than Memo and the Levantes. I sit in the recliner that Maria used to nap in.

Okay, motives first.

Let's say love is there at the top of their list, including your run-of the mill physical attraction, from a male most likely, I'd say, unless and until they find an indicator of Usaré having a different thing going on. Which still produces a long list of suspects, Rusic and Andre just the most obvious. Me and Jameson are there on the list too, I know. Some students as well, even Keanu, who was jealous, if not exactly drowning in guilt.

Then they have to consider money or power as a motivator, like how would the bad guy gain something from Usaré, either alive or dead. Pointing to Memo and his guys. Only them, seems to me.

And what else?

Burgoyne said anger—the perp lost his temper. Or *her* temper. A rejected lover? Maybe some girl whose boyfriend had fallen for Usaré. But that kind of rage is secondary, isn't it? The anger is *about* something—the perp didn't just have free-floating wrath unless he was a lunatic, in which case thinking about motive is a waste of time. So it's back to love or money.

Panic? Fear of discovery? That could be a stand-alone motive if the underlying secret has nothing to do with a relationship with Usaré. Which leads to Sullivan among others. But Sullivan seems überhetero, and so did Usaré. And Usaré had no real reason to out Nikki.

Envy? Somebody so resentful of Usaré that he'd kill her? Or she? More likely a she in that case, although Sullivan mentioned Canseco, which is probably a stretch too, but it's easy enough to check his whereabouts, I can have Santana do that . . . or some kid who didn't like the way she always got the limelight, though it's hard to imagine envy so green. I also doesn't fit the profile of kid-on-kid violence, which would have generated a buzz we'd have heard about.

Doctor Betterton's office calls about Francesca. Tylenol every six hours, rest, liquids, bring her tomorrow morning if the fever doesn't drop. Health care advice just as good as what you find on the Internet. When I check on her, she's asleep.

As I watch her, I can't help seeing Maria's shadows on her, her curly brown hair, which she keeps very short so as to avoid a losing battle with it, her smooth round cheeks and full eyebrows and bright front teeth, which I admit are a bit oversize for her thin lips and tiny mouth. For a moment, I remember paddling my fingers on Maria's face in the morning as we lay in bed, her smiling with her eyes closed and calling them 'fairy fingers.'

I go back to the recliner to pretend I'm a computer again. Okay, so as many as four motives then. But with the semen and the missing panties, the cops will keep thinking love put it all in motion. That's why they're stuck on Andre—his DNA, his texts. But they're still trying to put his lust together with access to E.

So they're also looking at eleven teachers, a secretary, four principals, four security personnel and something like ten coaches. Leave out all the women besides Nikki Sullivan, and they still have fifteen or more suspects on staff. That I know of. Might as well be half the school. But the cops are holding Andre right now, not Memo, because of the DNA. So how do they figure Andre got access to E? Well, they're probably going to search his stuff and hope they find the key and the missing panties, which they're betting was taken as a trophy. Good luck with that.

And Usaré! How they going to figure she got a key? Simpson and Bejarano haven't talked to any kids yet, so they don't know about Usaré letting herself in. Not yet. But they'll get to it. So will they decide the perp gave it to her? Will they figure the bastard got it back from her after he killed her? Or was that something he might've overlooked? Easy to forget a little thing like a key when you're adrenaline is going and you're trying to cover your ass on every detail of a crime. Maybe they'll think it's one of our notorious lost keys? Or some teacher like McNally lent it to her and forgot to get it back? Probably just have to wait, though I guess I could find a way to see who's lost a key.

And then there's opportunity. For cops, I guess that means you find out who doesn't have an alibi. Andre's is weak. Memo's is weaker. But hell, mine is weak too. Checking emails in my office, for Christ sake. But among the guys who have a key to building E . . . Amin has a solid alibi. So does Mayer. Rusic thinks he does, but he's in for a surprise.

"So all this tells me what?" I mutter. Not much. Pretending I'm a cold-hearted computer hasn't worked very well. I'm still thinking the cops should release Andre, wishing they'd go after Memo and his guys . . . or Rusic . . .

When Abuelita arrives, she is wearing tan bib overalls, soil-stained at the knees, and a darker tan nylon sun hat, reminding me of a mushroom. It was obviously a work meeting. Their club members maintain the little park in her neighborhood behind a strip mall, caring for flowering shrubs and perennials and planting seasonal flowers. She says, "¿Como está mi niña dulce?"

"She'll be mean as ever by tomorrow, I'd say." I smile at the old woman. I know she understands me.

"Tú eres un hombre muy malo. She have fever?"

"En serio, ella estará bien. Asleep now. Hay Sprite y sorbete cuando se despierte. En la nevera. Thank you for coming."

She slinks past me and looks in on Francesca and returns and picks up the remote control. "I watch SVU." Her favorite rerun series. She says she's seen them all a hundred times but still doesn't remember how any of the episodes end. It's also taught her some English. "Cuando se va a llevar a mi niño?"

"NJ has baseball practice. I'll bring him around six-thirty. Should I get a pizza?"

"Eres un hombre tonto. I make something."

With my grandmother-in-law's scolds echoing in my head, I return to Polk High School.

*****

Burgoyne says, "What's your idea, smarting off to Simpson like that? Trying to offer yourself up as an alternative to Andre?"

"Fuck him if he doesn't know a joke when he hears one. He's a prick."

Burgoyne shakes his head. "Cut the bravado, man. They go after a guy, they get him."

"Trouble is they got the wrong guy this time. You know it too."

He sighs. "Two of your teachers saw Andre on campus last week. Not just in his car either. During lunch."

This confounds me. I supervise lunch every day unless there's urgent business elsewhere. So does Amin and another security guard. I never saw Andre. And Amin knows virually every kid on campus and misses nothing. Nobody reported him on campus. "Rusic say that?"

"You know I'm not supposed to say."

In my head, I run through the staff who were interviewed. "So Mayer too, besides Rusic, since Mayer's the junior varsity football coach. I'm guessing Mayer's account wasn't compelling 'cause he was following a script that Rusic gave him. Rusic is building cover, am I right?"

Burgoyne doesn't answer directly, but he fills me in. McNally really wanted to help, so much so that Simpson didn't think she'd be a good witness, and yes, she might have seen me leave the gym some time between eight-thirty and nine or maybe ten, which contradicted Rusic, who would have sworn on his mother's soul that I couldn't have got out without him seeing.

The bastard *is* covering for me.

And yes, McNally was certain she'd seen Usaré with Andre a few times but that seemed like months ago, well maybe weeks, but no it couldn't have been days. She was able to produce her E-building key when they asked to see it. "In fact, they all could, the ones you said would have one—her, Rocha, Cook and the two coaches. But then of course the perp could've gotten it back after killing her."

Nuñez came across as a hell of a nice guy who likes kids but didn't know anything useful from Saturday night, though he did relate that Usaré came up and made some song requests, usually accompanied by some other kids. Trujillo, the punch bowl guy, gave a boring interview too, hardly noticed the girl, more interested in how much money his business club made on snacks and photographs, hated being there too—said the damn dances should end at ten-thirty or eleven.

Burgoyne goes on to say that Cook, the security guy, fit in a few pieces, namely that Rusic took his break early, a little before eleven, and that he never came back afterward, which Rusic later confirmed. This confuses me for a moment, since Rusic had told me he wanted me to cover for him, but I conclude he must have realized the lie wouldn't get past Amin. Either that or he thought it would make me look untrustworthy . . .

Cook also saw the girl leave, pretty soon after Rusic slipped out, with a black kid name o' Keanu Jones, later confirmed by Morales. They wanted to talk to the Jones kid right after, but they couldn't find me, and the other administrators weren't sure they wanted to let the detectives talk to him. They probably went to his house after they left here.

"Did Amin quote scripture?"

Burgoyne nods and smiles patronizingly. "Something like 'Break thou the arm of the wicked and evildoer.' Right when he sat down."

I fill Burgoyne in on Keanu's other revelations: the phony pickup on Park Avenue, her apparent rendezvous, the shifting shadows. Usaré letting herself in with a key.

Burgoyne says, "Well, there was no school key in Garcia's personal effects, so either they're like assholes and everybody's got one or the doer made sure to get it from her."

"Which means he probably lent it to her in the first place?" I say.

"It's good news for Andre. For Memo and his thugs too."

"There's got to be some other explanation."

We don't say anything more for a moment. The room suddenly smells stale to me.

I say, "One glitch in your theory . . . There has to be two keys now—one for the doer to let himself in and one for him to lend to Usaré."

He nods. A little grudgingly, I think. "But Simpson is definitely gonna focus on the two dozen staff who've been issued any kinda key that gets them into the E building."

"Santana can give you a list." I wonder briefly how fast Burgoyne will pass it on.

He tells me that none of the chaperones other than the two coaches could remember seeing Andre on campus for the last couple months. Morales and Rusic both admitted to contact with 'my girl' outside school hours but claimed it was always professional. They had excuses for being in her contacts, just like I did.

He shakes his head as if to call us all fools.

"Rusic referred to the wrestlers' cheerleaders, what'd you call them? Matmaids. Morales hung his explanation on this Mexican-American Studies Club, where she was president."

"Either one of them get fidgety?"

"Yeah. Morales. When we were talking about his texts and calls to and from your girl. Not the PE teacher though. He was cool as lemonade. Which reminds me. I saw a few of her texts. After the interviews, Simpson brought out transcripts of everything from the last month or so, wanted my take on some of them. The ones to and from Morales looked innocent enough, all about the cause." He intones 'the cause' like it's a bad pun. "But no texts or calls between her and Rusic."

"He was worried about them, so there had to be some. Can your guys surface the ones she erased?"

"I'm sure they will. They're also going to look at older ones."

"And the other ones you saw. Anything incriminating?"

"Not the way you mean. Some girl name o' Alma and some other number calling your girl a whore. Gossipy stuff too, about who's wearing what and who's doing the dirtiest things to whom. Several guys wanting to meet and telling her she was hot. Including both our friends Memo and Andre.

"There was one number called her two-three times the night she died, but she didn't answer and whoever it was didn't leave a message or send a text. And she'd put that number into her contacts as Paris. You know anybody around here called Paris?"

"Paris?" I shake my head. "How far back did that history go?"

"Couple months. No texts—just calls. In and out," he says.

"The teachers who saw Andre recently—did they say where?"

"One time in the senior patio. Once just strolling somewhere on campus with your girl. Couldn't remember the exact location or days."

"Course not. Too easy to verify." We seldom monitor the senior patio during lunch hour because there's never a disturbance there. The seniors keep underclassmen out and it is surrounded by classrooms with windows. "So anything damning for Andre?"

Burgoyne shakes his head. "Just his possible appearances lately. They'll probably ask him about that when they get back to the station."

"They still got him there?"

"Last I heard. Thinking about calling him a person of interest, but I don't think they'll hold him overnight on what they got so far. 'specially when they hear about the key. His man Lashawn showed up with a lawyer. They'll probably want to know how you failed to notice Rusic's disappearance though."

I shrug. "They show any interest in Rusic?"

"Yeah, they're gonna want to question him again. But Memo's name didn't come up. Right now, Simpson thinks the gang marks in the bathroom were there before your gal was lugged in there. He's gonna make a case against Andre until something contradicts it. The key might not be enough."

"I told you he was a prick."

TEN

Fred Garrison Park is a broad expanse of bumpy Bermuda grass barely kept green with a stingy sprinkler system and shaded in a few spots by giant Aleppo pines and eucalyptus trees. It reminds me of a pasture, and I know Fred Garrison used to graze his horses here before donating the parcel to the city just prior to his death some fifty years ago. The story is that his generosity was spurred on by a desire to prevent his heirs from selling it off to real estate developers. The city fathers added an irrigation system, concrete basketball and tennis courts, and lights for nighttime baseball. On its little league fields you can see dusty yellow circles where the outfielders usually stand. NJ is standing in the middle of one right now, sweating in the sunshine and waiting for the coach to fungo the ball his way.

I can't help wondering if he's enjoying himself. He and his teammates are practicing how to play this game in a much different way than I learned to play basketball. His team has volunteer coaches, inexperienced umpires and aluminum bats bought with the profit from a thousand snow cone sales at the concession stand. He's learning in a different neighborhood too, with parents who perch and provide advice and sometimes argue with the volunteers or with their kids or with each other. In the Polk neighborhood, we kids would gather at the outdoor school courts, every one of us dribbling his own ball, evenings in spring and fall, and work our way into the five-on-five game and stay on the court till we lost. We had plenty of arguments, but our parents weren't around to take sides.

It is late on a Thursday afternoon, a time when I would normally be in the middle of a twelve-step meeting, but the disruptions created by Usaré's death have completely destroyed my routine.

I watch NJ from a patch of shade on the aluminum bleachers. The shade is more comfortable than the sun, and it has brought together a small cluster of moms and dads who watch and wait. The coach fungoes a fly ball to left field, and NJ moves under it and catches it one-handed with a last-second backward lunge. I signal a thumbs up after he throws the ball back to the infield, but I see the dad in front of me shaking his head disapprovingly. The asshole. Time to call Eloise, I decide.

I drive around the park to let the air conditioning do its magic and then I place the call. I get a text back. She's in a meeting and will call me later. Is she talking with Burke again? Senior vice-president would be huge for her. For us, financially. Still, I hope he doesn't offer it to her.

One of the things I like most about Eloise, besides her stunning blond hair and the little twist in her smile when she wants to have sex, is that she doesn't mince words about what she wants. She might pause and say "I don't know" when I ask her opinion about where to go on vacation, but she really means she doesn't know, like she hasn't thought about it yet. But a thing like this, about a career move, she'll come home knowing what she wants, and she'll voice it right away. I smile, thinking about her evening shower, how I sneak in to look at her, never quite succeeding at the sneak part. She almost always grins at me, but sometimes, beneath that grin, there is annoyance with my adolescent behavior.

*****

I know I should call 911, but instead I press Burgoyne's number.

"This is Burgoyne."

"Jim. Something wrong here. Bad wrong. Can you come?" I find myself gasping, my heart accelerating and rattling the ribs beneath my nipple.

"Yeah. Where are you?"

"Home. Out front with NJ and the dog. Somebody's after my family. Just going in now."

"Hold on," he says, but I click off and hand the phone to NJ, who's kneeling on the driveway and holding Ursa's big head.

His eyes are wide.

"Call 911. Then Doctor Kay." He looks confused more than terrified. "Right now, NJ. First 911, then Doctor Kay."

I find Abuelita near the front door, on the floor wailing ¡Encuéntrala! I check every room, the back yard.

No Francesca.

I fight the panic that is surging up in me. My hands are shaking as I return to Abuelita, who has risen to her hands and knees and is now struggling to stand. I remember the threats from this morning, and I want to get into my car and race to Memo's house, find my daughter, and strangle anyone else I find there, but instead I help the old woman rise. I feel my heart again, palpitating now.

"¡Encuéntrala!" she says when she is erect.

"I will, Abuelita. I'll find her. What happened?" I hold her shoulders.

"¡Ve ahora mismo!"

"I can't go right now. Soon, Abuelita. I know how to find her," I lie. "Are you okay? ¿Está bien?" I lead her to Maria's recliner and make her sit. "What happened?" I can hear a siren now.

"Estoy bien. I just fall trying to chase them."

"They took her in a car? What kind o' car?"

"Blue. Dark, like zafiro. A Chevy I think. I see the bent cross. Recuerdo el número de placa."

"Arizona license plate? What was the number, Abuelita?"

When she recites it, I say, "How long ago?"

"Few minutes. I see the car leave, and then I fall. Soy una mujer de edad."

"I know you're old, Abuelita, but if you want me to bring Francesca back, you have to tell me what happened." I hold on to her to help me stop shaking, too tight I realize, and I let go her shoulders.

"Acaba de aparecer . . ." He just appeared . . . through the front door wearing a plain blue shirt and sunglasses and a straw cowboy hat and holding a big pistol in his hand, not pointing it but just holding it down by his leg. Then the second one showed up, going right past the first and calling him Manny. He tell him the dog was still eating. He had a pistol too, stuck in his belt.

"In English?" The siren is right on top of us now.

"No. En español. I ask them what they want with us." But the second one went past this Manny and straight to the dog door and blocked it with his leg. And you could see Ursa was trying to get in then, pushing at the little flap, and you could hear her growling. Then the other one, Manny, he came and pushed the table against the opening, the heavy oak one, and broke the lamp that was sitting on it. Then the second one, he ask me in Spanish when Enrique would be home.

"What did you tell him?"

"Seis y media. What you tell me. Then he say, 'Looks like we got time then,' and he went and got Francesca from the bedroom and carried her back to the living room, with her still in her school clothes but no shoes, with her kicking at him and trying to scratch him, but crying too because she was sick and scared."

The siren is off now, and I can hear voices behind me, through the open door. I can hear NJ pleading with someone and I can hear someone asking ". . . secure?" A paramedic appears, a young woman in uniform with city insignia, looking from corner to corner. She says, "Sir? I assume this scene is not active?"

That's when Burgoyne enters, his hand on his Glock, but he looks at me and says nothing.

"No, not active. But my daughter is missing. The lady is telling what happened." I look at Abuelita again and nod for her to go on.

He put Francesca down, the second one, and she ran over and stood by her great-grandmother and glared at the man. He came toward them and raised his hand, and she thought he was going to hit one of them, either herself in the chair or Francesca standing next to her and holding her arm. He said, "You got nice skin, little girl," touching her cheek with the back of his fingers and then stroking it with an open hand, smiling.

"Fue repugnante," she says. "She bite him and he pull his hand away. I look down and stare at his shoes, hoping he leave then."

"Shoes?" I ask.

"Sí, his shoes are extravagante. Naranja. How you say it?"

"Orange."

"Sí. Orange and black."

"Skinny guy? ¿Flaco? Short? ¿Pequeño? Like him?" I indicate Burgoyne. She's nodding, and I tell Burgoyne it sounds like Jhonny, Memo's brother."

The second man didn't smile anymore after Francesca bit him, hard enough to break skin, Abuelita says, because he put it to his mouth and then spit. He said, "Gonna be fun to bust you, little girl."

Ursa was barking then, not just growling, and then she would stop barking for a few seconds and butt her massive head into the dog door, trying to force her way in. Then she started slapping the sliding glass door with her forepaws as well, because she could see all of them through the glass. She tried the dog door, then the sliding door, back and forth, barking an angry bark in between battering at the doors. And she would disappear for seconds at a time, looking for another way in, Abuelita supposed. The barking and battering was thunderous enough that the two men couldn't really think about anything else for a few minutes, "Fascinado por el perro."

And then the other one told him he can bust her after they get where they going. And they better begin because of the long drive and because of the dog making noise and acting all crazy. He say the neighbors will look over the wall and they should have come at night.

"Hey Manny," orange-shoes said, "Fuck you."

Which didn't seem to bother Manny any. He shook his head mildly and went back to watching Ursa's assault.

"Purty soon, that dog gonna knock itself out or get tired and just shut up. And I wanna see the look on that big jodido carajo's face when he find me with his little girl."

Abuelita looked at the clock then, wondering how long it would be till six-thirty. Over an hour. She stroked Francesca's hair, remembering when she would see cruel men like these from a distance as a little girl living with her tia in Mexico, her tia constantly reminding her to run and hide from such men because they were 'hombres con enfermedad de alma,' men with sickness of the soul, and they could steal young girls and treat them as nothings, as rags for the dumping place. "The big one, Manny, he make me think of that because he talk like one from Mexico."

She had to decide what to do. Just let it happen like some insect, or try to change what happens, try to save her niña. She noticed she was breathing through her mouth and that her mouth was dry. She tried to think of a way . . . distract them and make Francesca run away . . . she knew she had the nerve but she needed an opportunity. Or get to a phone somehow, the land line in the kitchen or her cell phone out in the car, or was it in her pocket? She felt at her pockets—empty. Either one, just get a phone and call 911 and say nothing, let la policía answer and wonder. Maybe hide the phone then so the bad men didn't hear it.

The men didn't talk for a while, but then orange-shoes said, "Old one . . . anciana. Get us something to eat, uh?"

"What you want, hombre malo?"

"Enchiladas."

At first she was going to refuse but then she thought perhaps this was the opportunity. She rose and clutched Francesca and went to the kitchen, orange-shoes following, and said, "Why you here?"

"Just need to see Enrique." Making it sound like a social call. "What's he, your grandson?"

"No es, estúpido chico. He kill you."

Orange-shoes shrugged and made a spitting sound.

She could see into the back yard through the window above the kitchen sink, and sometimes see Ursa trot out and turn to charge into one of the doors. She could hear the growling and barking, and the intermittent crash when the dog tried to force her way inside. But Ursa's barking had grown sporadic too now, and she thought perhaps orange-shoes was right, that no one in the neighborhood would come to see about the noisy dog, and that the dog would grow tired of what was going on.

Abuelita put Francesca in a corner and told her to stay there and went to the refrigerator and retrieved a package of tortillas and some peppers and lettuce and a bag of shredded cheese and brought them to the counter next to the bowl where we keep garlic and onions. She took out the cutting board and a santoku knife and began chopping. The santoku is her favorite, she says, because it is like a cleaver but much smaller and sharp like a razor. She went to the pantry, near the wall-hung phone and looked at orange-shoes to see if he might turn away long enough for her to snatch the phone. No luck, but maybe when he eats, she thought. She took a bottle of cooking oil and cans of red sauce and refried beans to the range and began heating the oil in an iron skillet, which, it occurred to her, could be used to hurt the chico malo, if only she could swing it hard enough.

"Frijoles from a can for your last meal. You like that, tonto chico?"

He grunted, "We see about it, anciana."

She added the peppers, the garlic and onion to the oil. The sound of Ursa's assaults had stopped for a few minutes, and Abuelita wondered if she had knocked herself out, but Manny called from the other room, "Ay, chico, that dog is eating the door, the little flap on the doggie door."

"Buen provecho, perro," orange-shoes called back, grinning. "And don't call me that." But he went to the window and leaned over the sink to look, and Abuelita snatched the santoku off the counter and held it behind her for Francesca, who took it from her hand. She turned and knelt, shielding the girl, and whispered, "Hide it from him until he try to come for you."

"What are you doing, anciana?"

Abuelita rose and turned and said, "I comfort the girl. You scare her, tonto chico, you with the big gun."

"She's going to see lots of big guns, that one." He sat in one of the stools at the island bar and set his pistol on the counter in front of him. "Maybe we take you along too, anciana. For amantes de madurez." Grinning more.

"Diseased men like you, I cut off the barrel of their guns con mis dientes. Easy, they so soft and little."

Manny called again, "Ay, I'm gonna look around, see if there's a shotgun or anything."

She scowled at orange-shoes and added beans to the skillet and began stirring. She tried to think of other things in the pantry she might add, settled on oregano and found the little spice jar, but he was still watching her too closely for her to grab the phone. She opened the canned red sauce and spread some in the bottom of a glass baking dish and began rolling the tortillas around beans and cheese and placing them, seam-side down, into the dish. After she set the enchiladas in the oven, she left on the gas burner under the skillet and added two cups of oil, like that's what she always did. She thought, Maybe I can throw the hot oil on them.

In thirty minutes the glass dish would come out of the oven at 375 degrees, and she wondered if it would be another useful weapon, oddly thinking it would be a shame to waste the enchiladas, even if the beans and the salsa did come from cans.

She looked out the window at Ursa, who now lay prone on the patio, chewing at the thick panel it had torn away from the door, demolishing it and still growling. But in a moment, Ursa saw Abuelita and she rose and trotted back toward the house, her nose in the air, and she jumped at the window, her paws just below the outer sill, and gave a growling bark that

Abuelita thought could indeed have been a bear's bellow, and she wondered if the hundred-pound beast could leap high enough to reach the window if she opened the slider side, wondered if the dog was smart enough to try when the window opened, wondered if Ursa could penetrate the screen, and wondered if it would be obvious to orange-shoes what she was trying when she reached for the window latch.

Before Abuelita could process it all and decide what to do, Ursa trotted to the extreme farthest part of the yard, some twelve yards away, where she began to trot back and forth, not growling now but sniffing and somehow nodding her head. Three, four, five times she paced the little route.

Then she charged. At first Abuelita thought she would come straight at the kitchen window, and she wished she had opened it, but it was too late for that and she simply backed away.

But Ursa veered anyway and came at the dog door again, which no longer had a door, only the oak table blocking its opening. There was a huge lumbering explosion, and Abuelita knew that Ursa was in the house. She looked at orange-shoes, who was still confused by the noise, and smiled at him. She could hear the sound of Ursa's nails clacking on the Italian tile in the hallway as she gathered speed, and then she could see the lovely black and brown monster turn the corner and charge into the kitchen straight at the hijo de puta in orange shoes.

He had time to turn and see, his eyes wide and his mouth open, but no time to turn back and find his big gun. He raised his left arm, or his throat would have been torn away and he would be dead, but she could tell that the left forearm was hurt very badly, perhaps broken. The man was on the ground, and Ursa was not stupid, like so many dogs are, by just clinging to the arm after she had damaged it and wrestling with it, but instead she lunged in again and again, at the man's face, at his legs and crotch, at his throat again, tearing him, not bothering to growl, every bit of her energy going into the attack, a dog with both hatred and imagination.

"Estaba tan estúpida. I should have taken the gun." There are two more cops here now, uniform guys, listening as Abuelita goes on. "I could have shot both men."

His left arm practically useless to him, the man in the orange shoes put up his right hand to defend himself, but Ursa latched onto the fingers and tugged back at them, maybe pulling off the tip of one. "The bear-dog, que estaba loca, you say crazy. She would have killed the estúpido enfermo."

But the other, Manny, came in, and he shot his pistol. The first shot did nothing, and Ursa didn't even notice, but the second caught her in the side and knocked her down. She grunted out something like 'huh' and then she was up again, slower now, trying to come at Manny.

The paramedic interrupts to tell me they are transporting my dog to an animal hospital and that my son wants to ride along, and is that okay, and I nod.

I tell Burgoyne, "We found her out front with the hole in her. That's when I called you."

I have an overpowering urge to leave now, to race after my daughter, but I listen as Abuelita finishes.

Manny cursed the other boy and got him to his feet and told him to get to the car while he got the girl, Francesca.

Ursa tried to come after him, but he kicked her head and she went down again.

Francesca was smart and waited until the last second, pretending she was too petrified to do anything, or maybe for a moment she *was* that scared. She waited for Manny to lift her, and then she struck with the santoku, once on the face and then once on the arm when he threw her down, all angry and cursing and grabbing at his cheek, which was running red. "A mantener los cuchillos afilados, nieto." Then he carry my niña out the door, and Ursa follow.

I turn to Burgoyne and say, "My dog was lying on her stomach and trying to crawl forward on the concrete driveway. She was panting."

I remember the rest of it—Ursa's mouth dripping with saliva and blood, more blood still leaking from her side, a trail of the stuff leading toward the front door, NJ reaching her first and hugging her neck, and the bitch yelping and rolling onto her side, showing a tiny hole near her hip, oozing blood, panting with her mouth wide, her lolling tongue looking pale. "I called you and gave NJ the phone."

I turn back to Abuelita and ask, "And he didn't hurt her?"

Burgoyne says, "They're gonna take her to Mexico. She get the tag number?"

*****

We're sitting in his Crown Victoria, and he keeps telling me we have to wait, reassuring me that the Amber alert, the speed with which it was issued, will keep Francesca this side of the border, in one place.

"They know we made their car, so they'll probably need new wheels. And even if they only got half a brain between 'em, they know every cop in the state has their description. Besides," he says, "both of them probably need a doctor before they go too far."

Which reassures me in one way, but it occurs to me that it heightens the chances my daughter will be thrown away like a dirty rag, as Abuelita said, her bones found six months later at the bottom of an abandoned mine vent, or perhaps never, like the poor Robinson girl.

"I'm for going in now."

"You said that," Burgoyne says. "Too many guys in there right now. We got a better shot if one or two of the cars leave. Could be someone even walks out to one of the cars in orange shoes. Or Memo. Or a guy with a big bandage on his face. Easier to grab that one guy for questioning, just you and me and the asshole."

"Why don't you just get backup? We search the house. Maybe we're lucky and she's still here."

"Backup—you're watching too much Netflix. We'd need a warrant. 'less you think they'll invite us in. And since you didn't hang around to link the orange shoes to Jhonny Martinez, the County Attorney doesn't have cause to seek a warrant. Unless you want to go into headquarters." He swivels his head to look at me.

"And anyway, she's not in there. You already admitted that. We been through this. If you're right about this, Jhonny bein' the one, and I'm ninety-nine percent you are, then they didn't bring her anywhere near this place, headed straight for the border, or went somewhere to get stitches. Then, just like everybody else, they get the Amber alert on their cell phones and know they gotta slow down, hold her someplace for a day or two."

I attempt to visualize the place where they'd keep her—a garage? A closet? The trunk of a car? I wonder if they've hurt her, and I find myself shaking my head. I realize I'm glad Maria's not here to suffer this with me, but I wonder if she's suffering as she watches from God's heaven, which would be an odd feeling to get in heaven, I think. Then I wonder what she would want me to do.

"Thanks for getting me out of there," I say. "I noticed your guys in blue didn't want me to leave."

"Takes the department at least an hour to get up to speed, they already had the only witness there, and they wouldn't let you go chasing after your kid anyway. I figure, Why give these SOB's the extra time?" The way he says it sounds cold, like he doesn't really care it's happening to *me*, like he'd have done the same thing for anybody just so he could get a head start, acting like an ambitious cop.

"We can't just sit here, God damn it." I feel a certain insanity. This is not investigating the murder of some girl I was attracted to. This is a desperate need to find my little girl. I'm breathing fast, my guts wrung in a knot.

"Relax. It's gonna be fine." Trying to sell me but not saying *she'll* be fine, only that *it* will be fine, whatever *it* is.

The first ones out of the house are a couple of thugs, five-seven guys in creased cotton slacks and wife-beater shirts. They walk to an '03 Dodge Challenger, a dark blue convertible, with a shotgun air intake coming out of the hood, which I can't help thinking looks ridiculous. They walk fast and swing their arms too much, Mexicans acting like white guys, which I suppose shouldn't bother me, since I've been acting Anglo for a long time, but it does. No orange shoes, no bandages.

They drive away in the Dodge.

Burgoyne keeps watching the Martinez house, studying it, although we don't have a very good viewing angle, more than a hundred feet down the street, and nothing seems to happen there. No one is out on the high porch or the steps that rise to it, and the lights inside have not changed for the half-hour we've been sitting here.

I switch my eyes to the other side of the street where I can see the shrine for Usaré, brightly-lit in the gathering dusk; it has now overflowed the front porch down the walkway toward the street, like the flotsam and jetsam from a burst dam. But most of the flowers, even the arrangements, have drooped or lost petals from the day's heat. I wonder how many of the remembrances are from a Martinez. A hopeless feeling tries to seize me. This is what a girl's life in the barrio gets her: a portrait on the front porch, beads and crucifixes, dead flowers and neighbors who try to suck you into their terrible game. I thought I'd left the barrio long ago, but now I think that I have brought it with me.

I am terrified for my daughter.

Did the Garcías pray for Usaré's safety? Of course they did. I know the Catholic prayer: "Allow your Son Jesus to come now with the Holy Spirit, the Blessed Virgin Mary, the holy angels and the saints to protect her from all harm . . ." Jesus, Mary and all the saints and angels? Who could resist such an onslaught! I remember learning it rote as Maria began to lose strength. It's almost four years now since I lost Maria, but I still remember the words. The Garcías must have prayed it sometimes, or something like it, worried about an independent daughter, a girl who was unafraid and wanted to make her own way.

Like Francesca.

So here I sit, next to a faithless cop, wishing I had some confidence in the old prayer, anxious and terrified and wishing I were doing something to find my little one.

I text Abuelita: 'Is NJ home?'

She responds: 'Yes Where is my niña?'

I reply: 'We're getting close now Don't worry And Ursa?'

She doesn't respond for a time, and then in Spanish: 'Enferma de la perdida de sangre.' Sick from loss of blood.

A little later she texts: 'Policia want to know where are you.'

I find myself wondering, If Ursa dies, if our child is lost, will Maria, who never hated anyone, will she hate these men the way I do? And what will she think of me if I fail? Then I think of Eloise—should I call her or wait?

With the heat of the day lifting, the evening is clear and cool, but the moon has not risen. I should be home looking for constellations with NJ and Francesca and Eloise.

Rosa comes down the stairs. She is walking away from us down the crumbling WPA sidewalk, not fast, holding her phone to her ear, listening to a message on her phone.

I tell Burgoyne, "That's the little sister. Wait here a second."

I climb from the car and follow her, walking fast, but I still don't catch up to her until she reaches the cross street, where she faces left and looks for her ride.

"Hello, Rosa."

She turns to face me, not startled. "Allo," she says, "What do you want?" Not what do *you* want, just the question.

"My daughter. Just my little girl."

She looks at me as if I'm speaking Chinese. Convincingly.

"Did they tell you about her? What they did?"

Rosa is dressed as the cute innocent-looking girl tonight, wearing capris and a floral blouse and flat shoes. Her hair is dark and full of curls, parted in the middle and brushing her shoulders. I can smell her soap but no cologne. She says, "I don't wanna know why you're here, all right?" Her expression discourages me, void of feeling.

I keep watching her, thinking her face will change, that she will blink or smirk or frown, something to tell me she's going to help, but she keeps staring at me, cold, and I have to think hard about focusing on her eyes and not look away.

I start over. "I'm looking for a girl."

Her expression changes now, but it's colder still, with a little crook at the corner of her mouth. "Every guy who comes here is looking for a girl."

"No, it's my daughter. She's a little girl."

Nothing.

"Her name's Francesca, nine years old, brunette. Skinny like you, feisty like you too, smart like you. Only she was sick today."

"I didn't see no little girl, Mister Principal."

"Please, Rosa. I'm pretty sure your brother took her. Jhonny."

"I don't believe you, Mister. Is stupid." Not calling me names, I know, just making a comment.

"You *see* your brother today? Or Manny? They came into my house."

"I don't know no Manny."

"Really? Must be someone who comes around here. Maybe he uses a different name. How about, do you know some friend o' Jhonny's drives a blue Chevy? Sapphire blue."

She has blinked a couple of times, but she continues to stare at me, even now as she shakes her head. "I never seen nobody like that, Mister."

A Camaro approaches from the south, headlights on, and Rosa looks to see if it's her ride. The car pulls to the curb and idles, waiting. When she turns back to me, she says, "Jhonny wouldn't do nothin' like that. Memo'd kill him."

"Please, Rosa," I say again.

It might be the fading light, but her face looks softer now, warmer. "Gimme your cell, case I hear anything."

I give it to her. And then she is gone.

The hope that comes from giving Rosa my phone number only lasts for seconds, especially since she didn't even seem to listen as I gave it to her, and I desperately want to charge up the stairs at the Martinez house, but hopelessness wins out over rashness, and I return to Burgoyne's car.

"You get anything?" he says.

I'm shaking my head, but I say, "Pretty sure you're right—they never brought her here. She didn't know anything about it."

He says, "Them two guys were not in great shape when they left your place, hey?"

"Didn't sound like."

"Probly both need stitches. I'm thinking they wouldn't go to a hospital, you know? Or the urgent care in some strip mall, hey?"

"Okay . . ."

"But I'm betting they went somewhere this part o' town, some doctor Jhonny knows, a guy with just a shingle out operating outta his own house, accepts cash lotta times and doesn't report every little thing. Used to see these doctors' hand-lettered signs back in Chicago, just off o' Division Street. They'd take care of Puerto Rican families mostly. But some of 'em would treat a gunshot wound or a knife stick and never report it. What do you think? You see little signs like that around here?"

I nod. "Sounds like a better play than sitting here doing nothing."

He nods back, but I can tell he's a little impatient with me. Then he says, "So, you know the neighborhood . . . where we start?"

"I know a couple those guys. One stitched up my arm one time when I was a kid. My mom couldn't afford to pay him everything at once and he let her pay five dollars a month for a year or something. Doctor Rodriguez. Must be over seventy now, but I think he still sees patients."

I look toward the Martinez porch. "So we just give up on this place?"

"You watch a pot, it never boils, right? We'll come back in a half-hour or so. See if there's changes." He starts the engine and pulls onto the street.

I give him directions, then tell him about Humberto Rodriguez, who closed a gash about an inch from my brachial artery, which I suffered when I tried to climb back over the concertina wire atop the fence around a beer distribution warehouse. I'd already thrown three cases of Budweiser over to my friends, who had since disappeared. My mom was so ashamed of me that it ended my association with gangster types. I never drank beer or smoked cigarettes after that either.

The pickets around Doctor Rodriguez's house are freshly painted, but his signs look as if they haven't been touched in twenty years. One is the shingle with his name and the other warns people about his dog, which back then was a pit bull mix, I remember, and didn't seem to merit a warning at all, about as fierce as a bunny. Of course, it wouldn't be the same dog after all these years.

There is a new dog, a red-nose, just as friendly as the one I remember, who accompanies us all the way, wagging her tail. The porch light is on.

We come up the steps together and ring the doorbell, which has a sign saying to ring in case of emergency. Well if this isn't, what is?

The door opens and a woman appears, stately and handsome, almost solemn, Mrs. Rodriguez I suppose, and I wonder if I should remember her. She is wearing gold linen, or is it just yellow? The porch's bug light argues for gold. She sees Burgoyne's badge and lets us in. The front room is essentially a waiting room, much as I remember it, with rose-pattern wall paper and furniture that looks like it came from a thrift shop, an array of Spanish language magazines on a coffee table, a set of toddler chairs. The only sign of updating a wall-mounted flat screen television.

"Buena noches," she says.

"Buena noches. ¿Podemos ver al médico?" asking for the doctor dismissively, then realizing she might have been the first person to see Jhonny or Manny, or my daughter if the bastards even cared about how she sick she was. I think about calling Mrs. Rodriguez back, apologizing and starting over, but she is gone. The smell of their dinner lingers . . . fried whitefish, I think, and tortillas and something sweet, flan perhaps.

"Good evening, señores," Doctor Rodriguez says, entering from a dark hallway. I recognize him. His hair entirely gray now, but he has lost none of it, still keeps it long too. He wears a goatee, also gray, and you can tell he's losing a war with stubble all over his face.

"I was a patient of yours a long time ago, Señor Doctor. Enrique Tavish."

He nods, noncommittally.

"This is a friend of mine, Jim Burgoyne. He's a city policeman."

"I can see he is police. He has la emanación."

"We're looking for a couple sons-of-bitches," Burgoyne says. Now it is him who's growing impatient, but as much as I wish someone else was calling the shots, I stare him down.

"Do you remember me, señor? Me llamo Enrique Tavish. Usted me cosiste. You sewed me up."

"You were a stupid boy, but your mother loved you. Yes, I remember you. You were a very stupid boy, stealing beer for lazy boys."

"Esperemos que soy menos estúpido ahora."

"You do not need to speak Spanish," the doctor says.

"Hopefully, I am no longer so stupid," I say.

Burgoyne says, to me as much as the doctor, "I appreciate your stroll down memory lane, but these guys already have a head start."

Doctor Rodriguez stares at him, then at me. The stately woman has come back into the room and stands behind him.

I stare at Burgoyne. A half-minute passes.

Burgoyne nods.

I say, "We are looking for a man whose face was badly cut."

He tries to hide it, but his eyes flicker.

"And another man who had dog bites. Perhaps a broken arm. His name is Jhonny Martinez."

"¿Quienes son?" the woman says.

Doctor Rodriguez starts to shake his head at my question, but then Burgoyne says, "If you lie to this man, he will come back here and kill you, Doc. And there's no way to stop him."

My eyes narrow at Burgoyne, but he says, "And if you lie to us now, I will help him kill you. And we'll get away with it. ¿Entiende?"

This is not the introduction I'd imagined, but in a way, I'm glad to see this Burgoyne. I turn my head and stare at the old doctor, as if I agree.

The doc's eyes go blank. He doesn't believe Burgoyne. Or me either.

"They took my daughter, señor." I say. "Do you have a daughter?"

I turn my eyes toward the old woman now. "¿Tienes una hija? Estos hombres llevaron a mi hija. She's nine. Tiene diez años."

Then to the doctor. "If you know something . . . and you hold it back, I *will* kill you," I say, believing it myself now, still looking at the wife but talking to Rodriguez, wondering if I should repeat it in Spanish.

The old woman whispers, "Tienes que decir," but he is slow to answer.

Yes, they came. About seven o'clock. Very rude boys. They came one at a time, which he thought very odd, the first with an open gash on his cheek, which, though deep, was not bleeding badly and was not life-threatening, since he was pressing the tissue together with his crusty hand,

It was a young man he'd never seen before, large, perhaps six feet-two inches tall, with a powerful build.

The second was younger, and he remembered him of course, Jhonny Martinez, although he sensed the boy did not want to be acknowledged by name. He came with terrible dog bites, which the boy claimed were the result of careless handling of a hedge trimmer, and the wounds were deep enough for that, but it couldn't explain the weakness in his right arm, which I told him indicated a broken radius or ulna, or the claw marks on his arms. "I assumed they were caught breaking into a home. Did they hurt anyone?" When I glare at him, he adds, "I mean injure anyone."

"Let's hope they don't," Burgoyne says. "Where were they going?"

Of course, the doctor doesn't know, our threats notwithstanding. He stitched the one, dressed and splinted the other, Jhonny, who did not have time for a cast to be made, gave them both antibiotics, injections. And then they were gone, never saw a little girl, though he did give them a lot of ibuprofen as well as Percocet and more antibiotics, more than they needed, he judged, but 'que demonios.' There was a dark blue Chevy parked down the street, for sure, which he dared to look at when the second one left. "I was never fond of that boy. He was not merely stupid, like you were as a boy, Señor Tavish, but in some way conveyed malice . . . De un espíritu malo. Spanish expresses the idea much better in this case, don't you agree?"

"When?" Burgoyne says. "When did they leave?"

"An hour ago, I think," he says. "No, perhaps two."

"Can you be more exact?" Burgoyne says.

Doctor Rodriguez turns to his wife and says, "Cuando dejaron esos chicos?"

"Sobre ocho."

"¿Exactamente?"

"En punto. Sí."

"They left over an hour ago, eight o'clock," I tell Burgoyne.

He says, "They say anything about where they were going?"

"Qué dijeron dónde pueden ir?" I say, mostly for the doctor's wife.

The doctor shakes his head, but his wife says the second man talked about needing gas for the drive, two hours. "Si cruzan, luego tres."

"Two or three hours to where they cross the border, sounds like," I tell Burgoyne. "And they're halfway there."

"Not Nogales then." He bores into them with his eyes. "Anything else?"

Mrs. Rodriguez says, "Espero que los captura. Rezaré para su niña." She touches my hand.

ELEVEN

D o we guess or do we separate? Douglas, Agua Prieta, is just over two hours away, Naco a little less.

"And there's that Mexican highway that parallels the border, route two. They could walk over from a forest road if they know the way."

"As fucked up as they are? Carrying an uncooperative little girl? They'd rather castrate each other with a rusty knife. No, they're gonna try driving across."

"The Sasabe crossing's only an hour and a half," I say, sounding pitiful.

"Yeah," he says, acknowledging it. "But I still think they're holed up, so we got time."

"And they could go through Three Points or Arivaca, either one." There's a long silence before I say the last option. "Lukeville's the farthest, well maybe the same as Agua Prieta, two-and-a-half hours driving the speed limit."

I know I have to do something, now, and it has to be the right thing.

But I don't know what the right thing is. The desperation overwhelms me. My cell phone rings. Eloise. This time I message her that it's not a good time.

I say, "We'll pick a direction, east or west, take two cars; you let the department know which way we're going. They talk to the Cochise sheriff and Border Patrol about being extra vigilant the other direction, say over east, Naco and Agua Prieta. Maybe they get something that helps us while we're looking around to the west."

"Hundreds of miles to drive, thousands of square miles, looking for a blue car in the dark. We need something more." He starts the Crown Vic's engine again and turns a switch and police radio chirping begins right away. "SRO Unit Twenty-one here. Come back." He's driving now, toward the Martinez house, I'm thinking.

A woman's voice squawks, "What's your location, SRO Unit Twenty-one?"

Burgoyne ignores the question, and for the first time I understand he's probably violating half a dozen department procedures. Into the car radio he says, "I have a lead for the detectives on the Robinson case. Have them call me on my cell phone."

A male voice says, "What's your twenty, Officer?" A tone of annoyance.

Burgoyne says, "I'm on surveil. Gotta turn the radio off again. Have them call me. The Robinson case. Over and out." He switches off the radio again.

"They want you to bring me in, huh?" and he does something like a nod.

*****

He rolls to a stop in front of the Martinez house, directly across the street this time . . . studies again, saying nothing. There is just one car in the driveway now, a red Mazda, and two more parked down the street a hundred feet. The house lights look the same.

"C'mere," he says and gets out and goes to the rear of the car, where the trunk is already opening when I meet him there. "Waddya like better, the Glock or a pea shooter?"

All I do is stutter. I remember going to the rifle range with my uncle once, shooting a Winchester twenty-two rifle with an octagonal barrel, then a thirty-ought-six . . . remember a kid showing me a handgun he'd stolen from a house in the neighborhood when I was in eighth grade.

"Here," he says, tired of waiting. He kneels and produces a pistol from a holster above his shoe. It's barely bigger than the one I took away from Neto. He shows me how the safety disengages and then, when I don't take it from him, stuffs it into my belt. "I want them to see it, understand? 'cause they know you don't need a warrant like I would." He looks at me hard, seeing the terror in my face. "You're just asking questions, like you always do. Just let 'em see you got the piece."

"What are you hoping to get from this?"

"We want someone in there to crack and come out the back door. That's where I'll be."

I must look dazed because he says, "Your daughter, remember! This is the only play we got, arschloch! Let me get to the back door first." He considers me for a moment. "Nobody comes out, we'll just start driving, west, like you said." He lifts a shotgun from the trunk and trots toward the right side of the house and disappears.

I don't believe the gun showing at my waist is any help, but I leave it there and walk toward the porch, trusting Burgoyne, terrified.

A few stubborn or blind moths are flitting near the bug light and the screen door. There is beat music, hip-hop, but relatively low-volume, like Memo doesn't want any neighbors' complaints. Humid, half-cooled air puffs at me through the screen, and I can see Memo sitting with his stockinged feet on a coffee table and his knees up, working a little lap-top tablet. A blond girl sits next to him with one hand on his knee and the other holding an oversize soda cup from Circle K. They haven't heard me approach or they are pretending it. I can see pizza boxes, and I wonder if they're the same ones I saw the other night. Jesus, was it last night? Or maybe all these living rooms look the same to me, some truant kid sitting there with the door open, not expecting a visit from an assistant principal, screwing around on the Net and sucking down pizza. Except Memo's not a kid.

Instead of rapping on the screen door, I open it and step inside. Memo is momentarily startled, but then he recognizes me. The girl, hardly moving, says, "What the fuck!"

"Mind if I look around a little?"

"Chrissy," he says, "don't you know *the man*, you see a guy wearing a starchy shirt?"

"You got it all wrong. I ain't here to act like the man, just the papá. I understand, Mr. Martinez, your brother came by my house today."

Still sitting, Memo sets the tablet aside. "You see him with your own eyes over there?"

"I did, he wouldn't be walking around. Probably going away for twenty years as it is."

"Pfff. He'd just go back to juvey for a while." He glances at the gun, and I wonder if he takes it seriously.

"We're gonna find out," I say. "Your brother got a friend name o' Manny?"

"He gots lots of friends."

"This one's almost big as you and drives a sparkly blue Chevy."

"I mighta met him some time. You find him, you can tell him I say hi."

"You can tell him yourself when it all comes back on you. Police think he was mixed up with a previous kidnapping—that Robinson girl couple years ago—the one you see on billboards now and then."

Chrissy has been staring at me like she's wanting to say something, and now she does. "I don't see no police wit choo."

I say, "That's 'cause I ain't gonna bother with cops. I don't get my little girl back safe, you can bet I'll find the guys who took her and I'll kill 'em. I find out your pimp here had something to do with it, I'm gonna come back and kill him and you too." Trying to say the cruelest thing, hoping I sound like I mean it.

Chrissy gasps and says, "What choo sayin', mister?" but Memo silences her with a look.

Memo has twisted his face into a snarl by the time he turns to look at me. "You telling me my brother and some friend o' his came and snatched your girl?"

"I'm telling you I'll kill him if he did."

Memo stares, then brings a pack of Marlboro's from his shirt pocket, lights one and blows the smoke toward my face, like he's spitting at me. "It wasn't Jhonny. Who says it was?"

I say, "An old woman who's a lot smarter then you or your putana."

"She get his name from his driver's license?"

"Described him. Right down to his stupid orange shoes."

There's another warp in his face now, like he's angrier, but not just with me. "Maybe she mixed up. Just an old woman, ¿Me captas? My brother, he gets girls but never like that."

"He brings you a fifteen-year-old, you like it, he figures why not a nine-year-old. And somehow he knows the guy who snatched the Robinson girl." I shouldn't do it, but I mock him, "¿Me captas?"

He throws Chrissy's hands away, and stands up, chin out now.

I pull the gun and push the safety to red, the way Jim showed me. I don't point it at him, but he looks anyway, and he freezes. I don't know if he's scared, but I am terrified. I say, "I'm gonna look around now. Don't try to stop me."

The house was built in the forties, so there's barely any hallway at all, leading to a series of adjoining bedrooms, with a bathroom wedged in someplace. The only doorway connects to the kitchen. It only takes me a minute to go through the place, nothing to show for it, just the smell of burnt marijuana and a half-naked woman asleep in the rear bedroom. She doesn't even stir when I come through.

I am careful coming into the room where I left Memo, but he has sat down again. As I enter, he says, "You come here again like thees, you are a dead man."

I tell him I appreciate the warning, and then I leave.

Burgoyne meets me halfway back to the car, asking me with his eyes if I've got anything new.

"I have the feeling Jhonny did this on his own."

"No help then."

I shake my head. "You?"

"Nobody came out."

The desperation has been lying in wait for me like a lion in the tall grass and now it clutches me again. I feel it in my chest as if I've become wedged between two giant stones in a crevasse where I can't extract myself, and I can barely draw breath. My impotence reminds me of Maria's last days and inside my head I ask God the ancient question, Why do You hide yourself in time of trouble?

I put one foot in front of the other until we are at the Crown Victoria again. He sets the shotgun back in his trunk and I give him the pocket gun, my hand shaking now, and we return to the front seat, where he checks his cell phone and listens to a message.

"They bit," he tells me and dials a number.

I can hear voices coming through his phone but only one or two distinguishable words and some pauses. "This is Burgoyne . . . Because they're takin' her to Mexico, just like they did with *your* girl . . . Last I heard, you didn't have any new leads . . . Well, then *don't* follow up, you don't think it's related—then you can explain it to the chief, turns out I'm right." He clicks off, his jaw cut like carved oak.

"I don't know what to do."

Burgoyne fires the engine and says, "What we're gonna do is find those two boys. Then we're gonna kill 'em." He means it, I know, and he wants it to be an encouragement, but to me it sounds like he's writing off Francesca. He drives west, toward the junction for Sasabe.

"We're giving up on Naco and Agua Prieta then," I say.

"Give it a minute. Those guys'll call back. They can close that door."

I think about what he said earlier: hundreds of square miles, a blue car in the dark, a sapphire car beneath the starlit blue window of the sky, and I realize blue must be the color of hopelessness. Soon we are outside the city, and the night shrinks our car into nothing. The highway is two-lane, and I squint at every car that comes in range. At seventy miles per hour, we pass the receding lights from dozens of homes, and I know there are hundreds more I can't see from the road.

"She could be anywhere," I say, "same chance of finding her as winning the lottery."

I sense he's annoyed with me. He says, "By now, the department has faxed her photo and the perps' descriptions to law enforcement in seven counties. Border patrol too. Those detectives blew me off, but you can bet they've started wondering if I'm right."

"We just going to prowl around?"

"Three Points first, then Sasabe, then Ajo and Sonoyta. You got somewhere else you gotta be?"

It's time to call Eloise, I decide, and though I don't know what to say to her, I dial. Her voice is sweet and thick with a champagne loveliness. She's happy . . . a good day, but I don't give her the chance to talk about it. I tell her that Francesca has been taken, that I am following what I think is her trail, that I know who took her, that it will be resolved by morning and that she doesn't need to come.

She listens, then answers with a deep hurt in her voice, and I know that somehow I have betrayed her too. I wish I could crawl out of my skin like some molting reptile. She says, How awful! . . . how terrified Francesca must be . . . and NJ and Abuelita. She asks where I am now and how I know where I'm going but then says never mind and of course she's coming home on the next flight. We both know there is no comfort in words, and we do not talk long. I keep hoping that the detectives will call Burgoyne, but it is my phone that rings next, a blocked number.

"Ay, Mister Principal, that choo?" My heart hesitates when I recognize Rosa's voice. She goes on. "I don't know where they take her, you know? And I don't think it's Jhonny."

"You told me that."

"But I thought of this one house in that little town over by Ajo, you know the one?"

"Near Ajo. Town called Why, right? I been there."

"A green building, more like three buildings, all green and made of tin or something. Was there one time on our way to Mexico. Memo said it belonged to a good friend of his, and I think he meant a business friend. Smelled like ganja, you know?"

"Yeah I know the smell. They mighta took her there?"

"I don't know, Mister, but Jhonny knows the place and he could maybe go there if he didn't know what else to do, you know? He called before, but Memo wouldn't talk to him."

"Yeah." I turn on the speakerphone and turn up the volume all the way and hold it halfway between Burgoyne and me. "You got an address?"

"No, Mister. I got no address but I think you can find it. Like I say, it's all green metal and it's two storeys so you can see it from the highway. It gots a lot of windows, all up on the second floor cuz the bottom floor is jus a garage. You can see for miles from up there. There's a big yard and a pool, with a wall goes around it."

"You can see it from the highway?" I say, wondering if we'll see any lights coming from those second storey windows, turning and scanning for any sign of a moonrise. "Which highway, Rosa?"

"What choo mean? Only one highway I know there."

"Okay, well, is it coming into Why or as you leave?"

"When you're leaving. On the right."

"Leaving to go to Ajo? . . . or south to Sonoyta?"

"I'm not sure, Mister. I think maybe on the way to Mexico." There's a half-minute of silence. Then she says, "You still there, Mister?"

"I'm here. Hey Rosa one more thing . . . Why you telling me?"

"Cuz I don't want you to hurt my brother. I know you're chasing him, you and that mean cop from over to school."

"That's up to Jhonny. I just want my girl back."

"Jhonny wouldn't take no little girl. It gots to be this other one, this Manny, the matón with the blue car. I tol' you a little lie before. I know him. Un villano vicioso, from Culiacan. Jhonny listen to him too mush instead of Memo."

"You talk to him? Jhonny?"

"No. I tried his cell, but went right to voice mail."

"You talk to him, you convince him to give her up . . . Please, Rosa."

"I tol' you, Jhonny's not in charge. Manny just let him think so." Another pause. "Mister, you need to get her before they cross."

"Can I have your number?"

"No, Mister. That's all I got for you." And then the connection ends.

I say to Burgoyne, "What do you think?"

"Best lead we got. She ain't bullshittin'." He's been accelerating. We're doing ninety, but then he slows and sets a cherry top on the roof. When it starts flashing, he accelerates again.

It'll be less than two hours. I wonder if a rising moon will be friend or enemy now.

"You understand her directions?"

"Sorta. You?"

"I get it."

"I wanna kill them," I say.

We do not talk for a while. The Crown Vic races through dark flat desert, two-laned but broad and smooth, made for speeders, as if drivers are being hurried to their destiny. Every couple hundred yards, more frequent than any other highway that I know, there is a cross at the side of the highway, or two or three, death-marks, and I wonder how far back was the last place to buy alcohol before entering the rez.

Burgoyne is sure of where he's headed now, and knowing where to look gives me hope again. There's somewhere to go, not some nebulous, cross-your-fingers shot in the dark, something to look for besides a night-blue Chevrolet. But they've had all that time with Francesca . . . My skin writhes.

"Should we call the sheriff?" I say.

"Let's find the place first."

"You think they'll be looking for us?"

"You hear that girl?" he says. "Jhonny's probably messed himself. The other guy's expecting us too."

The Crown Vic has a good-sized engine, over four-and-a-half liters, thrumming along. Burgoyne leans his head back against the head rest and seems to relax, as if he's in his happy place and for a moment I hate him.

"I shouldn'ta said that."

Burgoyne pretends he hasn't heard me.

"About killing them."

After a long moment he says, "It's okay. You got more reason than most."

"I can't do that," I say.

He says, "This time you'll have to pull the trigger." When I don't answer, he says, "You better, motherfucker. I don't wanna die tonight."

"Have you ever?"

"Once. On the job."

I have questions about it, how it happened, the story behind it, how he felt about the guy, how he felt when he pulled the trigger, how it affected him—but even inside my head they seem like trite questions, with answers that are of little use, and I don't ask any of them.

He tells me anyway. "We stopped a car that fit the description of one used in a bar heist earlier in the day, told the guy to stay in his car while we ran his plates. White guy. The plate number didn't match the one from the robbery, so we approached, maybe a little too casual. I mean, we both unsnapped our holsters, but we didn't think the guy was the guy, hey? Just figured we'd check the registration and send him on his way."

I say nothing.

"Turns out . . . turns out he *was* the guy. He'd boosted the car, did the heist and then tossed the original plates and replaced 'em. Burns, my partner Burnsie, best lookin' guy on the planet, he asks for the registration and the guy goes into the console there to his right and comes out with a piece and puts two rounds into Burnsie. He was turning to do me the same favor, but I'd cleared my holster by then. Emptied my clip into the car. He was dead at the scene."

Again, I don't say anything.

"Burnsie made it. Lost an eye, poor bastard. Got his face caved in on the left side. His wife left him about a year later, said it was the rage he had now, but everybody knew it was 'cause his face was so fucked up. She couldn't bear to look at him after that. Most of the guys couldn't either."

For a long while we are alone in the night with the throbbing engine and the even road noise. Occasionally there are headlights or brake lights, which all pull aside for us. The moon rises about eleven o'clock, a quarter moon. Too much light? Not enough? I don't know.

"By the way, that's what you gotta do, Tavish. Shooting starts, you empty your gun, put in another clip, get ready to empty it again. That's what they teach you in the academy. We're not doing anybody any good if we're dead."

As we approach Why, Burgoyne turns off the flashing light, and moments later we pull into a park. Burgoyne says, "I gotta piss. You'd be smart to do the same." He exits and urinates near the rear of the car. How mundane it is to have to piss in the middle of the job we are on, but I get out and empty my bladder.

It's easy to spot Manny's fortress, just as Rosa said, the only two-storey place for miles, a metal building, light green you can tell when the moon hits it just right. There's a dim light in the second storey window. If anyone's watching, the approach will be difficult tonight, but impossible when the sun rises in a few hours. We drive past it, across a dry wash and then on for a couple miles and pull onto a dirt road where Burgoyne turns off the Crown Vic.

"Okay," he says, "look at me."

I do, and he says, "No bullshit now. No shaky hands, you got it?"

I'm sure my eyes are wide. I nod.

"Let's see if our phones work out here." He calls me; I call him. It's intermittent, but seems a little better when I call him. "Turn it off. We don't need a distraction."

"We'll come from the southwest, then over the wall and find the stairs." Like he's done the same thing a hundred times, then goes on. "If there's a blind spot, it's there. They're jittery, they're looking out at the highway and out front, which, looks like, is to the north. They won't be checking their back yard."

"I'm takin' the howitzer and the peashooter. You're gonna have my service revolver, but maybe you're gonna deny that later on—let you know after. I'll hit the door and go left. You follow, fast as you fuckin' can and look right. Lead with the Glock and look over the top of it. Hold it with two hands, underneath. It's heavy. Shoot everyone you see but me and your little girl. There's probably at least three guys in there. Jhonny and this Manny and at least one other guy."

I'm thinking he's surer than I am.

His eyes drill into me and he says, "Easy enough, right?"

"Simple," I say.

"She's gonna be fine," he says, but then he touches my arm and waits till he has my eyes again. ". . . because of what you're doing the next few minutes."

He starts the car again and maneuvers to face it north, just off the road, the lights off. After a few minutes, a northbound car passes, and he pulls in behind it and switches on his lights, close, like he's waiting for a chance to pass. Just before we reach the dry wash again, he brakes and veers sharp left and goes back to the parking lights and rolls the Crown Vic across the dirt to a place behind some mesquite trees and kills all the lights, fast.

When our eyes adjust, he gives me the Glock and two spare magazines and another lesson. He shows me the safety, which is basically just a pre-trigger, and the magazine release. He takes the Glock back for a moment and demonstrates. "Carry it. Don't put it in your belt. And don't touch the trigger till we're in." He racks the slide so that it's ready to fire and hands it back.

He takes the little pocket gun from his ankle holster and tucks it into his belt, right above his buttocks. He retrieves the shotgun from the trunk, shifts it to his right hand and starts carrying it like a garden rake, leads me west along the wash, confident in the cover afforded by the mesquites and palo verdes and desert brooms and creosotes. We wade into a cricket crescendo that recedes and softens as we pass. I see eyes glaring at us from the shadows, pairs of hollow globes, coyotes or ghosts or figments of my imagination. Finally, he breaks north through the brush, at a run toward some lights.

He's insane, I decide, but I follow him.

The wash is sandy but dry and easy to cross in the quarter-moon's light. There is cover at first, and I follow Burgoyne's path as he zigs from one scraggly tree to another, but after a hundred feet, the size of the water-starved brush becomes smaller and smaller, until it is virtually pointless to use for cover, and Burgoyne charges straight ahead toward a block wall.

Far to our left, a coyote yips suddenly through the silence, ferally and full of glee, joined by a few others in a matter of seconds. Their chorus reaches a frenzied cacophony and ends with the distressed and pitiful screaming of a rabbit.

It would be easy to trip on a scrubby young creosote as I run, but I glance up at the metal building for a second, wondering whether Jhonny and his friends have heard the coyotes, whether they might look out the window now and see me and Burgoyne charging. Nothing registers except light from the second storey windows, and I look down at the desert floor again and charge on. A hundred feet, then fifty, then ten, and then I'm next to Burgoyne at the wall. He's hunched down to stay below the top of the wall, and he's holding his left index finger to his lips, shushing me. He listens for several minutes, then raises his head and looks over the wall.

I stare up at the moon to keep my eyes busy while he studies the yard, feeling the weight of the Glock in my right hand. I remember Burgoyne telling me once that it weighs about two pounds loaded, but it feels heavier to me now, maybe because I've been lugging it.

In a moment, he taps my shoulder and motions for me to rise and surveil the yard.

The enclosed space is large and square, with a swept yard and round sage shrubs and a couple towering palms and half a dozen mesquite trees, trimmed to be umbrellas, projecting criminals who have pride of ownership.

I can smell the pungent sage in whiffs of breeze. Closest to us is a rectangular pool and a broad expanse of deck, pale yellow in the dim moonlight. Fifty feet away is the main building, just as Rosa described—no windows on the ground floor, just a broad garage door.

Burgoyne drops again and tugs at my sleeve.

When I squat next to him, I expect his voice to be hushed but it's not. "No fucking stairs."

I think about it. No. Maybe around to the right . . .

"I bet they're inside, goddamnit."

I get it. The only stairs are inside the garage. Makes sense if you're a drug dealer or a kidnapper.

"I'm gonna go aroun' front. Wait here." He runs north, hunched behind the wall.

Crickets are making their incessant noise and there is the whirring of a pool pump. I stare at the Glock, wondering what it's like carrying it around all the time like Burgoyne does. It projects power just sitting there on his hip, more than I imagined, because I've grown used to seeing it there, and even more in my hand now. For a minute, I wonder whether Burgoyne is aware of its effect on other people, whether he likes it. I think about practicing with it, using the magazine release and then jamming the magazine back in the way he showed me, pressing the pre-trigger just so far and no farther, but I decide it's not a good idea.

I remember what Burgoyne said, that Francesca was going to be all right because of what I'm about to do, what *we're* about to do, and I try to imagine the moment it's over, the moment I know she's safe, how it will feel, and frighteningly I have no sense for the emotion of it at all. Oddly, some speech from *Julius Caesar* comes into my head. It's just before the decisive battle in Act Five, and either Brutus or Cassius, I forget which one, is thinking out loud, wishing he knew the war's outcome that would be known at the end of the day and then reconsiders and says something like "but 'tis enough that the day will end and then the outcome will be known." I think that not only is it enough, but there's nothing you can do about it anyway. The day's going to end.

Burgoyne returns with a whooshing sound, like some kind of nocturnal falcon landing next to me. "The stairs are inside the garage," he says.

"You saw it?"

"Yeah. What we're looking at here is the rear garage door. There's a front one, buttoned up too, but I got in. Place reeks of weed. Humvee in there. Blue Chevy too. It's our guy all right."

I'm wondering how he got in, but I guess it doesn't really matter.

"Okay, look. All you gotta do is follow me, but I mean follow. Step where I step, go the same speed, and stop when I stop. There's motion sensor lights and if you get more than a couple feet out from the wall, you'll give us away." It's odd—he's wearing the same innocent face, but there's an intensity in his eyes, like a wolf's. "We'll be in the shadows most the way. No yapping." He scuttles away about ten steps, till he's under the eaves of the house, and turns to look at me, upright now and hugging the shotgun.

I follow, hunched low along the wall, but just as I'm about to sidle up to him, he scoots away again, in the deep shadow along the house's edge, scurrying like a roadrunner, seeming unconcerned with discovery now, then disappearing around a corner. Again I follow, consciously trying to imitate him, not just his steps but his demeanor too. Maybe that's what it takes . . .

Turning the corner, I hug the wall and look for Burgoyne, but I don't see him and I am more terrified than ever. For an instant, the two-pound Glock makes my arm sag and I wish the cops were here surrounding the place and I was just waiting, but then I feel like a Judas and a Capulet and shake away the wish and I spit.

I see a hand waving me forward, a disembodied hand waving me forward from beyond the next corner twenty-five feet away. My pounding heart shakes its way up my esophagus, but I try to sprint toward the hand, feeling like my stride is more of a jog. When I round the corner, I find him staring up at another second floor window, where there are TV lights flickering. There's a solitary first floor window, but it's covered with steel security shutters.

He keeps his voice low. "Okay, the stairs are directly to the left as you come in. When you get inside, I'm gonna close the door. Use your cell phone for light. It's pitch-ass dark."

"No garage door light?"

"Unscrewed it." He waits while I power on my phone again, then slips inside and I follow and he closes the door. In the low light of our phones I see the Humvee right in front of me, the stairs to our left.

He whispers now. "The stairs are made o' steel, vibrate like hell, so step soft. Can you do that?" He reads my expression in the light from his cell phone and knows I'm not sure. "It's easy, just put your toe down first and lift. Hold the rail. It's not a race."

He reads my face again and ascends, almost silently, his phone in one hand and his shotgun in the other, and I watch him till he reaches the landing. He aims the cell phone light down the flight of steps to help me see.

The garage has a high ceiling and there are more steps than usual, maybe twenty. I put my phone in my pocket and shift the Glock to my left hand. As I start the ascent, I am surprised at how silent I am, but then halfway up I stumble, sending out a wild ping.

I freeze, terrified and thinking I've betrayed us, looking up at Burgoyne, who's shaking his head, which I find encouraging. I rise slowly and ascend again, toe first and then lifting.

When I join him on the landing, he's staring at the door's lock.

"Dead bolt."

I don't know what the hell good I'm doing and again I wish someone else were here, someone capable.

He whispers. "Wood frame, not steel, which is good. But we gotta stomp it together. Use the bottom of your foot. Understand? I'm gonna count three."

I nod.

"But then the killing starts, you get that? Nobody gets outta here but us. Fucking nobody. It's how we save your girl." The one thing that will keep me from chickening out.

"I'll do it. Like you say." I'm so terrified, I can barely get the words out. It occurs to me that my bladder would be emptying now if I hadn't just drained it.

He sets his phone down to serve as a lantern. He holds up his index finger, One, and leans back against the steel hand rail with his right hand, holding the twelve-gauge in his left, getting ready to kick the door and looks at me to see if I understand. I've got the Glock in my right hand, so I grab the handrail with my left and get ready. Burgoyne says Two out loud. Then he rocks his head for Three and we stamp the door together. It explodes inward, and Burgoyne springs into the room, the shotgun at his shoulder and looking left, where an expanse of wall stretches for ten feet to an open door, and he runs toward it leading with the business end of the twelve-gauge. He shouts, "Police. Policía. Drop your weapons."

Leaving me to follow him and sweep the expansive greatroom that spreads to our right. I wish the roles were reversed, that he had the greatroom, but I know Burgoyne expects me to stick with his plan, and I do, holding the gun with two hands and looking over the top of it as I scour the room.

And there's a guy. Not Jhonny and not Manny, I think. Just some güero, light-skinned and surprised, sitting in a recliner and watching some soap opera in Spanish until the door caved in a couple seconds ago and now looking at me and the Glock, wondering for half a second what is going on. Then he looks around, like he's trying to remember where he left something, a gun maybe, but maybe a cell phone or a crack pipe or a cigarette to calm himself, I don't know, and I fire.

Empty the gun, Burgoyne said, and I start. I am not prepared for the percussion. I aim for the guy's chest, and I think I hit him there with the first shot, the way his body convulses and bounces forward off the cushioned recliner, but the weight of the Glock pulls my arm down after each round as I pepper him, and I think I'm punching holes into his gut and his groin and his leg, plus strays into the recliner. I hit him six times, at least, I can tell, his body shaking from each forty-caliber slug. My ears ring, and cordite fills my nostrils.

The guy is going to be dead, I know, but he's still sitting in the recliner, gasping and trying to talk, spitting blood instead of dying right away. He reaches toward me, like he's asking for my help, and now I want to help him, but I know from looking at him that he's beyond help, and I wonder if he's just some poor bastard caught up in somebody else's mess and suddenly I feel like I'm going to puke.

Then Burgoyne's voice penetrates my fog. I can't make out any words at first because of the ringing in my ears and because of the emotional speeches in Spanish coming from the television, but I can tell he's not talking to me anyway.

The TV speeches stop for a moment, replaced by low mood music and I think I hear Burgoyne say, "You need to relax, partner." I glance over at him, my stomach still trying to revolt. All I see is his back. He's holding the shotgun to his shoulder, aiming it into the next room, sighting along its barrel now. I am drawn to it now, to where he stands in the open doorway, but I don't know what Burgoyne would want me to do. There are other doorways that connect to the greatroom, though, adjacent rooms that have not been checked, and I move to one of the doors, a sliding glass outfit, before I can do any more thinking.

I hear Burgoyne's voice again, but I can't make out anything past "What I need . . ."

I can see through the glass doors ahead of me, but the quarter moon doesn't illuminate things very well. Just as I am about to operate the door's latch, I remember that the Glock is empty. I push on the magazine release button with my thumb the way Burgoyne showed me, and it gives a little, but the magazine doesn't eject, so I have to hold the pistol barrel with my left hand and push hard on the release button with my thumb before it will come out. After I put in a fresh magazine and rack a round into the chamber, I open the door and step out onto a wooden deck. A table and chairs and a gas grill and a potted queen palm. That's all. My heart is thundering like a storm inside my chest.

The outside air cools my upper legs, and I realize my fear has squeezed out some urine.

Inside again, there's a closet, with coats and nothing else, then another open door into a dark room. This time I get as low as I can and put the gun into the room first and then follow it, like I saw Burgoyne do, and I find the light switch. King-sized bed with glossy red sheets in disarray, massive

Mexican mahogany furniture. Nobody there though. Another closet. Another open door, another light switch. Bright porcelain and tile and polished brass and a wall niche with a santo of Francis and some towels clumped on the floor. Still nobody. I can hear actors arguing in Spanish on the television.

Only one more door, just a few feet from where Burgoyne stands, standing open, the light already on. Another bathroom, more porcelain, a niche with a santo—'Dismas' engraved below. And on the opposite side a second door, also open, connecting to a bedroom, where I see the guy Burgoyne has been talking to—Manny, I judge, from the bandage on his face, holding my Francesca by the hair, holding a pistol to her neck too. I wonder if Jhonny is in there as well. I move across the bathroom and into the open doorway, the Glock leading me, until Manny sees me and turns a few inches in my direction, and I freeze.

Francesca can see me now too. Her eyes go wide, like she's relieved I'm there, but full of a hatred that I've never seen before, and she gasps out 'Papa' and starts to cry, not pitifully but full of rage. Her face is haggard and fouled, from tears and dirt and her own phlegm. She has on the same floral print shorts she's been wearing all day, but not the matching top.

My ears are still ringing, but I hear Burgoyne say, "Look, I'm gonna back up a step and put the shotgun down." I can see him clearly across the room. He backs up and starts lowering the shotgun. "You're gonna get outta here, I promise, but not with the girl, you understand?"

"Bullshit, man. She's my *way* outta here. Looka that guy," meaning me of course. "He's gonna kill me he get the chance."

I wonder if he sees my wet pants, wonder if he'll laugh at me.

Sounds come from Francesca, low and almost guttural. At first I think she's groaning, but then I realize she's saying something, to Manny now. "I'm not going with you." She is standing barefoot between Manny's legs, twisting and straining against his grip on her hair. She can't break free, but she alternately kicks at him with her heels and slaps blindly at his left hand.

As Burgoyne sets the shotgun on the floor, I'm trying to understand why he's doing it, wondering what the advantage is.

I look at Manny again. The corner of his lip comes back and shows a dimple in his right cheek, and it makes me think the bastard is starting to grin. He points his pistol at Burgoyne and says, "Push it in here." As Burgoyne starts to bend he says, "With your foot."

Burgoyne puts his shoe against the butt of the twelve-gauge and pushes it forward half a foot, adjusts his stance, does it again. Manny has turned back in his direction, not concerned with me, and I think about taking a shot, but my hand is starting to strain from the weight of the pistol, the barrel pointing at Manny's waist now, and I see my hand quivering as I try to hold it steady with both hands. Someone told me once that the weight of a handgun, held properly, doubles every five minutes. I believe him now. Again, Burgoyne adjusts his position and pushes the shotgun so that it's almost entirely inside the bedroom.

"Thass it. Now back the fuck up."

He does and says, "You know you're not getting' outta here with the little girl, partner."

"You think this pendejo gonna stop me?" He stands now and faces me, points the gun at me too, and I flinch momentarily because I think he is going to fire, but Francesca starts slapping at his gun arm. "Coat it out, li'l girl." He dwarfs her by over a foot and by a hundred-fifty pounds, but she won't stop straining against him and slapping at his hand.

Burgoyne says, "You're in a fix, partner, ain't ya. Best choice you got is let her go to her papa."

He swats her with the side of the gun, once on her ribcage, and she stops slapping at his arm. But when he raises the pistol, she lifts her legs suddenly, just for a second, turning her seventy-five pounds into a dead weight, and Manny sits again. "Maybe I kill this man in front of you li'l girl, you like that?" She's on her knees now, and for a moment she stops struggling, and he's got the gun pointed vaguely in my direction, but not really committed.

I think that I've missed my chance, that Burgoyne has too, just then, when she went limp.

"I think he keel me he get the chance, eh, li'l puta who cut my face? He probly don't like so much what happen to you."

I say, "Her name's Francesca."

"This stupid boy, this Jhonny. His fault this all happen today."

"Where is your little friend? He coming back soon?" Burgoyne says.

"Good luck finding that one. You miss heem a couple hours." He pauses, thinking back to something. "He tell me we have a chance for a score. Little girl we take to Mexico. Easy, he say." He shakes his head.

"Not like the Robinson girl?" Burgoyne says, and Manny snaps his head around to face him. "Not so easy this time?"

I can't see Manny's eyes, but his dimple has disappeared and he's doing this tiny nod while he figures his next move, barely perceptible, or maybe I'm imagining it.

"Okay, me and the little girl, we leave now." He swivels his head back to me. "You, the papá, you so quick to shoot, you put you gun down now, like you friend. Then we leave."

I look across the open space to find Burgoyne, but there's no message I can read in his eyes. I lower my eyes to the Glock, which I've been trying to aim at Manny all along, and I realize it's pointing at the floor about two feet in front of him, and I let it drop to my side.

"My daughter stays here."

"You shoot my friend Chucho, and he a güero Mejicano like you. And religious. You don't see hees statues, man?" He shakes his head and pulls down the corners of his mouth, like he's going to spit at me. "No, you got no say in this, jodido coño. No, you toss the gun in here on the bed. Soft. There on the pillows." He nods toward the head of the bed

Francesca begins writhing again, slapping blindly at the back of her head where the massive brown hand remains tangled in her hair.

I look at Burgoyne for a sign, but he's got his eyes on Manny.

He says, "What good you think it's gonna do you to get outta here with the girl? Two seconds after you leave, there's gonna be cops all over the county looking for your car."

"Now you worry about me, that it?" He pauses long enough to bring the dimple back to his cheek. Then he says, "Nobody ever see me again after I leave here. I tell you what, I don't want this chica salvaja. Estúpido Jhonny think she come easy, like some pet, but she fight him all the way like a gata montés. Nobody pay nothing for her, you gotta hold her down for everything. You give me five minutes, I leave her for you a mile or two down the road."

"At the dry wash south o' here. You leave her there."

Now it's my turn to snap my head toward Burgoyne, and he's aware of it.

"Tavish ain't giving up the Glock, but I'll move away and stand by the unfortunate believer Chucho while you get to the garage."

Manny's eyes narrow as he thinks about it, but I know I don't like it. I want to tell Burgoyne it's crazy, and I don't know how Francesca will react. She's almost still right now, maybe thinking we're giving up.

"We trust you with the girl," Burgoyne says. "You gotta trust her daddy with the gun, Manny. It's the only way." Then he looks at me and says it again. "It's the only way."

"Okay. But he take out the clip and throw it on the bed. That give him one shot to cover you."

Burgoyne is nodding. "Give him the mag, Tavish."

Francesca screams now, "Don't let him take me, Papa. Shoot him. I don't care if you hit me." But she starts to sob, and for the moment, she quits writhing.

Manny says, "I tol' you she a crazy one, this gata montés."

Burgoyne says, "Listen, Francesca, both of you. It's gonna be fine. He gets to the bottom of the stairs and he's gotta make a choice between the car and the girl. No way he chooses the girl."

My heart is pounding in my throat, but I try to think about it. I can tell Francesca's thinking about it too.

Manny says, "You friend is right, pendejo. Thass why you only get the one round. I know you never hit me."

"It's gonna be okay, Francesca. All you gotta do is go to the stairs with him," Burgoyne says.

Manny stands up now and pulls upward on her hair. She's crying again, but she rises. Manny points his chin at me, reminding me. My hands are sweaty, and I have the same trouble ejecting the magazine, and I know the three of us are vulnerable for a few seconds while I grasp the gun barrel in my left hand so I can press in the magazine release. When it clatters to the floor, I pick it up and toss it onto the bed.

One more clip in my pocket, I remember, but I doubt I can punch it in fast enough.

Burgoyne backs away, out of my view, and Manny leaves the bedroom, glancing side to side, the wildcat girl compliant for now.

Francesca's eyes plead for me to be right about this.

I follow, the Glock hanging at my side, my finger outside the trigger guard. For a moment, I wonder if the terror I'm feeling slows my reaction time.

In a few seconds, Manny has reached the steel landing, and we inch closer to him, watching. He apparently uses the barrel of the gun to throw switches near the door. Lights come on behind him and the garage door's motor cranks. "Stay back," he says and starts down the stairway.

Perhaps it's because she loses sight of us—Francesca yells, "Papa, don't let him take me." I sense she's struggling to free herself again and rush to the door, but Burgoyne has beaten me to the landing. His right hand wraps around the pocket gun now, behind his back.

We both watch as Francesca tries again to free herself, breathing hard, almost grunting.

"Coat it out, puta," Manny says. He hits her in the rib with the pistol again and jerks upward on her hair. Before I can say Don't hurt her, Francesca throws her feet against the wall and pushes her back into him, knocking his back into the steel banister. It probably doesn't hurt him, but it surprises him because he finally loses his grip on her hair, and Francesca jumps away, moving up the stairs like a savannah cat.

Burgoyne's hand flashes forward holding the pocket pistol, and he fires as Manny bounces off the banister and tries to find his footing. The first round hits Manny's midsection somewhere, stunning him, and he stumbles to the side. Burgoyne is in no hurry now, aiming and firing into his middle again, then assessing the effect and pausing to tell Francesca to stay down, which she ignores, bolting up the stairs to grab me around the waist and start sobbing again.

Manny's pistol hangs uselessly at his side. His face is pale and expressionless in the overhead light. No dimple now.

Burgoyne watches Manny gasping for a moment, then he squares to look at me. "Maybe you wanna do this." He offers me the pistol. "Just don't shoot him in the head. I'd never do that."

Manny is gasping, trying to lift his pistol. Francesca is hugging me tight, but I look down at her and bring her face up to look at me.

She turns her head down and buries her face in my stomach.

I shake my head at Burgoyne, who walks down the staircase three steps and says, "How you like that girl now?" and puts four more slugs into Manny's chest.

TWELVE

It is noon before the sheriff's deputies finish with me, and even then I can tell they'd rather lock me up than let me take Francesca home. Burgoyne is still in some interview room, I know, because I see his Crown Victoria parked at the sub-station, right next to a city patrol car, both of them over a hundred miles from home. I know I'm in not a little trouble, and he may be in more.

The deputies separated me from Burgoyne right away, just as he said they would, but they were tentative about taking Francesca away from me, which Burgoyne had anticipated too. "They can remove her from you of course, and treat her as just part of the crime scene," he'd said, "but they'd prefer to get her permission first." She heard the whole conversation, clutching my neck, her tiny butt resting on my forearm.

"Not mine?"

"That'd be nice too, but you and me, we're suspects right now, and they'll pay a lot of attention to her interactions with you . . . how anxious she is about being separated from you for questioning, wondering if she'll be a good witness." I could tell he didn't want to explain very much with her there in my arms.

Since Manny had reverberated his way down the stairs, I'd been soothing Francesca, muttering "So glad I got you back" and whatever else came into my head, patting her, smoothing her hair, checking her skin for fever, rocking her. She would heave out sobs from time to time but otherwise remain quiet. Burgoyne watched us for several minutes, intently, which I thought peculiar until I realized he was examining her, assessing her bruises and scrapes and scratches, her reddened wrists and ankles, which had apparently been taped for a long while, looking for blood on her shorts too, I was sure.

He said, "You can help her wash her face, but don't let her take a bath." Moments before, I'd been terrified, but his new directive sent me into an even deeper wretchedness, and then Francesca began to moan. He moved toward the bedroom again, as if he were abandoning us.

I carried Francesca to the Saint Francis bathroom and set her down next to the sink and told her everything would be all right now, which sounded stupid even to me as I said it and made my heart sink again. She turned on the water and started bringing handfuls of it to her face and then lathering it with soap.

"I want to wash everywhere, Papa," she said.

"Soon, sweetheart." I handed her a towel. "After you see the doctor." She sobbed.

Burgoyne came in carrying a pillowcase, working at it with a pocket knife as he spoke. "Found her shirt, but it's all torn." He made cuts for Francesca's head and arms in the silky bag and handed it to her, and she pulled it over her head and went back to holding me.

"Found Chucho's gun too, right there in his hand." He stared at me hard. "Glock nine. Good thing you saw it when you did, or we wouldn't be talking now." He kept his stare on me. "Must've pointed it at you." He waited.

"That's just what he did," I said.

That's when he called the sheriff's office. "Law enforcement officer in need of assistance," he said. He told the dispatcher there were fatalities, gave the location, his name and position, said he'd meet them in front with his shield, clicked off, though I think they wanted him to stay on the line.

Then he told me it would be a good idea to let people know she was okay before they arrived and confiscated my phone. I texted Eloise and Abuelita. 'I have her, she's okay, more later. Probly tied up 4 a while'

I texted Augustine to tell him I wouldn't be at work. Then I called Eloise, which went right to voice mail, briefly told her the story, and told her we'd probably be in Ajo for a few hours.

The deputy in charge of the scene was named Barnes, Cheryl Barnes, who let Francesca decide about the ambulance ride. At first she told Francesca I would have to stay behind and talk to the other deputies, but she said she wouldn't go without me and Barnes didn't argue. Riding with her and holding her hand, I watched her wide eyes roam from pieces of equipment to me to the paramedic to a deputy who'd squeezed his way in, apparently to monitor any conversation between us. Her silence surprised me after seeing her struggle with Manny.

Her fever was gone.

In the exam room, they tried to isolate Francesca from me, but again she wouldn't have it. I stood next to her and held her hands when they draped her and put her in stirrups, thinking it should have been Maria who accompanied her the first time she faced those cold chrome things. Then they admitted her to a room in the ER and started an IV. She slept and Barnes took me away.

They questioned me at the substation, and they made me tell the story a million times. It reminded me of the way I question kids, starting with an open-ended hook. They asked me if I wanted an attorney and I said no. "So tell us what happened," they said. After I'd been through it several times with the sheriff's people, a border patrol officer arrived, and I went through it again. Then a city cop showed up, Lieutenant McCoy, a colleague of Burgoyne's, dressed in a shirt and tie, and I started over. Every time a new cop came in the room, he asked me if I wanted an attorney, and I said no. Each time I told the story, they went into the details, looking for admissions and discrepancies that might incriminate me or Burgoyne or both of us.

What made you think you'd find your daughter at that particular house?

Why did you trust the informant? Who was she?

How did Officer Burgoyne confirm you had the right house? That your daughter was present before you barreled in there?

Did Officer Burgoyne identify himself as a peace officer when you entered the house? In Spanish or English?

What did you think when Officer Burgoyne told you to be his backup? Gave you a gun?

Why didn't Officer Burgoyne call for local law enforcement for help?

The guy you shot, did he pose a threat?

What made you fire?

All nine rounds?

Did you realize you could be endangering innocent people, your daughter for instance?

I wouldn't give them Rosa's name, but I told them the truth, every bit of it, even the part that Burgoyne had helped me remember about Chucho's gun. And they asked more questions about that than anything else, every detail about it, like that was the part that would put me in lockup or not. I wondered if Burgoyne would confirm me in the details, but then I realized he wouldn't, that all his attention was focused on Manny and my Francesca.

After you busted in, how much time did the guy have to pick up his piece? Must have had the gun with him right there in his lap then, don't you think? Must have been expecting the cavalry then, right? But he still couldn't get off a shot. You suppose he was scared? Couldn't find the safety maybe? You sure he heard Officer Burgoyne identify himself? You said the TV was on, right? Something on Univision? You fired when he picked up the piece or when he aimed it at you? Or just when he seen it?

'Seen it?' for Christ sake.

Which hand did he pick it up with? You sure? What if it turns out the guy was left-handed?

Then they started in again, to see if the details changed, asking questions differently, in a different order.

You said the guy had three or four seconds to pick up his gun. That's kind of a long time for a stone killer, a gangster, sitting there all ready to pull his piece, and he still can't get off a couple shots. Maybe the gun was on the floor or on the table, and he forgot where it was. You think that could be? Did you see him looking for it or was it already there in his hand when you first saw him? Did you see him bend or twist before the Glock came out? Maybe he was just reaching for the gun when you shot him. You think maybe that was the way? The first officers on the scene weren't sure if the gun was in his hand. What did Officer Burgoyne say, exactly, when you broke in? Was it in Spanish first, or did he say it in English first? You think maybe the guy was asleep and that's what took him so long? To find his gun, I mean.

They took turns asking the questions, the three of them.

McCoy, the city cop, was the one most interested in Burgoyne. He said, "What about this school resource officer, this Burgoyne? He a friend of yours? . . . He have like a hardon for gangbangers, man? . . . You know your buddy Burgoyne didn't do this like he shoulda? . . . How long you know Officer Burgoyne? . . . He ever do something like this before— overstep his authority? . . . Maybe use a little too much force a time or two with the kids at your school?"

You got a heavy gang presence there at that high school of yours? What did you call it? Polk High School? The guy you were looking for, this Jhonny Martinez that you never found—he comes from up your way, yeah? Your home town? You met him before, yeah? He got a grudge going with you? Can you describe him? You have any indication that he'd worked with these dead guys before? The ones you and your buddy Burgoyne popped? You recognized Manny from one detail mainly—the bandage right?

"Cuz you never met him before tonight, right? And you had a description of this Jhonny Martinez, but what reason you got to think the guy you popped had anything to do with nabbing your daughter?"

McCoy said, "Looks like those two both got what they deserved, don't you think? How did you feel about it? Offing those guys that grabbed your daughter? That musta felt good right? Justified? We get why you did it. Who wouldn't have? I'd have popped both of them myself, know what I mean, if they grabbed my kid? What they did to her—"

It was pissing me off, the references to Francesca, but I kept answering. I thought more and more about the way they talked about her, especially McCoy, without using her name.

Finally I said, "What I want to know is who's out looking for Martinez while you're in here grilling me. Guy with a bunch o' dog bites and a broken arm, shouldn't be that tough."

McCoy didn't particularly like my answer. He asked me if I had problems with authority figures, by which I guess he meant himself.

"No sir," I said. "I'm just inquiring as to why you're pretending to care about my daughter, whose name is Francesca by the way, while one of her kidnappers is still ripping around the countryside."

"He might wind up being a witness against *you* if the county attorney decides to charge you for killing this Chucho."

"Well then you'd at least have to track him down to serve the summons."

They left me alone for an hour in the interview room. Then Deputy Barnes appeared and told me I was free to go. For the time being. She told me they had downloaded some data from my cell phone and returned it to me. As she drove me back to the hospital, she said it would be a good idea if I didn't plan any foreign travel in the near future.

*****

When I enter Francesca's room, Eloise turns and smiles faintly, and I begin crying. She is sitting alongside Francesca on her bed and she doesn't come to me, lets me sob alone, and I know that she is here for Francesca, and I am glad, but I keep sobbing.

Francesca is half-awake, sitting upright in her bed, her gaze on the television, almost watching 'Judge so-and-so'. She looks at me as I come close though, and I imagine that she has no idea why I'm crying. I know she's never seen me like this before, and I wonder if she sees me as some oddity, like the carnival's three-eyed man. She says, "I can go home now, Papa. They were just waiting for you to come back."

"Yes, I'm back now." I sigh and brush at my watery cheeks and force the corners of my mouth up.

"Look, El brought me some new things to wear." Suddenly, she sounds excited. She raises her arms to show she's already wearing a bright top, red and long-sleeved, with a gold graphic that says 'All Heart'. There are some more clothes at the foot of the bed.

"Cute," I say, knowing I'd never thought once about her needing clothes. I smile at her, then at Eloise.

"She put it on the minute I walked in . . . couldn't wait to lose that awful hospital gown. The nurse wasn't happy."

"How are you?" I ask Francesca.

"I'm better now," she says. Then she looks away from me, at some place faraway, and says, "They let Eloise take me to the shower."

*****

Eloise has driven up in my Camry because the three of us wouldn't have fit so well in her Beamer. She hands me the keys and sits in the back seat, assuming I think, that Francesca would sit in front with me, but Francesca climbs in back with Eloise, rests her hand on hers in the middle of the back seat. It makes me want to cry again, and it makes me want to smile. They talk intermittently. I text Abuelita as I drive and tell her we are on our way.

Francesca tells Eloise that the hills are pretty with all those spring flowers, that I seem to be driving pretty fast, that there are a lot of crosses along the highway—"They're for dead people," that she doesn't remember traveling this way before. Eloise agrees with her mostly. She tells Francesca the crosses are yes, for people who had bad accidents, that we came this way once to go see the telescopes, another time sort of this way to go to the desert museum, and did she remember those trips.

Francesca says yes she remembers, but she moves on to other topics. I keep checking her hand in the mirror, which rests always on Eloise's, even when Francesca points at something, and Eloise never budges either.

Halfway home, Francesca says, "I like that man, Papa, the one who came with you."

I catch her eyes in the mirror. "He's a good man, mija. His name's Burgoyne. Jim Burgoyne. He's a policeman."

"I knew that, Papa. Policemen always know what to do." It's not an accusation, but I feel like fathers who dealt treacherously with their daughters, like old Capulet, like Lear, like Polonius. I wonder what she remembers about the last seconds, about Burgoyne shooting Manny. Enough I decide.

I think back to my arrogant question to Burgoyne earlier: "You got a daughter?" and I ask myself if his having no children was the thing that made him know for sure what we had to do and how we had to do it in order to get Francesca out of the mess I'd made for her.

Then it occurs to me that forgetting my children for a few minutes, throwing Jhonny into the cool night air, was the sin for which my daughter will now pay, maybe forever, like a princess sold into slavery. I have not seen any tears in her eyes since she freed herself from Manny, but I wonder if she will cry secretly and bitterly in the night.

And then, oddly, it comes to me that no one knows my treachery, not Francesca, not Eloise, not even Burgoyne as far as I know. Is it best, I wonder, to confess to those I have hurt and seek redemption. As we say at addiction meetings, make amends? Or stay silent? Feign innocence?

The eighth and ninth steps in SAA tell me to determine all the people I have harmed and to make amends to them. My sponsor, a recovering porn addict who calls himself Willy, would tell me that confessing my behavior at the Martinez house, first in group and then to those who've suffered for it, is a necessity because it came from the same character defect that required me to get help in the first place—my arrogant impulsiveness. Not exactly what I want to do . . .

Six years ago, while I was attending a Five Star Basketball Camp in Philadelphia, I had a fling with one of the girls' coaches. I rationalized in the usual ways that philanderers do: it was just no-strings fun with an attractive woman that I would never see again; it was an opportunity to get some strange—after all, as Coach Jimmy once told me, nothing is more exciting than strange—he understood basketball motion and motivation a lot better than he did morality; and it wouldn't do Maria any harm—in fact, Maria wouldn't even have to know.

All bullshit, of course. The no-strings coach wanted to start attaching them the minute I unclasped her bra; the strange turned out to be very unexciting, Coach Jimmy's recommendation notwithstanding; and Maria found out about it when the no-strings, strange-but-unexciting coach started calling our land line.

It broke Maria's heart, and telling her the whole truth took more courage than anything I've ever done.

But this is worse. It's not Francesca's heart that's been broken . . . it's her artlessness, her naiveté, her trust in goodness . . . her nature.

The intermittent conversations between Francesca and her stepmother soothe me, a blessed interruption to my imaginings of the hysterical hours that passed for Francesca between the moment the two sons-of-bitches entered our house and the instant she freed herself and presented Burgoyne with a clear shot . . . six clear shots.

Evening is coming as we enter the city from the west. I wonder suddenly what's become of Ursa, and I suspect Eloise's silence about her for the past several hours probably answers well enough. I almost ask Eloise directly, but I don't, sensing a fragility inside my daughter that won't tolerate another distress. I don't know how to comfort her, and I pray that Eloise's presence has been enough, will be enough.

I think of Francesca saying how Eloise had accompanied her to the shower stall at the hospital and saying, "I'm better now," and it makes me remember a scene from a movie, a Western I think, where a woman tells a bandit and would-be rapist that she would wash herself in a tub of hot water after he finished with her and she would be exactly what she was before, with just one more filthy memory. Her speech convinces the bandit to leave her alone, but of course it was just a scene in a movie where bandits can be persuaded to act honorably. Still, I wonder about it as if it were real. If the bandit had raped her, is that how she would have framed it for herself—a thing that can be washed away and turned into 'just' a memory? Is that what rape victims tell themselves? Do some of them convince themselves? The woman in the movie, played by a beautiful Italian actress if I remember right, seemed to believe it, but of course she was acting a part, and probably following the directions of some man on the set and saying lines written be some other man.

Still, I wish I could plant the idea into my daughter's head and have her believe it.

On the way home, we pass Polk High School, where a couple dozen cars remain in the parking lot near the auditorium. Rehearsals for some performance, *Troilus and Cressida* perhaps. It surprises me a little because I know some of the kids in advanced drama were close to Usaré and they would have wanted to go to the viewing, which is also tonight. Then again, maybe they went early and came over for the rehearsal afterward. It's probably the first time I've thought of Usaré since I was sitting in Burgoyne's car near her house the night before. Tomorrow I have to go to her memorial service, and I wonder if I'll hear from Burgoyne before then.

"Papa, can we have pepperoni pizza for dinner?" Francesca asks, about a mile from our house.

"Of course, mija." I call it in.

When I turn into the driveway, NJ runs out to greet us, but after we roll to a stop he doesn't know what to do. He and his sister have not hugged each other since they were five years old, and so he just stares at her as she exits the car. I can see he's been crying, for Ursa certainly, and maybe for his sister. She smiles at him but offers no other acknowledgement and goes inside.

When I follow, I pick NJ up on the way and toss him onto my shoulder.

Ursa's bloodstains jump out at me as we walk past them.

NJ has to duck to avoid the overhang on the front porch.

Abuelita fawns over her great grand-daughter, tells her she is proud of her and offers, "Me alegro de que no te hicieron daño." She's glad they didn't hurt her.

The pizza is cheesy and greasy, and everyone's stomach is satisfied. When finally it is bedtime, we all kiss good night. Abuelita spreads a sheet on the couch for herself, and NJ drags himself away in his despair, but Francesca sits up in her bed listening to music with the lights on, buds in her ears. When I approach Francesca's room, I see Eloise's shadow and I stop and listen from the hallway.

"Can I listen?" Eloise says. There's a pause, and I guess Francesca gives her one of the earpieces. "Oh, I love this one," Francesca says and starts to sing a few words: " . . . you ever feel like a plastic bag . . ."

Eloise says, "Teach me," and I hear her trying to join in, trying to read lips I guess and to anticipate, but a half-beat behind: ". . . you just gotta get into the light and let it shine just own the night like the fourth of July . . ."

I decide there's nothing I can do any better than the singing, and I head off for a shower, but I find NJ sitting on my bed in his pajamas waiting for me. I've thought about Francesca a good deal, and myself and Eloise, and even Ursa, but very little about my boy. One minute he was fighting the sun to catch fly balls coming down from the sky, and the next he was holding a bleeding dog, his best friend. Now, his sister has come home, in one piece but different somehow than when he saw her last. His eyes, full of grief, ask me for rescue, for refuge and redemption. He must think I'm like a mule, without any understanding for him.

I say, "Trouble doesn't last, son."

"They killed Ursa." He remains on the bed, but now he begins to cry. "Doctor Kay said there was nothing he could do. I prayed for her, but there was nothing he could do."

I sit next to him and put my arm around his shoulder, but he shrugs it away.

He breaks down and talks through his sobs. "Why couldn't Doctor Kay save her, Papa? I prayed so hard." He sucks in these deep breaths and tries to stop crying. "Ursa loved Cheska more, even though she never paid any attention to her. She was *my* dog, not Cheska's."

"Ursa didn't love anyone more. She was fighting for all of us. She loved us and she would have done the same thing again. That's what you need to think about. That's what you need to remember, dude." I say, 'dude' to him a lot when I'm trying to convince him of something, but now it sounds stupid.

"I wish Ursa never got in the house."

I nod and reach around his shoulder again, and this time he lets me hug him. After a few minutes, I say, "Nothing could have stopped her, son . . . c'mon," and walk him to his room.

As he's getting into bed, he says, "Can we bury her by the big palo verde tree?"

"Of course. Listen, you wanna come sleep with me and Eloise?" He makes a little shake with his head and I kiss him. "Then I'm gonna lie here on the floor for a while, okay?"

He nods, almost imperceptibly, and I take off my shoes and lie down, regretting it almost instantly because of the smell from my socks. Despite his grief, or maybe because of it, he drifts off in about twenty minutes and I leave him to the torture of his dreams.

*****

As I approach the school on Park Avenue, Burgoyne says, "I thought you said she didn't matter to the other kids." He's in the passenger seat.

All the school parking lots are full, and they've opened up the football practice field for parking, and it's still not enough. Cars line all the adjacent streets, half of them jumped onto the sidewalks or otherwise illegally parked. There are groups of people moving along the walkways and across the grass toward the auditorium, slowly, like a stream of harvester ants, except they're in twos and threes.

It takes me a moment to come back through the fog of my thoughts about my family. When I do, I say, "No, I said they got over it awful fast. They only talked about the murder for about a day on campus, but, like you said, they were processing it on social media. She mattered a lot. She was involved in everything, seems like. Mat maids, drama club, Mexican-American Studies, debate team, future attorney's club . . . She was a beautiful girl who could work a room and make everyone feel like her best friend." It makes me think of Francesca, who always gets the lion's share of attention.

"Not to mention, she had the tendencies of a modern woman." His remark doesn't bother me the way it might have a couple days ago. He has not told me a great deal about his experience in the interrogation room out at the sheriff's substation, but from what little he has said, I gather he was grilled more rigorously than I was, especially by his own internal affairs people. He has been put on administrative leave with pay for several days, so when he called to ask me for a ride, he first asked how Francesca was doing, which both surprised me and twisted my insides, then told me he would not be operating in an official capacity, ". . . but of course, if you got questions, feel free to ask." He has also told me that the department did not ask for his badge and they issued him a substitute firearm, both good signs.

The road is hopelessly clogged with cars as we draw near the entrance to the school parking lot. We chug ahead a few car-lengths at a time as the cars ahead of us drop off mourners. When I look to my right, I see that there are a few cars and limousines getting special attention, disgorging VIP's, Oscar Benitez—school board president, which I might have expected, and Congressman Romero, which surprises me. The press is here too, some of them shooting video of the Congressman and anyone else they deem important-looking, then asking questions and shoving microphones at them. Four of the broadcast outlets have stationed their minicam vans near the auditorium, at least one of them in a fire lane. I scan for Laskeris but don't see him.

Thoughts about Francesca are like an earworm, more like an earsnake. For a few seconds, my consciousness abandons her, traitor that it is, and I feel only a general tightness in my abdomen. But then I remember what happened to her, and a horrible pang of regret seizes me, regret and rage and helplessness. She wanted the lights in her bedroom kept on, but we gave her half an Ambien at midnight, drug-abusive parents now, and she was able to sleep.

Burgoyne has told me that there will be patrol cars going by the house every half-hour or so, but I worry anyway. Jhonny is probably in hiding now, but I know Manny and Chucho were not just two guys who liked marijuana and santos.

I wish Ursa were still guarding my house.

"Lookit," Burgoyne says, pointing. "That car's pulling away from the curb. We can walk through the gate from here, 'stead of driving through. Easier to get out too."

The space is plenty big enough for my Camry and I pull into it.

Burgoyne says, "Hey, before I forget . . ." He pulls a revolver from an ankle holster and puts it into my glove compartment, along with a little box of ammunition. "I'd feel better if you had this. No paper on it—got it at a show."

*****

Inside the auditorium, most of the seats are already filled. On stage there are arrangements of roses and carnations and banners that read "In Memory of Usaré García" and "Our Precious Angel," along with a lectern for the eulogizers. The shell has been set up, and I speculate that there will be a performance by our orchestra or choir. Burgoyne has told me he plans to look for familiar people and keep his ears open, so he peels off toward one of the side aisles to begin crawling his eyes through the crowd. The conversational hum is louder and less somber than I expected, with unrestrained energy and occasional laughter from kids who are in no hurry to sit down.

The first teacher I see is Rocha, the special education teacher who helped chaperone the dance. "Della, how's it going?"

She leans forward to hug me, looking genuinely and deeply sad. She's wearing black, a narrow gown that stops at her knees, lace on the edges. She's tall and thin with reddish-brown hair going too early to gray. She asks about my wife and kids, and I wonder if news of my family's trouble has already leaked, but she doesn't wait for my answer, which relieves me. She takes on a look of devastation and talks about Usaré's death.

"She was so—" she shakes her head looking for the right adjective, aspiring for poetry I suppose.

"She was fabulous," I say, wanting to cut her off.

"Fabulous, that's the very word." She nods. "We're finally going to be back in our rooms on Monday I hear. The padlocks come off at six in the morning."

"Yes, I heard that too." I smile half-heartedly, wondering if she's a conduit for Jameson. "I didn't really conspire to keep you out, you know. No matter what Chris says." I try a broader smile.

"Now, Henry, c'mon. I thought you told us that sarcasm was the weapon of the weak."

"Just a line I picked up somewhere. But yeah, it was sarcastic. Sorry."

"It was hard on all of us. Chris was just carrying our water." It doesn't surprise me that she is defending him. She's a teacher with the perfect temperament to be a special education teacher. She puts a high level of energy into her work, and her work is tremendously difficult. The children assigned to her are all of low IQ, some of them very low. She writes individualized educational plans for all of them, as she is required, but what amazes me about her is that her plans are ambitious, and then she follows the plans religiously and documents them on almost a daily basis. She and her students maintain a vegetable garden in a greenhouse next to the special education building, and they're often bringing lettuce or tomatoes around for teachers and staff. I'd bet she never has a date night with her husband.

"Point taken." I don't see a smooth way to change the subject, so I just ask, "Usaré was in one of the classes where you're team teaching with Chris, I guess."

"Yes. Some of my higher functioning kids are in there that period."

"Did you ever notice anybody giving her special attention?"

"Special attention?" She snickers. "Everybody did. Especially the young men. You know that. You're starting to sound like that cop the other day, Simpson."

"Maybe it's my deep baritone." I try to make it sound humorous and not sarcastic. "You don't mind me asking, who or what were those guys interested in when they interviewed you?"

She stares for a moment, and I feel like I have to explain.

"They chewed on me for half-an-hour before they talked to you. Seemed to be zeroing in on Andre Carver. You remember him?"

"Sure I do. It surprised me at first, the way they suspected him, but the more I thought about it, the more it made sense. He *was* a little rough around the edges, poor kid. Plus she and Andre had their on-again, off-again history. I heard they already picked him up."

Somehow, I'd never thought of Andre as *poor kid*. "They released him too. Burgoyne told me. Not enough evidence to charge him." I decide to test my theory again. "What about Memo and his gang buddies? The cops ask about them?"

"That didn't come up."

I feel my liver producing bile. Doesn't Simpson know by now about Francesca, whose power to shape her own life was very like Usaré's? About

Jhonny, who held girls cheap? About Manny, who abducted them? I know now that I'm going to track Jhonny and find him.

I'm going to find him, and this time I won't let another man kill him.

"So what *did* come up?" I say.

"They mostly asked about the dance. Where I was . . . when my break was and where I was stationed for supervision . . . when certain kids came and left. Wanted to know if I saw Usaré leave, but I didn't. I heard she left early through a side door . . ."

"Did you tell Simpson that? What you heard?"

"Yeah, but they told me to stick to what I'd personally witnessed. Anyway, then they asked about whether any older boys tried to crash the dance . . . or if I'd seen suspicious activity in the parking lot . . . like if I'd seen Andre hanging around out there."

"Did you?"

"What? See Andre? I did tell them I saw a convertible cruise the parking lot a couple times, a few boys riding with the top down . . . told them it was blue and had those fancy chrome wheels, but they didn't seem all that interested in it. No Andre though."

"The convertible, did it have a funny looking thing coming out of the hood too?"

She nods, perplexed.

"Anything else they were interested in?"

"They also wanted to know all about the other teachers who were there, which I thought was odd . . . whether any of us left early."

"Did they? I mean, did anyone leave early?"

"Well, I was in the lobby the whole time. Just took a couple strolls through the dance to see how the kids were enjoying it. And of course I couldn't leave till Mr. Nuñez did. Our car is in the shop so Chris dropped me off and then Mr. Nuñez gave me a ride home."

"Did Chris hang around?"

"I don't think so."

"So, was that about it? What the detectives wanted to know?"

"They wanted to know if Usaré seemed clingy with any of us—the staff, I mean."

"Well, how about Usaré? Did she act interested in someone in particular?"

"You know her. She knew how to keep everyone interested, but she always paid more attention to the adults than anyone else. I guess you could call that clingy. She always wanted me and Chris to notice her and what she was doing."

"Yeah, I can see that. What did she do exactly? Ask a lot of questions?"

She nods. "She wanted feedback all the time on her work. She was doing a video bit about Mexican drug cartels. Senior mixed media project."

"Interesting topic. You put her onto that?"

"Don't know where it came from. I think she had some connection or something."

"Connection? Someone who dealt or something?"

"A lot of the kids know a dealer or two. No, I mean someone more important than a dealer, higher up. She had these notes she kept looking at, handwritten, which I thought was strange for her, being the tech-savvie thing she usually was." Della's face contorts then. "You don't think—"

"I do. Did you mention that to Simpson and Bejarano? About the handwritten notes?"

"No. I never thought about it till just now. You think that's important?"

"Could be. Course, by now, the detectives shoulda found them in her backpack or her locker."

"She didn't carry a backpack, Henry. You ever see her with one?"

I think about that. I stare mindlessly at the stage for a few seconds, and I'm sure I look like the last guy to catch on. "Somebody else would have carried her stuff, huh? Who would that have been in Jameson's class? Your class?"

"Chevy, I'd bet. Sat right next to her. Tried to get the attention of every guy who flirted with her. Kind of a rebound thing that worked pretty well for her."

I narrow my eyes at Della, and she understands it's a question.

"Usaré never dated guys more than a couple months. Usually, Chevy was there to lift their spirits when Usaré tossed them."

I am discovering that insinuations about Usaré no longer upset me. "Usaré dated Andre and probably Memo and maybe a couple other older guys. Chevy ever catch one of them on the rebound?"

"They were pretty secretive about that. I just kind of picked up on some things. And obviously you only see what's going on here at school. But Chevy tried to hook up with Andre, I heard, some time after Christmas . . . but he wasn't interested I guess. I think she was more successful with that newspaper man, forget the name."

"Laskeris? Jesus, Usaré dated him?"

Della nods. "I'm pretty sure. Then Chevy too."

"Son of a bitch should be in jail."

"Usaré had feminine charms. I bet you noticed them too, Henry."

I feel my face redden. "They ever talk about Memo Martinez? He's about Andre's age. Older maybe."

She shakes her head.

"Or the younger brother, Jhonny."

Another shake.

"You ever have occasion to read any of the texts she got during class?"

She gives me a puzzled look. "How would I do that? Kids don't let you see their texts."

I think back to what Jameson told me about seeing texts from Memo.

I say, "Well, I know you and Chris both do a lot of circulation during the lesson, just like they tell you to do in all the training. To monitor student performance, keep kids on task. I've seen you do that even when Jameson is lecturing. Just wondering if you might have seen something while Usaré had her smartphone sitting there on her desk."

Still puzzled, she says, "Usaré was very discreet that way. She'd sneak a look now and then, but we never had to tell her to put her phone away."

"Really? . . . So which teachers did you identify to Simpson as ones Usaré was clingy with?"

She stares for a long moment, then says, "The men, mostly. The handsome ones anyway—Chris of course, and her math teacher Steve Bergman and Pete Morales, the Mexican Studies guy. Even you, Henry, not so much this year, but a couple years ago there was some gossip about you and her." She seems a little embarrassed to add my name to the list.

I feel myself blush again.

"And a couple women too—Mimi and Nikki."

THIRTEEN

M r. Fontaine, our orchestra teacher, begins to assemble his string quintet to play some melancholy melody, and we both know the memorial is about to begin. Della smiles politely at me and moves to a seat that someone has been saving for her. I continue the slow descent down the aisle looking for an open seat, which is no longer easy to find. I am just about to give up and join the standing-room-only crowd along one of the outer aisles when Santana calls my name and stands, motioning for me to come sit next to her in the third row. It's in the center section, behind Usaré's family and closest friends, and among some of the VIP's. I wind up seated between Santana and one of the five members of our district governing board, an Anglo guy named Adams, who always smells faintly of beer and breath mints, and I wish Santana hadn't waved me over.

When he sees me, Adams takes on a look I can't quite classify as assumed sobriety or grief. I shake his hand and ask how his children are doing.

Fontaine's five kids are finished with their last-minute tuning and music stand adjustments. He is tapping the microphone, preparing to use it. He always exhibits a strong presence at performances—he tells everyone to silence their cell phones in a way that I never could, directly but without sounding like a scold. The audience grows quieter, some malingerers still chatting in the aisles. He steps to his own music stand, taps three times and directs.

It's "Dans Macabre," I know, because I've listened to them practicing the piece, and he's explained why he uses it in his program. His violinist, Hermione Vargas, is one of the best in the state, but she seldom places in competitions because Polk doesn't come up on any fine arts Google searches.

When the orchestral piece is finished, several of our girls come to the mike and simper through faltering tributes to Usaré, but it is Father John Walsh who gives the principal eulogy.

He is an old man now, gray-haired and gray-bearded and shrunk and stooped. He was something of a dandy, I've heard, when he first came to Saint Thomas as curate and headmaster of the school, young and handsome, with blond hair that ran to brown, hazel eyes, and ease in front of a crowd that endeared him to everyone. Oozing charm, he can still entertain the throng with humorous anecdotes and self-deprecatory asides, which help the crowd forget for a few minutes that they are here to mourn. Father John becomes the center of attention, which is, I suspect, his objective.

As I listen to him, I am reminded of Usaré, who had the same quality—people do not just like him; they want more than anything for him to like them.

There were ancient rumors about Father John's behavior with some of the Saint Thomas girls back in the day, the oldest of whom were eighth graders, but when we took our children out of the school, we paid no more attention to the gossip. I think about it now as he speaks, because I know two young parish women who've slept with him, one of them married, and I wonder how such a man decides when girlhood ends and womanhood begins.

I think of Francesca again, and my heart sinks, but I'm glad she left St. Thomas before puberty.

Then again, Della has just told me there were rumors circulating about me and Usaré not so long ago. Not without cause. Is Father John like Humbert and Rusic? Am I like any of them?

Father John speaks about Usaré's childhood, about her love for the ranch where her father cowboyed as a young man, her yearning to raise quarterhorses, her beauty, how her smile lit up a room for Christ sake, and I think of half a dozen people who could have eulogized her better—Mimi Nelson, John Klein, Amin, hell, even me—a brilliant young woman who wanted to change the world's trajectory and knew she could. He speaks of their personal relationship—her service to the parish, her devotion to the sacrament, which is a surprise to me. But then, the reputation of the dead is a hostage of the living.

He says that any good eulogy becomes a homily at some point, so he tries to salvage his remembrance by explaining how Usaré's life should instruct us, the friends and loved ones she has left behind. His text is Matthew, I think, the part where Jesus is explaining to his disciples that no one knows when the end may come, not the Christ, not Noah's neighbors who were partying until the flood came, and not our beloved Usaré. So we must be ready for the end by living our lives as she did, with deep loyalty to those whose lives we touch.

Loyalty? I think I would have focused on a different one of her attributes—her generosity, her warmth, her desire to lead her people—

loyalty not so much, but then I am not her priest, and no one asked me to extol her virtues at the lectern.

When Father John finishes, Usaré's parents ascend the stage and come to the microphone to thank us all for coming. Mrs. García needs help from her husband ascending the steps to the stage, and she can only stand sobbing at the lectern as her husband reads from a piece of paper. He says, "Mi mujer tiene tantas lágrimas que no puede hablar hoy. Usaré era nuestra hija de oro. Ella fue quitado antes de que ella creció." His voice trails away and he holds his hands to his face.

Adams leans closer to me and asks what the old man is saying.

"He says his wife can't talk because of her grief . . . that Usaré was their golden child and was taken away before her time."

Mr. García chokes back his sobs and reads again. "Ustedes son una especie de compartir esta tristeza con nosotros, pero sólo se puede preguntar por qué esto sucedió a ella. No hay respuesta. Mi mujer no puede soportar esto. Por favor, ayudarla."

Adams is still leaning, and I say, "He says we are thoughtful to share in their sadness . . . but why is there no answer to what happened. He wants us to help his wife with her grief." I remember what Andre told Burgoyne and me a few days ago, that Usaré's father always had a thing for her, an angle that Burgoyne and I haven't even talked about. Far-fetched to consider him a suspect though, since the murder happened in E building, even more-so after hearing him read.

They stand motionless at the lectern, heads down, though I sense Mr. García has finished reading his statement. He holds his wife close to him by her shoulder, as if he is waiting for something else to happen.

The mourners are silent though, not sure whether the service is over, and the silence lingers.

I am about to stand and go to help them wind things up, but it is Amin who rescues all of us. He appears from somewhere behind the curtains, steps to the lectern and embraces the two parents, then turns and speaks into the mike: "As we go forth now, into the bright sunshine, let us remember the words of Habakkuk, the prophet. 'Art thou not everlasting, O Lord, my God, my Holy One? We shall not die. O Lord, thou hast ordained them as a judgment; and thou, O Rock hast established them for chastisement. Thou art of purer eyes than to behold evil and canst not look on wrong.'"

He pauses, rouses himself and says, "Oh brothers and sisters, we shall not die, we shall not die, no we shall not die. Praise God, Usaré has not died, praise God, we shall not die."

Finally, there is an exodus, buzzing in conversation but filing out solemnly.

I nod to Adams and tell him I hope I see him again, which is only partially disingenuous. I thank Santana for the seat, but she tells me honestly she was saving it for Burgoyne until she saw him take a place along the auditorium wall.

I start to make my way toward the stage to thank Amin, who is still comforting the Garcías on stage, but then I see Pete Morales, chatting with a small group of kids, all Mexicanos, mostly girls, who would all have been students in MAS, Pete's Mexican-American Studies class. With them is an older woman, who is here to represent the Center for Latino Education and Defense. I recognize her from previous visits she made in support of MAS, but all I can remember from her last name is the hyphen. Morales is, was, Usaré's government teacher, an amorphous designation. Until last year, MAS was an elective class, but thanks in part to Usaré, thanks also to CLED, students can now take it in lieu of American History or American Government, which are required for graduation. I wait on the outer edge of their gloomy circle and listen. The kids ignore me for the most part, as does Pete.

The CLED woman glares at me hard and suspiciously, a litigation attorney's stare. I smile back.

". . . can't believe she's gone . . . she was everything to us . . . how could anyone do this . . ."

"We have our memories," Pete says. "Her spirit will always be there lifting us up."

"She was a wonderful young woman," I say. The students suddenly become aware of me and they begin to drift away in a cluster, looking back at the attorney expectantly. She keeps staring, so I offer my hand. "Enrique Tavish, assistant principal here at Polk."

After about five seconds, she extends her hand and says, "Pleased, I'm sure." She doesn't bother to introduce herself but simply draws away a few feet to rejoin the circle of MAS kids. I am the pariah, the Judas I suppose, the coconut who isn't even brown on the outside, the half-Mexicano who couldn't protect a sister—a kind assessment, I think, for the father who couldn't protect his daughter.

"Pete," I say, "how you holding up?"

"Not that great, actually. It's so crazy. One minute, she's here . . ." exuding sincerity.

"You're not alone, friend. Everybody's feeling the pain. All her teachers . . . I'm so sorry, man." The earworm is back. I think I should be pouring out my daughter's hurt instead of Usaré's.

He slowly shakes his head. "You don't know, man. My kids are taking this hard. She wasn't just a chica man, she was la alma, el corazón."

I nod gravely. Pete replaced Canseco, who left a year ago, and I wonder if he ever heard the rumors about Usaré and me. "She *was* el corazón," I say, "for the whole school."

Now it's his turn to nod gravely.

"So have the detectives talked to you yet?"

He nods.

"Yeah, me too. Was weird, don't you think?" I say.

"Bizarre. Talking about a dead girl." He's looking at the floor, shaking his head.

"Seemed like they already had a direction, don't you think? About who did it?"

"I don't know." Then Morales squints a little and says, "Yeah, at first they wanted to know about some guy named Andre, but then they started in on the teachers."

"Really. The teachers." Trying to do what Burgoyne does.

"Yeah. Asked me if she ever talked about any favorite teachers."

"For Christ sake. Did they ever ask about the Levantes?"

Pete shakes his head. "That street gang? Nah."

"Well, they didn't talk about them directly in my interview either. They asked about Memo . . . and Jhonny."

He's looking away from me, toward the MAS kids. "I don't remember any names like that."

"You sure? Jhonny Martinez? I'm sure they asked *me* about him."

Pete stares at me for several seconds. "What do you want from us, man? We're hurting." Like I can't know the depths of his grief.

I want to explain about Francesca and the reason I want to track Jhonny down, but Pete's pain shames me. "I'm sorry. We'll talk about it later."

Pete withdraws to the cluster of kids, who have been talking to the hyphenated woman. He hugs two of the girls.

Amin is helping Mr. and Mrs. García down the steps stage right, where a dozen or so relatives are waiting. The auditorium grows quieter as it empties. Only a few groups remain in the aisles and near the orchestra pit— Pete's group, the García clan, a couple others—dividing their grief in low tones. I look around for Burgoyne, but he is already gone, and I exit through the lobby.

On the patio outside, a pert blond reporter for one of the local television affiliates is interviewing Congressman Romero, and a few print and Internet reporters get as close as they can to listen. Not too far away, another affiliate, KIPP, is recording an interview with Oscar Benitez, governing board president. Nick Laskeris is listening to that one and taking notes on his tablet. Suddenly, I remember that Burgoyne intended to talk to Laskeris on Wednesday afternoon, but he never told me whether or not he did.

I know *I'm* not going to talk with Laskeris. I've read enough of his screeds to know that he nearly always injects a cynical tone into his articles, and the piece he did on Usaré was an exception. He considers gossip and hearsay to be quotable sources, and he doesn't adhere to any boundaries about a subject's personal life. In one column, he detailed the arrest of a thirteen-year-old boy to embarrass his father. Whatever information I get from Laskeris by chatting with him is not worth the risk of becoming the subject of one of his polemics.

Some people are heading for the parking lots, but most are making their way to the cafeteria where our staff is serving a lunch of green chile stew and tortillas.

I want to listen to what Benitez is saying, but I don't want to appear too obvious, so I pretend to watch the Congressman and the entourage that surrounds him, meanwhile drifting closer to the KIPP interview, straining to hear Benitez through the background noise. I don't pick up much: ". . . instructed the superintendent . . . school safety . . . accountability . . ." It's not enough to know who he's scapegoating.

When I give up and turn to leave, I see Burgoyne talking to Memo, who still reminds me of a kea bird, staring down at Burgoyne as if he were a sheep, and a guy in a plaid shirt, the two of them putting on a show for the cop. I wonder if they've heard about Chucho and Manny and the sheet metal house in Why. No need to be coy about listening to this interview, I think, striding across the concrete.

I say, "I see you found Mr. Martinez and one of his flunkies. You run the rest of his crew off?" Trying to keep the edge out of my voice.

Memo and the other guy look my way now.

Burgoyne keeps his eyes on the two of them, but he answers me. "Saw them across the auditorium. Came to pay their respects, I guess."

Memo is sporting his reptile boots again, cleaned shiny, and a long-sleeve shirt with a bolo tie. There's a toothpick stuck in the corner of his mouth. He says, "Yeah. 's too bad what happened, uh?" His sarcasm heats my blood, and I want to slap him.

Burgoyne takes a moment to remove his Ray-Bans, breathe on them and clean them with a fold of his polo shirt, somehow not squinting, his baby face implacable. "What I don't get is why you're here instead of running whores from your computer. Lot more money in that, hey?"

The two of them say nothing, staring at Burgoyne.

"No point beating around the bush, hey?" He puts his sunglasses back on.

Memo and his muscle guy still don't answer.

"I'm guessing my PD pals already talked to you, right?" He pauses, letting Memo make up his mind. "Last night or this morning. Am I right?"

"Yeah, I seen some cops. Couple times. It's cool," he says with a grin. "They wasn't interested in my escorts." Now he switches his gaze from Burgoyne to me.

Burgoyne, not wanting the focus to shift, says, "I'm told you're in some trouble with your Sonora friends. As of a couple days ago."

"Where you hear that?"

"From some friends of mine in Why. They told me you lost *two* big shipments over there. A hunnerd bales of grass . . . and something a little more dangerous."

Memo is forcing his grin now. He rolls the toothpick around with his tongue.

"Sounded to me like you might be in a little bind," Burgoyne says.

"Not as much as your friend here, the big one," pointing his hooked nose at me.

Burgoyne says, "Let me ask you something. You can't pay your debt, they just shoot you, or they give you a chance to buy them off? Maybe some girls for the grass? Your little sister for the fresh one that got away?" I don't like the way he refers to Francesca as the fresh one, but I keep my mouth shut.

"That what you're looking for? A payday?" Memo says to him.

I say, "The real question is what kind of payday you're willing to put out to stay alive. It's either me or your pals down south. All I want is a few bits of information, ya know? Like where your brother's holed up. I'm guessing the Sonorans want Jhonny's head and a whole lot more."

The guy in the plaid shirt raises his nose and sniffs.

Memo says, "You see that sign out there that says 'gun-free-zone'?" He points his nose at Burgoyne's new Glock and says, "How 'bout that?"

"I can pull it out if you want," Burgoyne says.

It gives them pause.

Burgoyne says, "Your brother's screwup is gonna get around and you'll be dead or out of business. Pretty soon, anyway. No more dope coming through there. No more girls going the other way."

The plaid shirt says, "You are nothin', man. You and you jodido güero."

"You wanna get into this?" Burgoyne says. "I'd be happy to break your kneecap for you. Tell me your name and what you're doing with this big son-of-a-bitch." Still the innocent face. "You wearing a bedspread, for chrissake. What's your name?"

"Spiritu." Proud of his name.

"I don't mean your street name, numb-nuts. I mean the name I look you up with."

He looks at Memo, who nods. Spiritu says, "Fernandez. Gonzalo. Want me to spell it?"

"You know how?" Burgoyne says, then to Memo, "Just tell me where Jhonny is."

"In Mexico, I think. Maybe Hermosillo," Memo says. "He still has friends there."

"Nobody believes that bullshit. He's down in a hole somewhere. Nogales, maybe. Too chicken to cross the border. You're bein' loyal to the wrong coyote, partner."

"My brother, he knows some trails across the border," Memo says.

Burgoyne says, "Somehow, Jhonny don't strike me as the outdoorsy type. Maybe he could get across with a guide on a nice bright sunshiny day, but he ain't had a good day since that dog ate his arm. Am I right?"

Silence.

"He been in touch?"

"He called my sister one day, I think." Memo grinning again, enjoying the chat.

"That makes sense," Burgoyne says, "Yesterday maybe. To find out what kinda mood you're in. Bet it wasn't good, hey?"

Silence.

"Was all Jhonny's idea, wasn't it? Going to Tavish's house . . . snatching the little girl . . . using the drop house to lay low. Was he in on it when those guys snatched the Robinson girl, or you guys just hear about it?"

Still silence.

"The detectives from the Robinson case scoured that place in Why yesterday too, after the first crew. Forencics guy's going over it again looking for her DNA. For any trace of her, really." He pauses to let it sink in. "You a betting man, Memo? I'll give you two-to-one they find something . . . a couple hairs maybe. Hairs are so easy to miss, you know— lay around for months. 'specially a place like that with all the plush carpet. Housekeepers don't really care, am I right?" He waits a couple seconds. "You probly strapped for cash though, I forgot, losing the shipment and all . . . a friendly wager then . . . say a dollar?" Burgoyne puts out his hand.

"You know, I think it's a sin to gamble with your life like that," Memo says.

"A sin? Really? You care about shit like that? I didn't think anybody talked about sin any more 'cept in church."

Memo swivels his hooked nose toward me and starts to peck."You talk to my seester, eh?"

"I talked with her."

"You like her a little too much, eh? Pretty girl, my seester." He's tried, but he can't shake the accent.

"Seems like a good girl," I say, recalling her standing unashamed in her panties when she answered the door a few nights ago, remembering her tip about the place in Why, thanking her for it in my head.

"She tell you how she work for the family, my seester? Thees good girl?"

"People do what they gotta do," I say.

"Yeah, I remember you pulling a piece on me the other night. I almost call the cops and tell 'em I got a home invader, man I'm terrified, could you shoot to kill the pendejo." He spits out the toothpick, aiming for me but missing.

If I had the Glock right now, I'd pull it. Instead, I pick up the toothpick and put it in my pocket and walk to the cafeteria. Inside, I look back through a window and watch Burgoyne say a couple more things to the thugs and then separate from them.

They wait until they are sure he will not look back and then they raise their hands and slap them together. It's not really a high-five for Memo, but he makes do. They are grinning and talking like two guys that just heard the best dirty joke ever told.

There are probably five hundred people in the cafeteria, half of them still lined up and trying to get their share of salad and tortillas and green chile stew. I have to admit, our cafeteria staff makes better Mexican food than most of the southside restaurants. It's all free today, paid for by several of the school clubs and a special donation from our local Pepsi distributor, who wants next year's vending machine contract.

Burgoyne finds me right away.

"What'd you think?" he says.

"I was gonna strangle one of them pretty soon."

He sees me looking out at Memo and his thug friend, and he turns and does the same. He waits.

"I don't know," I say. "I think he really doesn't know where his brother is right now, but he'll bail him out if he can . . . I worry about Rosa, the little sister."

"Yeah, you might have it right." After a couple seconds he says, "But he's gotta choose . . . between Jhonny and the cartel . . . I think he'd rather stay alive. And maybe he senses Rosa isn't quite trustworthy, but I doubt he suspects she gave you the place in Why. Or she'd be in a dumpster somewhere."

"Unless Memo's giving her up to the Sonorans for what he owes. Either way, there'll be some kind of contact with Jhonny pretty soon. Tomorrow. Maybe today. Don't ya think?"

"Mmm. Couple things you should know." He doesn't look at me as he says this, still stares out the window at the spot where Memo and Spiritu stood until a moment ago. "They like Manny and his friend Chucho for the Robinson abduction. All over it in fact." He's proud of this, because he's sure he guessed right, because he got them to take a fresh look at the case, "They'll wanna talk to you pretty soon . . . so they can compare it to what happened to Francesca." Not 'your kid,' but 'Francesca.'

I wait for him to go on.

"Simpson and Bejarano still want to talk to our boy Jhonny, but they don't think he did Usaré." We look at one another. "They still got a hard-on for Andre. If not him, maybe the wrestling coach. He left the dance right about the same time Usaré did. Then he lied about it. So they got him to give up a DNA sample."

I compare that to my visit with Simpson. "They ask for samples from anyone else?"

"Yeah, Amin, because he's the one contradicted Rusic."

"What do you think?"

"Rusic didn't seem to be concerned about it, so I'm guessing he didn't get too involved with her that night. As far as Memo or Jhonny, I'm not where you are, but I think Simpson's full o' shit about Andre."

I tell him what Rocha told me, about the blue convertible, same as the one we saw leaving the Martinez house, and his eyes widen. I tell him about the hand-written notes, about Laskeris being involved with Usaré, then Chevy too.

"I'd like a look at those notes," he says, and I start looking around the cafeteria for Chevy.

Chevy, though beautiful, is still a contrast to her poor deceased best friend, with dark skin, corn-row hair, a slim athletic figure and black eyes. She is a straight-A student, but she shows no inclination to lead a student movement or to get the attention of crowds. When we approach, she is standing with Mimi Nelson, Keanu Jones, a weepy Rachel Cruz, and half-a-dozen other kids—peer counselors. Chevy's only too willing to take us to her locker and give us the notes.

"You think there's something here helps you?" she asks, her eyebrows turned down, worried that she's betraying her friend. "I'da brought them sooner if I knew."

"Long shot, Chevy," I say. We're standing in hallway M, the math hall, at her locker. She's already opened her locker and handed over the yellow legal pads. Her eyes move back and forth between me and Burgoyne, whom it occurs to me I have not introduced. "Chevelon, I guess you haven't met Officer Burgoyne. He's our SRO."

"Hello, sir," she says, extending her hand a few inches. 'Sir'—still an honorific at Polk; adult women are addressed as 'Miss' most of the time.

Burgoyne shakes her hand for a moment, looking into her eyes with a faint smile, like an innocent child. "So happy to meet you," he says. "I think the notes may help. But you couldn'ta known."

There's an uncomfortable silence, but I finally say, "Did you see Usaré leave the dance?"

She's afraid now. She says, "No, she wanted to leave early and I didn't, so she left with my nigga."

"Your nigga?" I say.

"Keanu. He all up in her."

"All up in her?"

She smiles faintly. "I mean he like her, like he do anything for her."

"Why's that?" I say.

"Why any boy do anything for a girl?"

"When'd you leave the dance?"

"Jus' before midnight, same as everybody else."

"Except Usaré," I say.

She doesn't embellish anything, doesn't try to keep anything back. Keanu left the dance with Usaré to walk her across campus to the Park Avenue gate, where she was supposed to meet an older guy, Andre, she figured, since she knew Usaré had seen him Thursday and they were texting some in the afternoon, and, well, Usaré liked black guys, God knows why.

I say "One more thing if you don't mind, Chevy. Did you attempt to leave and come back earlier? With Usaré? Try to get one of the chaperones to let you do that?"

She hesitates, and I know the answer.

"Tell us about that."

"Well, I start my cramps all the sudden the middle of the dance, and I needed some ponies from out my purse in Marcus' car. Usaré, she say she and Mr. Rusic be cool, and he let her do 'bout anything she ask. Partly cuz she believe it and partly cuz she was showing off, the way she do. So we went to his door and ask if we can go out and then come right back."

"What time was that?"

"I don't know, Mr. Tavish. Like a couple hours before the dance end."

"Say ten or ten-thirty . . . Then what happened?"

"She's wrong about Rusic, cuz he won't let us leave and come back, and it piss her off, so she tell him he gonna be sorry, and some day she be there with bells on to tell everybody about him."

I say, "What did you think she meant by that?"

"It plain as day, Mr. Tavish. Don't you get it?" A seventeen-year-old girl making me look like a fool again. I look at Burgoyne, wondering if it's just me.

"Anyway, another girl give me some ponies, and I's all right."

"So that's when Usaré left?"

Chevy nods. "She say she gonna go meet someone."

"She didn't say who?"

She shakes her head. "I think it Andre. Maybe Memo . . . or maybe that reporter. She still see all them time to time."

"You notice which door?"

"It the one across from Coach Rusic. The south door where Mr. Morales was. He another one she think do anything she say." After a moment, she says, "Can I leave now?"

*****

We start examining the notes together in my office, but Burgoyne soon gives up, partly because they're mostly in Spanish and partly because he doesn't have much patience with a girl's notes: they're not neat, interrupted by superdoodles and tiny sketches of people that are not very good, Usaré being no artist, and clouds and stars and unicorns, and asides—notes to friends about boy X and teacher Z. I read aloud and tell Burgoyne what I think.

I thumb through, then come back to the beginning. "There's five of them that start with MM—Memo Martinez maybe?—with dates . . . not much on the first one—$45K/month . . . H but mainly mj—girls making K$/day—damn!"

I say, "Second one's longer, details . . . mostly numbers . . . 80b/month—bales?"

"That's my guess. Forty pounds apiece, maybe twenty grand each on the street. Serious money."

"Third one says 'Peligro!!!! Danger. CYA' Why's Memo even talking to her?"

Burgoyne says, "He's showing off, same way I would try to impress a hottie with my police work. Trying to get in her pants . . . or get in her pants *again* . . . or still trying to recruit her—show her how she's missing out."

After a pause, he adds, "You think that's Memo's, or whoever's, warning to her, or a reminder to herself? The CYA part."

I study the entry. "Says 'No puedes decirle a nadie, ¿ves?' That part like she's written it down word for word." I look up at a blank stare. "Means 'You can't tell no one, see?' Impossible to know but she's quoting him, I think."

"That girl had balls. What else?"

I study. "More numbers. It says, 'princ tuneles,' mostly tunnels, 'siempre cavando,' always digging. Twenty 'cruzadores,' crossers every week."

"Was there anything like a threat?" he says.

I thumb through it again, scanning. "March tenth—meet the Mexican—MI."

Burgoyne says, "Manny Ibanez. Our guy in Why. Any notes from the Mexican?"

I scan it more. "March twenty-fifth—MI—Sonoyta. Says I owe him now. More dollars in heroin—lower volume, less risk. Girls!! Glad Jhonny was there!!! There are a bunch of stars. Back in US at six AM."

"We gotta find that goddamn Jhonny. What else?"

I go back to the beginning and look through it again. "Numbers . . . dollar amounts . . . bales . . . I don't get it—why they letting her in on all this?"

"Good question, all leading to the same answer." He waits for me to see it.

"She won't be able to spread it around . . . dead maybe . . . or disappeared."

"Or they think they can recruit her with big money and heroin and fake promises."

"Pfff. Then they don't know Usaré."

"Yeah," he says. "A miscalculation maybe."

"So, maybe I'm right?"

He says, "I guess pigs really *can* fly," but he nods. "Anything else in the notes?"

I shake my head. "Unless your guys can figure something out." I hand them over and he nods. "What do we do now?"

"I'm gonna go talk to Laskeris again. He *did* make it inside the gym for the memorial, even though he was acting like a reporter."

"And that is important because . . ."

"If Jhonny wasn't the perp, then I'd bet you a hundred to one our guy was in there today."

"Over a thousand people there today," I say. "Memo was one of them."

"So were most of your teachers and staff. Morales, McNally, Jameson . . . even Amin."

"You see Rusic?"

He shakes his head. "You should go home and hug your kids after you drop me off."

"I want to." My heart sinks again, wondering how Francesca is managing.

He nods. "You might wanna keep your eye out for that convertible."

"Another hunch?"

"The connection to the Robinson girl was more than a hunch, Tavish."

"Nowhere near the same MO."

"No, but the motive was retaliation against the father, same as your case. And the missing persons dicks were always pretty certain there was a drop house in the Robinson case. So when your old Doc Rodriguez told us how banged up they were, I knew they had to be somewhere with their heads down. Plus, I figured Jhonny had the idea to snatch Francesca, but he didn't have the brains to get her across the border. He needed help from somebody who'd done it before."

"But this was so sloppy. In broad daylight, Abuelita getting their license number, apparently waiting around for me to get home . . ."

"They ran the tags yesterday—stolen car. And Manny wasn't intending to leave anyone around to tell the story. Your Rottweiler changed everything. Saved you and your grandmother-in-law. Maybe your boy too."

He lets it sink in, then says, "If you see it, get the tags on that car. Might be a link to Jhonny's whereabouts."

"How likely is *that*?"

"Those guys are watching everybody right now. Somebody's gotta pay for what happened in Why."

After I drop Burgoyne off, I decide to drive by the Martinez place on my way home, thinking there's some chance I'll see the convertible nearby. No luck.

What I do see, parked on the next block, is a white Mustang, air intake ports in the grille, Andre's car. He's sitting low in the driver's seat—still too distant to identify him, but I don't imagine it could be anyone else. I don't remember seeing him at the memorial service, but of course it was a big crowd. My first reaction is to try to disappear without him seeing me—my car is pretty nondescript after all—but making a Y-turn now would only attract his attention, so I keep going, thinking I'll turn at the intersection just this side of where he's sitting and pretend I haven't spotted him.

Impulsively though, I drive through the intersection and park my Camry right across the street from him and walk over to the Mustang. He glances at me, then gazes ahead like he's been doing it for a while.

"Kinda hot if you sit there very long, ain't it?" I say.

"I'm comfortable enough." He doesn't bother to look at me.

"Mind if I get in?"

"Door's open. You want a welcome mat?"

After I close the wide door, I say, "You parked here for some particular reason?"

"The cops think I's the one who did Usaré. You know that? Cuz o' that water bottle your boy Burgoyne took outta Lashawn's the other day. Matched my DNA."

"Yeah. Well, he's trying to clear you now. He knows you weren't the guy."

He glances at me for a few seconds, then stares down the street again. "What do you think, Mr. Tavish?"

"I think you were in love with her. And I think one of the Levantes killed her. Jhonny maybe, or Memo himself, or one of his goons."

"Seems like every man who met her fell in love with her. I bet you was too."

I wait before I respond. "So, that why you're here? You think it was one o' them?"

"I'd like it to be. Punk-ass gangbangers. They pee they pants they ever run into some gangstahs *I* know."

I believe him. His best friend in high school, a guy named Jimar, is still in the state prison on a murder beef. "So you're not convinced?"

"Not 'tirely. But I'm thinking it through, you know? And this the best place to do that. But I got questions, else maybe I already do something."

"Questions?"

"Like why they even want to do her? She jus' a nice looking girl trying to go places. I mean, so what if she doan wanna turn tricks? No skin off they nose. I doan get that."

"I know what you mean. Maybe she got to where she knew too much. You think that coulda been it?"

He considers this for a few minutes, silently, his eyes still fixed on the street ahead of him. "Memo know for sure she'd keep a secret. And there's the E building. Why Memo's boys do it in there? How they even get in? How they get her in there in the middle of a school dance?"

I think about what I know that he doesn't, and I think about telling him: that there are keys missing . . . that Keanu saw her let herself into the E building . . . that I also want Memo or Jhonny to be the perp, for my own reasons. I wonder what Andre would do with all that information: track Jhonny down? . . . kill Memo? I don't answer.

"So, what have you seen while you been sitting here? Anything interesting?" I say.

"Couple cars came and went."

"How 'bout a blue convertible?" I say it without thinking, then wish I hadn't.

He snaps his head at me. "That mean something?"

"It's been mentioned a couple times is all."

"Challenger, right? With an oversize intake? Who mention it?"

Now *I* gaze down the street while he glares at me. "It's probably nothing. Forget it."

"Mr. Tavish, I think you owe me. For letting that cop put it over on me."

I sigh. "I'll tell you, but like I said, it's most likely nothing." We're looking at each other now. "Some boys cruised the parking lot in it, the night of the dance. Don't know who or how many. Then I saw it pulling away from here the other night, Thursday, two cholos in it. Did you see it today?"

He goes back to gazing down the street. "Yeah, it come by. Two Mexican guys went in and come back out, five minutes, tops."

"You see the plates?"

He shakes his head. "Mr. Tavish, you think there's any way a teacher coulda done Usaré?"

"I'd hate to think so."

"Well, like I say, I been going over all this in my head, 'specially since those detectives grilled me—the brother and his Mexican sidekick. I keep thinking about the questions they ask me. One of the things was the key to that hallway. They musta asked me a dozen times if I had any keys to the school, if I knew anybody with keys, if I ever hearda anyone got keys. Well, o' course, teachers got keys, you principals got keys, monitors got keys . . ."

"Yeah, they asked me about keys too. They already talked to all the chaperones, and they're probably going to talk to everybody on the staff who's got a key to that hallway. They've been through her phone pretty thoroughly. I guess you got to the top of their list 'cause of your relationship with her. That and the recent contact."

He says, "Didn't know you principals made puns," and makes a low sound, almost a snort. "You know she always have a thing for older guys. She been with me and Memo. There's that newspaper guy. And they's stories about some of the teachers. Rusic, you musta heard those. And there's that one science teacher always trying to look down girls' shirts."

"Mr. Smith? You know how many times I've looked into that talk about him. That's all it is, Andre, talk."

"Well, I know it's more'n talk about Coach Rusic. How come you never look inta that?"

I don't want to blame anyone else or explain the principals' division of duties, so I say, "I did everything I could."

"Pfff. That guy ain't even a man. I swear to God somebody gonna pay for this, Mr. Tavish, but it's gonna be the right guy."

I know he means it. The silence, five minutes, is not comfortable. I want to tell him about my pain, about Francesca, but he has his own pain, and I realize he's right—I could have done more about Rusic, should have.

It's still hot when I leave, wordlessly.

I wouldn't be Memo now, not for all the tequila in Mexico—Andre just waiting to be sure.

*****

I expect to see Francesca bedridden and downcast when I get home, but she is in the back yard, toying with a soccer ball, looking for an opening as she goes one-on-one with NJ. She's still wearing the red 'all-heart' shirt. I watch through the kitchen window. This is when Ursa would be trying to join in, getting in the way, trying to eat the ball.

But of course Ursa isn't there. We are supposed to pick up her ashes Tuesday.

NJ doesn't have a chance. Francesca goes side-to-side a few times, feints hard enough to bring him out from his goal, the space between two oleanders, dribbles past him and scores. I get the feeling it's ten to nothing. Time to find her a counselor, maybe ask Ms. Nelson for a name. Meantime, I'll admire her resilience, whether it's pretense or not.

"Can I get you a whiskey?" Eloise asks, vaguely behind me. She's wearing a tee-shirt and walking shorts, no makeup—casual and unsexy and rare for her.

"Please." I see her holding a tumbler when I turn, a few cubes of ice in it, barely golden. "Let me get them. We can sit on the front porch . . . watch the sunset." I come and get the glass. "Rocks?"

"Whatever you do," she says.

I dump her ice and pour the whiskey neat, about a shot and a half, twelve-year-old, older than Francesca or NJ. I hand her the whiskey and sit next to her in an old-fashioned metal chair and say, "You're a blessing."

I can't help noticing Ursa's blood stains, remembering what Burgoyne said.

"I do love you, you know," she says.

"It's pretty obvious. Maybe it shows a lapse in judgment, but I'm thankful for it."

"You're a goof."

"You saved Francesca. Or at least you saved me. I never would have known what to do."

"Of course you do. You love her. As long as she knows that, she'll be okay. Anyway, it's not over. She looks like she's coping, but she's in some kind of denial or something."

"She seems so . . . okay. Monday, I'm going to ask Mimi Nelson to recommend someone—a psychiatrist or someone."

"Mimi—that's your school counselor?"

I nod. "I wish I would have come home ten minutes sooner. Maybe . . ."

"You can't bargain with the past, Ricky. If you'd come home ten minutes sooner, maybe I'd be going to a quadruple funeral and maybe Francesca would be in Hermosillo now. I may be the luckiest woman alive."

I sigh. "I thought women were from Venus."

"Not this one."

We both sip whiskey.

"I don't know what to do next," I say.

"Doll, you can't fix everything. I know you want to. Let Francesca be herself. She's probably tougher than you or me."

It's a minute or two before I speak.

"So, did Burke say anything interesting?"

Eloise is not a woman to hesitate. "He offered me Western District. Senior VP."

"Nice!" I say, hoping that I sound convincing. "Congratulations!" lifting my glass.

She says nothing, staring at a car as it rolls by, a rumbling blue convertible.

I don't react fast enough. For some reason, I feel as if I have to pretend the car means nothing, like Eloise and the kids don't need to worry, and I stroll out to look at the tag, still carrying my drink for Christ sake. The convertible speeds away, and I don't get the whole number.

Standing in the front yard, I call Burgoyne and leave him a message about what I have: "Didn't look like an Arizona plate, all white, hyphens, 'WCV-89-something. Two more numerals.'" Then I go back and sit down with Eloise.

"What was that about?"

Eloise doesn't like fibs. "Burgoyne told me to look out for a blue car."

"That one?"

"I don't know. I left a message."

There's a long silence.

"Are they coming back?"

This time I'm sure, and I set my jaw and I don't hesitate. "Not a fucking chance."

"Francesca doesn't need anything else to happen. Her nightmare isn't over. It may never be over," she says.

"You think I don't know that?"

There's another long silence.

"I won't let anything happen. I'll kill them if I have to." I think about Chucho and Manny. Then I realize this is not language she is used to—euphemisms for rape . . . talk about killing. "I didn't know this was gonna happen."

"We're going to be fine." She covers my hand with hers. "What you want me to do?"

I have the feeling this is a question she's never spoken in her life, and I want to cry. "If there was just some way to undo it," I whisper, and she pulls me down to her lap. "God . . ."

She strokes my head, says nothing for a few minutes, then, "I told Burke I wasn't ready."

FOURTEEN

My text alert sounds at 5:45, Sunday morning. It's from Burgoyne. 'Laskeris a possibility. Plate probly Sonoran??? Talk soon'
The house is still asleep. Soon a second text: 'Apt on 2nd St. See you at Mija's. 7:30'

I put on my shirt and trousers, the same ones I wore yesterday, and my sandals and go outside to the storage shed and find my dad's four-ten, plus the ammo for it. I remove the lock, load it with slugs and bring it into the bedroom.

Eloise is still half asleep when I come back, but she notices. "What's that?"

"Protection machine. Just for comfort."

"I like comforters." She smiles a little.

"Chances are we won't need it. Six shells in there, but the safety's on. You ever fire a shotgun?"

"My daddy used to take me duck hunting. I was the better shot too." She waits for me to look at her.

I set the gun behind the door, the box of slugs on Eloise's dresser. "I have to go meet Burgoyne. Should be back in a couple hours. That okay?"

"Some asshole comes to bother us, he'll wish he hadn't."

*****

Mija's is busy early Sunday morning, which I didn't expect, and I wish Burgoyne had picked another place. Congressman Romero is sitting in a booth with three men, labor guys I think. Two men I don't know are chatting with Board President Benitez. I feel like everyone recognizes me.

Burgoyne seems unconcerned with the pre-mass politics, assuming the face of an altar boy. Again.

"Who you think they are?"

Burgoyne says, "Not the Sonorans Memo's worried about, or they'd have already done something. Friends o' Jhonny's I think. Carrying messages back and forth from Jhonny. And keeping tabs on you and your family, other people too, just in case.

"In case?"

"Bargaining chip. For all we know, you're part of the price of getting Memo off the hook." He says it matter-of-factly, like I'm a piece of furniture. "Your family too."

I can't say his assessment doesn't bother me, but I continue. "Okay, that explains why we saw them the other night parked in front of the Martinez place, carrying a message one way or the other, but why were they cruising the parking lot the night of the dance?"

"Mighta been something random. But it fits your theory of the case, don't it? They're Levantes or allies of the Levantes. Jhonny may have even arrived with those guys. Your special ed teacher, Rocha, noticed the car and a bunch of guys in it. She probably couldn't describe 'em, but she put that car close to the crime scene. Damn close, hey?"

"How you like my theory of the case *now*?"

"Makes more sense now than it did. I wish we could get Jhonny's DNA, compare it to the samples from your girl."

"What about Memo's? Does that help?"

He tilts his head.

I reach into my pocket and produce a toothpick, well chewed on one end. "It's the one Memo spit at me yesterday. Course it's contaminated with pocket lint . . ."

"Put it down," he tells me. Then he calls our waitress for a doggie bag. "The chain of possession makes it worthless as evidence, but still might tell us something, gives us investigative probability." When the waitress returns with a bag that says 'Bones for Bowser' he uses it to pick up the toothpick and then ties it closed. "For now, let's just say I was the one who picked up after our friend yesterday."

"For the sake of argument?"

"It's more likely I can get the lab guys to put your toothpick at the front of the line and do their DNA-chip test that way."

"DNA-chip test?"

"It's faster than the usual process. They did it the other day with the semen too."

"Thought you were on administrative leave."

"I got friends at the lab, so the chief don't have to find out. If he does, I'll just say I felt like I had to go to the funeral and then I just happened to see the guy spit out the toothpick. Just made sense to pick it up, since the PD interviewed him the other day."

Burgoyne has an address for the convertible, and he came here thinking we would go watch the place and follow the convertible and see what developed.

"Guy's name is Gallardo, Leon Gallardo. Car's registered in Sonora, but he's got a local address. He crosses the border at Lukeville at least twice a month and the Homeland Security guys told him he needed to get a car with Arizona tags. That's how we tracked it down so fast." He shows me a photo of Gallardo, which looks like it was taken by some surveillance camera.

Burgoyne's more interested in the toothpick now, and he proposes swapping vehicles so I can stake out the address on Second Street while he goes to see his friends in the lab.

"In your Crown Victoria?"

He shakes his head. "I came in my pickup. They'll never recognize you in that, even if you're parked right across the street." I'm sure he's right since I've never seen him driving anything but the Crown Vic. When I look out through the window, he adds, "It's the Dodge with the deep tint. You better empty your bladder before you go. Take a cup to piss in too."

I take the gun from my glove box and swap keys with him. "What about the address?"

"I'll text it to you."

When I drive past the Second Street apartment building, I see the Challenger convertible right away, but I begin to have doubts about parking too close. The neighborhood is a sketchy one, and Burgoyne's truck may be flashy enough, black and new, to get Gallardo's attention. I wind up parking along the curb about a hundred feet west of the entrance. I text Eloise to tell her it may be more than a couple hours. She responds after a few minutes: 'Fine. Watching Fantasia.'

I sense some irritation and I reflect—am I dumping on her? I text 'How's Francesca doing? . . . what's NJ up to? . . .'

The apartment building is a tawdry, U-shaped one-storey affair, and judging from the cars in the parking lot, it houses residents who are none too prosperous. In the commons area, a prepubescent girl dangles one foot over a knee and talks on her cell phone, two toddlers near enough to her that I think she's been told to supervise them while they play. I can see the front side of the built-up roof, which is bare of its white coating in several areas, especially near the rusty evaporative coolers. A parking lot with older, paint-faded cars, peeling tawny paint on the walls, cracked mortar seams . . .

The day is getting warm, but Burgoyne's car is a luxury to me: almost new, plush bucket seats, Kenwood stereo. When I turn on the radio, I notice Burgoyne has it set to a country and western satellite channel. I find a classic hip-hop station, but I keep the volume low and try to keep my ears open as

I watch the building. There's not much to see. Occasionally, a car or some scruffy-looking pedestrians pass by.

I text Eloise: 'I owe you more than I can say.'

Nothing comes back. I nestle into the seat and listen to Cypress Hill, NWA, Run Doctor, thinking I need to drop some hints to Eloise about wanting satellite radio for Christmas.

A faded Ford Focus pulls in and jerks to a stop. The driver gets out, a twenty-ish guy, angry about something, and stalks toward his apartment, wearing a once-ironed white shirt and a red tie, carrying a black coat over his arm, not looking back. Half-a-minute later, a woman climbs out from the passenger side. She's pregnant and not moving fast. She opens the back door and retrieves a child in blue overalls from a child seat and follows.

Run-DNC sings about how tricky it is to make lyrics rhyme.

Two young women, tending to chubby, appear from Number Three and march to a nineties-vintage minivan and drive away.

I text Eloise again.

I study the pistol Burgoyne gave me. It's a Beretta, with a barrel shorter than the handle. The lettering on one side identifies the model, Tomcat. The safety is on the left side—operates by preventing the slide from moving, Burgoyne said. The magazine holds seven, but I could put one in the chamber if I want, so it's ready to fire. Not smart, I decide. The sun rises higher in the sky, heating the street around me, and I shift in my seat and start the engine and run the air conditioner until I get comfortable again.

About eleven-thirty, a squarish, old-model Ram pickup rolls to a stop and drops off six young Mexican guys, back from a Sunday morning job, toting work gloves and garden tools and a case of Budweiser into one of the apartments. I make them for Mexican nationals, border crossers working for cash on Sunday morning, just below minimum wage, to pay the rent. I wonder if guys like them really do hold down the cost of labor.

There must be a thousand landscaping outfits in this town—two guys, a truck, a trailer, some rakes and hoes, a leaf-blower—Angry White Dude and Son, LLC, working just *above* minimum wage, and bitching all the time. Call it ethnic pride or whatever you want—I always hire the guys with brown skin, no matter what the law says.

Leon Gallardo comes out of number six wearing a white tank top. He's short and slender. He walks like the guy I saw Thursday night, swinging his arms, and I assume he's the same guy. Right behind him comes some pal of his in a plaid shirt. What did Burgoyne call it—a bedspread?

It's the same little shit we saw at the memorial service—Spiritu.

I worry that I'll to have to make a U-turn to follow the convertible, but they make it easy, heading east, and I pull away from the curb and fall in.

It's a thing I know nothing about, following somebody in a car. Am I too close? Too far back? How long before he sees the same car in his rear-view mirror? Do I trail along close and hope he doesn't notice a big black Dodge, or do I hang back and risk losing him?

Leon uses arterial streets, south then west. I stay close but I still have to run a red light. When I get the chance, I voice-text Burgoyne: 'They're heading west side . . . following' When the convertible makes a left onto Sixth Avenue, Leon goes through on red, barely avoiding a compact sedan but catching a horn blare and a finger, and I start thinking he's spotted me, so I wait my turn at the light while he zips away. While I sit through the light, I text Burgoyne again: 'Going south now . . . they slipped me at a light. Hunch . . . Memo's?'

He texts back: 'Made you?'

'Looks like'

When I finally get the green, I stomp on the accelerator, trying to catch sight of them before turning into Memo's neighborhood. No luck, but my hunch is right. The convertible is parked on the street right in front of the Martinez house. Leon and Spiritu are not in sight, so I park again, far down the block this time, wondering whether they really knew somebody was tailing them. Wondering too, whether Burgoyne is right about these guys acting as messengers for Jhonny. Seems so primitive. Why not just use a throw-away cell phone? Afraid the cops are able to locate him? Burgoyne says they don't even need a warrant to track location in Arizona like they do in Illinois. But if he had a new phone, they wouldn't know it was Jhonny without listening in on Memo's conversations, which they can't do unless they get a warrant. And Memo's not a suspect in a crime.

Not yet.

So if they're go-betweens, they're probably extra careful about not being followed.

Are they in contact with the cartel guys too? It makes me think of Francesca, and I feel terrible again.

I glance at the García porch, where very little of Usare's shrine remains.

It's a few minutes after noon when Leon and Spiritu come down the steps from the house. At the bottom, they turn and look at Memo, who's come out now. Some parting words, Memo doing the talking and the other two seeming to agree. I start the Dodge's big engine. They finally pull away.

I'm still wondering how far back to tail them this go-round when Andre's Mustang appears from around the next corner. From the way his car is moving, I know he has no hesitation about staying close to the two Mexicans. I fall in behind him as fast as I can.

Our little parade goes west again, along US 86 now, and I wonder if Leon is leading us back to Why or to Ajo or if he's going all the way to the

Lukeville crossing. I fall back a hundred yards and let Andre make all the decisions about tailing the convertible, wagering he's done something like this before.

I start getting uneasy about Eloise and Abuelita and the kids . . . the way Leon drove by the night before . . . the loaded shotgun . . . the cops patrolling . . . Eloise's confidence . . . but then, the way she won't respond. I pick up my phone to call her, but I see there's a message and wonder why I never heard the alert. Going sixty-five, but I read it anyway.

It's from Burgoyne: 'Iffy on the toothpick . . . wasn't Memo maybe a relative'

I use the voice-to-text: 'Can you check on my family'

'K Where are you'

'Trailing the convertible west on 86'

After fifteen minutes or so, my phone vibrates.

"Hello?"

"Hi Ricky. Saw you texted." Eloise's voice sounds relaxed.

"Yeah. Just checking in. I should be there to make pancakes."

"Yes, you should." Scolding now, and I know they're safe.

A quarter-mile ahead, the Mustang slows, goes left, south on the road to Sasabe, accelerates. I concentrate on the turn and don't say anything for a moment.

"Are you there," she says.

"How's everybody doing?"

"Not completely perfect. NJ got teary about the dog, and Francesca slapped him."

"Not good."

"I sat with her, but she didn't want to talk."

I wish I could go back and finish Manny myself . . . take the threats seriously . . . unthrow Jhonny off the porch . . . "It's hard for her."

"I'm afraid it's going to get harder, poor thing."

"I'll get a referral from our school counselor tomorrow."

"Mimi?"

"Yeah."

"Hey."

"Mmmm."

"Thanks for sending that cop over . . . You're driving aren't you?"

"Yeah, I better go."

We are speeding. The highway's shoulder is narrow, perhaps eighteen inches in most stretches, and the pavement needs crack repair and resurfacing. I am driving seventy-five when the road allows, but the Mustang is a half-mile ahead and pulling away. I have no idea how far ahead the Challenger is. The route is fairly straight but hilly, and I have to slow down for every rise or risk being launched like some guy coming off a ski-jump. It's not long before I lose contact with the Mustang, and I decide to poke along at ten over the limit.

Since I am not watching taillights, I look around at the terrain, which is rugged and lovely, thick with creosote and mesquite, cholla and nopal. From the southeast, thunderheads appear, which surprises me, but then I haven't been watching weather reports the past few days.

Several cars pass me going north, one of them a Border Patrol vehicle, and I wonder what the BP officer did when he saw the two hot cars flying south. Ignored them? Radioed units down south? You can't drive very far without seeing another one of the green trucks, but it's their job to catch migrants and contraband, not speeders.

A dry wash or a dirt road intersects the highway every couple miles, but all I can do is slow down and squint into the distance looking for one of the cars, then keep driving.

At one of the dirt crossroads, I see a dust trail rising and dissipating, but I decide it's a better bet to keep driving south and look for the next mile marker so I can find the road again.

Somewhere north of the Arivaca turnoff the Challenger appears out of a distant dot on the road and roars past me going north. I slow at first, but I realize I'd never be able to stay on their tail, so I keep going south, expecting Andre to scream past me any moment. I try to call Burgoyne. No service.

I text him 'Leon heading north to 3 points' and watch the little circle my device makes on the screen as it tries to send.

A few miles farther south, near a narrow dirt road leading west, sits the Mustang, parked in a bare patch along the road. Andre's leaning against it, watching me through his pilot sunglasses, his arms crossed at his chest, still, like he could lean there like that all afternoon and never budge.

"Lose 'em?" I say.

He doesn't bother to answer. He strolls to the passenger side of the pickup and starts to climb in. He sees my little Beretta on the seat and pauses until I set it on the dashboard.

"They saw me for sure, but I pulled 'longside and made like I wanted to race. They bought it."

"You sure?"

He nods. "They beat me."

"So what are you doing here?"

"They went down that road right there. Had to slow way down, then gave 'em the fist when I went by. Hauled ass like I's goin' to Mexico."

I back up a few feet and look west. "You sure? Not much of a road."

"Got outta the car and watched from over the next rise. They went down that road, then come back after while and headed north again. You musta seen 'em." After a moment, he adds, "Go slow. Can't be far . . . I heard about your family, coach. That's messed up."

I turn off the road and we spend a few minutes idling up the trail, which is defined by two worn ruts winding through a thicket of scrubby mesquite and over little rises. We approach a hill and I say, "Maybe we should walk."

He nods. When he pivots to get out of the truck, I see a Beretta nine stuck into the back of his pants at the belt line.

I take the little gun off the dash and put it in my pocket. We walk slowly in the ruts, up and over the hill. The clouds are far away but building in earnest.

Over the crest and down, and another two minutes' walk, we see a building that must have once been a rancher's cottage, then a line shack when the homesteader got more prosperous or sold out to a neighbor, plastered adobe in need of a fresh whitewash, with a rusted roof. There's a propane tank in the clearing and a water pipe coming from a wellhead.

Jhonny Martinez is sitting with his legs extended on a lawn chair in the sun near the stoop, holding a brown bottle and listening to something through ear-buds, nodding his head to some beat. He's wearing dungarees, sunglasses and a stiff-looking wrap on his right forearm.

I'm remembering Francesca and Ursa . . . the way Burgoyne finished Manny.

"Sssst," Andre says. He taps his chest, makes a half circle with his hand. He's going to circle around.

I shake my head and point at myself. Andre makes a tiny nod and draws his pistol and moves to a spot next to a mesquite tree.

I fade back and start making my circle around the clearing, moving slow, stepping high in the range grass and watching Jhonny and the cabin appear and disappear in my line of vision, hoping my luck holds, until finally the corner of the line shack is between me and him. Then I advance, angling for the side of the shack, stepping high, hearing the whisking sound my trousers make in the grass and wondering what Jhonny can hear around his earbuds, looking down with each step to avoid twigs and trip hazards, glancing toward Andre's spot for any signs.

Under the eaves of the tin roof, I flip the safety down, wishing now that I'd put a round in the tube and wondering if Jhonny would hear me if I racked the slide.

Or that I'd thought to put some extra rounds in my pocket.

Too much thinking.

I run out and stand in front of him and point the pistol at his chest, but he keeps his head moving in time with some beat that's coming from his I-pod, so I kick the side of his calf. He pulls his legs back and starts to lurch up but sees the pistol and freezes. I liked kicking him and I am tempted to do it again. "Stay there."

He makes a face like he's going to spit. He still looks like a Harris's sparrow, but wearing sunglasses now to hide his beady eyes. "You ain't gonna shoot nobody."

"I wouldn't mind." I pull the pistol's hammer back.

His expression changes, but he still wants to act a part. "You dog bust my arm, man," like he's going to get even for it.

"Sorry. We taught her to go for the neck."

His sunglasses pivot a few inches, and I know he can see Andre coming across the clearing behind me. An odd feeling comes over me, confusion. I realize the uppermost thing in my mind has been to track down this son of a bitch, but I've not thought about what's next.

Andre enters the line shack, to sweep it, I suppose. Then he returns, tosses aside Jhonny's sunglasses and his I-Pod, and lifts him by the shoulder. He pulls him inside the shack and uses some cotton clothesline to tie his arms and legs to one of the stiff oak chairs near a little Formica table. He takes the nine-millimeter from the back of his pants again, forces it into Jhonny's mouth and pulls the trigger. Click! Then he puts the gun away behind his back.

"Mr. Tavish need you to tell him a few things now. I hope y'all show some respect." He pulls the gun again and fires a round into the back wall of the place. He's still wearing his sunglasses, but I imagine I can see the fierce glare he's putting on Jhonny. He's closer to Jhonny than I am.

I want to kill Jhonny, but as the ringing in my ears fades I remind myself to sound calm, even though my insides feel like a twisted towel. I move to a soiled sofa and sit and set the pistol next to me.

"So let's start with last Saturday."

Jhonny's eyes are wide from Andre's stunt, but he says nothing. After a minute, I pick up the pistol, point it at Jhonny's head and pull the trigger. Snap! Then I fire a round out the open doorway and set the gun down next to me again. "You know, you hurt a man and you can probably intimidate him, but you hurt someone he cares about, it can make a man kind of crazy, and it usually doesn't end well for you."

He says nothing, but I can tell he's not sure of me now.

Andre slaps him.

"I'm pretty sure you know what happened to your pals Manny and Chucho, but I tell you, I have one big regret about that night. Know what it is? . . . I had the chance to kill a man who hurt my daughter and I didn't do it. Believe me, I'm not gonna regret what happens here this afternoon. You got one chance."

"So what you wanna know?"

"Start with the part where you were cruising the parking lot. Go from there."

"Started about ten. Was four of us."

"Was Manny there? Spiritu?"

He shakes his head.

"Who was it?"

"Neto and two of his friends."

"The firebug? Where was Leon?" I say.

"He wasn't there, man. He lets Neto use the car when he's outta town."

"Leon was in Mexico?"

He nods.

"Leon tight with Manny's crowd?"

"No way man. Leon jus' a friend."

"What about Spiritu? He's getting' tight with your brother, you know." He doesn't say anything, thinking about it. "Spiritu's gonna carve you up, little man, and Memo's gonna hand him the knife."

"Memo's solid, man."

I decide not to argue. "So how many times you guys come through the parking lot?"

"Jus' twice. About nine. Then a couple hours later."

"So like twelve. Same crew?"

He nods again.

"What'd you do in between?"

He makes the expression like he's going to spit again. "Whatchu wanna know that for?"

Andre leans in and says, "What you do for a couple hours?" I'd have told him anything.

"Jus' hung out. Neto wanted to see my seester."

"So what were you expecting? When you drove by?"

"Whatchu think? Usaré said she be leaving early. Trying to hook up again."

I remember what Burgoyne said about the DNA. "Again?"

Jhonny starts this exaggerated grin. "Yeah, *again*." He dares a look up at Andre, who's still wearing his sunglasses, and I begin to wonder if Jhonny will survive the afternoon. I think I have mastered my own hatred for the moment, but I know I won't argue very hard with Andre if he doesn't want to let Jhonny see the inside of a police station.

"So you didn't see Usaré that first time. What did you see?"

"Nothin'. Everybody was inside dancing." He sneers.

"You get out of the car? Stroll around a little? Maybe near the E building?"

"¡Jódete! You ain't puttin' that on me. I never got outta the car."

"Oh, well that explains everything. I'm so relieved, I'm gonna come hug you. What you think, Andre? You wanna give Jhonny a hug?"

Andre says nothing.

"I got witnesses, pendejo. Neto 'n them."

"Okay, well tell me what you and your witnesses did the second time."

"We come by the E building on Park Avenue, pendejo."

Andre doesn't let this one go by. He slaps Jhonny on the ear, raising the chair legs under him. "You not hearin' so good when I say *respect*?"

Jhonny is wincing but he gets his answer out. "We come by the E building and I see a guy come outta there. Gringo guy."

"Well, sure, Pancho Villa. Sure it's a gringo. And I'm just picking on the poor Chicano now. What else you gonna say, Chocho? Next you'll be saying was me come outta there. Maybe James K. Polk his own self."

He's boiling with rage now, straining against the cotton ropes, pursing his lips. Andre slaps him again.

"You better quit making shit up, Chocho. I don't think Andre has much more patience. It was too dark to tell—gringo, Mexicano, black guy. You see in the dark?"

"Was a gringo. You guys can slap me all you want, and it'll still be a gringo. Walked like a gringo."

"I get it. Gimme a description."

"You tell me iss too dark then you want a description. Mierda."

Andre raises his hand, and Jhonny cringes.

"He was tall."

I wait and he sticks out his chin and says, "Taller 'n this nigger here . . . but shorter 'n you."

Andre does nothing. There's almost a smile playing around his lips, a hawk watching a strutting quail.

I say, "What else?"

"Walking fast. I dunno, man. He had funny looking arms. He was dressed all black but his arms stood out."

I think of Rusic. "Did he walk like a jock?"

Jhonny doesn't know what the hell I'm talking about.

"Kinda bowlegged?"

He takes a moment, thinking back, shakes his head, not meaning no but he's not sure.

"How 'bout his build?" He doesn't understand or pretends. "¿Que clase de fisico?"

"Flaco. Quizá regular."

"On the thin side," I say, mainly for Andre.

"What you mean saying his arms stood out?"

"They a different color, man, like white or tan or something."

"Anything else?"

He smirks again. "Your daughter, she a lot of fun, you know?"

I wait a few seconds, then pick up the pistol, walk over to Jhonny and put it in his face. He puts out his pouty lip, so I point the Beretta between his legs and pull the trigger.

It shocks me more than Jhonny, I think, and he is terrified, lurching back and throwing his legs apart. Too late. I can see a tiny hole in the pooched-out part of his jeans, and I wait to see if blood begins to seep through the cloth. His slick black hair still reminds me of a Harris's sparrow, but his eyes tell me he's a terrified sparrow now, and it gratifies me to see him that way, exhilarates me, even though I know I'll probably get in some kind of trouble now.

He grimaces suddenly and bends forward, straining at the cotton cords. From pain, I think.

Andre says, "You got more questions for this little motherfucker?" When I shake my head, he starts untying the rope and says, "Figger we'll take the chair along. It got a chunk a lead in it. Maybe leave it somewhere."

Now I'm the one who can't read Andre's eyes through his sunglasses.

"Too bad he come at you like that . . . 'stead of just coming along peaceful. He lucky you aim low." Jhonny is moaning, but Andre lifts him and ties his hands behind his back. "What's that mean, anyway? Chocho?"

"Pussy, more or less."

After he finishes his knot, Andre steps to a counter near the refrigerator and picks up a pistol, Jhonny's I guess. "Here," he says. "It's loaded." I put the little Beretta in my pocket again and take it from him. It looks just like Burgoyne's service gun, a Glock.

"Time to take a little walk, Chocho," Andre says.

"I'm shot, man."

"You're just boozy, Chocho. Start walking." He gives him a little shove.

Outside, he leads us to the spot where I first pointed my pistol at Jhonny and says, "Lemme see that thirty-two." When I hand him the little Beretta, he fires it into the ground a few inches in front of the lawn chair and hands it back to me.

It will be at least a month until the high temperature hits a hundred, but it feels hot in the sun as we walk along the dusty road toward the car. It occurs to me that we are an odd-looking troop, Jhonny leading the way, hunched over from pain or from the way he's tied, Andre carrying the little oaken chair and one end of the cotton rope, me next to him holding the big pistol.

We are silent for over a minute, then Andre says, "Important you know what I just seen."

I wait.

"I seen you jump out from behind the shack and get the drop on Jhonny here. Course I's far away and couldn't hear, but it look like you gave him a warning . . . and give me a chance to come up and help. But then I seen him kinda jump from the chair and come at you. And that's when you shot o' course . . . look like you drop your aim so's not to kill him.

"Look to me like it startle him more 'n anything . . . barely hurt him. But enough so's I could come help."

"You don't need to worry about me. I'll probably go to jail now, no matter what you say."

"I ain't ever worried. You might remember it some other way, but I'm jus' telling you what I seen, Mr. Tavish."

We don't say any more, and I wonder what Jhonny is making of Andre's recollections.

The southeastern sky has turned purple, its clouds laced with lightning. The road rises, and we all lean forward into the climb, knowing Burgoyne's pickup is just over the hill. Approaching the crest, I hear a motor running, grumbling, a truck's diesel engine, and a thrumming bass from some music. The three of us slow down at the same time.

Jhonny is three yards or so ahead of me and Andre, and he can see over the crest about a second before we can. As soon as he does, he drops like a well bucket. "Fuck. It's them."

Andre and I stoop now, watching Jhonny, whose eyes are wider now than when Andre stuck the gun in his mouth.

"We gotta get outta here."

Andre and I move up slowly . . . tentative steps . . . furtive looks.

Blocked by Burgoyne's pickup on the narrow road, sits another truck, modified into a red monster, at least two feet higher than the Dodge. Both its doors stand open, corrido accordion music blaring loudly from its speakers—Los Tigres Del Norte, and there are two guys in cowboy hats inspecting the Dodge and looking around.

Our heads down again, we fall back and to the right, into the thicket of mesquite that I negotiated earlier. Andre tosses the chair down, and the three of us kneel.

Clear of the road, Jhonny starts gasping out a rant. "Let me go, man. Those guys are sureños." If he's in pain now, he's ignoring it, terrified by the two men he's just seen. There's a dark spot around the hole I put in his jeans.

"Sureños? Cartel guys pissed off about losing all that grass?"

Jhonny glares back.

I think it, but Andre says it: "Be all right with me. Maybe we jus' put you back on the road there, uh?"

Jhonny strains against the ropes again, but they aren't giving. "They gonna kill you too, motherfuckers. You gotta cut me loose so I got a chance."

"Shut the fuck up or I'll kill you myself."

I say, "I'm gonna go check it out. Tie him to a tree or something." I leave them and move in an arc again, fast at first, then from shadow to shadow once I can see the men and their truck.

One of them is in the big truck again, trying to maneuver it around the Dodge while his partner guides him from the front, occasionally looking behind him up the hill and into the scrubby trees. The music is off now.

It's a late-eighties Silverado, square-looking, with massive off-road tires and chrome lifts. The path around the Dodge is completely blocked by a boulder on the right side, so the driver is trying to maneuver around on the left, where there is a drop-off toward a lollipop-shaped mesquite. My guess is he thinks he can power over the tree with his beast-truck, roll over it, then come back onto the road, get around Burgoyne's truck. It makes me think the men are stupid . . . or overconfident.

But it's a sure thing somebody's snitched Jhonny's location, Spiritu I'd bet, with Memo signing off to save his own ass from the cartel guys. I think about it some more. They drive here expecting to find Jhonny alone, the perfect sitting duck. They come up the road loud and careless. Then they find the Dodge blocking them. What do they make of that? They think it's picnickers? Johnny's friends? They still overconfident?

Sure enough, the driver starts powering his front grill and bumper against the mesquite. It barely gives, and the driver backs up a few feet and rams the tree's trunk. Instead of mowing down the tree, though, the maneuver lifts one of his rear wheels off the ground, almost tips his truck because of the skewed angle. He backs up to the road again, turns off the ignition and climbs down. They're going to walk in, but they don't know how far it'll be. Or did Spiritu text them about that too? Walk in. But how? Overconfident, right down the road? Or cautious, wondering who came in the Dodge, circling around through the trees and maybe bringing them right at me?

I look at the Glock, remembering Andre saying it's loaded, wondering if there's one in the tube, estimating Andre's location. Maybe a hundred yards back.

The sureños are getting ready to come. There's a short, stocky one, wearing a black cowboy hat, the guy who was doing the guiding. He reaches into the huge truck from the passenger side and comes to the front of the vehicle with a gun on a sling. I don't know a lot about such things but it looks like a machine pistol. There are two long magazines stuck into his belt. He lifts the pistol and racks its slide.

The driver is a thin guy wearing a tan hat. He's got a big handgun, like the one I'm holding, and a magazine stuck in one of his back pockets.

They advance along the road, not slow, looking side to side, scanning ahead. No worries though. They have firepower, so they own the road.

I head back to where I left Jhonny and Andre, hurrying, trying to figure out what to do. We could let them go past, get to the trucks while they're zeroing in on the line shack, rely on Andre to hotwire the big Silverado, back it out to the road and disable it, and hope they don't catch on in time. Too many ifs. Or sneak off cross-country a half-mile or so and hide, wait for them to give up and go home.

Or face down the machine pistol.

As I jog between tree shadows, I think about Andre and me—where we are right now, about Burgoyne out there probably looking for me, about Maria's poor dead Ursa, about Abuelita and NJ, about leaving my wife with a lousy four-ten shotgun to protect herself, about the terror Francesca will always bear . . .

I decide.

Andre has double-tied Jhonny's arms and then hogtied him.

"Should we gag him?" I say.

"He know his best chance is us . . . This way he can breathe okay and he don't die accidental."

"You gotta let me go, man," Jhonny says.

"You keep jabbering, they're going to find you here," I say. Then to Andre, "They're coming right down the road, not worried about anything. Like we're nothing."

He waits on me.

"I go down another hundred feet or so . . . Make 'em cover two angles . . . You wait on me . . . I come out first, behind their line of sight . . . Get as close as I can . . . We see how it goes . . . Whatcha think?"

He considers me for a moment. "Should work. Sun's starting down now, so it'll be behind us . . . affect their eyes when they turn."

I wonder, How do some people think of shit like that?

"I'll wait on you to come out . . . then I come," he says.

"There's one guy with an Uzi. Little fat guy. Black hat. I'm gonna put everything I got on him till he's down . . . I figure you got the other guy."

He gives me a tiny nod, and I'm off.

I barely get eighty feet ahead of Andre before I see them coming along in the two ruts. They're two guys out for a brisk walk, Sunday after all, looking mainly ahead at the line shack, figuring resistance will come from there if they get any.

I start thinking maybe we should have withdrawn several hundred feet. We had time. They didn't know where to look for us—they'd have left. Or maybe pretended to leave and then ambushed us. And anyway, here we are.

I begin to worry that I'll piss in my pants again.

But I don't like the idea of the sureños laughing at my wet trousers.

I study the guy with the machine pistol—carrying the gun with his left hand, so probably a lefty, and he'll have to reverse pivot, open up to his left when he sees me, drop to his knee maybe. But he's holding the gun one-handed and casually, like he's bringing in the newspaper so he can read it with his morning coffee.

Burgoyne loves Uzis, adores them in fact. He says they're the best small arm in the world and that all American policemen should have them. "But," he says, "they're worthless if you don't extend the shoulder brace—like throwing a handful of marbles up in the air."

I hope to God he's right. The fat guy in the black hat sure *looks* like someone who can handle a weapon.

I study the ground in the open field—grassy but flat-looking. I wonder about trip hazards—hidden dips and cattle turds.

I don't like the way the two cowboys are advancing, fast enough that it will be hard to close in on them from behind without running. I am seventy-five feet from the two ruts, standing behind a gnarly tree. When they come even with me, they will still be two hundred feet from the line shack. But it will be a challenge to close the distance on them from their flank, and if I can't get a lot closer my shots will be difficult, even if my own panic doesn't quake its way down my arm. And Andre's shots will be almost impossible because of the distance.

That's the flaw in my plan then—I'll be on my own for ten or fifteen seconds while Andre closes in. And these guys are going to shoot back, not like poor Chucho. My bladder threatens to explode, and now I have it in my head that I will start shaking when I'm trying to aim and fire.

The dry dusty air stings my nose. Is that what it smells like—dying?

When they are twenty feet past me, I know it's time to advance. The tiny mesquite leaves begin a sudden quiver and I feel a warm breeze on my face now. I have to force myself to step out from the cover of the trees, praying the cowboys don't see me right away.

I walk as fast as I can with the Glock extended in front of me, holding it with two hands. I notice a tiny white dot on the front sight of Jhonny's gun, and I focus on it, trying to keep it aligned with the middle of the scary, blurry silhouette of the guy in the black hat. The sight bobs up and down with each step, but the little dot helps me bring the heavy weapon back where it needs to be—on the fat guy's belly. He's just a blurry blob when I aim this way, focusing on the gunsight, but it feels right somehow, and I keep doing it, hoping I pick up the movement when he pivots.

My Nikes and my trousers are whipping through the field grass, making the whisking sound again.

I am vaguely looking at the black-hatted guy, but I stay focused on the little dot, centering it on his gut and waiting for him to turn on me.

Scared shitless.

Reminding myself. Empty the gun, midbody, one shot at a time, aim every shot so the gun doesn't drop, ignore the noise, ignore the other asshole . . .

It's hard not to look down. Once, I step into a depression and I almost trip as my body dips, but I keep walking, my arms extended. The gun is heavy, but I am not going to be the one to take the *second* shot. I wonder again if my bladder will release. They are slowing down a little as they come closer to the old shack, seeing the lawn chair, and I'm drawing closer . . . eighty feet away, then seventy-five, then seventy . . .

One of them hears something or sees something, and they pivot toward me.

I'm about sixty-five feet away when I take my first shot. I stop and put the white dot on the legs of the black-hat and fire at him. Then I walk again, not caring if I piss myself.

They start shooting back.

The first machine-pistol burst is off to my left, missing badly, and I fire my second shot, still walking this time, about fifty-five feet away now, lucky that the ground is level. Tan-hat fires at me too, and I want to dive forward and bury myself in the glorious dirt.

The Uzi's shots explode into the ground in front of me. Black-hat is fighting the pistol's action, probably knows he should have extended its stock. He drops to one knee and holds the thing with both hands.

I hear a shot from behind me, over to my right, and I know it's Andre's Beretta, and the cowboys look at him and fire in his direction, thank God, and I take three more steps. Andre fires again, so I know they haven't hit him.

I am forty feet from the Uzi man now. I stop and fire.

He lurches spasmodically and the Uzi sprays high into the air.

Andre and the tan hat are exchanging shots.

I drop to my knee, still holding the Glock with both hands. I remember how I let the gun drop when I killed Chucho and lift the dot onto black-hat's middle and fire. Twice. The second one, my fifth shot, hits him and he falls back with his arms over his head, like a gymnast starting a back-flip.

I swivel at the hips and fire at tan-hat, who's down on one knee trading shots with Andre. On the next couple shots, I know my aim is drifting down again, so I put the site on tan-hat's head and fire until the Glock is empty, but I keep missing him.

It doesn't matter, though, because Andre is finally close enough to his target and hits the guy. I can see three jolts—his hat flying off, a shoulder twist, then his middle. He falls and twitches once.

Rising from my knee, I finally look over at Andre, who's still standing and pointing his weapon, making sure the cowboy doesn't move any more. Then he removes the magazine.

That's when another shot crackles past my head.

It's black-hat, a smaller gun in his hand now. He's leaning on his elbow now, pointing the pistol my way, holding it sideways, but not really steady enough to aim. Another shot crackles past while I pull the Beretta from my pocket.

I drop prone, where I think he'll have trouble aiming at me, and steady my elbows on the ground and put three slugs into him.

My heart is racing when I stand. I look down at my pants, which are still dry.

Andre is right next to me.

I say, "What'd you see that time?"

"Same as you, I think."

FIFTEEN

I'm right. Andre does know how to hotwire the big Silverado. "The old ones are easy," he says. "And I don't feel like goin' through no dead guys' pockets." We leave it with the guys who brought it, at the clearing in front of the old line shack, where it's easy for me to turn the Dodge around.

The breeze is stiffer now, riffling the grass around the two cowboys. Let the dead bury the dead, I think.

At the highway, Andre stows the oak chair on his passenger seat and stuffs Jhonny in his trunk, saying, "He can whine all he wants in there."

It's four o'clock and the sky is rumbling when I can finally bounce a signal off a cell tower and get a call through to Eloise, who reports Francesca is holed up in her room listening to music. I tell her that I'll be at the police station for a while.

I text Burgoyne to tell him I'll meet him at the downtown police station, but he falls in behind me at Three Points and flashes his headlights, intending to follow me all the way in. He's been out looking for me.

I know that Andre is miles ahead, so I pull over.

I tell him about Jhonny and the cowboys from Mexico. I decide that Andre has probably disposed of the chair in some dumpster, and I don't mention it.

"Damn. Lend a guy a pistol and a pickup, and you wind up with anarchy." Then he chuckles. He wants me to go with him and have a look at the scene for himself, down at the line shack, but decides it's not a good idea. "The sheriff would put your ass behind bars this time."

After locking up the Honda at a convenience store, he takes over driving the Dodge and I move to the passenger seat, and he calls his headquarters to alert them that Andre is bringing in a fugitive on a child abduction warrant and that he's bringing along the other guy who apprehended him.

The highway stretches out before us, broad and black and flat, no shimmering mirages with the sun behind us. The bruise-colored clouds to the east keep threatening calamity.

Burgoyne calls the sheriff's office too and gives them directions to the bloody scene down south, tells them what they will find, tells them he'll have the shooters available for questioning at PD headquarters.

They want him to bring me to their office, but he says, "No can do. My people are gonna want to talk to him first." When he clicks off, he says, "Good thing we don't have the police radio squawking at us."

He turns up the volume for some music. He keeps it low, but beats emanate, the Geto Boys. "You like this shit?"

"Some of the old-school rap. I forgot to change the channel."

"They left the C off the beginning of that word," he says and finds his country channel. It's Sonny James crooning that he'll "never find another you," and it makes me think of Maria.

He has me go through the story a couple more times as he drives, asking questions from time to time about the whole sequence—who did what to whom and how and when, which seems totally redundant to me until I realize he's doing it to make sure I have my story straight. Whenever he glances my way, he's wearing a drawn worried look instead of his serene altar-boy.

He's driving five or ten miles per hour below the limit, and I notice the world passing by: the lavender line of hills rising behind airplane hangars at the rural airfield, palo verdes and creosotes gone gray in the drought, the mix of new ding-bat houses, scrabbly sixties-era hovels and decrepit sheds and trailers—all interspersed with flimsy modern burger joints, ninety-eight-cent stores and Circle-K's. It's not a beautiful collage, but I know I'll miss it when I'm in prison.

At the police station, he doesn't enter the parking garage right away; instead, he circles the block. Rain is starting to fall. Fat drops that spatter his windshield and fill the air with the aroma of creosote, even though we're downtown.

"Number one, call your lawyer."

"All I got is an estate lawyer."

"Yeah, but he'll know somebody. Number two . . . well, number two is up to you. But if I was telling the story you just told me, I'd mention that the Mexicans fired on me first."

I look at him, study his baby face, which has returned.

"It's a small thing, anyway—who fired first. Those guys were cartel executioners . . . settling the score for Manny and Chucho and their safe house in Why, not to mention a couple million in contraband. And more than that, letting Memo know his little band of thugs is nothin' to them. The big thing is they would have killed all three of you if you hadn't put them down.

"That's true, ain't it?" He's driving like a lost tourist, left, then right, right again . . .

I don't say anything.

"You didn't have a better choice either. Don't forget that." His eyes fix on me. "Its not like you were gonna say 'How can I help you?'"

"Memories are tricky anyway. The county's attorneys'll ask me if you made any spontaneous remarks while I brought you in. They call it an excited utterance. I'm gonna tell you one time what I recall . . . one time only—Enrique Tavish's excited utterance. And what I recall you telling me about the whole thing is that you *returned* fire . . . You and Andre were both there, involved in the same battle. He ain't gonna remember everything the same way you do, but I'm guessing it'll be his recollection that the guy with the Uzi just started shooting and you *returned* fire. You just went to talk to 'em, ask them to move their truck maybe, and the fat guy goes nuts with his machine gun.

"Good thing you were carrying a piece."

"I'll think about it," I say.

"You do that. Just know this. If the Mexicans fired first, then it might save everybody a lot of trouble. Not just you, everybody. The gutless county attorney don't have to defend herself for not charging you. There's no jury of dumbbells trying to decide if you feared for your life. And of course, you already shot a guy the other night. The word vigilante is definitely gonna come up. You'll be lucky to get home in three-to-five, let alone tonight."

"Not to mention I was driving *your* truck. I finished off that black-hat cowboy with *your* gun."

"Let me worry about that. You needed that piece for protection and I lent it to you. You wanted the truck so you wouldn't be made while you followed a suspicious car linked to your daughter's abduction."

After a few more turns, he says, "Number three. Jesus Christ, what did you make of Jhonny's description of the guy coming out of the E building?"

It seems like a thousand years since I last thought about Usaré and her killer.

"My first thought was he was telling the truth. He saw an Anglo guy walking fast to get away from there. Anyway, you can interview Neto, the little shit who tried to burn down the school the other day, and the other two guys that were in the car that night if you can track them down.

"On the other hand, if one of the gangbangers killed Usaré, they'd for sure invent a gringo perp."

"Suppose they didn't invent him."

I shrug. "A thin Anglo guy who was somewhere between five-ten and six-two, dressed all in dark clothes, except for his arms, which I guess means he was wearing a long-sleeve white shirt. Or he was bare-arm."

"And a spiffy vest. Like somebody might wear to a dance." We're approaching the police station again. "Was Rusic dressed like that? Or any of the other chaperones?"

"Not Rusic. He was wearing a white polo. I was wearing a dark sleeveless sweater, so it could have been me. Except I'm too tall."

"And not exactly skinny." He smiles.

I *am* putting on pounds.

"Mayer, the senior advisor, was wearing a light-colored, long-sleeve shirt, but I don't remember a vest or anything . . . Nuñez, the DJ was dressed about right, like a gambler, but he's chunky . . . Amin is black and was wearing black . . . I got no idea about Morales . . . Don't remember Trujillo, but he's got the right build, and he's light skinned."

Burgoyne is pulling into the parking garage. "Do you ever wonder why the girl's phone hasn't told us very much?"

"Well, if the doer was someone she was meeting on the sly, then maybe she purposely avoided putting in a name with the number, in case somebody saw it. If they ever texted, it was probably all cryptic . . . useless messages like 'Hi Doll.' From him anyway. If it *was* a him."

"Yeah, the forensics guys are trying to identify the cell towers associated most often with some of those nameless numbers."

The rain is falling steadily, and he's parking now. "I wonder where that phone is. The one he used."

Another topic. "You think the guy took her panties? . . . Like a trophy?" I say.

"I'd bet my retirement on it." He looks at me after turning off the engine. "You decide?"

I nod. I text Eloise to let her know I've arrived at police headquarters and ask her to get hold of Fred, our attorney. Then we enter the station where Burgoyne shows his ID to an officer sitting behind thick glass.

"The detectives are expecting this guy. Same investigation as Andre Carver." The sergeant consults his computer screen and nods his head.

"Scanlon. Fourteen-B." He presses a button, and Burgoyne leads me to meet Detective Scanlon. Burgoyne knows his colleagues will shortly find out about his own involvement with my latest escapade, and he tells me he'll be available when they want him, ". . . probably chatting with my union rep."

I tell Scanlon I'm waiting for my lawyer and he says, "Fine. I'm waiting on some people myself." Like I'm not going to like them. He puts me in a barren chamber with a mirror on one side, which I assume conceals a viewing and listening room beyond. It's a two-hour wait.

My first impression of my new attorney is that he's effeminate, with soft white skin, manicured hands and perfect brown hair, and I wonder if Fred thought very hard about finding a criminal lawyer for me. He puts out his hand in the most fastidious way to introduce himself, like he's welcoming me to some grand hotel.

"Hello, Mr. Tavish. I'm Aaron Altschul."

I rise in shock as much as for courtesy and shake his hand. His voice, a hearty tenor, and his name both surprise me. Everyone who reads the news knows that he represents some of the city's wealthiest and most colorful figures, recently the owner of a golf resort who'd allegedly hired someone to kill his grasping ex-wife. I know I'm going to be well-represented, and I know it's going to cost me.

"Thanks for coming."

"Freddy said you were in a bit of a fix." His voice is casual, like we're at a cocktail party.

"I think I am, yeah. I killed a guy."

"Did you? . . . The police and the sheriffs gave me an interesting tale. Would you mind giving me *your* recollections?" He gives me this faint smile, which somehow suggests to me that everything is going to be okay. He's Aaron Altschul, and I have nothing to worry about except how to pay my bill.

"Start with Thursday of course."

In the next hour, I tell him the story a thousand times.

When he finally lets me stop, his eyes are sad. He says, "How is your daughter now? Francesca?"

Just that. Like nothing else matters.

The emotions come to me like a gang of street muggers, and I don't think there is one that I miss: guilt, fear, rage, hatred, worry. Most of all, worry. What will happen to me? My poor Francesca? Eloise, NJ? Burgoyne, for Christ sake? Then I want to kick something.

"She's acting okay, but we're anxious," I say.

"You and Eloise? Understandable."

I don't say anything.

"Mr. Tavish, you're going home tonight. I don't know what the county attorney will do in a few days or a week, but I'm not going to let them hold you tonight." His eyes soothe me as much as his words. "What she will do is try to frighten you. Tell the story just the way you told me. If I don't like their line of questioning, or if they try to trip you up, I'll interrupt. You and your family are going to be okay." He pats my arm. "Francesca will be okay." I believe him.

He doesn't seem so effeminate now.

*****

I rebuke myself as we walk the hallway to the interrogation room. I shouldn't have tried to find Usaré's killer, shouldn't have rushed to judgment about the Levantes . . . shouldn't have saved Jhonny's life for Christ sake.

When I see the collected interrogators, however, I am stunned.

Simpson is sitting in one of the chairs, and I become angry and afraid. Simpson possesses an air of grave superiority, an air of 'gotcha.' He sits in his shirtsleeves, composed, full of contempt. On his left is Bejarano, on his right Scanlon. To Scanlon's right sit two sheriff department deputies. In the center of it all sits a young woman, alert and hard-eyed.

Scanlon motions for me to sit down. He explains that it is really Janet who is in charge now, Janet Wilshire, from the county attorney's office, because both the sheriff's department and the city police report to the CA.

Scanlon stands next to a chair, waiting for Wilshire to ask him to sit down I suppose, a sycophant. She nods at me, then looks at Scanlon and he sits.

"Nice to see you, Aaron," Wilshire says, for now more interested in him than she is in me. "Charity case?"

Altschul smiles, just a little, and sits. "I love these easy ones. But I need to be home before John Oliver comes on."

It's Simpson who speaks next. He and Bejarano are the only officers in the room who have had previous contact with me. "Tavish, we're close to making a decision here." He looks toward Wilshire now, expecting her to speak again.

She doesn't.

"Okay," I say, making them lay it out, even though I know what he's getting at.

Simpson says, "We don't know if your activities over the past few days have anything to do with the García case, but the county attorney is already considering homicide charges against you. You shoot a man in his own home Thursday night, and now this. At the very least, you're a vigilante."

Altschul was right—they want to frighten me.

It's working.

"Am I?" I say, trying to look calm. Under the table, I'm pressing together the tips of my middle finger and thumb.

Altschul looks my way, soft but not approving.

I say, "I told the officers Thursday night the reason I went out to Why. I pushed the wrong buttons."

Wilshire says, "I've read through the transcript from your last interview, Mr. Tavish. I understand how you could have been swept into a desperate rescue scenario. Until tonight, our office was inclined to forgo prosecuting you, providing your story was corroborated by the Martinez girl and others."

I think of Rosa and Burgoyne. And Memo, who would have described me as a crazy, angry gringo who'd burst into his house with a gun.

She says, "But your adventure today can't be explained away by desperation. Your child was safe. All you had to do was wait for the police to find Manny's co-conspirator."

"I guess I figured it would be a long wait." Still working my fingers under the table.

"My goodness, Janet, vigilantism?" Altschul apparently deciding I need to be reined in. "It would seem to me that this Martinez boy would be dead by now if my client were seeking base revenge. He and this other man, Andre is it? They saved his life."

"Is that your defense strategy, Aaron? Heroism?"

He smiles, not wide but confidently. "Janet, you haven't even asked him to explain what happened today. Have you and your boss already made up your mind?"

It's her turn to smile faintly. "I was just going to ask." She turns her eyes toward me.

I've related the day's events three times to Burgoyne, summarized them for Fred, then repeated them three more times for Aaron Altschul. It should be easy to tell it all again, a child's errand.

I start with Burgoyne lending me a pistol because I'm worried about protecting my family. I tell about Burgoyne's pissing match with Memo and the guy I'd never seen before—Spiritu . . . the toothpick, Usaré's notebook, the suspicious convertible driving past my house—the same one that cruised the school parking lot last Saturday night.

I explain it all the exactly the way I've rehearsed it: borrowing Burgoyne's pickup, losing Leon and Spiritu, lucking out and finding them again at Memo's, Andre appearing out of nowhere, trying to keep up with the muscle cars on the road to Sasabe, finding the line shack, capturing Jhonny, the gunfight . . . every detail.

The way I remember.

"Detective Scanlon has raised some questions about this investigation. There are some discrepancies between the stories obtained from the shooting victim and your associate, Mr. Carver."

Altschul doesn't let this one go by. "Forgive me, Janet, but no matter what your question is going to be, it's probably not appropriate to refer to Mr. Martinez as a victim."

"There are a couple of discrepancies between what Mr. Martinez told us and what you and Mr. Carver are telling us." She waits for me to respond.

"You want me to guess what they are?"

Wilshire purses her lips, but I think Altschul smiles a little. I'm still working my fingers, wondering if my stress is leaking out anywhere else on my body.

I add, "Like that old TV show, *I've Got a Secret.*"

"I think my client would appreciate your being a bit less circuitous," Altschul says.

"I'd appreciate a little less sarcasm. Mr. Martinez said you shot him while he was tied to a chair."

"That's quite a story but it doesn't surprise me . . . coming from him," I say.

"Would it surprise you if he said you and Mr. Carver conspired to hide evidence? To plant evidence?"

"Which one? Hide it or plant it?" I say.

"Hide evidence *and* plant evidence," she says.

"That *would* surprise me, yes."

"Would it also surprise you if there were forensic evidence to support his claim?"

My heart beats so hard that I think everyone in the room can hear it. "Yes. I'd be very surprised by that," I say, wondering what it could be. I wonder what Burgoyne's advice would have been had I told him about the chair.

"Mr. Tavish, how many rounds did you fire from the gun lent to you by Officer Burgoyne?"

I think it over carefully, counting, and I still almost screw it up. "Five, I think." This is true, strictly speaking. "Maybe six."

"Officer Burgoyne says he lent you a fully loaded gun. That's seven rounds. There's one left in the weapon. You told us you didn't reload. So you fired six times."

"I believe you."

"Tell me, the best you can remember, the order of those shots."

This is one of the traps Wilshire is exploring, and my attorney doesn't know it's a trap. I wonder what Andre said. As little as possible I'd guess, like he didn't remember.

"The one that hit Jhonny was the first one. I fired the rest at the cartel guy. I know I missed him once or twice." I realize I'm probably saying too much, saying it wrong.

She pauses for a moment or two, which I take as a good sign, either that or she's already sprung her trap. She switches to a different line of questioning.

"Tell me about the chair," she says.

"What do you want to know about it? It was a wooden chair. Andre tied him there, and we asked him some questions."

"Yes, now that's one of the things I don't understand. Why did you do that? Why not just walk him back to your truck right away?"

"I don't know. Andre didn't ask me or anything. He just did it. I went along. He wants to know who killed Usaré. So do I."

"You and Andre were thinking about killing Jhonny, I imagine."

"Janet . . ." Altschul warns.

"I can't speak for Andre. He might have been thinking about killing him. I had the feeling he was. I know I thought about it."

"Mr. Tavish," Altschul says.

"But we didn't kill him, did we?" I say.

"So, let's get back to the chairs. There were two of them, right?"

I shake my head. "I only remember the one. Unless you mean the couch . . . or the lawn chair out front."

She looks hard at me, waits. "Mr. Tavish, Aaron, we have some material evidence from the scene already. We think it may validate Mr. Martinez's story. If it does, you'll face felony charges for assaulting him. If you'd hit his femoral, he would have died and we'd be talking about murder two."

"What do you think you have, Janet?" Altschul says.

"We're looking for wood fragments in Mr. Martinez's clothing. If he was shot while he was bound to a chair, there's a good chance we'll find some wood particles in his trousers. I just want to give Mr. Tavish a chance to explain that."

She pauses for effect, and I pretend I'm calm, working the thumb and finger under the table.

"We've also found some slugs from the little Beretta, the Tomcat, three in the deceased gentleman from Sonora, just where your client put them. And one in the ground out in front of the shack . . . which ought to have some blood particles on it, Martinez's DNA maybe, if it's the one that wounded him. We're looking for the two slugs that are still missing. Your client better hope we find them in a place that fits his explanation. And we're looking for a chair that seems to have walked away."

"Janet, my dear, so many qualifiers," Altschul says. He uses an earnest, ironic tone that does not quite stoop to sarcasm or patronization. ". . . 'if' he was in a chair . . . there's a 'chance' . . . the bullet 'ought to' have blood . . . DNA 'maybe'. It seems to me you don't really have any evidence. You're just hoping some evidence turns up that will make your decision easy."

He tilts his head, his features soft and calm. "And for what? So you can prosecute a Latino man who has just been trying to protect his family from thugs the last few days? A man that risked his own skin to track down and apprehend a child rapist, then risked it again to ensure the rapist made it here alive so he could be jailed?"

He shakes his head. "I've never been cursed with the burdens of your office, Janet, but I doubt very much that your boss will want to hang her hat on the prosecution of Enrique Tavish."

The interview drags on for another half-hour, but it's easy to see Wilshire no longer has any appetite for locking me up. Not, at least, until she hears more from her investigators. I am out of the interview room by nine o'clock.

The spring storm is a deluge. Visibility is fifty feet; washes are overflowing; some of the arterial streets are closed. I see stalled cars along the roadway, and I think that perhaps I should wait it out. I don't.

On the way home, I think about the pain of discovering I cannot protect my own child. I can see that every parent at some point arrives at this reality, but my sense of impotence still overwhelms and humiliates me, seizing my soul like some giant shark. Just as with Maria's revelation to me about her cancer, I know that I have been experiencing denial about Francesca's abduction. And now, as then, I know I will react to my own powerlessness in episodes of deep anger. It's not right, after all, for my daughter to have been carried away and assaulted, any more than it was right for the gods to take Maria.

Then the truth of my denial comes to me, and I sense that Maria is nodding her head.

When your ten-year-old child falls from a tree and breaks her arm, you know what to do instinctively—rush to her, take care to protect the injured arm, soothe her pain, tell her it will be all right, dry her tears, get her to a doctor, a few days later talk to her about avoiding risks.

Some of those things I did on Thursday night and Friday morning—but I couldn't tell her everything would be all right because I didn't know myself if it would be, and I'm still not sure it can, and *I* am the one who needs to understand better about avoiding risks.

Old Lear had a poor reason for betraying his daughter, but he *did* have a reason. I had none, only my ignorance and vanity. I begot her, raised her and loved her; she returned the obligations as were fit, obeying me, loving me and honoring me. And for her care and duty, I betrayed her. Like the ancient king, I could not see the nature of the thing in front of me and became the fool.

I long to react by throwing and pounding and breaking . . . things. Rocks, sandbags, mesquite logs . . . driving my car into a lamppost. It's not hate that fills me, but a pure and perfect wrath. If I could just satiate this rage, perhaps Maria could forgive me, perhaps the despair would lift.

And now I can barely remember why I wanted so badly to find Usaré's assassin. To save her honor? . . . my job? To help Burgoyne become a detective? Because Usaré almost became my illicit-lover? Because I was responsible for her death the same way that I now am for Francesca's violation?

To make amends? If that's all it were, then I have already fulfilled an obligation to my daughter's dead innocence, and I should be able to lift myself from the terrible pit I am in. But I am not able, and it means that finding Usaré's soulless killer will do nothing to restore her or to lift her parents' pain.

But that's all there is.

*****

Francesca sits in the back yard on a broad landscape stone, the storm scourging her with thunder and heavy rain, despite the pleadings of her stepmother and Abuelita. Eloise tells me she has sat on that rock in the same place for the past half-hour, enduring the slanted pelts of sky water, braving the bolts of lightning and rolls of thunder, inconsolable, stubborn. I can see her out the patio door, in her nightgown, frail and naked-looking, rigid on the big piece of granite, looking up, defying the storm.

I should wear some rain gear, I know, but I do not, thinking maybe it shows some understanding. I approach her slowly, expecting her to make room for me next to her on the slab of granite, but she pretends I am not there. I am soaked before I get near her.

I nearly yell to be heard. "It's a fearful storm, Francesca, gonna blow the earth right into the sea."

She doesn't hear me or pretends so.

"We're gonna have waves here in a minute. The bears won't even come out and get their fur wet."

"Bears are stupid. It's not safe inside," she says, still looking into the sky. She starts to rock back and forth on the big flat stone. "The wind can break its stupid cheeks when it blows. I don't care."

I want to hold her, but I am afraid she won't let me. I am a man, after all, a repulsive man, cursed with the organ that violated her, the arrogance that enslaved her.

She yells at the sky. "Drown me, you stupid storm. Go ahead and hit me with your stupid lightning. Burn my stupid hair." Insanely, I want to tell her to use a different adjective.

She's crying now. "I don't care if the whole stupid world dies. I hope God spits fire on everyone." The sky brightens in a terrific burst and rocks out a peal of thunder, closer together than I'd like. Francesca rocks and sobs. She yells at the sky again. "Growl all you want. I never did anything to *you*!"

Uninvited, I sit next to her and put my arm around her shoulder, but it barely impedes her. She continues talking to the storm, sobbing. She pulls her feet onto the rock, her calves tight to her thighs now, and wraps her legs with her arms. She sways back and forth on the rock.

"You're stupid. You're on their side. I never did anything to you. You're on their side." The words sting me, though I know she's still talking to the storm . . . or the God who abandoned her.

I have to yell over the din of the rain, the cannonades of thunder. "Darling, I've never seen a storm like this. Let's go inside, okay? The lightning is too close."

"I didn't *do* anything," she wails. "I didn't *do* anything. I didn't, I didn't." Disconsolate, looking within her for the sin that exposed her to the malignancy that took her.

I hold her tighter, tentatively, unsure. She turns rigid though, and I loosen my embrace again, hanging one arm around her like a school friend might do.

"I've never seen such a storm, Angel. Let's go inside. We can talk there." Jagged streaks suddenly fulminate above us in a gigantic web, almost simultaneous with a deafening blare in my ear, sending a jolt of terror through me. The neighborhood's house lights are snuffed for a few seconds, then come back on.

Francesca doesn't seem to notice the fantastic lightning streaks or the explosion of thunder or the spasm of fear that I know she must have felt course through me. I know I should snatch her up and carry her inside, but I am more afraid of her response than I am of the storm.

"It's like heaven is with *them*, Papa, on *their* side. Ganging up. I didn't *do* anything!" Her voice is low and pitiable now.

"No, Angel, you didn't do anything. They were the ones who did something wrong. They did everything wrong." I start to think we'll both be killed by a lightning strike, wondering how much it will hurt.

"Maybe the storm is after the devil ones, the ones with something to hide. Like those men. Men who hurt people. Liars. People the police don't know about."

"I don't know, Angel. Maybe."

"Or maybe I'm crazy," she says. "NJ says I'm crazy, Papa." She's looking at my face now, really wondering I think. Pleading with her eyes.

I shake my head. "He didn't mean it, Francesca. He's just real sad."

"Am I?" she asks, my answer not direct enough. "There's a big storm in my head."

"No, Angel. You're not crazy. You're just sad, like NJ. But angry too."

She considers me for a long moment. Lightning flashes again, not as close this time.

"Carry me," she says. Her hands close around the back of my neck and she puts her head against my chest.

SIXTEEN

At home, Eloise wants my whole story, of course, from the moment I left this morning, was it just this morning?

But Francesca refuses to separate from us, so my zillionth telling of the story has to wait. Secretly, I'm glad, but Francesca's presence also stifles me from asking whether Eloise noticed any suspicious cars throughout the day.

Eloise hands me a slip of paper before she goes to sit with Francesca during her shower. Two phone messages to return—Santana and JV Muñoz, the superintendent, whose message contains a cell phone number and says 'forthwith'—not a word Eloise would use.

I'm thinking the supe has heard of my adventures by now, of Thursday's sojourn to Why at least. He knows he has a killer on staff. And he doesn't know quite what to do yet . . . or maybe he does. Will he wait for the press to interpret it for him? Does he want an explanation or my head? Am I a Latino victim, the way Altschul played it? A vengeance-driven dad? A lunatic? My stomach, my whole body, is in an uproar.

Some time tomorrow morning, for sure, I'll be on administrative leave. Call him last, I decide, before my authority evaporates. Forthwith, my ass. Decide the next step, not the next five steps. Santana's message says to call her before eleven, so I have about five minutes.

"Bueno." A standard greeting, terse, tension in her voice.

"Hello, Santana. It's Enrique."

"Hello, Mr. Tavish." Part of me always wants to tell her to call me something less formal. But I don't know if she'd be comfortable saying Henry or Enrique or Ricky, so I let it stand.

"Sounded like something urgent . . ."

She sends this soft, guttural chuckle through the phone. Her brother is a high school principal in a neighboring district, and I wonder momentarily if he'd hire me after I'm fired at Polk.

"Probably not urgent . . . just thought you should know before tomorrow . . ." She waits.

"All right. What's up?" I am tired, tempted to ask if I should expect the return of Emiliano Zapata, but I let the temptation pass. Santana is a friend, after all.

"Oscar called twice on Friday." Referring to Oscar Benitez, School Board President.

"Okay . . ." wondering if he called to try to fire me personally instead of waiting for Augustine or the supe."

"It's about his daughter's cell phone . . . Teresa?" Like I should know.

I do know Teresa, of course. Everyone does. Her parents nonchalantly take her on vacation for two or three weeks at the beginning of each school year, most recently to Cuba, then expect teachers to let her make up the work she missed, which board policy allows. It annoys her teachers of course, because they have to reconstruct curriculum that can't really be delivered properly outside the classroom, because they have to grade her work weeks after the rest of the class turned it in, and because Teresa infuriatingly gets A's all the time.

"Her English teacher, Ms. Dunham, confiscated it last Friday."

"So what's the issue? He can pick it up tomorrow from Helen."

"No, it's been locked up in the E Building all week, in the English office. Nobody can get in there except you and the police, you know?"

That's when it hits me.

The mystery phone!

Whenever teachers in the E building confiscate a phone, they lock it up in a filing cabinet drawer in the English office until the parent comes to claim it, figuring that if they inconvenience and annoy a parent sufficiently, they'll win parental support for suppressing texts and calls during class time.

I have serious doubts that their approach can work; it annoys the parents for sure, but it doesn't seem to have any effect beyond gratuitously creating a bunch of POP's—pissed-off parents. On the other hand, it is great camouflage—the perfect place to stash some teacher's throw-away phone, a burner phone.

Even if the police technicians encountered this drawer-full of phones, each in an envelope with some kid's name on it, they'd assume all the phones were just what they seemed to be—seized phones.

If Burgoyne is right and some Polk staff member was involved with Usaré, then he might have used a burner phone—a prepaid device that was purchased anonymously and which had no other purpose than to contact Usaré.

A phone, I think now, hidden in plain sight because it's locked up with four or five confiscated phones in a file cabinet in the English office, a phone that will probably be at the bottom of the lake in Center Park by tomorrow evening.

"Mr. Tavish?"

"Yeah, I'm here. I'm surprised Benitez didn't call sooner."

Santana hesitates. "He did, Mr. Tavish. I should have let you know. A bunch of parents called."

"You probably did, didn't you?"

She hesitates again. "I left a couple messages, yessir. Sorry, should have made them more prominent."

"Nothing to be sorry for, Santana. I just missed it. So what's his majesty expect now?"

"He wants you to give Teresa the phone, so he doesn't have to come in."

Ordinarily, I'd dig in my heels, the son of a bitch. The board writes policy, but it doesn't apply to them. Fuckers! "Of curse."

"Pardon, sir?"

"Of course. So should I call him?"

"No, sir. I said we'd have the phone for her at the front office. Seven o'clock. You'll probably have to go get it though, 'cause the English office won't turn it over to anyone except the parent or an administrator. Okay?"

So Santana knew I'd cave anyway. "We can do that. I'll send it up when we open," I say. Not the time for pride. "You remember the names of the kids whose parents called?"

"Not offhand, but I left a list on your desk Friday. Taped it to your computer screen."

I vaguely remember seeing the paper now, though I'd paid no attention to it when Burgoyne and I were looking through Usaré's notebook. "Thanks, Santana."

Next I call Burgoyne's number, but there is no answer. I leave a message to call me as soon as he's able, then I put off the call to the supe. Forthwith—immediately, not ASAP, but forthwith. Does he know when I'd receive this? Will he call Augustine now and get my cell number?

Forthwith.

Not yet, I decide. I'll give Burgoyne an hour. Till midnight.

I go to find Francesca, who's not in her room but in mine, ours, Eloise's and mine, straight-legged in the bed, not shivering now. Eloise is reading to her, some Harry Potter stuff it sounds like. NJ's door is closed, his room quiet, and I don't enter.

When I finally settle in, Francesca is lying between me and Eloise, snoring softly.

My phone vibrates just before midnight—Burgoyne. I press the answer icon and carry the phone into the living room. "It's me."

"I figgered. So what's up?"

I tell him about the phone.

"Makes sense about the hiding place. Our guys would ignore the whole batch, I'm pretty sure." I hear a long pause, then a sigh. Then he says, "Doesn't fit with the coach's profile. He used his own phone to contact the girl. And why does lover-boy . . . or lover-girl . . . keep the phone there in the first place? . . . And why ain't it in the lake already?"

"Because if it never leaves the school, his little lady at home never asks questions about it, right?"

"Yeah, that much makes sense. But you're saying he kept it there all the time. There's gotta be more accessible places to keep it—locked up in his desk or above the ceiling tiles ya know? He wants to knock off a piece of ass, he has to fish it out of the drawer every time . . . in front of the department secretary and whoever."

"Yeah, but he can just pretend he's returning a phone to some kid. Stick it back in with a new name later on. Then, the night she died, it was just a thing he forgot . . . I mean if it's still even there."

"And if he moves on the phone right away, you want me to be there to bust the guy."

"That's about right, I guess. Something you haven't taught me." I remember Chucho, who never really had a chance, and the cowboys in the grassy field.

"Mmm . . . Chief says if I get near the place, I'm suspended."

I've never heard Burgoyne sound intimidated. It's a new experience for me. Probably new for him too.

"Not great," I say, "but I know the feeling." I don't hear any response, and for a moment I think we've been disconnected.

"It's the only way though, 'cause I'm pretty sure we don't have probable cause to go snooping into a phone unless we're sure it's linked to Usaré's. It's just a fishing expedition. What else you need?"

I find myself shaking my head as if Burgoyne is there in the room. "I don't know. I'm going to take my phone charger along. See what calls and texts went in and out. Let me go find the phone . . . see if I'm even on the right track . . . call you back."

"Hey! Take some gloves along."

"Gloves."

"To handle the phone . . . envelope too. In case you're right."

It's an odd thing to leave your family in the middle of the night. Odder still to wake your wife and tell her you're leaving to trap a killer. Impossible with Francesca there. I decide to text Eloise after I've left.

I look under the sink and find rubber gloves, but they seem too small. Halfway back to the school, I buy a pair at Walgreen's, throw away the package and stuff them into a pocket in my sports coat.

The storm has stopped, but the pavement still glistens with rainwater.

'Urgent . . . had to get over to the school to check something B4 school opened' I text Eloise. 'Back when I can'

A high school campus can be a terrifying place for some kids at times, a point often lost on the adults who are charged with running it, but it's not lost on me as I remove the padlock to the E building. After retrieving the list of students from the computer screen in my office, I've basically retraced Usare's last steps on the night she died, when Keanu accompanied her through the darkness from the gymnasium to this very door. It is dark, though not exceedingly so, because of the campus remodeling project. I'm surprised to find I'm wishing for the comfort of one of the guns Burgoyne has lent me in the past few days. The occasional car zooms past on Park Avenue, perhaps a hundred yards east. Crickets buzz. The moon is rising, but the shadows from the buildings are deep.

I wonder what impulse drove Usaré to cross the dimly lit campus for the rendezvous she apparently had.

A guy's impulse, I think I'd understand—lust, ego, misplaced confidence.

A young woman's, I know I don't. Especially Usaré's. She had an outsized ego, for certain, and more confidence than anyone else her age, but I don't understand her motivation; she wasn't like Nikki Sullivan, who pursued sexual experiences for their own sake. For Usaré, I believe now, sex was only part of each arrangement she made with a man.

Admittedly, the risk of ploughing through the dim light was negligible when she left the gym with Keanu, but the cost of losing on the risk was high. The other kids adored her. Men worshiped her and desired her. The savory world was opening up to her like a ripe peach. And then it was taken from her. She crossed a darkened campus for a man who would ultimately kill her, not in the shadows at all but under the bright fluorescent lights inside a school building.

Not a boy or a woman or a gang, but a lone man, crazed with lust or jealousy or spite or dispossession.

My Nikes are soaked from walking through puddles of rainwater collected on the sidewalk, some of them an inch or more deep, and my steps make a squishy squeaking sound on the tile floor of the E building hallway.

The English office is warm and stuffy, since a timer ensures the air conditioning system can't come on between midnight and six AM, and I open a couple windows for air. Then I sit at the secretary's desk and open the tummy drawer where Cynthia Flores keeps her ring of keys. Rings—a one-inch ring for room and closet keys and a two inch ring for desks and drawers and storage cabinets. Thank God she labels them. I've seen her put kids' phones away and take them out when parents report to claim them. They should be in file cabinet fourteen—labeled FC14 on the key.

It's almost three o'clock Monday morning, three hours before teachers can return, three hours before Benjamin comes in to remove chalk lines from the bathroom floor and scrub the mirror free of blood and boot marks. I turn on Cynthia's computer and wait.

I consider the empty space where the department's sofa once sat. It was an ugly thing, etched with stains even before Usaré's secret Romeo scrubbed at his semen spot, and outdated, with a jagged pattern that used to be called flame, I think. The cast-off of some teacher, the soiled site of a girl's death, evidence now, carted away by the police.

The guttural blatting of two red-lining muscle cars bursts my reverie. Drag racing—not an infrequent Park Avenue contest, regardless of the hour. I put on the rubber gloves.

At file cabinet fourteen, I open the top drawer and extract seven bulky envelopes and compare the names on them to the ones on the list Santana left me.

Four of them match, the confiscated phones that invoked parents' ire. Three do not. I leave the four in the drawer and carry the three back to Cynthia's desk and log onto the computer with my own username and password.

My suspicion is that the burner phone bears the name of some fake kid, so that no one will ever come in to claim it. But I look up each name and find all three: Josefina Bojorquez, Yolanda Franco, two Yolanda Francos in fact, and Brian Jackson, all enrolled, all of them with more or less regular attendance.

Josefina's phone is an I-Phone, which I decide is unlikely to be a throw-away phone. Brian's phone looks relatively inexpensive, so I plug my charger into it and wait.

I decide to call Burgoyne while it charges.

"Hey," he says, "You find it?"

"I don't know yet. I'm charging one of the phones. Thought I'd see what the call record was. What should I look for?"

"You probably shouldn't be doing that at all. You're gonna queer the investigation."

"Let's just say I'm satisfying my curiosity. Besides, maybe something comes to me . . . how to steer you guys to it."

"You could just stay out of it. Simpson'll catch him eventually. Then the phone is just another piece of evidence."

My blood starts to heat up. "That's not good enough. This cocksucker has already cost me. He's gonna pay."

"Amen, brother. So, there are numbers to look for, Usaré's obviously. Did the cocksucker send any texts to that number? I'm guessing not. Or not many. Phone calls though. In and out both. Messages if you're lucky. The guy is careful enough to use a burner phone though, so my money says he erased everything as he went along. You'll be lucky to get anything."

"Anything else?"

"Hell. Check everything if you got the phone open—photos, locations on the maps app if there is one, the calendar. Look for unusual shit too. Patterns. Maybe there *is* a way to drop breadcrumbs for Simpson."

It's my turn to pause."You know, even if I'm right, it sucks. He's one of my teachers, the asshole. She probably didn't love this guy, but she trusted him."

"Brother, that's true in ninety percent of the killings out there. What are you gonna do when he figures out he's had?"

"I don't know yet. Punt."

"Call me when you know something about the phones." Burgoyne clicks off.

Brian' Jackson's phone finally has enough juice to function, and I turn it on and start looking around. A million calls, a jillion texts. Hundreds of photos, a couple sexty ones. Even a couple to and from Usaré. The most recent text to her says, 'whos bringing ya 2 the dance'. Apparently she didn't respond.

Yolanda's phone is password protected, so I call Burgoyne again.

"One of the phones is password protected."

"Mmm. No way for us to get anything then."

"No, but it makes sense the burner phone would have some kind of PIN or something. So I'm wondering. Did your techies ever find out anything useful about the cell towers?"

"Like what?"

"Well, you said they were researching Usaré's contact list—numbers that she might have used a few times but never attached a name to, or used a code name. Right?"

"Probably fifty or more."

"Well, what if there was one of those that always bounced off the tower that we got right here at the school? That'd probably mean the phone never left the campus, wouldn't it?"

"You never know about those damn things, but I guess it's worth a shot. Let me find out . . . see if I can get hold of 'em," he says, disappearing again.

I'm staring at Yolanda's phone, which has a Y painted on the back with pink nail polish, or maybe pink 'white-out.' Sitting there waiting, I try again to figure it out.

So Usaré gets herself involved with a teacher, more than one maybe, Rusic and someone from this hallway. I sure understand how *that* might've happened. Course, it's still possible it was just Rusic, and he kept the phone over here to throw everyone off. But that wouldn't make sense. Too much rigmarole to get in touch with her. And besides, he admitted he'd used his own phone to communicate with her, depended on her to erase everything, so he wouldn't do that *and* use a burner, would he?

If Yolanda's phone even *is* a burner phone. Or maybe this phone really does belong to one of the Yolandas, and even if Burgoyne gets the number from his techies, it won't ring when he calls. Well, if it doesn't, I can find out from Yolanda in a few hours if it's hers. The real burner phone, if there is one, will ring in Rusic's office or, hell, at his house, in which case Burgoyne won't even get the right number 'cause it didn't always ping the school cell tower. Or he already ditched the phone in some dumpster, and it's buried under a couple tons of debris out at the landfill. He's undoubtedly erased everything on his other phone by now for sure.

Now I'm the one forgetting Occam's razor. The simplest explanation is almost always the correct one. I'm just making a bunch of wild assumptions because, if the killer *is* one of the staff, I *want* it to be Rusic. So if the damn thing doesn't belong to Yolanda, then it belongs to some teacher who's in this hallway. And if it's the phone some teacher used to arrange trysts with Usaré, it steers us toward a motive. If he's discovered, he figures to lose everything—wife, family, job—might even go to prison, since Usaré was still not quite eighteen. So he kills her out of fear. But why did he think she'd out him? She hadn't even told Chevy about the guy. But we're back to Rusic then, because Chevy *did* know about him. He was on campus at the right time, he was involved with her, she even told him she'd out him. So if Yolanda's phone isn't a burner, he's the number one suspect.

Except for the Levantes of course.

Memo and Jhonny both got involved with Usaré. And she used them to meet up with this cartel guy. Dangerous shit. They had plenty to hide, for sure. And probably Jhonny's DNA inside her, somebody related to Memo but not Memo. From Saturday, if Jhonny was telling the truth about that. And he's a misogynist and a pimp like Memo. And she never would've become one of their escorts, and besides, they finally figure out it was stupid to let her meet the sureños and so they want to get rid of her. But where would they get the key to give her? Assuming she got the key from the same guy who killed her.

But they could've followed her.

Except then Keanu probably would have seen the perp go in. Keanu was undoubtedly outside the E building during the murder. Unless he's lying about that for some reason. Unless he killed her for instance. Which I doubt. Or he's got some reason to protect the Martinezes—fear again perhaps.

Yolanda's phone doesn't ring, but it starts vibrating faintly, as the screen brightens. I try to answer by swiping, but a box appears asking for a

PIN number. After perhaps a half-dozen buzzes, it stops, and my own phone rings.

"Well?" he says.

"Yeah. Was that you?"

"Yeah. That number's the one she called 'Paris'in her list of contacts. Forty-five calls and texts with that number in the last two months . . . most of 'em in-calls to Usaré's phone . . . all of 'em but two bounced off that school cell pole. Your hunch is right."

Silence for a few seconds.

"It just made sense . . . I mean if the guy was in this hallway."

"You know who it is, hey?"

"Pretty sure. Doesn't mean he killed her though." More silence. "Sucks."

"I told the lieutenant I needed to come over there in the morning and get some things outta my office while I'm on administrative leave. What's your idea?"

"Well, I can't sit in the English office and watch what's going on at six AM. It'd tip him."

"Ya think?"

"I'm going to go home and lie there with my kid and think about it. Rest some. Can you be here at five-thirty? The front office?"

"Rest is a good tool. Prevents poor performance better than proper planning. See ya soon." Then he's gone again.

I put the three phones back into their envelopes and return them to FC14 and then put the rubber gloves into my jacket pocket. After I've logged out of Cynthia's desktop computer, locked the file cabinet and closed the windows, I exit the building and head for my car.

The night is brighter with the moon higher now and the clouds dissipating. Water has already soaked through the mesh of my shoes, but there is enough light for me to avoid stepping in the puddles of collected rain. The air is cool and fresh.

I have not heard from Eloise since texting her, but I assume it's because she has not awakened since I slipped out. When I arrive home, she and Francesca look much the same as I left them, Francesca on her back asleep and Eloise on her side with an arm draped over her stepdaughter's chest, an intimacy that somehow lends me hope. I slip off my shoes and jacket, remove my belt and shirt and lie next to them. I cannot sleep, but I remind myself of Burgoyne's words—'rest is a tool.'

At four-thirty AM, I call Cynthia, to whom I promise overtime, and Amin, and Burgoyne, who promises to call Santana. Over coffee, I tell Eloise some of the things that happened yesterday, what I'm about to do. She doesn't exactly like it, and it's hard to make her understand in a few minutes why I've been doing any of the things I've been doing since she flew to San Francisco. I'm not sure I understand it all myself.

"What about Francesca?" she says. "Should I take her to school?"

"Leave it up to her, I think."

*****

I meet Cynthia in my office, and we walk together toward the E building, past the auditorium and the cafeteria, which both remind me of last Saturday, a bygone era now.

The groundsmen and custodians are clearing away pools of water with wide squeegies.

I caution myself not to share too much information with Cynthia, who's known for her round pretty face, her gossipy nature and her loyalty to the teachers she works with. My mind is set on getting all seven phones and giving a plausible explanation to Cynthia for her to pass on.

"So Teresa Benitez gets her way again," Cynthia says, suggesting I wasn't tough enough. "When did her daddy start calling?"

"Not till Friday. I guess he knew he didn't have any way to overrule the police. So it's not really her getting her own way, but him."

As we approach the hallway door, I see four teachers standing there waiting to get in—John Klein, Mac Gabello, Helen Dunham and Chris Jameson, who's wearing a sports jacket over his vest. No surprise, since they're all compulsively over-prepared teachers. It does surprise me that Nancy Horwitz is *not* there. The rest of the E teachers are, as Burgoyne would say, flexible.

"Fancy meeting you guys here," I say, hoping it lightens things up.

Nobody thinks it's funny. Helen smiles faintly. Mac and John are deadpanning.

Jameson says, "Are we finally going in or not?" It makes me bristle for some reason.

"If that's what you want." I remove the padlock and hold the door for them.

"After you," Jameson says. I turn my head and watch the staff, confident on their own turf. Cynthia, Mac and John go directly to the English office, Helen to her room. I step through the doorway, following, letting Jameson catch the door.

I talk at Jameson over my shoulder. "Leave the bathroom locked till Benjamin cleans up. He's due at six."

In the English office, Mac and John are hovering at the copy machine, discussing priorities as it warms up. Mac needs one-hundred-sixty copies; Klein needs at least a thousand and tells him to go ahead.

"Can you give me Teresa's phone then?" I say to Cynthia.

"Anything for Teresa." She smiles at me and unlocks the file cabinet.

Once the drawer is open, I more or less barge in and confiscate all the phones, stuffing them into my jacket pockets.

By way of excuses, I say, "May as well just call all the kids to the office. Santana had a lot of complaints last week."

She stares. I consider the possibility she finds me unconvincing.

"She figured it would look more consistent if we called everyone up there," I say, "instead of just Teresa," pinning the decision on my secretary. Secretaries talk, I know, but in a couple hours it won't matter.

When I leave the English office, Mac is running his copies, Klein is waiting impatiently for his turn, and Jameson is entering.

We start an announcement after I am back in my office, Santana speaking over the PA system: "Students, if you need to reclaim a phone which was confiscated over a week ago, please come directly to the Activities Office." She reads it out every twenty minutes.

Burgoyne calls me on the school phone from his office. "What does Santana know about this clusterfuck?"

"Just about everything," I say."You know she's golden."

"I'm not worried about *her*."

"It's all I could think of." Apologizing. "Like I said, I couldn't sit over there all morning staring at that file cabinet."

"But why the announcement?"

"I wanted our doer to know I'd taken the phones. Otherwise, maybe he doesn't find out for hours. No guarantee Cynthia tells him 'cause she's usually the one who returns the phones when parents come in. Saves the teacher having to get in verbal judo with some angry parent."

Nothing to do but wait now, so I call the superintendent. It's after seven o'clock, and I can't ignore his 'forthwith' any longer. I know there's a good chance this will be my final administrative act for quite a while. At the very least, I think, he'll put me on leave for a few weeks.

When I call his school number, the receptionist answers of course. Every month, JV addresses the administrators in a meeting at the Catholic Services Center, and every month he begins his inspirational address by giving us his direct number. It's about as direct as a jackrabbit's escape route, however. Whenever I've called it, I get the district receptionist, same as if I'd been John Q. Public calling in. It's no different this time. The receptionist, a soft-spoken bilingual guy named Luis, answers in Spanish, which he does about half the time.

"Buenos dias. Digame."

"Hi, Luis. This is Enrique Tavish, over at Polk High School. I have a message here from the superintendent. He's expecting my call."

"Ay, señor. It's too bad what happened over at your school. We all feel so bad about poor Usaré. And her parents. ¡Qué lástima! Have they caught the bad men yet?"

"Not as I know of. There's some detectives been here every day though. Just a matter of time."

"A lot of us believe it was Los Levantes, Señor Tavish. What do you think?"

"Could be. I just don't know." There is silence for twenty seconds or so, like he's waiting for me to say more.

"I'll put you through to Dr. Muñoz's office."

Bernadette, JV's secretary answers and tells me he has a breakfast meeting scheduled and won't be in for another couple hours. She doesn't offer to give me his cell phone number, and I don't ask for it.

*****

The tardy bell rings at eight o'clock, and all the students' phones have been claimed. Except Yolanda's.

"So now what?" Burgoyne asks. Santana has already filled him in, apparently.

"Just what I was wondering."

We listen to each other's silence for a few moments.

"What about calling the two girls up here? See if it maybe actually does belong to one of them," I say.

"Eliminates a possibility, for sure," Burgoyne says.

"Or just wait on his next move. He's gotta be squirming. Wondering if anybody's been able to get into the phone."

"Mmmm. I'm guessing he's squirming some, like you say. But he also knows the phone is just sitting up here in your office. If we'da got in, that would've happened a week ago and he'd be in lockup. So he might sit tight. Figures if nobody claims the phone, he's in the clear."

"Can't we get his DNA and compare it to what we find on the phone?" Then I remember our clearance cards. "Or fingerprints. His prints are on file with the Department of Public Safety, same as mine. Same as yours too, I guess."

"Nah, there's no link established between the phone and the crime. Not part of the crime scene because it was locked away. You gotta think of a way to force his hand."

"So the guy walks away . . ."

"Think of something soon. I can't wait around much longer," Burgoyne says.

"If I give the girls another hour, maybe he'll just fuck up. Or maybe I think of something."

"You need to put him in a situation where he has to make a decision in a matter of seconds. Like when you get a kid to lie to you, and he's stuck with the lie he told."

I look up the Yolandas on my computer again. There's Yolanda *Valencia* Franco and there's Yolanda *Hipolita* Franco. Based on their class schedules, I want the *Valencia* girl. First, I have Santana verify Yolanda is in her first period class, and then I pick up the PA microphone. The teachers always hate it when we call for a single kid over the public address system instead of sending a call slip, but I want everyone in the school to hear this announcement.

"Yolanda Valencia Franco: please report immediately to the Activities Office." I say it twice.

Yolanda is an extremely thin girl and I wonder if she's anorexic. She also doesn't look much like the picture of her in her student record because she has bleached her hair after photos were taken. She's wearing a brown G-unit tank top and jeans that she paid too much for so she could sport the worn and ragged look. There's a small white purse hanging from her shoulder. She smells faintly of marijuana, as if she took a couple hits off some other kid's joint on the way to school, which surprises me a little because she's a B-plus student.

I bring her into my office and close the door, but Burgoyne knocks and I let him in as well. I can tell she doesn't like it that he's showed up. He sits in his usual spot on the far side of the room, and I invite Yolanda to take a chair right in front of my desk.

"Am I in trouble?" she asks, narrowing her eyes a little.

"No, you're not," I am quick to say. "Officer Burgoyne and I were hoping you'd help us with something."

She's suspicious.

"We're trying to find someone."

"You gonna use me for a dope bust?" she says, thinking we're after her dealer maybe, and wanting nothing to do with it.

"We think somebody in your second period class might have information about Usaré's murder," I say. "Did you know Usaré?"

"Her and me was best friends in middle school," her face taking on a sorrow-torn look. "We still hung out once in a while. What you need me to do?"

"Well, I'm getting a little ahead of myself. I need to know if you had a phone confiscated here at school the last few weeks."

She looks confused, shakes her head.

I put on my gloves and bring the phone out of its envelope.

"So this isn't yours?"

She shakes her head again.

"Okay, then here's what I want you to do. I'm going to give you this phone to take with you to your next class. I want you to keep it in your purse until it's close to the end of second period. You with me so far?"

"I'm not as stupid as your teachers you know." Her voice reminds me of Jody Foster's, hearty and deep.

"Sorry, didn't mean to patronize." I actually did mean to patronize, and she knows this and gives me a dismissive look.

"So keep it in my purse till the end of class. Then what?"

"I need you to leave it behind. Face down, so that pink mark shows. Like you forgot it. Like you were distracted or whatever. Pretend you thought you had it and leave."

"Sir, I get it. Act it out. Then what? Just go merrily on my way? Ain't too convincing."

"No, come back in half a minute. If it's where you left it, just grab it and go to third period. We'll come get it. If it's disappeared, then ask about the phone. Ask any kids in the room. Ask the teacher. You have to be convincing though."

"Sir, I gotta tell you, your plan is stupid."

I stare at her, and Burgoyne is staring at me over her shoulder.

"I gotta show the phone around some, quiet-like you know, to my friends. Like I tricked you guys, you know? I mean, you thought it was my phone, and called me up here to give it back to me. So I gotta church it up some. Tell my maggs 'Look what I got for free, fool.' Cuz the phone ain't mine, you know?"

She waits for us to catch on, then says, "I can do that. That teacher always lets us get up and do an activity halfway through the period."

"Smart teacher. Well, be discreet. Don't let the teacher catch you showing the phone around. Might confiscate it. Then our plan is out the window."

She smiles at me like I'm stupid. "It'll be fine." She pops up from her chair. "Anything else?"

"Yeah," Burgoyne says. "Dawdle before you leave. Don't be the last one out of the room, but say, before the last six-eight kids beat it out of there. Pay attention to who's still in the room when you leave too, 'cause we'll want to know who they were. Then come back and look for the phone." He wants her to think we're after a kid, I guess.

"Okay." With a little less confidence now. "What if somebody follows me?"

"Follows you," Burgoyne repeats, like he always does, making it a question. I look at his face, which is still soft and innocent, as if the last week hasn't happened.

Yolanda glances over her shoulder at him, probably wishing the cop weren't in the room, then back toward me. "A lot of us kids think it was one of the Levantes killed Usaré. Jhonny Martinez, maybe. What if one of *them* follows me."

"It'll be fine. They just want their phone back and you're leaving it for them," I say. "And anyway, Amin will be there in the hall along with me and the officer here. Amin can tail you, make sure there's no one."

She nods and I hand her the phone. She slips it into her purse and then she's gone.

"Smart kid," Burgoyne says.

"We need a meeting. Amin and one more. Let's say Frank. He's got more sand than I thought."

Burgoyne waits.

"But you need to do the logistics," I say. "Should we really make a show of following Yolanda?"

"Probably should. Not *much* chance the Levantes did your girl, or that they're interested in the phone, but still a chance. Burn one of your guys on following her. The teacher probably ain't armed, but you never know with a gangbanger. 'sides, if the teacher was packing, one more security guy don't make a difference. We're probably giving him too much time though . . . thirty seconds."

"Well, let's find out. Set the timer on your phone."

Burgoyne does it and says, "Okay, talk me through it. Go."

I lay it out the way I've visualized it:

"Of course, he's spotted it already and he's thinking about grabbing it . . . wondering if it's smart to grab it . . . wondering if she'll come back before the last goddamned dawdlers leave . . . praying no kid asks him some stupid question about the lesson . . . finally deciding yes, this may be his only chance to grab it . . . he's already moved close to it standing there next to her desk to block the dawdlers' view . . . then he's alone and he doesn't know for how long . . . seconds? . . . half a minute before another batch of kids starts filing in? . . . not even enough time to go take a piss . . . so he grabs it and stashes it, no time to look at the phone records right now or turn it off. He stashes it . . . How long was that?"

"Forty-eight seconds."

I wait.

"He'll probably assume the battery is dead anyway, after a week," Burgoyne says. "And she's already back in there, looking for the phone. Good call. He says 'No, never saw the thing,' and she leaves and he's in the clear. All he has to do is get through the day and then ditch it. Get your boys in here."

I use the radio. "Amin and Frank, please report to the activities office."

They both roger me.

Burgoyne says, "We gotta be right there so he doesn't have time to open the phone and switch to silent or power off . . . you charged it, right?"

I nod. "He's overconfident, but I don't think he'll risk logging into the phone. Like you said, he's got a short decision-making window. He's still thinking about getting it stashed, not worried about her specifically, 'cause he knows the phone ain't hers, but he's still anxious."

"So he'll stash it where?"

"Well, he ain't gonna be stuffing it up above the ceiling tiles, standing on his desk . . . so in his desk or in his closet."

There is a long silence.

"Terrible thing, a guy like that," he says.

"Lost his soul."

*****

At nine-fifty, we are all in place: Frank at the east end of the E hall acting as if he's doing nothing, living up to his reputation but waiting to follow Yolanda where we expect her to exit the building, Amin outside the west end, and me waiting in the hallway with Burgoyne, looking into classrooms from time to time—the few we can see into without opening the door.

Half the teachers have filled in the narrow door-windows to their rooms with collages or poster strips or blank paper so nobody can look in. It's against regulation, but we administrators don't enforce the reg because it helps teachers manage their classrooms. At any given time, there are twenty kids roaming the hallways at Polk High School, and usually they are looking for opportunities to interact with friends who are stuck in class. It's a pain-in-the-ass interruption for teachers, so most of them keep their doors closed during class, and the little windows covered.

The superintendent's office has not called back for me, nor has Burgoyne so far heard from his lieutenant, and now we've both turned off our cell phones. I've told Santana I can't be disturbed, and I know she'll find a way to deflect JV and Augustine if they call.

As dismissal time approaches, a few kids are leaking from classrooms where their teachers either don't have strong student management skills or are simply more than ready for second period to end. One senior English class in particular, Mr. Navarette's, emits a steady trickle of seventeen- and eighteen-year-olds. If I didn't have something else to do, I'd send them back to class. But most of the teachers in this hallway are strong teachers. Klein, Jameson, Dunham, Gabello, Horwitz—their kids have been taught to stay involved in the lesson until the last possible second.

"So what do we do if we're right? Tackle him before he swallows a cyanide pill?"

Burgoyne doesn't answer right away. "You do the talking, hey?"

The bell rings, a pinging sound actually, and a flood of students gushes into the hallway. Half the teachers post themselves outside their doors to monitor student behavior and greet their third period classes. In the flow of kids, some guy with a Los Levantes tattoo actually does emerge from Yolanda's classroom. I watch him exit west, toward Park Avenue, the same direction that Yolanda will likely go.

"Tavish to Frank," I say into the radio." When he responds, I say, "Eyes on the double-L boy now exiting your end. That's double Lima."

He rogers me.

About a minute after the dismissal bell, when the tide of kids in the hall has ebbed to forty or so, Yolanda appears from her classroom and walks toward the west end as well, slow, counting her steps I think, the little purse dangling from her shoulder, her eyes glancing toward Burgoyne and me. She winks. After about a dozen paces, she stops and opens her purse, pretending to look for something, acting the part for me and Burgoyne, and Burgoyne says, "I guess we were able to make her think we were after a kid."

Now she whirls and goes back and opens the door and disappears inside, and Burgoyne and I move to a place just outside the door to wait for her to emerge again. I raise Amin on the radio and tell him to come into the hallway. The classroom door opens again, and a group of kids files past us, quizzing us with their eyes but asking each other about some algebra assignment.

Kids who've come from other buildings are arriving now, sometimes soloing in, sometimes in clusters.

When she comes out of the classroom this time, I ask Yolanda if she's got the phone.

She shakes her head. "Nobody seen it." She heads west again.

When Burgoyne and I come in, Chris Jameson is standing near his closet door, his hand on the knob, and he turns to look at us. He's not wearing his jacket any longer, just the vest.

"Hello, Chris," I say.

"You boys hot on the trail of some hapless drug entrepreneur?" he says, trying to smirk but not quite succeeding. He looks stiff, his hand still on the closet doorknob, his tanned face looking a shade lighter than it usually does.

I say, "Wondering if you've seen a phone. Has a pink letter Y on the back."

"A cell phone?"

The door opens behind us, some kids starting to come in. Chatting about some party.

"Yeah, we thought it belonged to Yolanda Franco, gave it to her a little bit ago. Turns out it wasn't hers, so we wanted to retrieve it."

"Can't say I have. Maybe you could come back later though. I have a lesson to present." His stance shifts, but his hand doesn't move from the knob, like it's stuck there while he waits for us to leave.

We're standing in the fluorescence, me and Burgoyne and this teacher who's just picked up a phone from Yolanda's desk. Kids keep spilling into the room, filling it with young voices, Jameson becoming more apprehensive by the second, his droopy eyes not so droopy now and looking suddenly troubled.

Marcus Lee approaches and presents a form to his teacher. "Mr. J, I need a release to go to a chess tournament."

"Put it on his desk, Marcus," I say.

The door opens again. More kids babble into the room, Amin following them.

"Is something wrong?" Jameson manages.

"You sure you don't know where that phone went? We already talked to Yolanda. She swore she left it in here." I try to sound inquisitive rather than accusatory, not succeeding, afraid he's had time to silence the phone.

The warning bell sounds. One minute to the tardy bell, and kids stream in, and most take their seats. I think of my evaluations of Jameson over the past few years, reminding me of the phrase "good mastery of his students' behavior."

Burgoyne takes his cell phone from his pocket, turns it back on. He has grown impatient with my interview.

"If you'd just let me get on with my class . . ." Jameson says, no conviction in it.

"We'll be out of your hair in a few minutes, but we need to do a preliminary search for the missing phone. It's pretty important. Only take a second."

While I wait for Burgoyne's phone to fire up, I ask Jameson, "You dropped off Rocha to chaperone the dance?"

He nods, knowing I know.

"That's damn nice of you. Did you have some other reason to come all the way over here that night? Work on your lesson plans? You take her home too?"

He shakes his head, waiting. We're all waiting. The class has grown quiet, sensing tension. The tardy bell rings.

Then Burgoyne presses his touch screen a few times.

I use my teacher voice to the class, "I need silence right now. We have an important announcement."

Then we hear the buzzing. It's muffled but only a few feet away. It buzzes twice. The buzzing seems to come from inside the closet.

Jameson tries one last gambit, stepping away from me and Burgoyne, finally releasing his grip on the doorknob.

"Okay, class, let's begin with a review of yesterday's lesson. So who killed Hector?" A few hands go up and a few kids blurt out Achilles. When he stops talking, we can hear the buzzing again, and I move toward the closet. Jameson makes a quick step toward the closet door, like he's going to intercept me, but Burgoyne blocks him.

"Amin," I say.

"I need the class to come with me," Amin says. He's using his preacher voice. They obey, stand, start exiting, something they're doing just as quickly for him as they would for me.

When I open the closet door, I see Jameson's jacket hanging there on a clothes rod. The jacket buzzes.

Amin touches each kid on the way out, counting and reassuring them.

"It's not what you think," Jameson says.

"I sure hope not," I say. I put on my rubber gloves again and lift the jacket off its hanger. The buzzing has stopped, so Burgoyne clicks off and presses redial.

"It's not what you think," he says.

When the vibrations begin again, I begin going through its pockets. Jameson has backed away from Burgoyne, and he sits in the chair at his desk.

I reach into the inside breast pocket because I think that's the source of the buzzing. It's not. Instead, my hand comes out with a pink and silky thing: strands of elastic . . . a triangle of fabric. A girl's thong panties. I show it to Burgoyne and lay it on Jameson's desk. Finally, still buzzing, out comes Yolanda's phone.

"Oh God," Jameson says.

It's an odd appeal from a soulless man, I think.

"Stand up and turn around, please," Burgoyne says. He binds Jameson's hands with a set of plastic handcuffs and pushes him back into his chair and starts reciting the Miranda warnings.

After I lock the classroom door I use the radio. "Tavish here. Amin, did the sub meet you in the chorus room?"

"Roger that."

"Come on back to the classroom then. We're going to need some help. Frank, if you got Yolanda where she needs to be without incident, we can use you as well."

"Roger that."

Burgoyne is talking to Santana on the radio as well, using a different channel. He asks if Simpson and Bejarano have arrived. When she apparently says no, I think he's happy about it and he tells her to call 911, tells her to ask the cops to park on the west end of the E building. He extracts small evidence bags from a pocket, inserts Yolanda's phone into one, the dainty thong into another.

We have maybe three minutes before the police patrol cars will arrive. I sit in one of the student desks near Jameson.

"She was gonna expose you?"

He has lowered his head, and he keeps it low.

"Tavish, shut up," Burgoyne says. I ignore him. He's standing just behind Jameson, and he turns on his phone to record.

"That why you did it? She was gonna out you? You knew you'd lose your wife, your job? Maybe go to jail. Freaked you out, I bet." Then I wait, giving him space to talk.

His head hangs low. We can't see his eyes. He shakes slowly side to side. "She was kissing me off." His head comes up. "Leaving me." Like we'd see then.

That it was the only way.

"Right," I say. "She told you it was over. Shit happens, bro."

He is trembling. His eyes are full of tears and he drops his head again, hiding his eyes with his hands, leaning onto his desk. "We were supposed to talk. That's why I gave her the key, so we could be alone for a while and talk. It was gonna be fine. I just needed more time."

"For what? You think she was going to move in with you."

The classroom door opens, and in come Amin and Frank.

"I got her an apartment. Was gonna help her out while she went to the U."

The hum of the fluorescent lights is the only sound for a half-minute.

"But she wouldn't listen?" I say.

"She loved the idea . . . at first . . . But it wasn't enough. It was all I had, but it wasn't enough . . . She found something better."

I don't say anything, remembering that day sitting with her on the sofa, our fingers so close.

"She was an hour late." He faces me again, his eyes droopy and teary. "Then all she said was we could do the dog one last time. That she had to move on." He shakes his head.

"You used a condom?" Burgoyne says.

He nods.

"And afterward, you pushed her face down into the pillow. Held it there," Burgoyne says.

Jameson drops his head into his hands again and starts to sob.

"Came off, didn't it. The condom. As you smothered her. Left your junk on the sofa. All that trouble you went to . . ."

"Frank, secure the hallway doors. Nobody else comes in," I say. "Amin, go up and down the hallway and tell the teachers we need all kids kept in class till I give the all-clear. No emergency bathroom trips." As he opens the door to exit, I call to him again.

"Make sure Navarette and McNally understand. No emergencies."

He nods and leaves.

There's a lot I still want to ask Jameson, but I don't say anything. None of us do.

When the patrol officers arrive, Burgoyne tells them to take Jameson, the jacket, the two little evidence bags. He'll meet them at the station.

He tells me to seal the room in case the crime scene techs want to look for more evidence.

"I'll get the district locksmith over here," I say. "Change the lock."

"Crazy, him carrying the thong around like that," Burgoyne says.

"Probably had it all last week too. In his jacket. It was more than a trophy, like a token of remembrance. You think there was anything wrong with the search?"

"Nope. I couldn't have done it like that, but you're golden. His lawyer will argue of course, but the county attorney will show you were entitled to search the jacket."

"I feel bad for his family."

SEVENTEEN

I have only been inside the superintendent's office once before, the day he offered me the contract to become assistant principal at Polk High School. Instead of the institutional green on the walls of most of our building interiors, it's painted a soft shade of yellow, which he mentioned to me at the time is called humble gold.

"It's to remind me about what kind of leader I set out to become," he said. "The kind of leader you should be." I paid no attention, of course.

It was a day of promise. I remember thinking that I would become the principal of one of the district's high schools inside three years, four tops. Our librarian, John Tevis, told me if I hadn't made the jump by then, I'd be an AP forever.

So here I sit seven years later. The humble gold looks fresh, but the mood is very different.

There are five of us, including JV Muñoz of course, Governing Board President Benitez, George Peña, the district's PR guy and Larry Farness, the district's in-house counsel. JV and his two staff guys are wearing silk suits. Italian, I'd bet.

"Why didn't you give us a heads-up?" JV asks. "After you killed this man Thursday night . . . Friday morning."

"I'm sorry, Dr. Muñoz. I should have. It was all a normal investigation, me assisting Jim Burgoyne and the two detectives . . . Then, Thursday I couldn't think about anything but getting my daughter back."

He says, "Yes, that had to be a terrifying thing," waiting for me to go on, giving Benitez a sideward glance, reading him. A superintendent is a creature of the board, after all.

"I spent all day Friday and Saturday getting my family situated. Except for the memorial service, of course."

"You shot a second man yesterday," Benitez says. "Like some kind of Elliott Ness."

I can tell JV doesn't like this. I'm guessing he told Benitez he could attend as an observer, that he has no standing with any employee except the superintendent. I think that if I were in the same circumstances as JV right now, I'd remind Benitez of that.

Tough to project though. JV needs three out of five board members on his side at all times or, poof, he's gone.

Humility is a good goal for a man like JV to strive for, but I think very few people rise to a high position without a fair amount of its opposite, and I suspect I have more than my share of that.

"No disrespect, sir, but I shot *two* men yesterday . . . A punk who used to come to school here, Jhonny Martinez, who's still alive, and another guy who was shooting at *me*."

"And what you think they gonna do, the friends of that stone-cold killer? The guy shooting at you and that other boy. Uh? Jus' say have a nice day. The whole school in danger cuz of you."

"I'm hoping they're still mainly interested in the Martinez kid, which is who those sureños were after in the first place. My daughter's kidnapping was Jhonny's idea."

I wait a few heartbeats, hoping that JV jumps in to rescue me, but of course he doesn't.

"I know the school faces some risks, along with me and my family, so I'm prepared to tender a letter of resignation if Dr. Muñoz asks."

It disarms Benitez, placates him to a degree, and he lets the superintendent regain control.

"With all deference to the board, we don't think that's a good idea right now. Though perhaps in a few weeks it could become necessary." JV is looking at Benitez. Then he goes on. "George, do you want to explain our thinking?"

George Peña has been smiling since I entered, a perpetual smile that he's groomed to project certainty and guilelessness. Everything about him projects careful grooming—the moussed hair, the arranged red kerchief in his breast pocket, the warmth in his voice.

He says, "Dr. Muñoz, Mr. Benitez, we think it would prove counterproductive for Mr. Tavish to resign right now. As all the circumstances come out about these incidents, the press may very well portray Mr. Tavish as a victim. A hero even." George continues to smile as he says this, conveying a sense of assurance that I don't think is merited. But then, he's the high-priced PR guy, not me, and his words start to soothe me.

"Hero," Benitez says. It reminds me of Burgoyne, repeating the one word.

"The first stories are already out on some blogs. All on Mr. Tavish's side so far. The twelve-thirty news will be doing a five-minute piece. We won't know for sure until we see all the stories, but we sense most media will take the same spin as our press release regarding the events in Why:

'School leader and policeman team up to rescue child.' They've already asked permission to interview district personnel."

"You won't be making any direct statement," JV says to me. "When they do contact you, you need to respond about its being an active investigation and so forth." His eyes are stern. At first, it makes me wonder if I'll get reporters coming by the house, which I don't think will be good for Francesca and which Eloise will detest, but then I realize JV is actually appealing to Benitez to keep *his* mouth shut.

"So what are we doing about the rest of it?" Benitez is white-knuckling now. He likes attention, given to saying things for sound-bite quality, but often as not the reporter catches him in an exaggeration. Since I haven't been watching the news, I wonder what he's said in his most recent interviews.

"As you know," George says, "the district has not been in the most favorable light since the poor García girl was found, and our troubles will be compounded by Mr. Jameson's arrest. But we think Mr. Tavish's actions are going to help us turn that around."

"Like I said, what are we *doing*?" Benitez says.

"I've prepared a second press release. Stated the obvious about events this morning . . ."

Nobody helps him, but George doesn't seem to mind. He reads. "'City police have arrested district teacher Christopher Jameson in connection with the recent murder of student Usaré García. The school's internal investigation, led by Enrique Tavish, assisted police in apprehending the suspect, and district officials are offering all available resources as the investigation continues.' Of course, it helps us that Tavish was the one who actually tracked down the girl's alleged murderer. We're going to make the most of that. And naturally we'll keep rolling out press releases with each piece of news."

Benitez says nothing for a few moments, accepting the sense of JV's approach, but not liking it.

"So what's the internal recommendation then?" Benitez says. "About your administrator."

JV has his answer ready. "It starts with indefinite administrative leave for Mr. Tavish. But George will continue issuing press releases that highlight his resourcefulness uncovering the truth about the Garcia girl's murder . . . as well as some not insignificant bravery in apprehending the kidnapers. We're also bringing on additional security at Polk . . . off-duty police officers. Your concern for the school is certainly on point."

I think about my Francesca and NJ and Eloise, wondering what kind of protection I can arrange for them.

JV's folded his arms across his chest. It's his signal. The decision is made.

I hold the door open, playing sycophant, letting the others leave and intending to follow them out, but Muñoz holds me back as I'm about to exit.

"Come sit down."

When we sit, he refers at first to the table where we are sitting. "Birdseye maple. I had it built by the district carpenter shop right after I arrived. In those days, the pressure from the state to reduce spending was just beginning, but the board wanted me to maintain the full staff at maintenance, so I created a few projects for them." Beating around the bush. What I am expecting is for him to insist I resign. No pressure. Just doing what's best for the district.

"Do you like it?" he says.

"It's a beautiful piece," saying what's expected and wondering what his point is.

"Sometimes a superintendent obeys the will of the board, and sometimes a superintendent shapes the board's will. A head has to roll for this," he says.

I nod agreeably, wondering if Eloise's promotion could still happen.

"Do you think you could handle the principalship at Polk?" He's straight-faced.

I am confused, so I say nothing.

"Do you?"

"Yes, sir. I do," telling myself to keep the answers short.

"It sounds as if Mr. Rusic had also been involved with the girl. Did you know that?" His arms are folded again, his back straight, his eyes unwavering.

"Yes, sir. He basically admitted it to me last week."

"And what did you do about it?"

"I reported forthwith, sir, as required. To Jim Burgoyne." After a few seconds, I add, "Which I'm guessing you already know."

"I'm putting this Rusic on leave as well. The police are already interviewing him. We don't want to overdo it, so we'll leave it to some enterprising reporter to read the police records and discover that you were the one who reported Coach Rusic as a sex offender."

There's nothing for me to say.

"Two of your colleagues knew about it long before you did."

"Sir?"

"Your boss, Augustine Oropeza, and Will Bentsen. They're going to be gone too."

"It's too bad it's turning out this way."

"It's going to be a lot worse than merely 'too bad.' It's going to look like Polk High School is run by a den of whoremongers and killers. If George can even make us look even half-normal in the media, it will be a major accomplishment."

I nod, wondering if he's thinking of me as part of the den of killers. The board president apparently does.

"The district needs a hero, Enrique. I can't offer it to you yet, but if the media portrays you the way George anticipates, I'll want you to assume the principalship at Polk. I can name you interim without board approval. Will you think about that?"

"Yes, sir. I will. Do you think the board would support me staying there beyond the interim?"

"I don't know about Mr. Benitez, but I'll make sure you have three votes. Unless you screw it up." He sits a moment longer with his arms crossed. "I'll be assigning two of the directors to help Sally at Polk for a few days, people with site experience. I suspect you'll be back there in a week." He stands and extends his hand and says, "Things can change quickly, Enrique. Stay humble." It's just before two o'clock when he sends me out the door.

*****

"Wanna have a chat?" Burgoyne says. He's sitting in his pickup in the district office parking lot, apparently waiting for me to come out of my meeting.

"I got a couple updates you may be interested in." There's an expression on his face that resembles a grin. "First, your boy Jameson talked like a precocious five-year-old. You only just got him started. The interrogators couldn't shut him up."

"I detest him but I pity him."

"He didn't mean to do it, he said. He only wanted to talk to her, didn't even think they'd have sex. He was just gonna talk her out of leaving him. That was his plan anyway. This was around ten or so. He waited there after he dropped the other teacher off at eight for her chaperoning duties at the dance. What's her name?"

"Rocha, the special ed teacher."

"He parked in the main parking lot, figuring his car would blend in with the rest. We're bound to find him on the security camera for that area. One of the few places on campus that ain't a blind spot. Exiting his car and then returning.

"Then he waited. In E building. According to him, she'd promised to come by before ten," Burgoyne says. "So he just fiddled around, looked at book counts and such, department business, trying to read some Shakespeare play, fidgeting apparently, until she showed."

"He probably thinks of himself as Othello now, and her as Desdemona, but it's pathetic more than it is tragic, more like the story of Troilus and Cressida."

Burgoyne is not familiar with either play, apparently, and goes on. "He'd found an extra key to lend her, thanks to your great security over in the key department."

The comment irritates me, but I say nothing.

"Then she's late, of course, and it starts getting him riled up. He's thinking he should postpone the whole thing, go home. She's not coming, so he calls her from the burner phone, and she never answers, of course. He puts the phone back then, figuring to use it again in a week or so.

"But then, just before he's gonna leave, he hears the outer door open, and he knows it's her. He starts going over in his head what he's going to say, how he's going to take care of her. Has the place picked out and leased already, under a phony name, cute brick one-bedroom on tenth street, a bank account for her. He's figured out a way to pilfer a few dollars for her every month. In his mind, this is gonna get her back.

"She comes in twirling her panties, the thong, smiling at him but getting ready to dump him. He knows she's just offering a gratuitous goodbye fuck. But he figures he'll hear her out first, and afterward convince her that he's still her ticket to ride at Easy Times University.

"He said he should have turned back then, knew it deep down. Shoulda sent her back to the dance. Still coulda canceled the lease. Nobody woulda found out. He's a sophisticate, after all, knows just how far he can press things without going too far. Knows how to cover his tracks.

"But she gave him the look. The eyes, you know, the parted mouth. So of course he couldn't resist, and he told himself that he would do her and then maybe he could convince her, figuring it was easiest to persuade her after she'd orgasmed. He's telling himself he'll just do her this one last time and then forget her if she's still past persuading. Come to work Monday like there'd never been nothing between 'em. They've both been pretending this long, and he knows he can do it forever. Go back to being just her teacher. And to hell with her.

"But some time, while they're fucking, he decided she'd been using him, that it wasn't right, that she'd probably used a dozen men before him, and that she'd probably betray a hundred more after him, and he suddenly wanted to hurt her, make an impression on her, teach her a lesson.

"Went crazy the way people can in the middle of sex. 'cause he knew she wouldn't change her mind, that everything he'd risked was for nothing. That's how he put it off on her, made it *her* fault when all was said and done."

I remember Andre's story about Usaré. Jhonny's story too. I recall the accusations about Usaré's father, about Memo. And I recall that long moment during the retreat, Usaré's fingers an inch away . . . the look she gave me . . . the times I did a drop-in observation on a teacher just so I could observe *her*, yes, even after I met Eloise and even after I was remarried . . . that first time she came to my office and paused to tell me she was infatuated with me . . . and the past year with her in the office as an aide every day . . . the swell of her breasts always reminding me she was a woman . . .

"Stupid SOB didn't even want a lawyer. Simpson kept asking him too. It's all on tape. Her skirt was up. She was holding her skirt for him, naked below the waste of course. And she kept moaning. He kept talking about how she moaned. Christ, he was reliving it as he told us about it in the interview room. Which is why he probably didn't ask for a lawyer.

"And then he came inside her, except not really inside her but in the condom. And he knew it had to be then, while he had the leverage to hold her down, her face in the cushion, to punish her, to show her he still had power even though his erection was shriveling . . . Jesus! . . . She tried to fight but couldn't get any purchase on the sofa, and he used most of his body weight on her thighs while he pushed down with all his strength on the back of her head. Until she went quiet."

"Said it just like that?"

"Pretty much. He had a certain coldness as he looked back at his rage. Like he didn't understand it any more. But you could tell that for him lust and potency were all mixed together."

"Most men see it that way . . . partly. Don't you think? An erection means power."

"But the balance was gone for him, like with a rapist."

"Why'd he move the body to the bathroom? I mean, if he'd have just got her outside the building—"

"I know, right? Then the keys would have meant nothing. Course, he didn't have a plan for that because he didn't plan on killing her. But his condom had come off sometime while he was smothering her and he knew it'd be impossible to get all his DNA outta that sofa. And then he remembered seeing the graffiti earlier in the day, and he thought it would look like there had been a struggle in there, and maybe we'd put it off on the Levantes. Made no sense 'cause he knew she'd died from asphyxiation by smothering, and there was nothing in the bathroom to smother her with. Not a criminal mastermind, your Jameson."

"He morphed. I'm guessing he fell in love with her," I say. "Then went mad when it turned out Usaré wasn't who he thought she was. Did you ever meet her?"

He doesn't answer for a long moment. "Guess I'm glad I didn't. Sounds like the short road to hell." But he doesn't understand. Just like Jameson, he's putting it on her.

"Just missed the turn myself," I say.

"I wanna hear that story some time."

"You'd have to get more than one whiskey in me."

He nods, knowing that would be impossible.

"You said a *couple* things," I say.

"Not quite as interesting to you, I imagine. They located the second accomplice in the Robinson case, the guy who helped Manny snatch the girl. One Alonzo Peña de Gradillas."

"So is he talking?"

"Unfortunately, Mr. Gradillas is currently locked up in a Mexican calaboose and unavailable for questioning unless our boys can work something out with the Mexican Federal Police. Charged with kidnapping, which is apparently damn big business south of the border."

"So no way of knowing if the girl's dad was in on it," I say.

"Looks like not. But the techies are trying to hack into the computers and phones that Chucho and Manny left behind down in Why. Something may still turn up."

I don't want to sound cowardly, but I have to ask, "Do those sureños know who killed Manny and Chucho? . . . and the other two guys?"

"We kept it out of the police report . . . but Jhonny will give it up, I'd say, to save his ass."

*****

After Burgoyne leaves, I finally have the time to call Mimi. I try her office number first.

"Hello, this is Mrs. Nelson," she says, professional, a welcoming tone in her voice.

"Hello, Mimi. It's Enrique."

"Just a minute." Her voice has an edge now. I hear the thud of her phone being laid on her desk, the sound of her office door closing. "Oh my God, Enrique, what the fuck is going on at this school?"

"Maybe it's the water," remembering a factory some of my neighbors had sued a couple decades ago for pouring radioactive waste into the sewer and contributing to developmental problems for their children. It's a tasteless joke, and Mimi doesn't get it anyway, since it didn't affect her neighborhood like it did mine.

"It didn't surprise me to hear about Coach Rusic, but, my God— Jameson? His wife is so sweet," she says.

"I know. It's no good."

"No wonder everybody's taking their kids to charter schools."

"Listen, Mimi, I need to consult with you about something, and it's going to take a few minutes to explain. I was wondering if we could meet this afternoon."

Mija's is my idea. Mimi has never heard of the place, but she meets me there at four o'clock. They're closing in an hour.

The first ten minutes, she grieves and pours out her surprise about Polk High School, about Rusic and Jameson, like a relative at a funeral who's just found out her dead cousin was a narcissistic bestial pervert. I listen. She is a small, pretty woman with long eyelashes, and except for all the worry lines that are fighting for control of her face, she reminds me of a young Liz Taylor.

"Augustine *knew*, Enrique. He knew about Coach Rusic!" Her eyes probe me.

"Looks like."

"Who else knew?"

"I don't know that, Mimi. I'm actually here about something else."

She doesn't say anything. I'd assumed she'd heard about my family's trouble, making this all a little easier to explain. Apparently, she hasn't.

"It sounds like Will knew. Maybe a couple of the coaches. A few kids for sure," I say.

"How long was this going on? I can't believe nobody found out." Accusing me now.

"You've known Usaré for over three years. As well as anyone. Did *you* have suspicions?"

She hesitates, then says, "Of course not."

"The main thing is there won't be any more," I say.

It creates a pause, and I start talking. I start with the fire alarm, Neto Arregon, the threats that I didn't take seriously enough, the wrestling match in my office. The rest of it, the things I need her to know, the mad dash to Why, until I'm explaining Francesca's vile violation and her reactions since, watching Mimi's face, which acquires a broken look—as if I've twisted something inside her, then tears puddling in her eyes until she soaks them up with a napkin. She's an empath.

This is why our kids bring her their pain and worry and disappointment. She touches my hand on the table, her eyes focused on mine, unflinching, still leaking tears but sturdy, like a dam's spillway.

I tell her about NJ's pain—the death of his best friend, the strange alienation of his sister, my failure to comfort him. I tell her the way Eloise surprised me by coming back and seeking out Francesca and saving her from an incompetent father, the way it shamed me too, for not having enough faith.

That's when I ask her for the name of a counselor for Francesca.

She sheds more tears, then prints out two names on the back of one of her cards and slides it across the table to me. Her breathing is hard, deep.

"I don't understand these monsters. Who are they? Why did they come after your daughter?"

It's difficult to answer. "I pushed some people a little too hard when I shouldn't have."

"These Levantes? Who are they?"

"You wouldn't know them, probably. Memo and Jhonny Martinez."

Her eyes widen as if a predator has just appeared. "Martinez! Rosa's family?"

"Her brothers, yeah. Why?"

There are deep furrows between her eyes. "She's been in to see me. Three times in the past week. She's frightened. Terrified really. She seemed to want to talk again at the memorial service on Monday but there were too many kids around."

She's looking into me for an insight.

Now I worry too. "What was she afraid of?" knowing the answer.

"She didn't like living there, with everything that was going on around her, especially since their mother died, the things they expected her to do. She wanted out of the house but didn't know where to go."

"It's always tougher for kids than I think . . . tougher than I remember. And her situation may be worse than you think." I tell her about her defiance to Jhonny, about her giving me Memo's number, and how I found the drop house in Why.

She has locked her tiny fingers around my wrist like an over-tightened handcuff. Her face has gone white. "Oh my God, what if they know that?"

"I doubt they knew. They probably blamed us showing up there on Jhonny's stupidity."

But even so, I think, she might have been the sureños' price.

Mimi's face is still strained with worry.

"Do you know if she was in class today?" I ask. She shakes her head, so I call Santana's cell phone. She knows she's not supposed to work any overtime, but I know she often logs out officially, then spends half-an hour or more tying up loose ends.

Santana's voice is low and calm. "Well, you and Sally are the only ones left. You do still have a job here, don't you?" I can tell her question is only partly a jest.

"Yeah, it's going to be fine. I need you to look up a student record if you can though."

"Have to be on your computer, Mr. Tavish, or we'll get in trouble with the Feds again." I can tell she's already on her way to my office. "You haven't changed your password, have you?"

"No. I just need you to log in and check today's attendance for a student. Rosa Martinez, freshman."

"You never turned off your computer. Just take a second . . . You know when you're coming back? There's all these rumors. They're putting Sally in charge for the rest of the week, which is *not* a rumor."

"You know more than I do then, but yeah, don't let the movers come in."

"Here it is. Martinez, Rosa. Negative. Rosa didn't make it to school today."

"Then I need you to call the school security office and get them to do a home visit. A wellness check." I'm shaking my head at Mimi. "Or have Sally do it. I'm on administrative leave, or I'd do it."

"I'll do it. Sally went home."

"Santana, this needs a forthwith."

"I'll try, but they don't always drop everything they're doing for a secretary."

"Tell 'em it comes from Sally. I'll give her a heads-up."

After I've hung up, Mimi asks what else we can do.

"Nothing but just wait. I'm sure it'll be fine." Wondering how convincing I sound. "Want me to call you when I hear from school security?"

"The second you know something, okay?" Her response is palpable worry; mine is near panic.

*****

The day's end possesses an odd and mystifying normality for my family, which doesn't mesh with the surreality of my own day or the anxiety I'm feeling about Rosa. Francesca had wanted to attend school, and Eloise dropped her and her brother off on her way to the Astrobank office.

When I pick the kids up at Abuelita's place, they chatter and spat in their usual way on the way home, disagreeing about some new kid in class, Tommy, who hails from southern California and is either a dork or a netfreak, depending on which of my kids is talking. One thing they can agree on is that they want pizza for dinner again, and I almost give in, even though it will be the third night in four, because I am afraid not to give Francesca anything she asks for. I don't though, because I want to stay busy until I hear from the school security office, and I say, "I think we'll stick with what's on the Monday menu, which is jambalaya if I remember right."

They groan, but they don't argue.

When I get all the sautéing and seasoning done, I combine everything and add the broth and rice. While it simmers, I use my phone to look up the names Mimi gave me. I am anxious to call one of them and get an initial visit scheduled, but of course it's too late in the evening for that. I wish I had asked her more about the two names. Maybe when I call her back tonight, I think, but that gets me started worrying about Rosa again. Why *did* she help me? Hatred of what her brothers are? Because she likes me? Teenage independence? Because I mentioned Francesca's age, only a few years younger than Rosa?

I don't know. I just want her safe. She saved my daughter, after all, more than me or Burgoyne or anyone else. I don't really know why she did what she did, but I owe her.

During our dinner together, NJ is expressing his jealousy over Francesca's teacher, who has started the fifth grade pre-algebra unit weeks ahead of his own, who has her class doing social studies for two hours a day.

"Can you talk to Mrs. Skinner, dad? I don't want to learn the names of all the Civil War generals."

"All knowledge is worth having, son," I say, but I'm thinking two hours of social studies every day is dreadful for NJ, and probably most of his fifth grade classmates as well.

"Mrs. Kane told us the Southern generals were better than the Union ones," Francesca says. "That's so, isn't it Papa?"

This is the old Francesca, letting her brother know that she has the better teacher and that she had no trouble learning about Civil War generals. I'm always happy and hopeful to see this Francesca now, but it's a tenuous feeling, infested as it is with the fear of her next breakdown or outburst and with a pervading doubt of my own ability to help her.

"It's hard to say, Mija. The winning side must have had some good generals too, or they wouldn't have won. How's everybody like the jambalaya?"

Eloise thanks me for making it and says she likes it, though I know it probably has too much cayenne for her taste. The kids are less enthusiastic.

My cell phone rings just after eight o'clock.

"Mr. Tavish?"

"Yes sir.

"Officer Tanner, school security detail." His voice is hoarse and gravelly. After a brief pause, he says, "I called Mrs. Jelinek, but she told me you were the one who needed to know this."

"If you're calling about Rosa Martinez, then that's right. Some of her friends are worried about her."

"Well, she wasn't home. The guy there, I guess her brother, said she'd gone out on a date last night, Sunday, and hasn't been home since. He let us look around in the house, so we know she wasn't there."

"And he hasn't heard from her since?"

"No. We asked whether she'd done that before, and he said yes, only he didn't seem like the most trustworthy bastard I've ever met. We asked if he's tried to find her, like check with her friends or if he'd contacted the police or anything, and he said no. Strictly from gangsterville, but there was no one else there to talk to."

After a brief silence, I ask him if he has any other information.

"Well, we watched for about an hour, surveilled from down the street you know, thinking she might come home, or somebody else comes by we could talk to, but no luck. So what we did do is we checked with four of the closest neighbors. One of them, guy named Olivas, confirmed seeing her leave last night. He said she seemed kind of wobbly, like she's already tied one on, leaning on the arm of the guy she left with and not too sure of herself coming down the stairs."

"He remember the car?"

"Convertible."

"Dark blue?" I feel a sinking sensation within me, as if my organs are turning to stone.

"Maybe. Not a light color anyway . . . Is there anything else we can do?"

"You'll make a report to the PD, right?" He sighs in agreement. "Then nothing. Thanks, Officer." I think of a Shakespeare ditty: 'He that is thy friend indeed, he will help thee in thy need.'

I turn to Eloise and say, "I'm sorry. I have to go."

She can read the grief in my eyes, and she nods grimly.

On my way toward Leon Gallardo's apartment, I call Burgoyne and explain what I think is going on, praying he'll know what to do.

"You don't have a piece, so I wouldn't go knocking on Gallardo's door. Sit on it. I'll see what I can find out."

"I owe her, you know."

"Don't go all sentimental, okay?"

There is no convertible at Leon's place, no light on in his apartment. It's a relief, really, since I probably won't have to confront him, and since, even if I did, there would be no way of predicting what might happen as a result. I set to wondering, again, which things would be different, less painful, if I had not paid that first visit to the Martinez house a few nights ago. I wanted to activate the basketball, thinking I could force the Levantes into some mistakes, which I undoubtedly did.

But tossing Jhonny off that porch was the sole fixed point of a multi-rod pendulum, producing a thousand and one results, only a few predictable, many of them probably still not actualized, but all of them evidence of the Chaos that is always only half a step away.

I have the windows down for the night air, but with it come the neighborhood's greasy smells and jangling sounds. There's a biker bar about two blocks north, I know, and I can occasionally hear the sound of a chopper revving as its rider prepares to park or to leave. Somewhere to my right, men are arguing and cursing jocularly about major league baseball players and who is going to win the West, white guys I think, their voices slurring to varying degrees.

I imagine them sitting in lawn chairs in somebody's yard, wearing tank tees and gulping from forties in brown paper bags. The amount of traffic is surprisingly high for a side street, cars and pedestrians both, and I keep checking my mirrors, hoping to see the convertible. I'm not comfortable. I text Eloise to say I love her. No answer.

Evening passes, and the baseball aficionados quit talking. Evening becomes night time. Burgoyne calls just before midnight.

"Hey," he says.

"Hey yourself," I say.

"They got her across last night. Used the Nogales crossing." He doesn't say he's sorry.

"They got it on video or something? . . . I mean, you sure?"

"Border cam got them. Just before ten, Gallardo driving, the Martinez girl asleep in the passenger seat."

"Doped up, more like." As if someone has crushed my lungs.

"There was a short chat with the agent. You can read the agent's lips, asking if the girl is okay. He says some bullshit, and the BP guy buys it, of course, since they look like a Mexican couple who've just had too much fun for one night."

"So she's gone then?" I can almost see Burgoyne nodding his head at me.

"No way you can track her, partner." He sighs. "Which is probably a blessing. Keeps you from getting the same thing your dog got."

His bluntness unsettles me and comforts me at the same time. He's right. If there's not a single step that I can take to rescue Rosa, then there is no possibility of my taking it.

Still, if there were . . .

*****

There are very few positive things about being placed on administrative leave, but I hope it gives me the time I need to start realizing the extent of my emotional debts.

Most men don't think too deeply about what it means to grow into manhood as it's happening, only when they're looking back.

Hell, I don't even know if I've arrived yet—Abuelita says no one is really grown until they're into their fifties.

But I think one of the most important things is to acquire an awareness of the value you place on those around you, loved ones and strangers alike, perhaps best measured by the risks you're willing to take not only *for* them but also *with* them.

By that measurement, I know I have failed. I owe more to Eloise and NJ and Francesca than I can ever discharge, of course.

It makes no difference that I didn't know I had been risking their lives; in fact, that makes it worse.

And then there's Rosa, a girl who destroyed herself, gave herself up, to save my daughter, God alone knows why. And just as with my family, I never gave her precariousness a thought until now, after she's been thrown into an abyss—rewarded by her older brother for taking pity on me and my daughter. I imagine her disappearance will haunt me as much as my own daughter's violation, and I feel guilt for that too.

I will find a way to liquidate the debt I owe to my family, to make amends, but I have no idea how to repay Rosa.

I'm indebted to Andre and Burgoyne too, of course, but it's not the same.

There are some ugly things about being put on administrative leave too, but the worst is that everyone presumes you've done something wrong. Happily, George's press releases have mitigated that notion over the past few days.

I have this feeling there's something I've done wrong, for sure, but when I go over the events in my mind, I can't figure out what it is.

In my head, I go through this series of justifications, which are perhaps only rationalizations: Chucho—he was just sitting there in his favorite chair watching TV, scared shitless as soon as he saw me and Burgoyne burst in, and he never had a chance . . . but then the house turned out to be deeded to him, a drop house, stuffed with marijuana, and he's letting Manny and Jhonny hole up there, letting them destroy my daughter's childhood there, so I wind up thinking I'd have done it the same way all over again; then Jhonny—another guy sitting in a chair, tied up this time while Andre slapped him, tied up when I wounded him and which I lied about to the police, letting Andre misremember for me too . . . and then I remember Jhonny's tough talk, a guy who stole my daughter, penetrated her immature little vulva and then spit it back in my face, so I'm glad Andre was there slapping him, and I'm glad I put a nick in his penis, and I'm glad he's locked up—Burgoyne is positive Manny's friends will kill him in lockup, and I'm glad about that too; and then the cowboy, the black-hat, Jesus! I'm just relieved he's not still shooting at me.

But it does no good. I still feel an oppression that I suppose must be guilt.

There's an irony to it, of course: I trivialized the innocence of three girls; I shot three men in three days, and two of them are dead; I stretched the truth to the police three times as well.

So I am portrayed as a hero and rewarded with a principalship.

Go figure.

ABOUT AUTHOR JIM CHRIST

Jim Christ holds a degree in Literature and Writing as well as two masters' degrees. He taught English composition and literature in Arizona schools for twenty-five years. The author of several non-fiction books, Christ wrote his first novel *The Day Hal Quit* in 2014. He lives with his wife in Tucson.

THE DAY HAL QUIT
AN EXCERPT

Caje'eme's uncle had told him many times that he was named after a great man. On Friday, he was riding on the back of a flatbed north-bound for Sasabe with a load of half-seasoned mesquite firewood, wearing a bandana over his nose to block the dust and holding a duffel bag on his lap. It did not make him feel like a great man. But if he were home, what would he be doing after all? Working in a restaurant, or reading in the university library perhaps, or maybe having fun with the girl, so no, this was better--getting money so he could keep going to the classes and keep being with the girl. Maybe be like that first Caje'eme in a few years.

When the flatbed slowed to turn northwest at Saric, where the road separated from the shoulder of the Rio Altar river bed, Caje'eme jumped off, clutching the duffel. He twisted his ankle as he landed, and rolled into the powdery dust. Wincing, he pushed himself up, slapped the dust away and made his way to the clay bank and then into the sandy river bed. As he had on the previous trips, he continued the trek north in the mostly-dry Rio Altar, treading as much as possible in dampened sand, where it was cool and gave only slightly to his weight. He trailed along the western bank where the shade from cottonwoods and mesquites was just beginning to lengthen. About halfway to El Busani, he began to wonder if he'd broken something in his ankle or foot. He set the duffel bag down and knelt to tighten the laces on his Converse high-tops and limped on, but he knew he could not walk all the way to the border now. He needed the steps left in him for the hills beyond the border.

When the river bed turned sharply east and told him he was just south of El Busani, he climbed the bank, continuing north through the thick mesquite and onto the alluvium, under the highway bridge, and still north.

Broad farmland stretched to his right, but Caje'eme trailed the tree-lined north-bound road until he reached the town.

At the little dark cantina in El Busani, he ate a burro of beans and carnitas and bought a gallon jug of the local mescal. Then he waited fifty yards away in an adobe ruin, with his right leg raised up on what used to be a window sill. He lay back on the duffel as if it were a cushion. His thick black hair lay flat and smooth on his head, his nose was hooked like a bird's nose and his mustache was fine-haired and wide, rounding the look of his smooth brown face. He wore a long-sleeved white shirt. He would be late now, and he would have to call the girl, he knew, or she would have to wait. He thought about the girl, tall and lithe and blond. She always called him Caje.

After four o'clock, men began entering the cantina, locals, he assumed. He watched the little parking lot, powdery dust rising as each set of tires rolled in, the Sonoran darkness descending. Finally, a little after eight o'clock a vehicle approached from the north. He heard it before he saw it, a noisy clatter coming in from the dirt road. He watched its headlights until they blinked off as the old pickup truck rumbled in. A floodlight beamed out into the darkness from above the cantina's door, and he could see two men get out of their faded red truck. They looked like braceros, with their sinewy arms, hard dark skin and relaxed gait. They would have to be the ones to give him a ride. He limped closer and waited on the outer perimeter of light. He clutched the duffel. A half-moon rose, and the temperature dropped. He opened the duffel and extracted a dark blue sweatshirt and put it on. He waited.

Two hours later when the men came out, their gait was unsteady. Caje lifted his duffel and the gallon jug and approached them. "¿Me puede dar un paseo al norte? ¿La frontera?" The men's eyes were glassy but steady.

"Vamos a El Cumaral," one said.

"¿Es cercano a la frontera?" He held up the jug. "Por favor."

They nodded at the bed and took the mescal and got into the cab. Caje sat in the straw-strewn bed with his back against its side. He rested his right foot on a smooth spare tire. The truck bumped along for several miles, then turned east, crossed a creek and turned north again. He had not crossed the border east of Rio Altar before, and he wondered where he would find himself. He had over an hour to think about it as the little truck made its way slowly among the ruts.

They stopped at a fork, where Caje could smell livestock and water. He saw several low adobe buildings. The engine idled, and one of the men got out from the passenger side of the truck and said, "Es El Cumaral. Jorge le llevará sobre el filo."

Caje said, "¿El filo . . . La frontera?" He could smell mescal on the man's breath.

The man nodded and walked toward the buildings. He had left the truck door open, and Caje climbed out of the bed and into the cab. The truck turned at the fork and began climbing. Caje bounced on the bench seat, clutching the duffel.

In fifteen minutes they were descending again. There was a road of sorts, but it seemed to open up only a few feet ahead of them in the headlights between scrub oaks and piñons. Branches screeched along the sides of the truck and over its roof. Then they came to a small meadow, where Jorge circled around a tall ponderosa. As the truck came around, Caje saw a barbed wire fence with two small signs. One read 'Coronado National Forest,' the other 'United States-Not a Port of Entry.' Immediately to the left of the sign there was wide gap in the wire.

Jorge said, "No entrada," and smiled at Caje.

Caje smiled back and got out of the truck. "Muchas gracias, señor. ¿Donde esta Ruby?"

Jorge pointed. "Norte recta y un poco este. Seguir la huella. Pero tenga cuidado. Hay hombres malos."

"Okay, Jorge. Tengo cuidado." He slung the duffel onto his shoulder and moved toward the signs, limping but moving quickly. The truck's lights shone directly on the gap in the wire, and as he approached it, Caje could see curls of the wire twisted back and wound haphazardly around the T-posts on either side of the gap. He wondered how many times the strands had been cut and repaired and then cut again. He could hear Jorge revving to start the ascent again, and soon the lights of the truck disappeared. A few yards inside the fence, he stepped into a thicket of oak and sat on the thick duff. He checked his watch and waited for a half-hour, moving once to raise his right leg onto the duffel. He remembered his uncle saying that a Yaqui could wait longer and quieter than anyone—better than an Apache. He listened for engine noises, for footfalls, for voices, for dogs, for anything that did not belong to the night. He heard the fluttering of bats, the padding of a coyote and the swishing of puffs of breeze through the leaves. At eleven o'clock, he took a canteen from the duffel and drank and then set out on the trail again, limping.

The moon had risen, just edging over into a waning stage, and he could see the trail about ten yards ahead, twisting between scrub oak and clusters of rock, sloping down to a creek and then following it. He stopped every hour and rested with his ankle raised up on the duffel. At one clearing along the trail, he saw signs of a camp—rocks circled for a fire pit, broken glass, a few rusting pop-top cans, diapers, a torn shoe . . .

At dawn, he came to a rocky earth dam on the creek with a silvery camp trailer parked in a flat spot on the far side of the pond. The pond looked still and green and cool, inviting him. There was no car or truck at the camp though, and the trailer stood silent. The campers' fire pit looked cold among a pair of camp chairs and a heap of firewood.

He circled wide to the west, upslope and beyond the dam, and found a wide crevice of granite behind a manzanita bush. He pulled his canteen out and stuffed the duffel into the crevice. He studied the place so that he could find it later—the purple-barked Manzanita lush with blooms, the giant twisted trunk of a dwarfish oak, the towering rocks that leaned together in a kiss to form the crevice. Then he walked downslope again to the trail. He could see that the trail was joined by a narrow road on the far side of the dam. It arced over a hill to the east. He knew it must lead to the Ruby Road, but remembered Jorge had told him to stay on the trail. He walked up the creek trail to the dam. There was still no sound from the camp trailer.

Caje stooped to fill his canteen, then sat on a low rock on the dam and started to unlace the sneaker from his throbbing foot, but he saw the swelling there and thought better of it. Instead, he worked from the bottom of the laces and tightened them even more and retied the sneaker. Then he swung his foot out into the pond and leaned back on his elbows. The morning air was cold, and wisps of vapor rose from the tiny pond. His ankle throbbed. He could call the girl when he got to Ruby if they had a phone there, but where could they meet now?

Perhaps he dozed, or perhaps he was thinking of the girl again, but he did not hear the approaching car until it was turning in at the camp to his left. It was a two-tone El Camino with two men in it, no more than a hundred feet away.

Caje could see the passenger stare at him. He turned slowly on the rock, picking up the canteen, and lifted his wet leg out of the water, standing and testing the foot as water bled from his sneaker.

"Mornin!" the man said, but it was really a question, like 'Who the hell are you?' He opened the car door and stood. He was a big man, well over six feet, with long black hair in a ponytail and a beard. He wore a heavy army shirt, sleeves torn away to make it a vest, over a red shirt, jeans and boots. A name patch on the shirt read 'Hicks.'

Caje smiled faintly and nodded. "Buenos dias." Time to act lost, he decided. He fought the urge to run. "¿Donde esta Calabasas?"

The driver from the El Camino went to the camp trailer and tried the door—locked. Then he came around the car and stood next to Hicks. He was shorter, about Caje's size, with a crew cut, in an oversized white tee shirt, and baggy fatigues and sneakers. He wore a revolver in a holster on his belt. His tee shirt covered his belt line except where it was tucked behind the holster. "What's he want?"

"Says he's looking for Calabasas. Just a wetback I guess." Never glancing at the smaller man, he smiled at Caje.

One may smile and smile and be a villain, Caje remembered from his lit class. "¿Donde esta Calabasas?"

"Northeast. Follow the road." The big man motioned behind him with his thumb. "You alone? Solo?"

Caje nodded. "Si, estoy solo." He smiled and moved forward along the dam to where the two men stood, trying not to limp. His heart pounded but he moved ahead. "Gracias." When he got close to them, he moved left toward the road. The big man leaned at him suddenly, and he almost broke into a run. He nodded and said, "Muchas gracias." He listened as closely as he could, walking up the road as it rose to the east.

*****

The two men turned and silently watched Caje distance himself along the road until he neared the top of the ridge. "So if that asshole's a wetback, where's his stuff?" the short man said. "He's hiding a pack somewhere."

"Yeah," the big man said. "Get up to the perch and see what gives."

The smaller man hurried to unlock the camp trailer and went inside. When he returned, he was carrying a set of binoculars. Over his shoulder, on a sling, was a Ruger Mini-14. He scrambled up the hillside.

"Well, don't shoot him," he called. "Not unless he's already carrying something," he added to himself.

The small man reached an outcropping of rock and stepped to the edge, raising the binoculars with both hands. In a few minutes he came down again. "Still ain't carryin' nothing but he left the road."

"Which way?"

"Back to the west."

"Little shit! He's a mule for sure."

"Circling back for something. Gotta be."

"Okay. Lock up. Let's get on up the trail. He'll probably come back that way till he gets close." He ambled to the spot where the trail touched the road's dead end and waited.

The small man locked their trailer and joined him. "How you want to do this?" They were both looking north, up-trail.

"You get ahead of me with the rifle, and then go off-trail to the right. I'll stay on the trail and meet him coming back. Gimme the handgun."

The small man handed him the revolver. They started together, and then the small man climbed away to the right. He stopped after a few steps and brought the rifle's sling over to his right shoulder, and then resumed. When he was twenty yards away, he waved back to the big man and started making his way parallel to the trail.

The big man had put the revolver into his belt at the middle of his back. He walked slowly, knowing that his partner would have to set the pace. The trail was rough, barely visible in stretches, but still easier to negotiate than the hillside. He began counting his steps, stopping every twenty paces to let the small man get ahead again, looking hard up the trail for any sign of movement and checking to his right to find his partner.

*****

After he had cleared the top of the rise, Caje continued walking along the road for a quarter mile and then turned uphill to his left. He was glad he had not been sitting with the duffel bag at the pond, but he knew he had to retrieve it as fast as he could. The man in Hermosillo and the other man in Tucson did not forgive.

He moved cautiously, staying in the shade when he could. He climbed with difficulty. His ankle hurt, and his shoes kept slipping on the duff. If he had not twisted his ankle, he thought, he would be having an easy walk in the dry wash bed. He would wear boots next time . . . or he would not be careless and twist his ankle next time . . . or maybe he would not do a next time. Safer to study literature . . . easier too, he thought. He passed the crest of a hill and stood in the shadow of a twisted oak. He scanned to his left for movement, but there was none. He listened and looked hard down the hillside for some sign of the trail.

He removed his sweatshirt and tied its arms at his waist. He looked at the sky and the shadows. He knew that he was going in the right direction, so he would hit the trail at some point. Over the next ridge or perhaps the one after that. He planned his route down the hillside. There was cover, but the hillside had a good deal of duff. He started down the slope, sideways to keep from slipping, facing south and scanning. He held the canteen in his left hand. Leading with his right leg was painful, but it was better than falling or losing control of his speed, and better than turning his back to the south, where the two men might be. In a few minutes, he reached the bottom of the slope and began to ascend toward the next crest, now straight ahead, stepping on rocks and other breaks in the duff.

At the crest, there was a promontory of granite. When he crawled onto it, he could see the trail about fifty yards below him. He raised his eyes, just slits, to the south horizon and crawled them slowly back along the route he imagined to be the trail. There was no movement. He checked his watch and lay there listening. He would wait, he told himself.

But he was becoming anxious about the duffel bag. His hiding place between the kissing rocks was a good one, but what if they found it? He sidled down to the trail and began to trace it back toward the duffel.

*****

Hicks stared uphill and waited for the small man to look at him. When he did, Hicks pumped his right fist, telling him to move faster, but the small man responded by stopping and signaling 'fuck you' with his left. He smiled up at him and nodded. It really was as fast as his partner could manage along the slope, but Hicks was starting to wonder if the mule had avoided them somehow. He looked back along the trail, but he could not see past its last hook around a piñon tree. He estimated that they had covered about three-hundred yards. He looked uphill, where the small man had now disappeared. He peered along the trail ahead of him to the next bend and took twenty more steps—still nothing. Then twenty more . . .

The next time the small man came into sight, he was crouching and holding his left fist up. Yeah, I'm paying attention, he thought. Standing still, he pulled the revolver from his belt and stared ahead to where the trail curved out of sight, ready if their quarry came into view. After a moment, he looked uphill, and the little man was motioning him forward again, out of his crouch and moving out of sight. Nothing.

Hicks put the revolver back in his belt and went to counting steps. In the next four hundred yards, the small man raised his fist twice. Once he even held his left hand up to his eyes. Each time, Hicks pulled the gun from his belt and readied himself, but there was only the momentary pause and then the signal to move ahead again. He jogged forward until he saw his flank man again and waited for eye contact. When the small man stayed in his crouch and did not look at him, Hicks called to him, "Come on down."

The small man stood and glared down. He held his left palm up and moved it side to side.

Hicks waved for him to come down to the trail. "I'm thirsty."

The small man shook his head. He pointed at Hicks and put his hand over his head in the cover sign. Then he pointed at himself and pointed ahead, crouched and moved on.

"All right, ya son of a bitch," Hicks said to himself, "but sure as shit, we missed him." He squatted to wait.

*****

At ten o'clock, Tara said she would not let herself worry until noon, even though Caje was over an hour late. She asked herself again if she might be in the wrong place, waiting at the wrong arroyo while Caje stood scratching his head and wondering where she was. But no, she could see all the markers he had shown her. To her left was the giant boulder sitting atop the three smaller boulders, shiny with mica, where the road crossed the wash. To her right, buried to its window in sand, was the rusty, bullet-riddled car hood. She was sitting on the same blanket in the same shady spot she'd waited on that first time two months ago, when he had arrived fifteen minutes late. She had carved his name into an oak tree while she waited, and he had asked her not to do that again because it had offended the tree's spirit. She found his name there on the tree. He had smiled and said the only way to heal the tree's spirit was to make love in its shade, and so they had.

But it was one o'clock now and way too hot for outdoor lovemaking, and she was worried. Her thin eyebrows straightened as she focused her blue eyes as far up the wide sandy wash as she could manage, hoping for a man's form to appear suddenly from the mesquite and desert broom that stretched along its course. Waiting, she had intermittently heard gunfire, and though she knew the area was a prime hunting area, she also remembered the stories Hal and Johnny told about Ruby and Arivaca and the hard people who lived out here.

She thought about driving the road again, thinking that maybe it was Caje who had taken a wrong turn. She had already driven Tres Bellotas Road for five miles in each direction, stopping at each arroyo crossing, turning off the engine and calling both ways, scanning for him. She wished now that she had brought his Jeep instead of her MG. She had already scraped bottom half a dozen times on the rough road, and she could not take the MG off road. Well, she thought, I have to do something.

She rose abruptly and stepped out of the shade and jogged back to her car. She pulled her wavy blond hair into a tight pony tail and wound a band around it behind her head and climbed into the little car. She turned it around and drove northeast, toward Arivaca. She looked for straight-aways where she could make a little speed, but there were almost none. The engine wound too tight to stay in first gear, and she shifted into second whenever the road permitted, but she kept having to stop the little convertible for low spots and ruts in the road, and she cursed the MG for not being synchromesh into first gear. No synchro, no air conditioning, no headrests—should have listened to her father that time. Of course, he doesn't like Caje either, she thought. "Fuck it," she said and ground the transmission into first again.

It was hot, over ninety degrees, and the sun hit her bare thighs and arms relentlessly. Sweat gathered in her armpits and ran down her neck between her small breasts. In one straight section of road, she got the MG into third gear and rested her arm on the door, but it burnt her, and her arm recoiled. As the altitude dropped, she saw more mesquite trees and whitethorn acacias. She kept hoping Caje would step out from under a clump of the brush and smile at her.

*****

Caje was thinking about food as he walked, guessing it was now about eight o'clock and trying to calculate how long it had been since he had eaten the burro in El Busani, and he heard a voice and froze, listening. He looked ahead first and then right and left. And there it was—a slant of white up the hill far to his left. It did not move, but it did not belong there either. His heart pounded as he took one backward step, slow, then another, feeling exposed on the open trail in his white shirt but afraid to turn quickly. With his eyes never wavering from the slant of white, he shrank slowly into a squat and pulled the shirt over his head and held it in a ball in his right hand. Then, finally daring to snap his eyes away, he started duck-walking to his right. He made for a twisted multi-trunk mesquite, whose hanging branches swept near the ground, resembling a giant parched weed. Twenty feet away, then fourteen, then six and then finally in the mesquite's cover. Caje turned slowly and searched the hill side for the slant of white.

It was several minutes before he saw it again, closer now, perhaps eighty yards down-trail and moving slowly. He knew he was still too close to the trail, so he turned slowly and planned a route. There was another weedy mesquite about thirty yards away, but he would have to move slowly, crouching behind manzanitas and dwarfish junipers, though the man in white drew closer every moment. He wanted to leave the shirt and the canteen, the sweatshirt too, but he decided he could not. Not this close to the trail.

He waited until the slant of white went invisible again, behind a cluster of trees, and then he scooted, bent at the waist, to the next cover and turned and found the white again and waited for it to disappear once more. And so he made his way to the mesquite. By the time it took Caje to get in a squat behind the tree, the man in the white shirt never changed in his pace, never came closer to the trail. To Caje, that meant that so far the man in the white shirt had not seen him. He was a man now, and not just a slant of white cloth, forty yards away, with a rifle slung over his right shoulder.

The mesquite had two huge trunks separating in a vee about two feet off the ground. A lot of its new spring growth hung near the ground along with its tangled dead branches. Good cover from the trail. Caje folded the shirt in half and laid it out on the grass and the duff beneath the tree, and he lay on the shirt with his arms holding him off the earth so that he could see through the vee. Then he was still.

The man negotiated the hillside slowly, stopping repeatedly to scan and then moving ahead again, maintaining his distance from the trail. Caje began to wonder where the big man was. If they were tracking the trail from opposite sides, then the big man would approach him on the right, and there would be no way he would miss his hiding spot. But he knew he could not move to a new place with the white shirt so close. Maybe I should have run, he thought, remembering his high school cross country team for an instant, state champions—but not with the bad ankle, not while the man held the rifle. He waited until the white shirt disappeared behind a clump of brush before he rotated his head to the right to check for the big man. Not there. He crawled his eyes back between the notch in the mesquite, and saw the man in the white shirt now straight across the trail from him, motionless and scouring with his eyes. The man looked far down the trail and then brought his head around, peering closely. The man's head stopped, aiming at the mesquite below Caje and then rising to scan. His head stopped several times, squinting closely into the shade of every big tree, seeming to stare momentarily into Caje's eyes.

Finally, the man looked back along the trail, waved 'come,' and started forward again, keeping his distance from the trail. Caje watched him thread his way, now farther with each of his steps. Caje moved his head right, past the old tree trunk's mass, and watched the trail.

The trees did not stir. The big man came along after a few minutes, walking upright, scanning right and left, but not intently as the man in the white shirt had, stopping sometimes. The protective shade was deep, but Caje knew that there would be a few moments when his blue jeans and his brown skin would be exposed to the big man's view, his white high-tops too. He breathed slowly and tried to blink only when the big man looked away. He became aware of an itch on his shoulder blade and then another on the bottom of his foot. His forearms were beginning to hurt from the constant pressure of his upper body, and his hands tingled from restricted circulation. The itching was especially irksome. It reminded him of a book he had read, but he could not remember the story that went with it. He was thankful when he heard a dove's love call and tried to concentrate on that. And still the man inched along like a giant worm.

Finally, the man passed, ten yards up trail, and then twenty . . .

As quietly as he could, Caje rolled over on his back, wriggled his back against the rough ground and extended his arms to his side to let the blood return. He would have to stay off the trail to return to his duffel.

Caje heard a voice again, and this time he could hear the big man's words as he called, "We missed him." He lay still and listened. After a few minutes, he could hear two voices, low. He knew they were coming back along the trail.

"Maybe he went back across the road after you come down from the perch. Went the other way."

"Yeah, or maybe he's just holed up."

"Yeah, watching the road waiting for us to leave, the little shit."

"Reminded me o' chasing gooks."

"'cept a gook woulda shot us."

"Yeah,'specially when you hollered at me," his eyes calling the bigger man stupid.

"Well fuck you and him both. I'm hungry."

There was a short laugh. "Well we oughta at least drive around after breakfast."

Then the words turned into fading tones and soon there was only the sound of the dove again. Caje rolled back up on his forearms and saw the two men ambling down the trail toward their camp. After counting slowly to nine hundred to measure his wait time, he rose and began climbing to the next crest. It would be a slow hike back to the duffel.

– Excerpted from *The Day Hal Quit*